PROLOGUE

BULL RUN, VIRGINIA – JULY 21ST 1861

Colonel Thomas Jonathan Jackson of the Army of the Confederate States of America was tall with dark curly hair and a short beard. He looked out across the open terrain where the battle was about to be joined. Wearing a grey uniform as he sat on his horse, he peered through the mist while subconsciously reaching down to his left side to extract his personal firearm from its holster. The richly engraved silver-plated 12mm Lefaucheux M1858 pinfire revolver was a work of art, but its purpose was sinister and deadly. He looked down to inspect it one more time, despite knowing that it was exactly as ready to fire as it had been earlier that morning when he had meticulously disassembled, cleaned and loaded it.

Once again, he lifted his gaze to the wide open field in front of him, contemplating with a heavy heart what was shortly about to unfold. Soon, in a perverse and orchestrated symphony of mayhem and bloody death, soldiers would be marching, bullets would be flying, cannons would be roaring, and bayonets would be piercing the frail bodies of young men in uniforms. Hundreds would likely die.

Brother against brother, Jackson mused bitterly to himself as his bright blue eyes peered towards the enemy lines through the low morning fog that was still hugging the ground.

The notion of brother fighting against brother had long been a euphemism for civil war, but Jackson knew firsthand how this was true in a literal sense in what was now the American Civil War. Staring at each other from behind ramparts and fortifications on battlefields across the United States of America and the newly formed Confederate States of America, there were now men from the same towns, villages and families, each having chosen their side in the conflict.

One such man was Joseph Lightburn, who had been one of Jackson's closest friends since the two of them were young boys. The pair had spent much of their childhoods together fishing and playing in the woods, and the Lightburn family had embraced Thomas as one of their own. To Jackson, it was a painful truth that Joseph was now fighting for the Union, whereas Joseph's brother John had joined the Confederate Army instead. Brother against brother. It was a dark and inescapable reality of this war, but Jackson had been forced to close his mind to the true horror of it. It was the only way for him to continue to command his troops in the battle to come.

When the United States of America had been born with the Declaration of Independence in 1776, no one could have foreseen that it would one day come to this. No one could have imagined that the original thirteen colonies of the British Crown, which had fought together out of a desire for freedom and self-determination to successfully tear themselves free from under the yoke of the English monarchy, would then descend into violent internal strife less than a century later. But that was what had happened. And this was why thousands of young armed men were now facing each other across this battlefield at Bull Run.

It was a very long and complex series of events that had eventually led to this tragic state of affairs. However, as an educated man, and as a result of his officer training, keen interest in history, and general thirst for knowledge, Thomas Jackson had a better understanding of the historical background than most.

Having studied his young country's history intently, Jackson knew that the colonisation of the North American continent had begun as far back as 1492, when the Spanish first settled in the Caribbean and soon after pushed further east to settle in what was to become Mexico in 1518 after making contact with the Aztecs. Over the following century, the colony of New Spain expanded to cover much of Central and South America, and the Spanish also created a separate settlement in northern Florida in 1595. The French, in turn, settled first in Port Royal, far to the north in present-day Nova Scotia in 1604, soon followed by Quebec, and the first English colony of Jamestown was established in 1607 in what was to become the state of Virginia. It was named after King James I, and it barely managed to sustain itself until it began growing tobacco, for which it soon brought in slave labour from Africa. The Dutch were also attempting to assert themselves, and they established the colony of New Amsterdam on Manhattan Island in 1626. During these years, the English and the French clashed regularly over control of territory.

The assassination of King James I and the resultant civil war in England provided for more autonomy in the English colonies across the Atlantic Ocean, and it stoked a rising desire for independence. When Charles II eventually usurped Oliver Cromwell and restored the English monarchy in 1660, he enacted legislation to force the colonies in North America to send raw goods back to England. This did nothing to improve the already resentful attitude of the settlers with regard to 'the old country'.

During the next decade, either through purchases or military action, England managed to take over all of the former Dutch colonies along the northern east coast of America. This included Manhattan, which was soon renamed New York. After Charles Town was founded in South Carolina in 1670, the English Crown now controlled almost the entire eastern seaboard, all the way north to the city of Boston. These colonies would eventually constitute the future United States. Charles Town grew rapidly through the use of a slavery system similar to that employed in the sugar plantations on the Caribbean Islands, and this laid the foundation for the use of slaves across the English colonies. Thomas Jackson had himself grown up in a household that owned several slaves, so the concept was both familiar to him and an accepted part of life.

In the decades leading up to the year 1700, the French carved out an enormous area for themselves, stretching from Quebec in the north through much of the central North American continent and along the entire length of the Mississippi River to the Gulf of Mexico. This expansive territory, which was roughly the size of all the English territories combined, was then known as Louisiana, named after the French king. Similarly, the Spanish expanded north from their colonies in Central America to take control of much of the southeastern part of North America. They had now also taken over all of Florida.

Around this time, there were roughly a quarter of a million people living in the English colonies. Over the next decades, Britain became a significant maritime power, and it took over both Nova Scotia and Newfoundland from the French. It also stopped Spanish expansion in the south with the establishment of the settlement of Savannah in what was to become the state of Georgia. Around 1750, the population of the British colonies had risen to around one and a half million.

In 1763, after having had its North American colonies blockaded by the Royal Navy as part of the Seven Year War in Europe, the French Crown finally relinquished control of most of its North American colonies to Britain. Spain was given the western part of the enormous territory of Louisiana in exchange for western Florida, which from then on became part of the British Empire. However, the war with France had cost Britain dearly, so it began to levy taxes on its overseas colonies. This led representatives of the British colonies to assemble in the city of Philadelphia in 1774 for the First Continental Congress. Here they agreed to petition the English king to address their grievances regarding taxation, legislation and a lack of representation in the English Parliament.

This unresolved tension eventually culminated in the outbreak of the American Revolutionary War at Lexington, Virginia in April of 1775 where the first armed clash between the colonists and the British Army took place. The rallying cry on that day was *"No taxation without representation"*.

The colonist militias soon organised themselves in the Continental Army under George Washington and drove the British out of Boston, but the Royal Navy soon returned with twenty thousand soldiers that landed in New York intent on quelling the rebellion. Then followed the Declaration of Independence in 1776, and after many hard-fought battles, often with support from an opportunistic France, victory was finally secured. The result was the creation of the United States of America on September 3rd, 1783. The fledgling colonies had finally won their independence after a long and bloody war. Four years later, the Constitution of the United States was created, and of its roughly four thousand words, the first three would come to reverberate through time.

'We the People...'

Those words were written roughly forty years before Thomas Jackson was born, and the history of the United States was just beginning. In 1803, with the Louisiana Purchase of the remaining French territories that encompassed most of the Midwest, the United

States almost doubled in size once more. Just over a decade later, Florida was purchased from Spain and annexed into the Union. In 1836, a civil war in Mexico led to Texas seceding from the Spanish Crown and declaring its independence. It was then immediately recognised as a state by the United States, and it joined the Union ten years later after the Mexican-American War, which also resulted in Mexico being forced to cede the huge territories of California and New Mexico to the United States.

During the 1850s, divisions began to form within the young and rapidly growing nation. The main schism was ownership of slaves, with the more industrialised, urban and liberal North pushing for abolition, and the more agrarian, rural and conservative South wanting to retain the right to hold slaves. Playing into this divergence of cultures and economics were the South's general anxieties about being governed by a distant, centralised federal government. These anxieties echoed the time before the Revolutionary War, when the original thirteen colonies had been ruled from London. As more states were added to the Union, which now stretched across the continent to the Pacific Ocean, great care was initially taken to add as many free states as slave states in order to maintain the balance between the two sides in the Senate.

However, when Abraham Lincoln, who was a vocal opponent of slavery, was elected president in 1860 in an election where his name was not even on the ballot in many southern states, the South became convinced that it was a matter of time before the North would attempt to impose abolition on them. As a result, seven states, beginning with South Carolina in December 1860, decided to secede from the Union to create the Confederate States of America. It was no accident that the Confederate flag, the 'Stars and Bars', with its three alternating red and white stripes and its circle of thirteen white stars on a blue background, echoed the design of the original flag of the Continental Army that a century earlier had fought against the British Crown and won independence for the colonies.

Abraham Lincoln then set out to raise seventy-five thousand soldiers from the remaining states to invade the South and quell the rebellion. However, this caused four more states, including Jackson's home state of Virginia, to secede from the Union. Faced with this situation, men like him felt that they had no choice but to join the Confederacy. With President Abraham Lincoln in the Union capital of Washington, and Confederate President Jefferson Davis in Richmond, Virginia, less than a hundred miles to the south, the situation was as tense and combustible as it was possible for it to be, and war finally broke out. The first shots were fired at Fort Sumter in South Carolina on April 12th 1861. Before long, battles would be fought across much of the young nation.

And so here they all were at Bull Run, facing each other down across an open field. Unionists against Confederates. The North against the South. Brother against brother. During those moments of eerie calm before the storm of the coming battle, Jackson allowed himself to cast his mind back to his childhood in Virginia, and everything that had happened since then that led him to this moment. This battle. This first direct armed confrontation with what until just a few months ago had been his fellow countrymen.

The great-grandson of an Irish immigrant, Thomas Jackson had been born in Clarksburg, Virginia in 1824. At the age of three, his father, who was an attorney, died of typhoid fever less than a month after the same fate had befallen his infant sister. His mother, suddenly widowed at the age of 28, remarried to a man who did not like Thomas and his two siblings. His older brother went to live with an uncle, and Thomas and his younger sister were sent away to live with their doting grandmother, who by all accounts spoiled them both. However, five years later in 1835, their grandmother died, and only a year later, their mother also died from complications in childbirth. Jackson then went to live with his half-uncle who owned a grist mill. Here, he helped with the sheep and the crops. After four years, he was sent to live with his aunt whose husband disliked Jackson, so after less than a year, the boy ran away and made his way back to the grist mill across eighteen miles of wilderness. He remained there for the next seven years, becoming a strong and determined young man.

It was likely his tumultuous and painful childhood that eventually caused Jackson to become attracted to the discipline, rigour and regimented qualities of a military career, and in 1842 he was accepted to the United States Military Academy at West Point, New York from where he graduated four years later. During his time at the academy, he initially found himself badly prepared, and he struggled to keep up. However, he soon gained a fierce reputation for determination and hard work, and he ended up graduating near the top of his class. It was also there that he came across a phrase that was to become one of his life's tenets, and which he wrote down in a small notebook that he always kept with him.

"You may be whatever you resolve to be."

These were words written by a Connecticut minister in a publication called '*Lectures to Young Men, on the Formation of Character*'. Reading them at West Point, those words resonated with Jackson and appealed to his already strong and independent spirit, and they likely helped shape the man he was to become.

After graduation, Jackson served with distinction as a second lieutenant in the 1st United States Artillery Regiment during the Mexican–American War, which had resulted from the formerly independent state of Texas joining the United States in 1845. During this time, he was promoted several times and ended the war with the rank of major. It was also here that he first met Robert E. Lee, who was later to become the most famous of the Confederacy's generals.

After the war, Jackson returned to his home state of Virginia in 1851, where he taught at the Virginia Military Institute. He was by most accounts a terrible teacher who had trouble engaging with his students in a meaningful way. However, a grudging respect for his knowledge and experience as well as his character began to materialise. After a particularly dull lecture, one of his cadets wrote in his notebook. *"I can't stand the way this man teaches, but if I ever have to go to war, I want to go with him."*

Like many people with troubled and emotionally deprived childhoods, Jackson wanted nothing more than a family. In 1853 he married Elinor, about whom he had said that he could not imagine being happier than if he were to marry her. But their happiness was short-lived. A year later, Elinor gave birth to a stillborn boy, and within less than an hour, she too passed away from severe haemorrhaging. This was a devastating blow for the man who had become an orphan at a young age, and on the night of the funeral, Jackson was found lying in the pouring rain, clawing at the earth of his wife's grave, trying to bring her back. Jackson eventually recovered and married a woman named Mary Anna three years later. But fate proved no kinder to them. Mary Anna gave birth to a baby girl in the spring of 1858, but the child died less than a month later.

This tragic event was now three years in the past, and Jackson had managed to keep himself together serving as a Colonel in the Confederate Army. He had always followed his own lodestar, and this had led him to turn his back on the Union and instead join the Confederacy after its formation in 1861. As much as he had been a Union man who was educated at its premier military academy and who initially opposed the secessionist movement, Jackson was first and foremost a Virginia man.

Born and bred in that first colony of what was eventually to become the United States of America, Virginia had been his home and the home of his wider family for generations. When President Abraham Lincoln ordered the mobilisation of soldiers from across the northern states of the Union to put down what he saw as a rebellion in the South, Virginia seceded in the spring of 1861, and Jackson decided unhesitatingly to join the Confederacy. He was not willing to fight for the Union against his home state.

Now standing by his brigade's thirteen short-range cannons at the top of a wide, gently sloping open field called Henry Hill, Jackson and his men had set up positions near a tree line behind the infantry lines and facing the Union Army. Surrounding them as far as the eye could see was the wooded, undulating countryside of Virginia, roughly forty kilometres west of Washington D.C. With a maximum effective range of about half a mile, their smooth-bore cannons were currently unable to reach the enemy forces. To their right was a battery of newly developed rifled cannons with an effective range of just over a mile, and in the distance on another wide-open slope called Matthews Hill, Union and Confederate forces were embroiled in a vicious clash of arms.

The battle had now flowed back and forth for hours, and Jackson's brigade had been brought up and instructed by Generals Johnston and Beauregard to hold the line in the face of a dangerous flanking attempt by Union forces. As the Confederate infantry units from South Carolina across the shallow valley faltered and broke from Matthews Hill, the lines of Union soldiers fought their way ever closer, approaching and threatening to overwhelm Jackson's artillery position and thereby rout the Confederate army. If this happened, the entire Confederacy could be lost almost before it had begun.

Looking around, Jackson could see the fear in the eyes of his men. He could sense how they now wavered, and he realised that they were all looking to him for guidance. They were looking to him for the strength that was rapidly draining away from them.

At that moment, the Union's long-range artillery off in the distance let loose a heavy barrage of shells. As Jackson looked across to them, smoke and fire spewed from their cannons. After a couple of seconds, the sound of the incoming fire reached him and his men, and moments later, one of the shells slammed into the ground just a few metres away. It struck the roots of a tree where it exploded with a deafening clap, and shrapnel and splinters of wood flew in all directions. None of his men suffered any injuries, but a piece of shrapnel ripped through the air and caught Jackson in the hand, slicing through his glove and nearly severing a finger. But Jackson held firm.

'Steady, men!' he shouted through the clamour of the battlefield.

Grimacing through the intense pain, he took several long strides through the line of cannons towards the enemy in the distance. Then he turned around to face his now badly shaken artillerymen.

'Compose yourselves!' he shouted, his face covered in a spatter of mud as he gripped his bleeding hand tightly with the other. 'We will remain right here. We will not falter this day, you hear? Reinforcements are on their way. All we have to do is hold on for a while longer. So, keep firing and let's give those Yankees everything we've got!'

His men looked at him for a moment, stunned and awestruck at the apparent lack of fear and the sheer determination of their commanding officer. Then, in a flurry of activity that rippled through the battery, they re-organised themselves after the near miss and began opening up on the approaching Union forces yet again. Upon seeing this display of courage and perseverance, the remaining Confederate units took heart and formed up around Jackson on Henry Hill, and together they held off the Union forces until reinforcements finally arrived. What had now become an infantry battle continued for the rest of the day. Several more waves of Union attacks were launched against the Confederate lines, but all of them were repelled. In the end, the Union army lost its momentum and was forced to retreat, and as more and more Confederate reinforcements arrived, the retreat turned into a rout and ultimately a clear victory for the Confederacy.

When the battle finally ended, reports of the heroic and successful stand against the onslaught of the Union army spread like wildfire across the Confederate states. *"Yonder stands Jackson like a stone wall"*, the reports from Bull Run said. Soon, Jackson had acquired the name by which he would be known for the rest of the war until his death in 1863 at the age of 39.

General Thomas 'Stonewall' Jackson.

★   ★   ★

RICHMOND, VIRGINIA – FEBRUARY 1865

There was a palpable sense of gloom in the Confederate capital. It was now almost four years since the civil war had broken out, and after several early successes in its military campaign, the Confederacy was now losing badly. There were many reasons for this, but it mainly boiled down to the simple truth that the North had more resources than the South. The North was more heavily industrialised, and it had a much more developed railway network that allowed it to move armies and supplies around on its territory in ways the South simply could not. But possibly the most important factor was sheer size and the ability to raise and equip armies.

When war broke out, there were around 22 million people living in the Union. The Confederacy's population was only 9 million, and almost half of those were slaves. And whereas the Union could muster just over two million troops, the Confederacy could only manage about one million. In addition, the Union was able to use its navy to blockade Confederate ports, making it difficult for the South to receive assistance provided by European powers such as Britain, which was sympathetic to the Confederacy because of its dependence on cotton for its textile industry. As time passed, this asymmetry increasingly began to make itself felt across the nineteen states where battles between the two sides took place. Now, in early 1865, the North's advantage in terms of sheer numbers, logistics and economic might was becoming virtually impossible for the South to overcome. If things continued the way they had been going, it would not be long before the Union armies would be at the gates of Richmond.

As has been the case in warfare since the dawn of time, armed conflict was a great catalyst for technological innovation, and the American Civil War was no exception. Earlier in the century, muzzle-loading cannons had been replaced by breech-loading artillery, and over the previous few decades, huge strides had been made in the development of artillery shells, mainly with the introduction of explosive and incendiary shells. This, in turn, had forced warships to adapt since both types of shells represented a mortal danger to any ship constructed out of wood. Without protection, they would either be torn to shreds by the explosive shells or set on fire by their incendiary counterparts. The result of this adaptation was warships clad in metal plating, and the newest naval innovations were the so-called 'ironclads'. These were an entirely new type of warship with very low-profile hulls that often only just protruded from the waterline, and the exposed parts of the hulls were covered in iron plating that was often mounted at an angle. This design protected against the new types of artillery shells by either deflecting or absorbing the blast of their explosive charges and rendering the incendiary shells ineffectual. Almost three years earlier in March 1862, two of these new ships had clashed in a naval battle in Virginia that was already famous throughout both the North and the South. The Union ship, the USS Monitor, with its rotating cylindrical dual gun turret, had engaged in a close-range firefight with the Confederate CSS Virginia, whose sides were all sloped at a roughly 45-degree angle. The two ships had slugged it out for three hours, firing shot after shot, but none of them had been able to deliver a killing blow to the other, and eventually, both ships had to return to their respective ports. In another incident on the Mississippi River, a single Confederate ironclad had forced a Union flotilla of thirty-eight ships to withdraw. Just one year earlier in February 1864, the Confederate submarine, the H.L. Hunley became the first submarine to sink a warship when it sent the wood-hulled USS Housatonic to the bottom of Charleston Harbour.

Other innovations included the Gatling Gun, which was a rapid-fire rotating, multiple-barrel machine gun. It was hand-cranked and prone to jamming, but when it worked correctly, it was capable of laying down devastating fire on advancing enemy troops. An equally significant innovation was the rifled barrel. This allowed firearms to be employed at much greater range and with much better accuracy compared with smooth-bore muskets, which until then had been the main infantry weapon. In addition, new technologies such as the battlefield telegraph and aerial photography added whole new layers of sophistication to the way campaigns could be conducted and troops deployed across the warring states.

Late on a gloomy, overcast afternoon in Richmond, Virginia, Professor Richard Sears McCulloh was sitting at his desk inside his laboratory at the Confederate Nitre and Mining Bureau. As a part of the Confederate Ordnance Department, this agency was, among many other things, responsible for procuring saltpetre. This oxidiser, also known as potassium nitrate, was an essential chemical reagent in gunpowder. With the Confederacy on a full-scale war footing, efficient production of gunpowder was self-evidently essential in order to keep the war going.

Born to Southern parents in 1818 in the Northern state of Baltimore, McCulloh had held the position of

Professor of Natural and Experimental Philosophy and Chemistry at Columbia College in New York for ten years. During this time, he had acquired a reputation for exacting standards and for never holding back on his students to the point of cruelty. Other professors who observed his lectures recorded private notes in their diaries.

"I have never seen a class so awfully mauled."
"His method is very severe, in fact, merciless."
"No one was spared."

A fervent yet secret supporter of the Confederacy, McCulloh resigned suddenly from Columbia College in October 1863. His resignation letter was short and to the point.

"I hereby resign the Chair I have held at Columbia College. It should incite no surprise that one, born and reared a southerner, prefers to cast his lot with the South."

This caused both shock and indignation at the college, and at the following meeting of the Columbia board of trustees, Richard Sears McCulloh was unceremoniously expelled from his professorship on the grounds of him *"abandoning his post of duty"* and for allying himself with those now in open rebellion against the government of the United States.

Immediately thereafter, McCulloh had made his way to Richmond, where he offered his allegiance and expertise to the Confederacy. With his credentials as a respected scientist specialising in chemistry, he was received with open arms. Soon he was given an offer by the Confederate Secret Service to head up a special task force inside the Ordnance Department. One of the main tasks of this agency was to seek out alternative clandestine warfare options to help tip the balance in favour of the South. The objective had been very clear and simple. Develop a weapon capable of winning the war for the South by any means necessary. More specifically, he was ordered to…

"…go beyond the limits of the Confederate States, to engage in the destruction of the enemy's property on the high seas or the rivers, lakes, and harbours in the United States or the Confederate States of America."

McCulloh, like dozens of other scientists working to develop improved guns, bullets, mines and warships, was now at the forefront of a frantic military innovation effort. As always in warfare, new and better weapons could be the key to victory, and as the saying goes. Desperate times call for desperate measures. So, here McCulloh was, working with his assistant in a last-ditch attempt to decisively turn the tide of war in favour of the Confederacy. With the Union Army besieging Petersburg less than twenty miles from Richmond, the hourglass of the Confederacy's war effort was haemorrhaging sand, and he could sense the walls beginning to close in on him.

His goal was to develop a viable weapon that could be used, not on the battlefield, but in the Union capital of Washington D.C. It was a weapon that was very different from those being developed by his other colleagues in the Confederate Ordnance

Department, yet it was theoretically much more destructive. In fact, if McCulloh's efforts could be brought to fruition, his weapon had the potential to decapitate the Union's leadership in one fell stroke, thereby handing the Confederacy absolute victory in a single day.

The weapon was a deadly chemical gas. The intent was for it to be used against the government of the Union in its seat of power in Washington. If this gas could be released inside Congress in the Capitol Building or in the presence of President Lincoln and his whole cabinet, the Union leadership would be wiped out all at once. As a result, the Union would almost certainly collapse into chaos and disarray, allowing a cessation of hostilities and for the South to force a settlement that would be to their advantage. Or at least, so was the thinking in the Confederate Secret Service.

McCulloh's efforts were viewed as some of the most important work in the Confederacy, and even its president was kept abreast of its progress. On the 11th of February 1865, the Confederate Senator from Texas, W. S. Oldham who received regular updates on the weapon, wrote a letter to the Confederate President Jefferson Davis informing him of the latest developments.

"The combustible material consists of several preparations and not one alone and can be used without exposing the party using them to the least danger of detection whatever. The preparations are in the hands of Professor McCulloh, and are known but to him and one other party."

The plan was to covertly transport the weapon to Capitol Hill and deliver it to the congressional chamber for release at a time chosen for maximum impact. However, it first had to be tested, and for this purpose, McCulloh and his assistant had constructed an air-tight glass box roughly one cubic metre in size. Inside the box had been placed a cat, and the design of the box allowed McCulloh to drop a chemical substance in solid form into a liquid. The two compounds would immediately begin to react, filling the glass chamber with a deadly toxin in gaseous form. McCulloh and his assistant had already performed a dry run, as well as one with another cat. The test had gone as they hoped, and the creature was now very much dead and buried.

Today, however, was when the viability of the scheme was to be demonstrated to the decision-makers in the Confederate Army. A delegation of high-ranking officers had arrived to watch the test, and it was headed up by Brigadier-General Nathaniel Templeton, who was the liaison officer between Professor McCulloh, the Ordnance Department and the Confederate Secret Service who financed the project. Templeton was a stocky, heavy-set Texan with a rosy complexion, short salt-and-pepper hair, bushy sideburns and a thick and well-manicured moustache. His wide jowly neck made him wear his grey uniform with the top button on the raised collar undone, and in addition to the revolver by his side, he also carried around with him a protruding paunch that pushed visibly against the lower front of his jacket.

As Templeton strode into the lab, followed by a junior officer whom McCulloh knew to be his personal secretary, the professor rose from behind his desk and rushed to greet the general. Wearing glasses and a white lab coat over a pin-striped grey waistcoat, McCulloh looked every bit the natural scientist.

'General,' he said effusively, using both of his hands to grip Templeton's outstretched right hand. 'It's a great pleasure to see you again. Thank you for coming.'

'Good to see you too, Professor,' said Templeton in a slow southern drawl, looking around the room as if inspecting it for the first time despite having visited on several previous occasions. 'As you can imagine, I am very keen to see the weapon in action. As is the rest of President Davis's war cabinet. Not to mention the general staff of the Army. Lord knows we need a miracle, and we're counting on you to come up with one.'

McCulloh swallowed and gave a thin and uncertain smile as he gestured for his two guests to move further into the lab.

'Uhm, well,' he said. 'I'm glad to report that I believe we have made very good progress. Hopefully, my demonstration today will convince you. Please come this way.'

McCulloh led his two visitors across the wooden floor of his office into a small side room that sported windows on three sides. The open door to the room was made of riveted metal plates. In the middle of the room was the glass chamber that McCulloh and his assistant had built. It was sitting on a raised metal platform that had been made to measure, and above it hung a single wide pendant lamp whose incandescent lightbulb cast a yellow glow over the centre of the otherwise murky room. Inside the box was a grey cat, and as the three men approached, it turned to look warily at them.

'A cat?' said Templeton, sounding mildly surprised. 'You're demonstrating this on a damn cat?'

'A cat is as good as any other creature for this purpose,' said McCulloh. 'It's a stray that has been hanging around the lab for a while. I figured I would make good use of him.'

'Alright, Professor,' Templeton shrugged. 'If you say so. Please proceed when you're ready.'

'Certainly,' said McCulloh, stepping up the box and pointing to a small metal tray on the floor of the box. 'This tray contains a liquid that by itself is virtually harmless. However, when mixed with a special chemical compound that I have developed, it produces a highly toxic gas. As you can see, there is a small fabric pouch hanging suspended over the tray. When I cut this string, the pouch will drop into the liquid, and the chemical reaction will begin. And as you will shortly observe, this will rapidly cause the chamber to fill with the toxic gas.'

'Ok,' said Templeton matter-of-factly, with a note of impatience in his voice. 'Let's see this thing in action.'

'Very well,' said McCulloh as he picked up a pair of scissors. 'Now, please watch carefully.'

McCulloh placed the scissors on the string and snipped it. The pouch immediately fell into the liquid, some of which splashed out onto the floor of the glass chamber. When it landed, it gave the cat a jolt, and it darted into one of the chamber's corners, where it glared at the tray for a moment before looking out at the three men. For the next few seconds, nothing happened, but then a visible white mist began rising from the pouch. It was slow and gentle at first, but as more and more of the liquid seeped inside the pouch and began reacting with McCulloh's compound, the thin mist quickly became a rising plume of roiling gas that began to fill the chamber.

Almost immediately, the cat reacted. Its head jerked from one side to the other, and it blinked rapidly several times before baring its teeth and hissing. When it next inhaled, it suddenly jerked further backwards into a corner of the chamber, where its entire body soon began to tremble as it hissed and sneezed. Without warning, it suddenly gave a loud wail and launched itself forward into one side of the chamber, thudding heavily against the glass. It immediately repeated its attempt at escape and smashed into the glass several times in quick succession as it sprinted furiously from one side of the chamber to the other while screeching and yowling ever more desperately.

By now, the chamber was filled with a thick white fog, and the cat seemed to be a grey blur of motion inside it. As it slammed into the glass, it left smears of blood and frothy mucus mixed with hairs. After another few seconds, the cat once more smacked into one side of the chamber, bouncing off and landing on the floor as its body spasmed and convulsed. A thick white liquid was streaming from its eyes, and its mouth was open in a long silent scream as its lungs seized up and its heart stopped. Then it slowly sagged and lay still.

'Hot damn!' said Templeton with a grin and a chuckle, sounding impressed. 'Now, that's what I call having a bad day. Eight more lives to go, I guess.'

'It's very effective,' said McCulloh, taking his eyes off the dead cat and turning to the general with contentment and even a hint of pride on his face.

'Well, yes,' said Templeton pensively. 'But as impressive as that was, how do we know if it works on people?'

'Oh, it works,' said McCulloh confidently. 'This gas is lethal to anything that breathes. With enough gas, we could eliminate the entire Union leadership. Cut off the head of the snake.'

'What about delivery?' said Templeton. 'How do we get it into the Capitol building? And who's going to deploy it?'

'I am sure we can find sympathisers on the inside,' said McCulloh. 'And all it takes is for one of them to make it up to the gallery overlooking the congressional chamber and then throw a device containing these two chemicals down onto the floor. Everyone present will be dead in a matter of minutes.'

'Hmm,' said Templeton, stroking his moustache while looking thoughtful and not entirely convinced. 'As you might know, the congressional chamber is a big room. I've been there myself several years back. How do we know whether there'll be enough gas to do the job? We need to take out all of those damn bluebelly bastards.'

'We simply calculate it,' said McCulloh, as if the answer was self-evident. 'It's easy to do if you understand how the chemical reaction works.'

'I see,' said Templeton, nodding sagely. 'Good.'

After a long pause during which he exchanged a sideways glance with the junior officer next to him, he finally spoke again.

'Professor, I need you to carry out another test,' Templeton said, levelling his gaze at McCulloh. 'You see, I need to know for a fact that this gas works on people. Do you understand what I'm telling you?'

McCulloh blinked a couple of times as the implications of Templeton's orders settled inside his mind. Then he nodded.

'Right,' he said eventually. 'Yes, I think I understand. But… how do you propose we carry out a test like that?'

'Well, I assume it works as well on black folks as it does on whites,' said Templeton, squinting briefly as he leaned forward to study the dead cat in the glass chamber. 'I don't suppose there's a difference?'

'No,' said McCulloh, giving a quick shake of his head. 'There's no difference at all. Like I said, it is equally deadly to all living creatures. Animals and people.'

'Very good,' nodded Templeton approvingly. 'In that case, I think I've got an idea for your next demonstration.'

ONE

REVELATION, TEXAS – PRESENT DAY

Eddie Barton pushed through groups of boisterous young men near the main doors and made his way deeper inside the High Jinx Tavern in the small Texas town. Some of them turned around looking eager for a fight, but when they saw Barton, they thought better of it and merely swore under their breaths. The sounds of clacking billiard balls, up-beat country music and clinking beer bottles filled the room as the former soldier proceeded inside. The atmosphere was relaxed and jovial, but Barton knew this could change in a heartbeat.

Located some thirty miles southwest of Sweetwater in Nolan County, about a hundred miles from Fort Worth, the sleepy town of Revelation was situated on the arid southwestern plains of the Lone Star State. It was surrounded on all sides by dry, flat and mostly brush-covered high desert, except towards the south where wide undulating hills gradually rose up in the distance. To the north were several of the wind farms that had now increasingly taken the place of the many oilwells that used to be dotted across the most southerly state in the union.

In his mid-thirties, Barton had a stocky muscular build, but he was light-footed and moved smoothly through the crowd. He was wearing an army-green short-sleeved shirt with small white buttons, a pair of beige cargo shorts and brown leather hiking boots. Over his short, sandy-coloured hair was a black linen baseball cap with the peak pulled down low in front of his face, and in his front shirt pocket were the aviator sunglasses that he always wore in the blinding Texas sun. He had a neck like a bulldog, and both of his powerful arms were covered with tattoos. Most of them were in memory of past military units. Others were in honour of fallen comrades. He had never been accused of being good-looking, but what he lacked in looks, he made up for in personality.

With his slightly protruding jaw, his short, blond full beard, square teeth and wide smile, he had always been known for his cheeky grin and his dry sense of humour, ribbing his squad mates every chance he got. He was the type of person who would always help keep his team feeling loose and upbeat. Even in the face of imminent danger ahead of an insertion into enemy territory, he would find a way of easing the tension with a barbed but good-natured dig at someone else or a joke about himself, and his fellow soldiers had appreciated that quality in him.

Halfway to the bar at the back of the large, busy main room, Barton did a quick turn to check if he was still being followed. Beads of sweat were trickling from his forehead, and not just because it was an unusually warm and humid Texas evening. Until a few minutes ago, he had been running from his pursuers. He wiped his brow with the back of his hand and steadied his breathing. He had spent most of his professional career being the hunter, Now being the hunted was an uncomfortable feeling, to say the least, especially because he knew the men who were after him very well. And those men were among the best-trained special forces soldiers in the world. As he looked behind him, he was relieved to find that he could see no familiar faces.

He turned again and walked to one side of the vaguely horseshoe-shaped bar area, trying to look as relaxed and carefree as he could manage. People were ordering drinks and talking loudly, and he had to make an effort not to appear out of place. He sat down on a bar stool that was partially hidden from the entrance behind a large wooden support pillar from where he could watch the room. He scanned the drinking hole's interior and looked around at the other patrons. Threat assessment was second nature to him, and it only took a few seconds to map out his surroundings. There were a couple of obviously single guys at the bar drinking beers and checking out the female clientele. There was a loved-up couple holding hands and sharing a bottle of white wine. At the far end of the bar was a gaggle of middle-aged women on a night out drinking cocktails and looking like this was the only time of the year they managed to get out of their houses. Most of the other patrons looked like they were wearing their regular clothes and were simply here for a few drinks with their friends after a hard day's work. Nothing unusual.

After a few seconds, a barmaid came over. She had an attractive face, and she was wearing a tight-fitting black shirt and matching jeans. Her straight, black hair was done up in a high ponytail that swung from side to side as she moved her head.

'Hi there, Eddie,' she said cheerfully as she approached. 'What'll it be tonight?'

'Hey Charlene,' said Barton in his low, husky voice as he shot her a quick smile. 'I'll have a Bud, please.'

Barton had now spent several years in the US, but as he spoke, his northern English accent still came through clearly.

'Coming right up,' said Charlene and reached back into a small glass-fronted fridge behind her. 'You look kind of jumpy? Everything alright, honey?'

'Sure,' said Barton tensely, eyeing the entrance. 'Just a little trouble at the ranch.'

Charlene shot him a glance as she twisted the cap off the beer bottle and placed it in front of him. Her demeanour now seemed more apprehensive.

'Trouble?' she said, looking concerned. 'What kind of trouble?'

'Nothing I can't handle,' Barton shrugged, giving her an unconvincing grin.

'Alright,' she said. 'I won't pry then. You just take care of yourself, now. OK, Eddie?'

'Always,' he said, and then he lifted the bottle in a quick toast and took a large swig as she gave him a nod and walked off to serve another customer.

Barton savoured the taste of the cool beer and felt himself beginning to relax. It looked as if he had got away. Scanning the room once more, all he could see were men and women mostly in their mid-twenties on a night out with friends. Some were now dancing on the small dance floor near the bar. Others were at the pool tables. Most of them were sitting quietly at their tables talking, drinking and laughing. He had been here countless times over the past many months, and everything seemed just the way it always did. There was nothing to indicate that he was in any danger. However, the other patrons would have been shocked to learn that just a few minutes earlier, the bearded man with the black cap sitting at the bar had been shot at just a few hundred metres from the High Jinx Tavern.

A former Royal Marine with 40 Commando, Eddie Barton had spent four years based at their headquarters at RM Norton Manor in Somerset, from where he had been sent on countless overseas deployments to a host of conflict zones around the world. Growing up in Monkswood in Leeds, like most of his peers, he didn't do very well in school. He wasn't academically minded, and he didn't like being told what to do. And he also didn't much like teachers. He figured that respect was something that should be earned and not just simply assumed. This strong rebellious streak naturally didn't endear him to his teachers, and since he was hanging out with the 'wrong crowd' after school, he was probably well on his way to a life of crime. However, he was physically strong and had an aptitude for endurance sports despite being bulky. He especially enjoyed running and going to the gym.

After dropping out of school, he worked several dead-end jobs for a few years, but nothing stuck. One evening, he randomly ended up talking to two Royal Marines in a pub in Leeds, and he instantly knew what he wanted to do. He wanted to be like them, except better. And he had all the youthful self-confidence to make him believe that it would be possible one day.

At nineteen years old, he signed up for the Potential Royal Marines Course along with 59 other recruits. The 36-week selection course, the longest in the world, took place at the Commando Training Centre Royal Marines near the town of Lympstone in Devon. He initially had trouble adapting to the strict regime and to being shouted at by only slightly older corporals who served as instructors. However, he soon found inside himself a discipline and inner strength that he never knew he had. Through the many courses in physical training, navigation, weapons handling and troop tactics, he excelled, and he soon came to embody the four elements of the so-called 'Commando Spirit'. These were courage, determination, unselfishness, and cheerfulness in the face of adversity. This ethos was repeatedly drilled into him and the other new recruits, and he did everything he could to mould himself into the perfect commando. As the course progressed, 60 recruits dwindled to only 12, and he drew strength from seeing other people quit and from realising that this was finally something that he was really good at.

During the course, the instructors regularly made notes about each recruit, and Barton's records reflected his determination and physical prowess as well as his general aptitude for soldiering. However, there were a few things that were held against him. His army files carried mentions of "a certain inherent disrespect for authority". He would occasionally attempt to ignore the orders he had been given in favour of a shortcut that he thought was a better solution, and he would generally struggle to fall in line as effortlessly as most of his peers. As much as his instructors valued resourcefulness and ingenuity, he was spoken to several times about this tendency. During these talks, his CO spelled out to him that on the battlefield, men would die unless everyone followed orders. He knew this instinctively, but his deep habit of self-reliance got him into trouble with his superiors more than once.

They were roughly halfway through the course when Barton and his troop first met someone from the special forces community. It was a captain from the SAS who had come down to Dartmoor from Hereford to teach a survival course. This was something every commando needed a certain level of proficiency in, and the Special Air Service was renowned for being experts at it. The anonymous captain showed them how to build make-shift shelters and evade enemy capture. He had also demonstrated several techniques for unarmed combat, specifically how to sneak up on, disarm and take weapons from enemy soldiers should the need arise. It had been an eye-opener for Barton, and by the end of that day, it was clear to the young recruit that this man was a special breed of soldier. So impressed had he been that he had promised himself to one day apply to join the SAS, if ever the opportunity presented itself.

Barton eventually graduated as a Royal Marine Commando by completing the last challenge of the course. The gruelling 30-mile winter yomp across boggy Dartmoor in under 8 hours while carrying full kit and weapons. This display of extreme physical and mental endurance finally earned him the coveted Royal Marines green beret. He was then sent off to 40 Commando at RM Norton Manor, which specialises in rapid amphibious deployment and mountain terrain operations as well as artic warfare. During his time there, he took part in several deployments overseas to the mountainous northern Afghanistan as well as various hotspots in the Middle East.

After four years as a commando, he felt that he was ready for the next step. Ready to pursue the path he had glimpsed on that foggy day on Dartmoor. He talked to his CO who wished him good luck, and then he filled out the paperwork and sent in his application to join the SAS.

Joining the Regiment was far from a seamless experience. Getting accepted onto the punishing 10-week selection course turned out to be the easy part. Completing the course was the hard part, and it was much more challenging than the longer commando selection course. First, there was the gruelling hills section. Then followed the draining jungle training. After that, he had to complete the course in escape and evasion, and finally, the all-too-real section designed to demonstrate the ability to resist interrogation. Despite intense physical fatigue, mental exhaustion and a few scrapes, including a dislocated knee and a broken collarbone, he completed the course successfully and was finally badged. Then followed the continuation training designed to get him ready to be sent to a squadron. This included a dive course, parachuting and finally a long CQC course designed to hone close-quarter combat skills. Only once all of those elements were completed was he sent to join 22 SAS at Hereford.

Like many new joiners at the SAS headquarters, Barton already had a significant amount of combat experience, although not in a special forces role, and he generally felt that he knew what he was doing. But joining the Regiment was not as simple as that. In many respects, he was as capable as the men already there, but that counted for nothing. It was very much a learning-on-the-job experience, trying as best he could to follow the lead of his much more experienced Tier-1 colleagues and trying to absorb as much of their expertise as possible. In addition, like all new arrivals a Hereford, Barton had to earn the respect of the other operators, and he immediately understood what that meant. He had to prove himself, and not just in terms of his prowess with weapons, his physical fitness or his mental toughness. He had to prove that he was capable of slotting into the unit and being part of a tight-knit team.

He was only too aware that most of the operators that were already there had lost colleagues in battle, and they were naturally reluctant to accept what they saw as 'replacements'. Barton quickly understood that the best thing he could do was to keep his head down, work hard, try to absorb as much as possible and make sure he didn't get in anyone's way. So, if someone told him to go and fetch something, he would do it. If someone told him to scrub the toilet, he would do it. And if someone told him to shut up and go and stand in a corner until the grown-ups had finished discussing tactics for an upcoming mission, he would do that too. This ability to read the room and fit in amongst like-minded but more senior colleagues meant that he was able to integrate quickly, and after a few months, he was a fully accepted and trusted member of 22.

One of the men who were first to drag him in from the cold and start treating him like an equal was the captain he had first met on Dartmoor years earlier. A man by the name of Andrew Sterling. One of the best in the Regiment, Sterling was always level-headed, even under enemy fire, and he was always both willing and able to lend a hand and provide support to his slightly more junior colleagues. Sterling soon became Barton's most trusted senior officer, and he quickly took on an informal role as a sort of mentor to him.

After a time, the distinction between Barton and the other members of the unit disappeared. Under the guidance of Sterling and a couple of other experienced operators, Barton became the best warrior he could possibly be, and he was finally a fully-fledged member of 22 SAS. He quickly became known as a joker. Always able to pull out a comment that would lighten the mood and make his colleagues smile.

Barton deployed alongside Sterling on more than one occasion, and it happened several times that the captain would lay out a plan for the strike team for an upcoming mission, after which Barton or one of the other soldiers would interject, make suggestions or even point out potential weaknesses in the plan. Sterling would then often scratch that element and incorporate any new and better ideas presented. This attitude led Sterling to be highly respected among his men. Eventually, however, Sterling left to join a new special unit in London under the command of Colonel Strickland, dedicated solely to preventing terrorists from acquiring weapons of mass destruction. It was mainly an intelligence unit, although Sterling would often be the tip of the spear in subsequent strike missions. Barton remained at Hereford and continued his deployments with 22, mainly in the Middle East. But the two men stayed in touch and managed to meet up for a beer once every year or so.

However, Barton's tendency to push the boundaries of what was acceptable persisted. After a particularly risky and dynamic deployment to Mali with intense and sometimes costly missions almost every night, he was rotated back to RAF Akrotiri for a short break to decompress. But he quickly became bored and ended up being severely reprimanded for running a private entertainment business involving vodka and a cadre of Russian women out of the base in Cyprus. Boredom and greed had got the better of him, and from then on, it was as if a black cloud was hanging over him. He suddenly sensed that his superiors didn't quite trust him the way they had in the past, and that his future opportunities in the Regiment were now limited.

The Yorkshireman had finally decided to leave the SAS for better pay in the private sector. The goal was to work in private security, but despite his capabilities, it was much easier said than done. He had no way in, and he ended up taking menial jobs here and there. He hated it, and he was struggling to accept what he saw as the lack of commitment he encountered in his civilian colleagues. Worse still, he missed being part of a tight-knit tribe like the SAS. Having come out of military organisations that instil the pursuit of excellence in their members, the average person on civvy street seemed like a bad joke to him. And yet, he was the one struggling to get ahead. This caused a measure of resentment against 'normal' people who Barton felt had never been at the sharp end of anything meaningful, and who he thought deserved success a lot less than he did. When he saw people much younger than himself driving around in expensive cars and living the high life, his resentment only grew. At the age of 34, he felt lost, bitter and washed up.

Finally, out of the blue, an old contact who was plugged into the private contractor scene got in touch. He had a lead on a job with a private security provider in London, and Barton got the job. He then worked in corporate security in the UK for several years, mainly cushy jobs in the City of London for bigwig financial types before being recommended to a US-based head hunter. Thinking that he needed a change, he decided to take the leap and travel to Florida for an interview with the recruiter. There was then a second meeting with a cagey representative of the end client, but within a few days, he had been offered a job with a company in Texas called Ironclad Tactical Solutions.

Ironclad, or ITS as it was sometimes referred to, was based on a remote ranch in the southwest of the Lone Star State. He first began working in corporate security, babysitting pampered Dallas corporate executives in expensive suits, but he soon found out that this was only a small and relatively uneventful part of Ironclad's activities. After a few months of being a glorified chauffeur with a gun, he was inducted into what turned out to be the Ironclad's main business, which was its black ops team. And it was a world away from cushy but dull jobs in the city looking after corporate types. In fact, it was more like the SAS than anything he had ever thought he would encounter in the private sector. Ironclad offered its security services mainly to shady enterprises and African and Central American tinpot dictators, as well as anyone else prepared to pay the elevated fees for its prime services and no-questions-asked approach to doing business. Most of the tasks involved protecting corporate assets and executives in volatile countries, and some of which included more so-called 'kinetic' operations, which was military jargon for live firefights.

The job had brought with it equal amounts of action and money, and Barton had relished the rush that he thought he had left behind after his exit from the Regiment. Although he was the only foreigner amongst what were mainly former SEAL Team and Delta Force operators, he had managed to fit in pretty well, even if the Ironclad team was not quite as tight-knit a group as his squadron in 22 SAS had been.

Now, sitting in the noisy bar in a small town in Texas, Barton reflected on the recent events that had led him to this place. As he finished his beer and ordered another, he began pondering what to do next while eyeing the entrance. Once again, through hubris and naivety, he had ended up overplaying his hand and underestimating what he was up against. His plan had seemed so simple and straightforward. He had thought that his employer would fold and pay up just to make the problem go away, but that was not what had happened. Not even close. In hindsight, he should have known better. The boss was simply not that kind of man, and Barton was kicking himself for being so stupid. But what was done was done. And now they were coming for him.

Fuck, he thought to himself and winced.

He took another large swig of his beer and gave a small shake of the head. There was no way back. What he needed to do now was to get the hell out of town. Get out of the damn country and lie low somewhere for a very long time. He briefly considered going back to Blighty but then ruled it out. With the sort of people he was up against, there was every chance that the boss had a way of somehow tapping UK intelligence services. They would then hand Barton's location to his pursuers. Or perhaps they would simply arrest him at the UK border and extradite him back to the US on some fabricated charge. After that, a few envelopes full of untraceable cash would change hands, and shortly thereafter he would be six feet under, pushing up daisies or whatever other flowers grew out here in the arid high desert of southern Texas. Not an option. He needed a different plan. Perhaps he could get himself to somewhere in Southeast Asia. Thailand maybe. Or Vietnam. Somewhere he could disappear until they stopped looking for him, if they ever would.

He reached around to his back pocket to pull out his recently acquired foldable smartphone, wanting to look up flights from Dallas to Bangkok. But his hand felt only an empty pocket, and then he remembered that he had been unable to find the phone when he had headed out that evening.

He lifted the bottle from the bar counter and was about to put it to his lips when he caught movement out of the corner of his eye that somehow didn't fit the pattern. It was erratic, and bodies were moving too fast for it to be part of the normal hustle and bustle of the tavern. He turned his head towards the entrance to see two tall, burly men with beards make their way inside and push through the crowd. They wore caps, blue jeans, heavy boots and grey T-shirts over bulging muscular torsos. Their demeanour screamed ex-military, and Barton instantly recognised them both. One had a tattoo of a spiderweb on the right side of his neck, and the other had the tip of his beard tied into a knot with a small leather strap meant to evoke a certain Viking look.

'Shit,' Barton mumbled to himself as he put down the beer bottle.

Moving as calmly as he could, he swivelled on the bar stool and stepped off to make his way towards what he knew to be a door to the back of the establishment. With a bit of luck, they might not see him. A sign on the door said 'Staff Only', but he ignored it and pushed through just as he heard shouting behind him. He instantly recognised the voices of the two men. They had spotted him.

He ran through a narrow corridor with an office and a couple of storage rooms on one side. The corridor continued on for about five metres until it reached a corner where it turned right at a ninety-degree angle. He rounded the corner and kept going until he reached the backdoor to the alley behind the tavern. He gripped the handle and pushed. It was locked. Behind him, he heard the door to the main bar slam open, followed by the sound of heavy boots on the concrete floor. As he took two steps back in order to get a run-up to the door, Barton turned his head to see his two pursuers coming around the corner. Due to their bulk, they swiped the opposite wall as they did so, and they were practically clawing their way towards him with bared teeth and grimaces like predators. Barton turned back to the door and propelled himself forward with all his force, ramming his shoulder into the door. The lock instantly disintegrated and spun off into the air as the door flew open on its hinges and slammed into the exterior wall next to it. Surprised by how weak the lock had been, Barton's momentum carried him forward out into the alley where he stumbled and fell to the ground. Dust kicked up into his face as he rolled once to clear the door and get back up. By the time he was on his feet again, his two pursuers had caught up. They swiftly stepped outside and curved menacingly around him to cut off his only escape route towards the street. He looked around. There were a couple of dumpsters and a broken air-conditioning unit lined up next to the tavern, but nothing he could use as a weapon. If only he had brought his gun from the barracks, but there had been no time.

'Listen, guys,' he said, showing his pursuers the palms of his hands. 'It doesn't have to happen like this.'

'It's gonna go down the way it's meant to go down,' said the one with the spiderweb tattoo, his accent marking him as a Texan. 'Orders straight from the boss. Now, you can either make it easy and come with us, or you can make it hard. Don't matter to us.'

'You know what he is fucking planning!' said Barton heatedly, looking at both of them in turn. 'Right? Are you actually prepared to go along with that?'

'We're following our damn orders, is what we're doing,' said the Viking icily, also in a southern drawl. 'Something you seem to have forgotten how to do.'

'I can't believe this piece of shit was part of the team,' said the tattooed one. 'Fucking traitor.'

'Hey,' said the Viking. 'Don't question the boss. Shit like this happens sometimes, alright? The important thing is, we're here to put it right.'

'Damn straight,' said the tattooed one and began reaching around to the small of his back where a semi-automatic SIG Sauer P320 pistol was concealed under his T-shirt.

Barton had clocked the hand and body movement before it had barely begun, and he immediately launched himself at the man and barged into him before he could draw his weapon. Slamming him back against the wall and winding him, Barton then grappled for the gun as the Viking moved in. The tattooed man was still holding onto the weapon, but with gritted teeth, Barton managed to twist the weapon so that it pointed roughly in the direction of the Viking, and at that precise moment, the gun went off. There was a dry crack as the SIG Sauer fired, and the bullet struck the Viking in the face. The loud report bounced off the walls and reverberated through the narrow alley and up into the night air. The Viking crumpled to the dusty ground and slammed his already bloodied face into the dirt, jerked once and then lay still. He was already in Valhalla.

With a furious grunt, the tattooed man pushed back against Barton who lost his footing, and the two men spun and crashed to the ground next to the Viking whose blood was oozing out into a pool around his dead body. The two powerful men were now fighting over the weapon, and the winner would walk away alive. The loser would die. Amid furious punches to faces and throats, knees to groins, teeth biting at anything within reach, and the frantic clawing at eyes or anything else that might incapacitate the other, the two men rolled around in the alley in what might from a distance have looked like just another drunken brawl, but which was, in fact, a fight to the death.

The tattooed man somehow managed to force the muzzle of the gun up towards Barton's face, but the former Royal Commando wrenched it to one side just as his attacker squeezed off another shot. Barton felt the hot exhaust and the wake of the bullet on his skin as the 9mm super-sonic projectile tore through the air uncomfortably close to his face. Then followed the sharp smell of cordite. He pushed the gun out and away from himself and punched the guy in the gut twice as hard as he could eliciting a pained grunt through gritted teeth.

Barton was then able to roll on top of him while gripping the pistol with both hands, one around the barrel and the other around the man's right hand, which was firmly locked around the pistol grip. Using his weight and every muscle in his powerful arms and hands, Barton slowly pushed the weapon down so that it was close to his pursuer's chest pointing up towards his face. He then began tightening his grip around his attacker's hand. Realising what was happening, and with spittle and blood playing on his lips, his enraged would-be killer glared furiously up at him and snarled.

'You goddamn English motherf…'

The gun went off with a deafening blast mere inches from the heads of the two men, and the muzzle flash lit up their faces. The 9mm copper-jacketed bullet punched up into the tattooed man's jaw, and in a split-second it tore up through his brain, punching out of the top of his head and taking a spatter of blood, brain tissue and skull with it that sprayed onto the ground with a wet slap. Barton felt something hit his face. It was hot and sticky on his skin. In an instant, the man suddenly stopped moving, and he went completely limp. Barton slumped down onto him, panting heavily. With his heart beating out of his chest, he quickly rolled off the dead man and lay on his back, gasping for air and squeezing his eyes shut as he grimaced.

'Bloody hell,' he wheezed through gritted teeth.

At that moment, a police cruiser with its lights and siren on appeared and screeched to a halt in the street at the end of the alley. Two officers immediately scrambled out of the vehicle, one gripping his service revolver and the other holding a pump-action shotgun. Wearing sand-coloured short-sleeved shirts with police insignia, matching slacks with a black stripe down the side and shiny black leather shoes, they took up positions behind the relative safety of the cruiser's open doors with their weapons trained at Barton. The officer who had been behind the wheel then yelled to him. He looked to be in his early thirties, and there was a nervous tremor in his voice.

'Stay down!' he shouted. 'Don't you move a damn muscle now, ya hear? Put the gun down and get onto your front with your hands on your head!'

'Okay,' Barton shouted breathlessly. 'Dropping the gun now.'

He let go of the weapon, and it slipped out of his sweaty hand and clattered to the ground. He then rolled slowly away from it and onto his front with his legs splayed out and his hands folded on top of the back of his head. He was in no mood to fight a pair of local cops who were no doubt just as trigger-happy as everyone else in Texas seemed to be. And given his current predicament, getting arrested and being locked up in a jail cell was almost certainly the safest place for him to be right now.

Once in position, he lay perfectly still and waited. The officers approached cautiously, not taking their weapons off him for a second while he remained immobile but panting. The adrenaline was still pumping through his veins, and he tried to calm his breathing to make sure he didn't come across as some drug-crazed lunatic who might suddenly launch himself at the officers. The officer with the revolver reached for a pair of metal handcuffs attached to his belt and approached Barton warily while the other officer covered him with his shotgun.

'You just lie perfectly still now,' he said as he knelt down next to Barton and flicked open one of the handcuffs. 'We're gonna have to bring you in. So, don't you do nothing stupid, alright?'

'Yes, sir,' said Barton calmly. 'I think I like the sound of prison right now, if I am honest.'

As he was pulled to his feet and led back towards the cruiser in handcuffs, two more police vehicles and an ambulance arrived at the scene, all with flashing lights. The other officers and the ambulance crew shot him wary glances as they approached the two dead ex-soldiers lying in the alley. Barton could see the blood on the ground glistening in the lights mounted on the exterior wall at the back of the tavern. After he had been put inside the back of the cruiser and the door had been slammed shut, he glanced out of the window to see the new arrivals huddled around the corpses. Two of the officers were kneeling next to the Viking, and one of them looked back up in his direction. His face said it all. Who was that homicidal maniac in the back of the cruiser?

An hour later, Barton was in a holding cell in the sheriff's office near the centre of town. He was bruised and battered, but it was preferable to being hunted on the streets of Revelation. The process of booking him in had been swift, and there had only been a skeleton crew there to do it. The sheriff himself seemed to be absent, but then it was late on a Friday night, and he had probably gone home many hours ago.

The cell was cramped, and it had a metal bunk bed on one side and a tiny washbasin on the other. The walls were white-painted concrete, the door was made of thick black iron bars, and it was locked with an old-fashioned iron key. Barton was in the cell by himself, and as far as he had been able to ascertain when he was brought in, the other two holding cells in the Sheriff's lockup were both empty that evening.

Before he had laid down, he had taken off the two British Army dog tags that he always wore on a metal chain around his neck. Like countless servicemen before him, they had been issued to him shortly after joining the army and had remained with him ever since. Originally instituted by the Roman legions who crafted theirs out of lead, dog tags had only been introduced into the British Army in 1907, before which soldiers carried the much more perishable paper identification cards. A set of black rubber sleeves for the steel tags were an optional extra, but Barton had always preferred being able to feel the two cold metal discs against the skin on his chest.

The chain was tucked under one of the slats in the bunk above him, and the tags were now suspended over his head, languidly swaying and turning as they gradually lost momentum. Being standard issue army tags, they were made of stainless steel, and on their front were engraved his service number, blood group, surname and initials. He wasn't much of a sentimental character, but those tags were now part of his history and had become part of who he was. On the rare occasion, when for whatever reason he suddenly found himself not wearing them, he felt strangely naked.

As he lay there watching the tags sway like tiny pendulums, he thought back to the encounter with his two former colleagues. In hindsight, it occurred to him that the cops had turned up surprisingly swiftly. Or perhaps someone in the High Jinx Tavern had called them as soon as they saw the two-man hit squad chase after him. He thought back to the gunfight, going over every detail and playing it back in his mind as if watching a movie, and he knew that he had been acting in self-defence. But he also knew that there was no way for him to prove that. There were no witnesses, and he didn't know if there were security cameras at the back of the tavern. As far as the police were concerned, he was now a double murderer, and that meant that he was about to be dropped in a world of hurt.

Soon to be accused of two murders in a state where the death penalty was not only regularly enforced, but which carried out more executions than anywhere else in the United States of America, Barton had quickly realised just how much trouble he was in. So, when the duty officer had offered him his one phone call, secured under the 5th and 14th amendments to the US Constitution, Barton had not called a lawyer like most people did. He had called the only man he thought might be able to help him. The one man he felt he could reach out to, and who he knew would come to his aid at a desperate time like this. His old friend and SAS troop leader, Andrew Sterling.

Now, lying outstretched on the bottom bunk with his eyes closed and his hands behind his head, he could only lament the fact that Andrew had failed to pick up the phone. He had left a voice message where he had explained in broad strokes what had happened that night. However, he had been unable to tell Andrew exactly what had been going on in the days leading up to today, or why he had been running from his former colleagues who had tried to kill him. All he could do was ask for Andrew's help and then wait and hope for the best. It was going to be an uncomfortable wait, however long it lasted. As he lay there thinking back to a much simpler time when he had been part of 22 SAS, he suddenly felt an immense wave of physical and mental exhaustion wash over him, and within a couple of minutes he had slipped into a deep dark well of tiredness and fallen asleep.

★   ★   ★

Pulled from the dark depths of sleep, Barton awoke to the sound of a distant metallic rustling. Then there was the sound of rapid shuffling as he began to come to, and then he suddenly felt rough hands grabbing his arms and shoulders. Before he was able to properly wake up and orientate himself, a hood was pulled over his head and he was pushed forcibly to the floor. His arms were twisted around to his back and he felt restraints being put around his wrists, but these were not metal handcuffs. They were zip ties that cut into his skin. Once they were secured, he was yanked back onto his feet and pushed out of the cells.

From his walk into his holding cell, he remembered the layout of the cell corridor and the rest of the sheriff's office, and even though he was unable to see anything, he realised that he was being led along the corridor but not out of the front door. Instead, he was hustled to one side and through another door after which he heard the voice of what sounded like a young man, possibly in his early thirties. A local man who sounded anxious and stressed.

'You can't be doing this,' he said. 'This ain't lawful.'

For the first time, one of the two men holding Barton by his shoulders and walking him through the back of the building spoke up.

'Shut up, Billy Ray,' he said in a terse, husky voice that seemed familiar to Barton, although he couldn't place it. 'This ain't none of your business. If you know what's good for you, you'll forget this ever happened.'

After that, no one spoke again, and Barton heard the sound of a metal door on rusty hinges swinging open up ahead. A few moments later, he sensed that he was being led outside. The air was warm and dry, and the only sounds he could hear now were the rustling of clothes, the crunch of boots on the dusty ground and dozens of crickets in the bushes. Then he heard a car door opening and sliding along its rails in front of him. It had to be a van of some sort. He was bundled roughly inside and onto the floor, and then the two men behind him followed. Finally, the door slammed shut. Barton felt the weight of the van shifting as a third man got in behind the wheel and started the engine. He could sense the proximity of the men next to him, and they smelt of sweat, alcohol and aggression.

'Alright,' said the husky voice. 'Let's go, boys.'

Moments later, the van exited from behind the sheriff's office, pulled out onto the main road and headed for the high desert.

Two

THE WEST END, CENTRAL LONDON

It was mid-morning, and Andrew Sterling left the gym under the HQ of the London-based SAS unit to which he had now been attached for several years. From its modest offices in a nondescript building on Sheldrake Place near Holland Park, and under the firm and even-handed leadership of Colonel Strickland, the unit had been responsible for thwarting numerous attempted terrorist attacks both in Britain and abroad. Specialising in combatting terrorists hell-bent on acquiring and using weapons of mass destruction on both civilian and military targets, it was a heavily intelligence-led enterprise that had saved countless lives, although none of those efforts would ever be publicly acknowledged. Andrew had been with the unit almost from the beginning, being hand-picked from 22 SAS at Hereford shortly after Strickland had left to form and head up the new covert entity.

Although much of Andrew's work happened behind a desk, he insisted on never allowing his fitness levels to decline, and he prided himself in being able to make occasional visits to Hereford to take part in the most demanding physical exercise regimes and the never-ending CQC exercises inside the 'kill house'. While there, he also made sure to always catch up with old friends in the Regiment.

Taking the elevator up to his office on the 4th floor, he then made his way along the corridor, and as he passed by his secretary Catherine, who was fielding a call on her headset, he gave her a quick salute and she shot him a smile and waved. He sat down at his desk and went through the emails that had arrived since he had left for the gym about an hour earlier. There was a note from Strickland about an upcoming briefing on a recently launched UK spy satellite with infrared capabilities well beyond any existing technology currently in orbit. There were also a couple of reports from human intelligence assets working covertly in deep cover inside various Middle Eastern NGOs suspected of being fronts for terrorist organisations. The emails all contained valuable intel, but none of them required urgent action. He then picked up his personal smartphone to see that there was a missed call from a mobile phone number with the country code '+1'. The United States. There was also a voice message waiting for him. It had come in several hours earlier, but he must have missed it.

He frowned as he looked at the number on the phone screen. It was a rare occurrence for him to receive calls from US mobile phones. He was in regular contact with various US intelligence agencies, but they were always conducted via secure landlines, and he never took calls from overseas numbers that he didn't recognise. He also wasn't aware of anyone he knew who was currently in the US. He pressed the speed dial for his voicemail, leaned back in his chair and held the phone to his ear.

'Andy,' said a gravelly, tense and despondent-sounding voice with a thick Yorkshire accent that Andrew immediately recognised. 'Mate. It's Eddie here. Listen, I am in a jail cell in Texas. A small place called Revelation. Great fucking name, isn't it? Anyway, I have been living there for a while now, and I am in a spot of bother over here. I could really use your help. I killed two guys. They were trying to take me out. I can't tell you the details, but it's a fucking mess. You know I wouldn't ask you unless I was in real trouble. Call me back as soon as you get this, alright? I'm relying on you, mate. Thanks. Bye.'

Stunned by what he had heard, Andrew placed the phone back on the table and turned his head to stare out through the slatted blinds to the leafy trees outside. In the distance, the faint undulating wail of a police car washed over the West End. He had always known that Barton could be a bit of a rogue, and he had been sad to find out that he had more or less been forced out of the Regiment. But a double murder? What could possibly have led to this?

'Eddie,' he muttered as he gazed out. 'What the hell happened?'

He then picked up the phone again and attempted to return the call, but he simply got a pleasant-sounding recording of a female voice with a southern accent saying "Sorry. The number you have called could not be reached". He tried again, but with the same result.

He spent the rest of the day attempting to work and focus on the tasks at hand, but his mind kept circling back to Barton's voice message, and he listened to it several more times during that afternoon. He couldn't remember ever hearing Barton sounding like that. Through the timbre of his voice, he had sounded defeated. Even anxious. This was not the Barton that Andrew remembered. Something was very wrong. That much was clear.

At one point, he picked the phone back up and opened an image gallery he had created with photos of places he had been and people he had worked with throughout his career. After a couple of seconds, he had found what he was looking for. It was a photo of Barton on a leafy footpath walking casually towards the camera while wearing military fatigues and holding the silenced SA80 rifle that was the standard issue for Royal Marine commandos. The picture was at least ten years old, and it had clearly been staged, probably so that Barton could send it back to England to impress some girl somewhere. But Andrew had kept it because he thought it captured everything that Barton was. The stocky frame. The tattooed arms. The cheeky grin and the carefree demeanour. That's how he remembered him. He sighed, turned off the phone and caught a glimpse of his own reflection in its dark screen. He looked concerned, and there was an uncomfortable frown on his face.

As he drove back to Hampstead that evening, he pondered what to do. By the time he entered the house and made his way to the kitchen, there was really only one possible option.

'Hi Andrew,' called a female voice from the living room as he entered the open-plan kitchen.

It was that of his girlfriend Fiona Keane, historian and archaeologist with the British Museum, problem-solver extraordinaire, owner of a sometimes-terrifying eidetic memory, and all-round gorgeous Irish hothead. The love of his life.

'Hey,' he said wearily, dropping his bag on one of the bar stools by the kitchen island and walking to the living room to join her.

She was reclining lengthways on a large white sofa with her feet up, a thick, leatherbound book resting on her stomach, and a steaming cup of coffee within arm's reach on the coffee table next to her. She was wearing a white figure-hugging top and dark grey jeans, and her auburn hair was done up in a bun with two chopsticks poking through it. As he entered, her green eyes locked onto his, and she flashed him her winning smile.

'Tough day at the office?' she said, a mild teasing note in her voice.

'Not really,' said Andrew with a sigh, lowering himself into an armchair and leaning back with his hands behind his head as he stared up at the ceiling.

'What's wrong?' she said. 'Are you alright?'

He proceeded to tell her about the message from Barton, and she remembered him having mentioned the Yorkshireman a few times in the past.

'Shite,' she said empathetically once he had finished. 'Have you tried calling?'

'I can't reach him on the phone,' said Andrew. 'I've tried several times this afternoon, but it can't connect. It's as if his phone isn't even switched on anymore. Something's not right.'

'What are you going to do?' she said.

'I have to go over there,' Andrew replied. 'He asked for my help, and he wouldn't do that unless he was in way over his head.'

'I think you should sleep on it,' said Fiona. 'Give it a few more hours. He might call you back.'

'Maybe,' said Andrew. 'I doubt it.'

'Come on,' she said, placing her book on the coffee table, swinging her legs off the sofa, and getting to her feet. 'Let's go get a pizza at that new place you like. Take your mind off things. I'm sure he'll be alright.'

Andrew said nothing for a few moments, but then sat up and nodded.

'OK,' he finally said, reluctantly. 'Maybe you're right. I'll wait a bit longer. If he hasn't called by the time we get back, I am booking a flight over there.'

Three hours, a bottle of red wine and two pizzas later, the two of them returned to the house, and Andrew's phone had been as silent as the grave. He sat down inside his small home office, and within a few minutes, he had secured a business-class seat on a flight from Heathrow to Dallas Fort Worth International Airport, departing the following morning at 10:40 a.m. and arriving just after 3 p.m. the same day. With a six-hour time difference between the UK and Texas, he was going to be experiencing a bit of jetlag, but that was the least of his concerns. Still, he decided to try to get as much sleep as possible and went to bed early, following the age-old military mantra. Eat when you can. Sleep when you can.

It took some time to fall asleep, but after a while, he finally drifted off into oblivion.

★   ★   ★

Opening his eyes after too little sleep, Andrew blinked a couple of times and looked up at the slats in the bunkbed above him. It took him a few seconds to remember where he was. The sounds of diesel engines outside the barracks, a helicopter passing overhead and the commands shouted by an officer in the distance quickly anchored him in both time and place. It was mid-morning, and he was in a forward operating base in Mali as part of an international effort to suppress fundamentalist militants in the south of the tortured and unstable African desert nation.

The FOB was a lot smaller than the bases the Regiment had been operating out of in Afghanistan, but it was large enough to have its own wooden barracks buildings, recreational facilities, mess hall, tactical operations centre and helicopter pad. The sprawling compound was well protected by high walls constructed from large heavy-duty fabric-lined wire mesh containers filled with rocks and dirt. The boxy-looking so-called Hesco barriers had been ubiquitous in Afghanistan, and despite their simple construction, they were practically immovable and extremely effective as defensive fortifications against all but the heaviest of artillery, which neither the Taliban nor the Mali militants possessed. On top of the walls, behind low berms of smaller sandbags, were covered machinegun emplacements every twenty metres or so. There were also heavy mortar positions ready for use in all four corners of the base.

The FOB was located in a sparsely populated part of the country. It was a mostly flat terrain dominated by orange sand and red dirt, as well as the occasional brown, craggy ridge jutting up a few dozen metres. Aside from that, it was a featureless parched desert brushland with only a few small bushes and trees clinging to life under a huge blue open sky above.

The team from Hereford had rotated in several weeks earlier, and the operational tempo had been high, often with more than one mission per day. Linked to and funded by al-Qaeda, the Islamist militants in Mali were conducting regular and brutal raids on government facilities and villages all over the province. With excellent intelligence provided by US satellites and loitering drones overhead, the SAS team was in high demand in the multi-national effort to stamp out the extremists and protect the civilian population.

The FOB's prefab barracks buildings, although built from heavy-duty timber and large sheets of plywood, were sturdy enough to take a beating from the violent sandstorms that sometimes blew up here. Providing shelter from the scorching sun during the day and the desert cold during the night, they were also surprisingly cosy inside, and Andrew found that he often slept better here than back at their HQ in Hereford.

'Hey Andy,' came a voice from the top bunk.

It was gravelly and languid, and it had a strong Yorkshire accent.

'What?' said Andrew, rubbing his eyes and sitting up in the bed.

Eddie Barton's head appeared over the edge of the bed above him. He was holding a thick book in one hand. Its title was 'Three Millennia of Military Tactics', and Andrew recognised the cover. For several days now, Barton had been reading it during downtime between missions. The Yorkshireman had that look on his face that told Andrew that he was about to tell him something he found amusing.

'Do you happen to know why they call it infantry?' Barton said with a wry smile.

'Go on. Tell me,' said Andrew mid-yawn, still tired after the night mission they had completed only a handful of hours earlier.

'It's Latin, apparently,' said Barton. 'Comes from 'enfant', which literally means without speech. As in, an infant that's too young to do anything useful, or in this case, too young and inexperienced to be fighting from a horse. So that's why the infantry fights on foot.'

'I thought you never liked studying?' said Andrew with a wink as he swung his legs out over the edge of the bed.

'Doesn't mean I don't like to learn new stuff,' said Barton. 'It's never too late, is it?'

'Fair enough,' said Andrew, getting up from the bed.

'Just don't tell the lads,' said Barton, putting the book aside and producing a grin. 'I have a bad reputation to maintain, you know?'

'Your secret is safe with me,' said Andrew.

At that moment, a red light mounted above the wooden door came on, along with a claxon mounted on top of the tactical operations centre about thirty metres away. The claxon produced a brief squeal and then fell silent.

'Fuck me,' said Barton. 'Already?'

'Duty calls,' said Andrew, grabbing his gear and opening the door as Barton jumped down onto the floor. 'Let's see what they've got this time.'

The two men left the small barracks building and crossed over the dusty open space at the centre of the FOB. Suddenly, there was a bark coming from their left side, and a small and skinny German Shepherd raced towards Barton. Spotting the dog, he broke into a wide smile and knelt down to pet it as it came close and pushed up against him.

'Hey Asbo,' he said kindly, ruffling the dog's ears as it wagged its tail and tried to lick his face. 'How are you, boy?'

The dog was a stray that, for a long time, had taken to coming sauntering into the base as if it owned the place, and it was now becoming a semi-permanent resident. Barton had named him Asbo due to his fondness for doing the exact opposite of what was expected of him as an unofficial base mascot and for generally being anti-social to everyone except Barton.

'You know, you won't be able to bring him back with you, right?' said Andrew, chuckling at the sight of the hard-as-nails Yorkshireman showing his soft side.

'I know,' said Barton, reaching into a pocket of his combat trousers for one of the dog treats that he had started carrying around with him. 'There you go. Good doggy.'

Shortly thereafter, they were inside the operations centre, where a multitude of wall-mounted screens were showing various live drone feeds. A handful of techs and intelligence officers were monitoring the feeds and communicating with the drone operators. Along with the rest of the small SAS team, Andrew and Barton converged on a large table in the middle of the room. The other three team members were a burly Scot named Duncan who excelled at breaching operations, a lean and wiry marksman from Kent called Taylor, and a Welsh all-rounder with a black goatee by the name of Evans.

'OK. Listen up,' said the operations commander. 'We have picked up mobile phone chatter about an imminent raid on a village about forty klicks from our location. The staging area used by the militants is supposedly at this compound right here, a couple of klicks from the village.'

The commander pointed at a monitor showing a still image of a small group of dilapidated buildings in a shallow valley. The surrounding terrain looked much like everything else in that part of the country. Orange sand, red rocks, the odd butte and clumps of small anaemic-looking trees and bushes clinging on for dear life in the parched and arid desert.

'Andrew,' said the commander. 'Your team is going to clear out the compound before the militants can launch an attack. You will be helicoptered in by a US Army Black Hawk and dropped behind this ridge. You will then make your way over the ridge to move in from this direction behind cover of these trees and bushes here. Once you have cleared the compound and grabbed any high-value targets, you will extract from this location over here. Any questions?'

'Any particular HVT we're looking to nab?' asked Barton.

'No,' said the commander. 'There is limited intel on the composition of their forces at this point, so you will have to improvise. Anything else?'

No one else spoke up, so the commander nodded and clapped his hands together.

'Alright, chaps,' he said. 'Wheels up in ten. Get yourself ready.'

Just under an hour later, the Blackhawk flared out and landed inside a whirling cloud of orange dust, roughly a kilometre from the target. As soon as the team of five operators had disembarked and taken up defensive positions around the landing site, the chopper took off again and pulled back to a safe location. It would wait there for the call to come back and extract the team along with any high-value targets they might have captured.

Once the chopper had cleared the area and the swirling veil of orange dust had dissipated, the team ripped off the clear plastic goggles they had been wearing during the insertion. They then converged on Andrew, who led them through the bone-dry brush towards the low ridge about a hundred metres away. Each man was cradling a suppressed Heckler & Koch MP5SD as well as a pistol in a thigh holster. Barton, who was directly behind Andrew, also carried a sawn-off 12-gauge Remington 870 pump-action shotgun loaded with large-diameter buckshot shells. This weapon often came in handy during breaching operations, and during a close-up fight, it was capable of eliminating an enemy with a single blast.

It was now close to midday, and the heat was stifling. These were far from ideal conditions for a mission like this, with most of them taking place during the night or early morning. However, due to the time-sensitive nature of the operation indicated by the available intel, command had determined that it should be carried out without delay before an attack by militants on a nearby village could be carried out.

As they crested the ridge, the five men kept low behind cover as much as possible. Andrew used his binoculars to scan for movement below them, but he saw nothing. That didn't mean that the compound was empty, and there was always a chance that one of the many local informants had heard the chopper and alerted the militants. If that was the case, then they were about to walk into an ambush. The Islamist group might be a ragtag bunch of deranged religious extremists, but they knew this terrain like the back of their hand, and they were not afraid of dying. In fact, they welcomed it with open arms. This made them a very dangerous enemy.

The small team of operators made their way down a narrow trail, mostly out of sight of the compound, and began to spread out in a vague crescent shape as they pushed up towards the main building with their weapons in front of them, ready to engage. At one point, a dog that appeared to have been sleeping inside an outhouse came barreling out and sprinted off in the opposite direction. Perhaps sensing what was about to unfold, it didn't bark but merely disappeared in a cloud of dust behind one of the buildings. Silently, Andrew glanced over at the rest of the team and used his hand to indicate for them to push forward except for Taylor, who was directed to take up position on a small bluff overlooking the compound. From there, he would be able to provide covering fire if needed.

They formed up along a wall next to the door to the main building. Andrew and Barton were on one side, and Duncan and Evans were on the other. No one spoke a word. The wooden door in front of them was relatively flimsy and did not appear to be locked. At Andrew's signal, Duncan detached a flashbang, pulled the pin, kicked the door open and tossed the stun grenade inside. About two seconds later, the flashbang exploded with a deafening blast, and despite the glaring midday sunlight, a brilliant white flash of light spilled visibly out through the doorway to the outside.

The debilitating explosion was still reverberating through the ramshackle building when the team filed swiftly but silently inside with all the speed and aggression that characterised a good breaching operation. With their weapons up and ready to fire, they swept through the entire building in a matter of seconds, clearing each room in turn. However, it quickly became clear that the place was empty. It wasn't abandoned because there were obvious signs of it having been used recently, including a stash of canned food, some blankets and a small weapons cache. But of the militants, there was no sign.

They quickly checked the outhouse and also a small barn, but those bore no sign of having been used for a long time. Once he was sure that there were no threats, Andrew assembled the team in front of the main building, including Taylor, who had climbed off his sniper perch. He then reached up to activate his helmet-mounted mike, relaying their status back to the tactical operations centre at the FOB.

'TOC 1, this is Alpha 1,' he said. 'The compound is empty. I say again. The compound is empty. No sign of militants. I think we might have been played.'

'Alpha 1, this is TOC 1,' came the voice of the commander. 'Roger that. Bad luck, chaps. Prepare for extraction. Chopper inbound. ETA is two minutes.'

'Roger,' said Andrew. 'Awaiting extraction. Two minutes. Alpha 1 out.'

Barton came over and joined him with his arms spread out to his sides.

'I thought we had good intelligence people?' he said with a smirk. 'Where the hell is everyone?'

'That's how it goes sometimes, Barton,' shrugged Andrew. 'Cheer up. At least no one is shooting at you.'

'No tea and medals today then,' Barton grinned.

'Alright, lads,' said Andrew, addressing the whole team. 'The chopper will be at the LZ in 2 minutes. Let's move out.'

The designated landing zone for the helicopter was located about one hundred and fifty metres from the compound on a small, slightly raised plateau further down in the valley. On its eastern side ran a steep, rocky escarpment that was roughly thirty metres tall.

When they arrived, they saw that a dirt road ran across the open area of the LZ, and a small thatched-roof earthen hut was sitting on one side of it near some withered-looking trees. They assembled near the hut, taking up defensive positions while they waited to be picked up by the Blackhawk and flown back to the FOB. Within seconds, the familiar distant thudding sound of rotor blades washed over the terrain. Shortly thereafter, the large dark helicopter flared out above them and touched down in a furious tornado of dust and debris. Moving in a tight formation, the team pushed through the pale orange whirlwind and began boarding the chopper, whose side doors had already been slid open. Inside was a US Marine door gunner manning a Gatling rotary machinegun, and in the cockpit were a helmeted pilot and a copilot eyeing the SAS team and waiting for them to board.

As was always the case, Andrew was the last man in, crouching on the ground next to the door while his teammates scampered up into the helicopter's rear passenger cabin. Suddenly, the ground near the chopper seemed to come alive with puffs of dust, and he instantly realised that they were taking incoming fire. The pilot seemed to have spotted it too, and he immediately increased the revs of the turboshaft engines and began increasing the collective in preparation for a rapid take-off. A split second later, a couple of bullets smacked into the cockpit glass, almost hitting the copilot.

'Ambush!' Andrew shouted as his teammates shuffled inside the cabin to make room for him.

With the Blackhawk's landing gear suspension flexing as the aircraft began to lift from the ground, Andrew got to his feet, turned around and started scrambling up into the cabin, helped by Barton. The chopper's wheels finally lifted off as he began to haul himself inside. At that moment, a militant fired an

RPG from the top of the escarpment. Trailing white smoke and sparks behind it, it streaked through the air and narrowly missed the tips of the whirling main rotor blades. It then slammed into the ground and exploded just metres from the chopper's fuselage, peppering it with metal fragments, flying rocks and debris. Miraculously, the powerful blast did not cause any serious damage to the engines or the rotors. However, when the shockwave slammed into Andrew, he lost his grip on the strap he had been using to haul himself inside, and he was shunted violently sideways into the Gatling gun's mount. The impact caused one of his ribs to crack, and a searing pain shot through one side of his torso. An instant later, he was falling backwards, and then he thudded painfully into the dusty ground below as the chopper lifted off into the air. As he landed, the back of his head smacked into the dry compacted earth, causing his vision to black out for a few seconds and an intense pain to shoot through his skull.

Seeing what had happened, and with no time to call out to the pilot and make him set the helicopter back down, Barton launched himself out of the doorway and crashed into the ground next to a badly winded Andrew as the chopper lifted clear of the LZ and peeled away under enemy small arms fire. Still inside the whirling dust cloud created by the chopper's downwash, Barton gripped the back of Andrew's ballistic vest and began dragging him across the hard ground towards the small earthen hut roughly twenty metres away. As soon as the militants up on the escarpment realised that two of the soldiers had been left behind when the helicopter took off, they opened up with everything they had. Bullets whistled through the air, peppered the area around them, and smacked into the ground left and right as Barton dragged Andrew across the open ground and into the hut. Just as they passed the threshold, one of the shooters got lucky, and a bullet punched through Barton's left thigh. He crashed onto the ground inside the hut with a protracted grunt, while Andrew managed to scramble away from the doorway and get his weapon out. He was still groggy from his fall but was now beginning to recover.

'Are you hit?' he shouted, turning to Barton.

'It's just a scratch,' said Barton with a pained grimace as he gripped his thigh with both hands and pressed against the wound.

Blood was seeping through the fabric of his combat trousers and oozing out between his gloved fingers.

'Sit down,' Andrew ordered, reaching for his emergency med kit. 'Don't move.'

Evans had been the team medic, but he was now in the back of the chopper, probably threatening the helicopter pilot with murder and mayhem unless he returned to the LZ. However, both Andrew and Barton knew that there was no way the pilot was going to turn the bird around and come back into a hot area like that until it had been cleared of hostiles.

Andrew ripped open the medkit and grabbed a roll of thick gauze, while Barton tore open his trouser leg, exposing the wound. The bullet had gone right through and seemingly missed major arteries, but there was still a lot of blood. Working quickly, Andrew applied the bandage and then used another one on top to try to maintain as much pressure on the wound as possible until Barton could receive proper medical attention. That was if they managed to get out of this alive.

Outside, most of the gunfire seemed to have died down. There was only the occasional crack from what sounded like AK-47s echoing through the small valley. If the militants knew what they were doing, those shots were an attempt to provide covering fire for an advancing force that was about to arrive at the hut. Andrew moved to the doorway to take a quick peek outside, but he was immediately met with a barrage of incoming fire and quickly retreated back inside the hut.

'TOC 1, this is Alpha 1,' he called into his mike. 'Alpha 1 and Alpha 2 are not in the chopper. I repeat, not in the chopper. We're taking cover in a hut near the LZ under heavy enemy fire. Request close air support. Over.'

The comms equipment crackled briefly, and then the commander's voice came on the line. He sounded tense yet calm and composed.

'Alpha 1, this is TOC 1,' he said. 'We are aware of your status. CAS has already been called in. ETA six minutes. Repeat six minutes. Be advised. Danger close.'

'Roger that,' said Andrew, and glanced out of the doorway. 'Danger close. Six minutes.'

Six minutes was an impressively short response time for the rapid reaction force in the form of two AH-64 Apache helicopter gunships that were flying in from an operation nearby. But for two isolated soldiers under intense enemy fire holed up in a small earthen hut in the deserts of Mali, it was an eternity.

'CAS is six minutes out,' said Andrew, turning to his wounded teammate who was on the ground, propping himself up against the hut's back wall.

'Great,' said Barton tensely. 'Let's go outside and ask those fuckers to cease fire for a few minutes. I'm sure they won't mind.'

'Three full mags. Two grenades,' said Andrew as he checked his ammo pockets. 'You?'

'About the same,' said Barton, crabbing his way across the floor of the small hut with gritted teeth. 'I'll take up position on this side of the door.'

'Alright,' said Andrew. 'Let's hope those militants take longer than six minutes to…'

A mind-numbing explosion suddenly shook the ground and blasted a large chunk of the thatched roof off the hut as well as some of the walls, leaving them looking up through a cloud of dust at the open sky with their ears ringing and their eyes watering. Another RPG had been fired from the top of the escarpment.

'Fuck me!' shouted Barton, spitting dust from his mouth.

'We got lucky,' Andrew coughed. 'Bastard missed by a couple of metres.'

Taking cover behind what was left of the hut's crumbling walls, the two soldiers prepared for the inevitable final assault. It would either come in the form of several more RPGs, one of which was bound to hit its mark, or in the form of a wave of militants carrying old but very lethal AK-47s.

A few seconds later, they heard the sound of several car engines approaching, and they both knew what that meant. Toyota Land Cruisers with machineguns mounted on the back, also known across the African continent as 'technicals'. And they were sure to be bringing a whole bunch of trigger-happy, blood-thirsty militants with them.

'Things are about to get interesting,' said Andrew tensely. 'Are you ready?'

'As ready as I'll ever be,' wheezed Barton as he slapped a fresh magazine into the well of his MP5. 'If today is going to be the day, then let's take as many of those bastards with us as we can.'

'Roger that,' said Andrew. 'Try to conserve that ammo. Make it count.'

'Contact!' Barton shouted at the sight of one of the technicals pulling up about fifty metres away in partial cover near some large boulders.

In addition to the driver and the passenger, a handful of militants jumped off the back of the vehicle and began advancing towards the hut while firing badly aimed bursts. The gunner manning the heavy machinegun fixed to the vehicle's cargo bed swung the bulky weapon around and took aim. Then he squeezed the beast's two triggers, and a hailstorm of hot lead tore through the air towards the hut, slamming into the brittle earthen walls and chewing them up.

After a few seconds, the machine gun appeared to jam because the firing suddenly stopped and the sound of angry shouting reached the two SAS operators inside what was left of the hut. The two men looked at each other, and without a word, they both rolled out from behind cover into the doorway and trained their submachine guns at the militants that were advancing towards them on foot. With short three-round bursts that hit their targets with surgical precision, they cut down first two, and then four of the militants. The men crumpled to the ground in clouds of dust, and as a fifth man turned tail and began to run back towards the technical, Andrew tossed a grenade as far as he could towards the vehicle. The live grenade sailed over the head of the runner and landed between him and the vehicle, less than a metre from both. The runner had no time to react, and when the grenade exploded, he was lifted off the ground and blown backwards landing in a bloody heap on the ground with a mangled face that oozed blood. The technical was shredded by hundreds of pieces of shrapnel, and dozens of metal fragments tore through the body of the gunner standing in the cargo bed. His arms flailed up and around, and then he spun and fell lifeless onto the back of the vehicle.

Both SAS soldiers used the momentary disarray to reload their submachine guns. They had barely finished doing so when another technical pulled up behind the smoking wreck of the first one. Another group of militants jumped off the back, and the rear gunner took aim across the bonnet of the disabled vehicle in front of him. Only Andrew had a clear line of sight to the new arrivals, and he managed to squeeze off several short bursts that sent two of the militants sprawling in the dust before the belt-fed heavy machine gun on the back of the technical opened up. And this one didn't jam.

Amid a furious cacophony of heavy gunfire and fiery muzzle exhaust, it sent a torrent of copper-jacketed lead screaming through the air to smack into the remains of the earthen hut. Large-calibre bullets ricocheted off the hard ground and zinged off into the distance with high-pitched whines. However, most of the bullets hit their mark and rapidly began chewing up the walls of the hut. In a matter of seconds, there would be nothing left of the small fragile structure, and Andrew and Barton would be shredded like so much meat in an abattoir. Lying inside the hut in the chaotic maelstrom of flying metal and clouds of dust, both men realised that they had no option but to risk it all and try to break out and make a run for it. Hugging the floor behind the crumbling walls, they both managed to toss out their remaining grenades in the direction of the technical, but none of them made an impact. The firing continued, and it would continue for as long as the machine gun had ammunition.

'We need to go!' shouted Andrew through the noise and the chaos.

'My leg is fucked!' shouted Barton with a bitter shake of the head. 'I can't run. You go! I'll try to hold them off.'

'Not happening,' Andrew shouted back.

There was not a snowball's chance in hell of Andrew leaving his wounded comrade behind just to try to save his own skin. However, he didn't have an alternative plan that might get them out of this situation alive. This was going to be the end of the road for both of them.

Suddenly, two AH-64 Apache gunships crested the rocky escarpment and hovered menacingly in the air. One of them immediately used its under-mounted 30mm M230 machine gun to tear into the militants still positioned at the top of the escarpment. With a rate of fire of about six hundred high-calibre rounds per minute, the gun peppered the ground and made short work of the armed men. The other Apache immediately locked onto the technical with an AGM-114 Hellfire missile designed to take out Russian main battle tanks. The almost two-metre-long missile came off the rail with a loud whoosh and streaked up into the air, after which it immediately curved down steeply to slam vertically into the technical. The missile's high explosive warhead detonated with such force that the vehicle disintegrated entirely inside a bright spherical fireball that sent thousands of fragments of metal, rubber and plastic flying in all directions. The gunner was vaporised instantly, and a black and orange mushroom cloud of smoke and fire roiled up from the scorched crater where the technical had been just moments earlier.

Pieces of the vehicle were still falling across a wide area and thudding into the orange dirt like hundreds of tiny asteroids peppering the desert when both helicopter gunships directed their machinegun fire at what was left of the militants. There were only a couple of them still alive and on foot, and as they attempted to run away, they were cut down and dismembered by the bullets spewing from the gun pods mounted under the noses of the two choppers.

'Bloody hell!' grimaced Barton as the sound of explosions and gunfire ended, and all they could hear was the sound of the two terrifying apparitions hovering over the escarpment while they scanned for stragglers. 'I want one of those!'

'That was damn close,' said Andrew, getting to his feet and waving to the two chopper pilots. 'Are you alright, mate?'

'I am alive,' said Barton, patting himself down. 'I think.'

'I am going to call in medevac now,' said Andrew, kneeling beside his teammate to make sure he was ready to be moved onto a stretcher and into a chopper.

He then got onto the comms to the tactical operations centre to ensure that Barton was brought out of the valley as fast as possible.

'Thank you,' said Andrew, fixing Barton with a meaningful look. 'For jumping after me. I'd be dead otherwise.'

Barton gave him a small, dismissive shake of the head.

'You would have done the same for me,' he said, grimacing again as the pain lanced through his leg.

'Absolutely,' nodded Andrew, placing a hand on his teammate's shoulder. 'Still. I owe you.'

*   *   *

Andrew woke up from his dream with a start. It was the middle of the night, and bright moonlight over Hampstead cut into the bedroom through a large window next to the bed. Those last words of his, spoken years ago in a desert in Mali and replayed in a dream that had felt all too real, were now echoing inside his mind. I owe you.

He rubbed his eyes, swung his legs over the edge of the bed and stepped out onto the wide wooden floorboards. Fiona was still fast asleep beside him, but he knew it was useless for him to try to go back to sleep now. He moved quietly to the bathroom where he took a shower, and then he went downstairs to pack a few things and get ready to leave for the airport just after sunrise.

Before leaving, he would need to explain to Fiona why he had to go. She had been by his side many times in the past, and she had saved his life more than once. She had proven an invaluable resource during their various quests for legendary historical artefacts, but this time was different. This time it was personal, and he couldn't risk having her along in case things spun out of control. He had no specific reason to think that they might do so, but he couldn't shake the feeling that something was seriously wrong and that Barton was in a lot more trouble than he had let on during his call.

The evening before, despite having already booked the flight to Dallas, he had still found himself wavering about whether to run off on such short notice without understanding what he was getting himself into. But not anymore. His dream had made things crystal clear in his mind. He was going to Texas.

THREE

THE ALTAMIRANO ESTATE, CENTRAL AMERICA

The sun was approaching the horizon, and evening was closing in around the luxurious and sprawling compound sitting on a large private estate by a lake inside what could best be described as a private tropical forest. The estate, with its perfectly manicured flower gardens, tennis courts and swimming pools, was owned by Fernando Lopez Altamirano of obscure but very old nobility from a time when the New World had first been settled by the Spanish Crown. Like his father, grandfather and great-grandfather before him, he had only ever known a life of significant wealth and political influence, moving in circles that had made his life comfortable and safe to a degree outside the realms of possibilities for the vast majority of his fellow countrymen. After having received his education at one of the most prestigious and expensive business schools in the United States, he had returned to his country of birth to take over the running of the oil exploration and trading company that his grandfather had established more than a century earlier.

Like most evenings at this time of year, the air was warm and humid even inside the main residence, whose mid-century modernist angular shape was broken up at each end by two tall and round medieval tower-like structures that housed VIP bedrooms for important visitors. At its centre was a large wedge-shaped edifice that protruded out towards the gardens like the bow of an oil tanker. The enormous mansion was lit up by warm lighting spilling out of every one of the large windows, and placed at the top of the two towers were flagpoles with white flags bearing the old colourful Altamirano family crest.

In the trees of the dense forest that surrounded the estate, exotic birds were singing and squawking to their hearts' content. Wrapping around the back of the mansion were wooden porches and an outside dining area by a glistening, lit-up swimming pool. Away from the mansion stretched several gravelled paths that meandered through the gardens, lit up by regularly spaced metal bollards. On the porches and along the paths strolled armed guards who were patrolling calmly, as they did every day and every night. No one had any inkling that the peace of the forest was about to be shattered.

Fernando Altamirano was in his study, sitting by a large dark wooden desk and surrounded by tasteful furniture and other décor, tall mahogany bookcases and several large oil paintings of his illustrious ancestors. As the sole heir to the family fortune and the serving CEO of the PetroDorado company, he had taken over the reins from his father more than a decade ago. Since then, he had confidently steered the company forward through a difficult and ever-changing operating environment and ensured its continued growth, often at the expense of smaller rivals. By all accounts, he lived a charmed and relatively carefree existence, but this evening his brow was furrowed as he read through the latest update from his finance team based on information provided by his brokerage firms. It was now crystal clear that someone was quietly buying up PetroDorado shares on the stock market, and it had proven impossible to discover the identity of the buyer. The unusual activity had begun several weeks ago, and it had been carried out through foreign brokers on behalf of shelf companies registered in various opaque tax havens in the Caribbean. It wasn't obvious what the purpose was, but something was definitely amiss. He could feel it in his bones.

He looked up to gaze absentmindedly out of the window towards the garden. As he did so, one of the guards walked past, and Altamirano could hear his weighty footsteps on the floorboards of the porch outside. The man was a large bulky figure with short-cropped hair. He was wearing a dark suit, he had an earpiece sitting in his right ear, and he was cradling a submachine gun in his hands. Altamirano couldn't remember his name. He was just one out of a large security team on a constant rota system, but he knew that he had seen him many times before. Whoever he was, he was certainly well paid. Running a successful multi-billion-dollar corporation in a country like this required a certain level of personal protection.

Kidnappings for ransom were a regular occurrence, and Altamirano had spared no expense in protecting himself and his family.

★   ★   ★

Sixty kilometres away, at an altitude of seven thousand feet, the Bell V-280 Valor aircraft was approaching the estate at just under four hundred kilometres per hour. The sleek, black-painted dual tilt-rotor aircraft had taken off more than three hours earlier and had spent most of its journey heading south across the Gulf of Mexico. Designed specifically to replace the Blackhawk helicopters in the US military, it was capable of vertical take-offs and landings. However, it also had the ability to tilt the two large three-bladed rotors at the ends of its wings forward during level flight, thereby drastically increasing its effective range to several times that of the Blackhawk. The first of the Valor aircraft were only just coming off the production lines, but the owner of this particular one had secured one for himself through his close personal relationship with an intermediary tasked with liaising between the military and the manufacturer. With a range of almost three thousand kilometres, it had been able to easily cover the distance from Texas to the target area.

The hybrid aircraft was now less than ten minutes from its destination, and the pilot hit the switch to signal for the team in the back to get ready. A red light came on inside the passenger cabin, and three of the four men unbuckled their straps and got up from their seats. The team leader, an imposing-looking man by the name of Cormac, was a large bald former SEAL Team operator who sported a thick black moustache. Like most of his colleagues, he had a chest like a gun safe, tattoo-covered biceps like tree trunks, and hard penetrating eyes.

'Listen up, people,' he said in a gravelly, baritone voice with a thick Texas drawl. 'It's showtime. Ten minutes. Prep your gear. And somebody wake up Knox.'

Knox, also a former Navy SEAL and a fellow Texan, was still asleep in his seat. Short and muscular, he had blue eyes and a short, blond beard. His head was resting at an angle against the vibrating fuselage, and his hands gripped the suppressed Heckler & Koch HK416 assault rifle fitted with a 4x ACOG sight that was lying across his lap. The Advanced Combat Optical Gunsight was the standard medium-range optic used by U.S. special forces, and it allowed highly trained shooters like Knox to consistently land rounds on targets at ranges up to about 300 metres.

The man sitting next to him was a lean and wiry former Delta Force operator named Tyler who hailed from Alabama. With his wild eyes, distinctive hooked nose, narrow face and black ponytail, Tyler looked more like a gang member than anything else, but he was a highly experienced and decorated former Tier 1 operator. He was leaning back in his seat with his right foot resting on his left knee, using an oversized combat knife to clean dirt from under his fingernails. The knife was his most cherished possession, and he kept a running tally of the number of men he had killed with it. Getting up from his seat and sheathing the large blade, he turned around, leaned over and punched Knox hard on the shoulder.

'Yo! Knox!' he shouted over the noise of the cabin. 'Wake the fuck up, man. We're coming up on the drop zone. Ten minutes.'

'Yeah, alright!' grunted Knox groggily as he woke up with a grimace. 'Keep your damn pantyhose on, Tyler. There's plenty of time.'

'On your feet!' shouted Cormac in the authoritative voice he had employed during his almost two decades serving as a master chief in the Navy Seals. 'Get ready.'

'Yes, sir,' said Knox, immediately getting up and setting about preparing his gear for the drop.

'I thought you'd never wake up,' grinned the fourth man in the team.

He was another burly but clean-shaven former Delta Force operator from Texas by the name of Willis. With a weathered face and piercing blue eyes, he had a small tattoo in the shape of a teardrop below his right eye, and tufts of black hair were sticking out from under a Confederate flag bandana tied around his head. As the banter continued between the team members, their various Southern accents filled the cabin.

'I'm telling you, man,' grinned Knox. 'Sleeping is the best way to travel. I learned that a long time ago. You should try it.'

'Nah, dude,' said Willis, swiping the bandana off his head to reveal a head of black hair slicked back over his head. 'I'm too wired to sleep. I just want to get out of this damn flying coffin and get back into the action. It's been a while since I was in Central America.'

'You'll get your chance soon enough,' grunted Cormac from under his moustache. 'Just get yourself ready. Remember, this is the last hit before the big one. Let's make the boss proud.'

'Fuck yeah,' said Knox, pumping the air. 'Payday.'

Wearing all-black tactical clothing, the small team of former special forces operators put on black balaclavas with full-size white skulls printed on them, their maniacal skeletal grins giving them a truly menacing appearance. They then donned helmets with night vision goggles mounted on them and checked and double-checked their weapons. They were wearing no insignia, the way a regular military unit would have done. Instead, they each had a single patch velcroed onto both shoulders. They were black and circular with gold trim around the edges, and in the centre was the gold-stitched image of a scorpion's stinger raised and ready to strike. Underneath the logo was a single word stitched in gold letters. 'Nightcrawlers'.

Finally, the men fastened their various weapons to their bodies, checked their comms equipment and helped each other strap on the parachutes securely. They then lined up by the rear sliding door on the left side of the aircraft and waited for the signal from the cockpit. About a minute later, the red light changed to green, and Cormac slammed the button for the door. It slid open, and with cold air blasting through the cabin, he moved up to it, his backpack slung low between his legs for the duration of the jump.

Behind him, the three others waddled forward and prepared to exit the aircraft after him. Cormac looked back and got a thumbs up from all three team members, after which he turned towards the door, gripped the doorframe on either side and launched himself out into the dark void. Seconds later, all four men were out, accelerating rapidly towards terminal velocity and watching the forest below race up to meet them. When they were at about a thousand feet, they pulled their cords. Almost instantly, their black rectangular high-manoeuvrability parachutes shot out of their packs and unfurled, slowing them down violently. Less than a minute after that, the black-clad quartet touched down silently in a small moonlit clearing on the opposite side of the estate's artificial lake where they quickly folded up and disposed of their chutes.

'Everyone good?' Cormac said, in hushed tones.

Knox, Tyler and Willis all nodded and whispered a quick 'Affirmative' as they unhooked their suppressed assault weapons, inserted fresh magazines, slung the straps over their shoulders and gripped the weapons firmly with both hands, ready to move out.

'Alright,' whispered Cormac. 'Let's do this.'

With Cormac taking point, the quartet activated their night vision goggles and began pushing slowly and quietly through the dark trees around the left side of the lake towards the brightly lit mansion. A few minutes later, they arrived at the edge of the gardens and crouched down behind a clump of topiarised bushes near a footpath. While the others took up positions around him, Cormac activated the encrypted link back to the ops centre in Texas.

'Alamo, this is Voodoo 1,' he said quietly. 'How copy? Over.'

After a couple of seconds and a brief burst of static, the familiar and slightly hoarse voice of a middle-aged Texan man came through their headsets.

'Voodoo 1, this is Alamo,' he said. 'We copy you, five by five. What's your status? Over.'

'Alamo,' said Cormac. 'We have eyes on the mansion. Flags are up and the lights are on. Looks like our target is at home.'

'Voodoo 1,' said the voice. 'You are cleared to engage. Repeat. Cleared to engage. Alamo out.'

'Roger,' said Cormac.

He terminated the comms link and turned to Tyler, using his index finger to make a whirling motion in the air next to his head.

'Let's get eyes on,' he said.

Tyler nodded, reached into a side pocket of his jacket and extracted a small, black palm-sized drone which he unfolded and activated. He placed it on his hand and held it up in the air, and a couple of seconds later, making virtually no noise, the miniature surveillance vehicle took off vertically and ascended to about fifty metres. Then it began moving across the lawns and flower beds while sending a live feed from its infrared camera back to Tyler's phone.

'Two pairs of tangos patrolling the footpaths on this side of the house,' he said quietly as he studied the incoming greyscale feed. 'Submachine guns, by the looks of it. Two more guys confirmed patrolling on the porches. Probably several more inside.'

'Looks like a tight setup,' said Cormac. 'They only move in pairs, and they are well-armed. We need to assume that they know what they're doing. Options?'

'I say we ambush the first pair of walkers in the shadows under those trees over there,' said Willis, pointing to a clump of tall deciduous trees with wide crowns about fifty metres to their right. 'We can hit them there and dispose of the bodies before anyone realises what's happening. Then we move on the mansion.'

'Sounds good to me,' said Cormac, nodding and looking around at the other two. 'Any objections?'

Knox and Tyler both shook their heads.

'Alright,' said Cormac. 'Let's get over to those trees. Move out.'

Shortly thereafter, the team had split into pairs and had taken up two separate positions in the shadows. They waited for a couple of minutes as the two guards approached. The men were smoking and talking quietly as they walked, with bright orange glows and puffs of white smoke visible in the murky darkness every so often. While the assault team sat immovable and hidden behind foliage, Cormac waited for the perfect moment when the guards were out of sight of the mansion before giving the order.

'Execute,' he whispered.

Immediately, their suppressed weapons clicked and popped as four high-velocity bullets smacked into the two unsuspecting guards, who would never know what hit them. Each man was hit once in the chest and once in the head, and as they dropped onto the footpath like marionettes with their strings cut, the gravel crunched briefly under their weight. Then they lay still.

'Good work,' said Cormac calmly. 'Drag them into the bushes.'

Having hidden the bodies, the team proceeded along a footpath up towards the mansion which sat slightly elevated above the lakeside. Cormac ordered Tyler and Willis to push left through the garden while he and Knox curved right. Moving low and without a sound, the two pairs pincered in towards the long porch that wrapped around the entire mansion facing the lake. Nearing the open area with the swimming pool, Tyler suddenly stopped, crouched and raised a clenched fist, signalling to Willis to stop and get down low.

'Lone tango spotted off the footpath,' he said into his mike as his crosshairs moved onto a lone figure roughly fifty metres away. 'Looks like he's about to take a leak. Want me to reach out and touch him?'

'Roger that,' said Cormac. 'Take him out.'

The words had barely left Cormac's lips before Tyler's assault rifle popped once, sending a copper-jacketed 5.56mm projectile tearing through the air at just under 2,500 kilometres per hour and impacting a fraction of a second later. It carried such force that it punched through the guard's torso, splintering bones and ripping through tissue to exit a fraction of a second later and sending the man crumbling forward into the bushes in a bloody heap.

'Tango down,' said Tyler, cool and calm as if he's just fired a practice shot at the range.

'Willis,' said Cormac into his mike. 'Move around the perimeter and wait for his buddy to come look for him. Then take him down real quiet-like.'

'Got it,' whispered Willis. 'Moving.'

He crouched low and proceeded along a hedge to an area near the dead guard that was in full shadow.

He then took up position by a tree that left him in full shadow, enveloped by darkness and invisible to anyone who wasn't wearing night vision goggles. Soon after, the other half of the guard pair showed up, clearly looking around for his buddy. As he passed Willis, the former Delta operator slid silently out of the shadows and approached the guard from behind, holding a long hunting knife with a black, anodised and razor-sharp blade in his right hand.

Wrapping his left arm around the guard's neck, with lethal efficiency, he then brought the knife around, slit the guard's throat and then plunged the blade into his chest near the heart. The guard spasmed for a brief moment, produced a gory gurgling noise and then stiffened as life left him. Willis was already dragging him backwards out of the light and into the undergrowth where he placed the body quietly on the ground and wiped his knife on his suit jacket.

'Tango Two is down,' he said.

'Alright. Keep moving up,' came Cormac's hushed voice over the radio. 'Two external guards left.'

Another few seconds later, he and Knox were by the porch on one side of the house, and they spotted one stationary guard and one patrolling lazily along the porch.

'You take the guy standing by the railing,' whispered Cormac. 'I'll take the walker.'

'Roger,' said Knox, bringing up his weapon and taking aim.

Cormac lined up his own rifle and took two slow breaths while lining up his own ACOG sights on the guard that was strolling obliviously towards them on the porch. Then he whispered to Knox.

'Three. Two. One. Execute.'

Their weapons popped at the same time, and both targets crumbled to the wooden floorboards with enough noise for the two shooters to think that the remaining guards might have heard it. However, after about ten seconds, all was still quiet, and Cormac got back on the radio.

'Garden cleared,' he whispered. 'Everybody move up to breach positions. Go.'

The team converged quietly on the double doors that had been designated as their main entry point during the mission briefing back in Texas earlier that day. The door was locked, so Tyler placed a long strip of adhesive breaching charge that was more than powerful enough to blow in the wood-framed doors. The four men stepped aside and hugged the exterior walls of the mansion, and Tyler then clacked off the explosives.

The directed charge detonated with an ear-splitting crack that blew both doors inward and ripped them off their hinges. Without hesitation, the four men filed through the smoke into the large dining area on the other side with their weapons up and ready to engage. Almost immediately, two more guards emerged from a large adjoining kitchen. They both looked shaken, but they had their submachine guns raised, and as soon as they spotted the intruders, they opened up. None of the Nightcrawlers sought cover but instead aimed and fired mid-stride as the guards appeared. The fire exchange took less than a second, but during that time, several dozen bullets traversed the dining room, and by the end of it, both guards crashed to the floor dead.

'Fuck,' grunted Knox, clutching his left shoulder. 'I'm hit.'

While Cormac and Tyler covered their teammates, Willis immediately checked Knox's injury. A 9mm bullet from one of the submachine guns had sliced through the top of his deltoid muscle. Blood already oozing out and soaking his black clothes, and as Willis examined the wound, Knox grimaced and flexed his hand to check for any impairment.

'It just nicked you,' said Willis. 'Nothing serious.'

'Alright,' said Cormac. 'Suck it up, Knox. You're a frogman. We'll get you patched up once we're back at the ranch. Form up on me. Upstairs.'

With Cormac taking point and a lightly wounded Knox bringing up the rear, the team filed swiftly and quietly up a sweeping staircase and proceeded along a corridor towards what they knew to be Altamirano's office. At that moment, a terrified-looking woman in her forties appeared from a room on one side of the corridor. She was wearing a black and white maid's uniform and holding a silver tray with a set of teacups. When she spotted the menacing black-clad operators advancing swiftly but silently towards her, she let out a shriek, but before it had barely left her lips, she was cut down by several bullets from the assault rifles of Cormac and Tyler. The encounter did not slow the team down, and they pushed swiftly forward towards the end of the corridor and their quarry.

'Stupid bitch,' whispered Cormac as they passed her dead body, her vacant eyes still open and staring up at the ceiling.

When the team was less than five metres from the CEO's office, the door was suddenly torn open by a large man in a dark suit holding an Uzi in each hand. He raised the weapons and was about to release a torrent of lead from the two small rapid-fire weapons when several bullets punched into his chest and sent him flailing and crashing backwards onto the floor of the large office without getting off a single shot.

Maintaining their momentum, the Nightcrawlers pushed inside and fanned out in a matter of seconds, covering the entire space with their weapons. Behind the desk was a distinguished-looking middle-aged man with a short greying beard and glasses. He was wearing a white shirt and an expensive dark suit, and he was sitting in a dark leather office chair. He appeared frozen to the spot at the sight of his guard being cut down right in front of him to now lie on the floor in an expanding pool of his own blood. Cormac moved up to stand in front of the desk, pointing his weapon at the bearded man who was looking up at him with terrified eyes.

'Fernando Altamirano?' Cormac said, evenly. 'CEO of PetroDorado?'

'Si,' replied the man with a trembling voice as he nodded nervously. 'I am Fernando Altamirano.'

Without hesitation, Cormac pulled the trigger, and a single bullet slammed into Altamirano's forehead and exploded out of the back of his skull, taking a red mist of blood and brain tissue with it. Then Cormac lowered his weapon and watched as the dead body of the CEO slumped down onto the wooden desk with a thud. A dark, glistening pool of blood oozed from his mangled head. With the rest of the team arrayed around him looking dispassionately at the dead man, Cormac reached for his mike.

'Alamo, this is Voodoo 1,' he said calmly. 'Jackpot. I say again. Jackpot. Over.'

'Voodoo 1, this is Alamo,' came the gravelly voice. 'Copy Jackpot. Return to base. Over.'

'Roger,' said Cormac. 'RTB. Voodoo 1, out.'

He then turned his back to Fernando Altamirano's corpse and looked at his men.

'Alright, boys,' he said as he began moving towards the door. 'Let's call the bird back in for exfil. We're leaving.'

FOUR

REVELATION, TEXAS

Andrew had left the enormous Dallas Fort Worth International Airport around three hours earlier and driven his Jeep Cherokee rental car almost due west along Interstate 20. The black muscly SUV was large and comfortable to drive, and Andrew had found himself enjoying the country music that seemed to dominate most of the local radio stations. Climbing up into it had been like mounting a horse, and the high driving position gave him a good view out of the windscreen. He had then slung his small backpack onto the passenger seat next to him, started the throaty V8 engine and set off, the four wide tyres hugging the interstate as he cut west through the increasingly dry landscape.

Continuing west through Fort Worth to the city of Abilene, he had then spent over an hour on a virtually straight road until he got to the town of Sweetwater.

From there, he had turned southwest and continued for another hour or so along smaller roads across the arid high desert and scrubland of southwestern Texas, and a dome of beautiful pale blue evening sky hung over him during the final stretch of this journey. As the warm breeze died down and the temperature dropped slightly, only a few wispy clouds were hanging high above in the orange sunlight. Now, as he approached his destination, the sun was descending below the horizon, and its last golden light poured in through the Jeep's windscreen. When he passed the sign by the side of the road bidding visitors 'Welcome to Revelation', dusk was settling over the small Texas town.

Unlike many towns in the state whose populations were falling almost every year and who often had a decidedly down-at-heel look to them, the town of Revelation seemed to be thriving. Even now, just after dusk, there were a fair amount of people walking along the pavements in the town centre, and along most streets were cars and pickup trucks parked on both sides. The blacktop roads seemed relatively new and well-maintained, and Andrew drove along the appropriately named Main Street, which was short but lined on both sides with neat, independent shops, often under awnings carrying their names and logos. Many of the buildings had been built in a distinctive Southern Colonial architectural style with colonnades, porticos and tall windows with wooden shutters, emulating the mansions that once stood on the Lone Star State's many cotton plantations. However, these were much smaller versions of their predecessors, and they were mostly two-storey wooden structures, many with first-floor balconies.

Their storefronts had large lit-up windows, and these were often emblazoned with lettering across them that was touting the various wares for sale inside. There was a general store, a bank, a homewares store, a bakery, a pharmacy, several outfitter shops selling clothes, boots and hats, a hardware store and a couple of shops selling hunting and fishing equipment. Their wooden storefronts were painted in cheerful, light pastel colours, and many of them had small flagpoles mounted outside at a 45-degree angle with either the Stars and Stripes or the Lone Star Flag.

There were also a number of bars and restaurants, mainly steak houses and burger joints, and they all seemed to be busy as Andrew drove slowly past them and took in the scene. All in all, it seemed that Revelation had been able to buck the trend of decay and depopulation that had swept across most of rural America for decades. Somehow, the town had been able to remain vibrant and affluent, so there was clearly money flowing in from somewhere.

His plan had been to pay the sheriff's office a visit at the earliest opportunity, since this was the place from which he had last heard from Barton. But when he pulled up in front of the building, which was built vaguely in the style of a small 18th-century Spanish mansion set back from the street by about ten metres, it appeared to be shut for the day. With darkness closing in, he decided to find a place to spend the night, and so he turned the car around and headed back along Main Street to a motel he had passed earlier on the outskirts of town.

Mike's Motel was by the side of the road just as the edge of town became open scrubland, and it was impossible to miss on account of its large red and yellow neon sign spelling out its name in bright swirling letters. The motel consisted of two one-storey wooden buildings with low-pitched roofs set back about fifty metres from the road. All of the rooms had red-painted front doors facing the road, and above each one was a small light that seemed to be switched on regardless of whether or not the room was occupied. As Andrew pulled into the parking lot and the car's headlights swept across the motel, it looked to him like it might have around twenty rooms, most of which had no lights in the windows.

He parked up, grabbed his backpack and climbed out of the SUV to walk across the nearly empty parking lot to the small office building that was lit up from the inside by another yellow neon sign. As he pushed through the glass doors and approached the front desk, a young man who looked to be about eighteen looked up from his phone where he appeared to be watching a movie. He pulled his earphones out and got to his feet.

'Evening, sir,' he said with a bored expression. 'Looking for a room?'

'Yes,' said Andrew, pulling his wallet from his pocket. 'Just one night for now.'

'Gotcha,' said the teenager, reaching across the desk for a keycard. 'That'll be 34 dollars.'

'So, who's Mike?' asked Andrew casually as he extracted the banknotes from his wallet.

'What?' asked the teenager.

Andrew jerked his head vaguely towards the neon-lit sign on the wall behind him.

'Mike,' he repeated, handing over the cash. 'I assume he's the owner?'

'I dunno, man,' shrugged the teenager, sounding disinterested as he gave Andrew the keycard. 'I only work here. You're in Room 14. Over there at the back across the yard.'

The youth pointed through one of the windows towards the far side of one of the buildings. Andrew pocketed the keycard as he looked across to his room.

'Alright,' he said. 'What's a good place to get something quick to eat around here? I'll also need breakfast in the morning.'

'There's a place in town,' said the teenager. 'It's called Donna's Diner. You could try that. It's pretty good.'

Andrew almost attempted a good-natured joke about the apparent naming convention in the town, but he decided against it. The young man didn't seem to have much of a sense of humour.

'Thanks,' he said with a nod as he headed for the door.

'Sure,' the teenager said as he returned to watching the movie on his phone. 'See you around.'

Andrew exited the office and strode over to his room. He swiped the keycard, and an electronic beep sounded followed by a metallic click. Then he gripped the spherical metal doorknob and pushed the door open. The room was of a decent size and had the standard motel layout with a low double bed a couple of metres from the front door and a bathroom at the back along the rear wall of the building. The walls

were painted off-white and the décor and furniture
were varying shades of brown and pale yellow. Across
the bed was a checkered red and brown bed throw.
All in all, it looked clean and comfortable enough,
although a bit drab. But then, people didn't come here
to spend time and enjoy the interior design scheme.
They came to sleep so they could be on their way
again the next morning.

As Andrew dropped his backpack on the end of the
bed, he wondered for how long he would be there. It
all depended on precisely what Barton had got himself
mixed up in, and whether there was anything Andrew
would be able to do about it. He would have to wait
until morning to find out. First, though, he needed to
eat, so he had a quick shower, left the room, got back
into the SUV, and set off. Dusk had now turned to
darkness, but it was still warm, and as his black Jeep
Cherokee trundled slowly along Main Street, he had
the window rolled down to breathe the pleasant
evening air and to get a better look at the town.

As he looked out at the seemingly calm setting,
with both sides of the street lined with shops whose
warm light was spilling out onto the pavements, it was
difficult to imagine that this had been Barton's home
turf "for a while now", as his friend had referred to it.
And it was even more difficult to reconcile the
tranquil scene with what Barton had relayed to him
about a double homicide and ending up locked in a
jail cell.

Andrew bit his lip at the thought of his friend's
predicament and at the palpable frustration at having
to wait until the next day to get any answers. He tried
to shake off the gloom as he pulled over in front of

Donna's Diner, pulled the handbrake and stepped out of the car. There was nothing he could do right now except make sure that he had himself a good meal and then some sleep.

The diner had clearly been designed to evoke the nostalgia of 1950s small-town America, and its name was emblazoned above the storefront in swirling yellow neon letters. Underneath was a smaller sign spelling out what appeared to be its tagline. 'The Best Burger Joint in Town'. The diner had three large windows, and as he approached the entrance located at the far left of the storefront, Andrew could see that behind each one was a comfortable-looking four-person booth with red vinyl seats adorned with thin white piping.

He pushed the door open and stepped inside where he was greeted by an interior that was full of red, pink, white and other bright colours. On his left was a classic jukebox, from which emanated a soft 1950s ballad. As he glanced down at the machine, he could see that it was packed with songs by various 50s rock 'n' roll icons such as Buddy Holly, Jerry Lee Lewis, Bill Haley, and of course, Elvis Presley.

The diner had a classic black-and-white checkered tile floor, and the walls were adorned with vintage posters of various movie stars such as James Dean. A long aluminium-edged bar ran opposite the windows, and it was lined with about ten barstools upholstered with the same red vinyl as the seats in the booths. It seemed that all of the staff were young women, and they were wearing outfits that matched the mid-century vibe of the diner's décor.

As he stood there for a moment taking in the scene and enjoying the vague sense of being in a time warp, a petite young woman wearing a waitress uniform approached him and greeted him with a confident look. She was pretty with shiny auburn hair and blue eyes and dimples, and her plastic name tag read 'Donna Cooper'. She wore an easy smile with perfect teeth, and she had red lips to go with the short-sleeved shirt and the flared skirt of her red-and-white plaid uniform. This was clearly the woman behind Donna's Diner, and as she smiled and greeted him, it struck Andrew that, no doubt, many a truck driver had had their day brightened by the sight of her approaching with a plate of burgers and fries, or perhaps a breakfast tray full of hash browns, bacon, sausages and pancakes with maple syrup.

'Hi there,' she said with a cheerful smile in a charming and gentle Texas twang that instantly made Andrew feel welcome. 'My name is Donna. How are you today?'

'Not bad,' said Andrew, returning her smile. 'Nice place you've got here. It comes recommended.'

'That's nice to know,' said Donna. 'Well, it ain't exactly the Ritz, but it's all mine. Would you like a place to sit?'

'Could I have one of those booths over there,' said Andrew, pointing. 'I'd like to be able to look out onto the street.'

'Sure thing,' said Donna. 'Right this way.'

She turned and sauntered past the first two booths that were both occupied to the far end of the diner where she quickly leaned in to place clean cutlery and a fresh napkin in the last booth. Then she picked a menu off a holder on the wall next to her.

'This OK?' she asked.

'Perfect,' said Andrew, and sat down.

'And here's your menu,' she said, handing him a red, padded plastic menu with colourful pictures of the various drinks and dishes available. 'Can I get you a drink?'

'I'll have your best beer,' said Andrew. 'Whatever that is. You decide.'

'One beer coming up,' smiled Donna. 'I'll get you a bottle of Blood & Honey. It real popular. You just have a look at the menu, and I'll be right back to take your order.'

'Great,' said Andrew as he scooted in and made himself comfortable.

As Donna walked back along the bar towards a tall fridge near the other end of the diner, he noticed that several sets of eyeballs belonging to a number of the male patrons followed her all the way. She was stunningly beautiful, but she carried herself as if she were blissfully unaware of the effect she had on her audience. Andrew placed the menu flat on the table and leaned in over it to peruse the options. A minute later, a red skirt entered his field of view again.

'You ain't from around here, are you?' said Donna as she placed a bottle of beer in front of him that had a label showing two old-style six-shooters and the name Revolver Brewing emblazoned across it.

'No. I'm British,' said Andrew. 'I am here to find an old friend of mine. Another Brit. Supposed to be working here. You wouldn't happen to know him, would you? Ex-army. Big guy. Lots of tattoos. Always has a smile on his face.'

'No,' said Donna, looking up and to one side as she appeared to think of someone matching Andrew's description. 'We do have a lot of military types come in here. There's some kind of private military contractor out in the desert. Someplace called Stonewall Ranch. Maybe that's where your friend works?'

'It's possible,' said Andrew. 'What do you know about that ranch?'

'Nothing really,' Donna shrugged. 'Those guys come into town every so often. Sometimes in here too. Most of them don't seem so bad, but some of them are real assholes, if you don't mind my saying so. I'm not sure I ever heard any of them talk like you, though. They all sounded American. Anyway, there was a shooting about a half a mile from here a few nights ago, and I think they detained someone. I hope your friend's got nothing to do with that?'

'I hope so too,' said Andrew darkly, deciding not to divulge any more than he had to. 'I am going to try to speak to the sheriff tomorrow morning. Maybe he can help.'

'Sheriff Hogan?' said Donna, raising one eyebrow. 'Knock yourself out, my friend. He's a bit of a character. My older brother works for him as a deputy. Hogan ain't really that easy to get along with, but you can give it a try.'

'Alright,' said Andrew. 'Sorry to ask you about all this, but I think my friend has got himself into some trouble, and I want to try to help him.'

'Well,' shrugged Donna. 'That's mighty nice of you. I guess that's what friends are for, right? Good luck with that.'

'Thanks,' said Andrew.

'So, anyway, what can I get you?' said Donna, pulling a small notepad from a pocket.

Andrew ordered a burger and some fries, and as Donna disappeared off to serve another customer, he leaned back in his seat and looked absentmindedly out of the window at the cars and pedestrians passing by while a fast and upbeat Jerry Lee Lewis song came out of the speaker system. If it had not been for his unwelcome reason for being here, this town would have made for a nice holiday destination for Fiona and him. It seemed like an idyllic place. A place with one foot still in the good old days, whatever that meant. But his mind kept circling back to the idea that two people had been killed by Barton in this town just a few days ago. He shook his head at the apparent absurdity of it just as two throaty Harley-Davidson motorcycles slowly rumbled past outside.

What could possibly have led to this? he thought.

A few minutes later, his meal arrived, and he took a big bite and savoured the rich and salty flavours of the meat, cheese, ketchup and bacon. The Blood & Honey beer went perfectly with the burger, and after twenty minutes, he shifted in his seat and nudged the empty plate away from the edge of the table. With a belly full of burger and beer, the jetlag was suddenly beginning to catch up with him, and he decided to flag down a waitress to settle the bill.

As he handed over the money, he spotted Donna standing near the jukebox at the other end of the bar.

She was pulling a phone from a pocket in her skirt, and she then touched the screen a few times and put it to her ear. With her right hand holding the phone and her left arm wrapped tightly around herself, she stood silently for a while, evidently waiting for someone to pick up her call. As she did so, her face was lit up by the phone's screen, and it took on a worried look as she stood there, gazing first down at the floor and then out of the window. As Andrew observed her across the diner, she suddenly looked very different from the seemingly carefree young woman he had spoken to half an hour earlier. There was obvious concern in her facial expression, and she shifted uncomfortably on her feet several times as she waited for the call to be answered. Eventually, she removed the phone from her ear and put it back into her pocket with a dejected look and a small shake of the head. As she turned to head back to the serving counter, a respectable-looking older man with short white hair and a grey tweed suit came in. He appeared to be a regular patron because Donna's face lit up when she saw him.

'Hi Arlan!' she called with a smile. 'How's our town mayor this evening?'

'Oh, I just thought I'd stop by for some coffee and cake before heading on home,' he said, making his way to one of the barstools. 'You know how much this place reminds me of when I was a kid.'

'Have a seat, then,' smiled Donna. 'I'll be right with you.'

As she turned to walk back to the bar, her face abruptly fell again and was taken over by what could only be described as anxiousness, or perhaps even fear.

Moments later, a large grey Chevrolet Silverado pickup truck with dark tinted windows pulled up in front of the diner and parked at an angle across two parking bays. Heavy metal music was blaring out of speakers inside it, and on top of the cab was a row of the type of floodlights that were used to light up the desert at night.

Two large men stepped out of the bulky truck and headed for the door to the diner. The larger of the two was wearing dark blue jeans, a white t-shirt and a light beige Stetson hat, and he had a black pointy goatee. The other sported a short-cropped black mohawk, and he was wearing dark brown combat trousers and a mustard-coloured short-sleeved shirt. They both wore military-style leather boots and had tattoos spilling down their muscular arms. Both of them also had the unmistakable look of hard men with whom no one in their right mind would tangle. Andrew suspected that this was intentional, and from their easy swagger, as they moved towards the entrance to the diner, he figured they were used to coming here and treating it like their own backyard. As he observed the two new arrivals, something about them told him they were very comfortable in each other's company. Like they might be used to working as a team. He decided that they were almost certainly ex-military, and he began to wonder if they might be from that place in the desert that Donna had mentioned.

As the two men stepped inside, the occupants of the booth next to Andrew's vacated their seats, and the next few moments that were about to unfold suddenly played out inside Andrew's mind. The two men were going to be heading for that exact booth, and that gave him an idea. He reached into his jacket pocket, pulled out his phone and quickly attached a small surveillance device to the appropriate port. It was a battery-operated combined camera and microphone that was housed inside a matte black plastic casing about the size of a standard die. It could be used while attached to the phone, but it was also capable of being left somewhere for days while recording. The final special trick up its sleeve was its ability to identify and connect to local WiFi networks and use those to send sound or image recordings back to his phone. They had originally been developed for MI6, but his boss, Colonel Strickland, had secured several of them for his investigative unit, and Andrew never travelled without one now.

Andrew sat up straight, placed his phone on the table in front of him, and leaned in over it pretending to be reading something on its screen. Then he placed a wireless earphone inside his left ear and tweaked the position of the phone so that the directional microphone was pointing towards the booth next to him. While he pretended to be absorbed in the phone screen, the two men slumped down heavily in the adjacent booth and waved over a waitress. The man with the Stetson and the goatee took off his hat and placed it on the table to reveal a clean-shaven head. He then leaned back and spread out his muscly arms to place them on the edge of the seatback on either side of himself. After a few seconds, the distinct smell of booze and cigarettes wafted over Andrew, despite him being several metres away.

A waitress came over and asked for their order with a hesitant smile. She was short, slim and blond with blue eyes and light pink lipstick. She was quite pretty, and as he glanced up, Andrew could tell from the looks on the duo's faces that they were busy undressing her with their eyes. She seemed to ignore them and did her best to remain friendly and welcoming. From her somewhat tense demeanour, it seemed to Andrew as if she already knew these two men.

'Evening boys,' she said cheerfully. 'What can I get you tonight?'

'Well, I can sure think of a couple of things, Sugar,' said the bald cowboy in a baritone and lecherous voice, which caused the mohawk guy to grin and chuckle.

'Guys. Are you ordering or not?' said the waitress, sounding mildly irritated but calm.

'Oh, come on now, Paige,' said the mohawk guy reasonably. 'We're just having a bit of fun, that's all. Ain't nothing wrong with that.'

Paige just looked at him without saying a word, and she raised her eyebrows slowly as if to say 'Get it over with'.

'I'll have the 20-ounce steak with fries,' said the cowboy, taking his arms off the seatback and placing his elbows on the table.

'Same here,' said the mohawk guy. 'And a couple of Buds.'

'Steaks and Buds. Coming up,' said Paige, and then she turned and walked away.

'Man, she something, ain't she?' said the mohawk guy, leaning to one side to gaze at her rear as she walked away.

'Almost as hot a little Donna,' said the cowboy. 'I'd sure like to show her a good time, if you know what I mean.'

'Oh yeah,' said the mohawk guy with a smirk. 'Shame about her stupid brother.'

'Well, he had it coming,' said the cowboy quietly and shrugged. 'Should have minded his own damn business.'

A few seconds later, Paige returned with two beers, which she placed on the table before walking off without a word.

'Things might get kind of dicey,' said the mohawk guy. 'Think the boss will be able to keep a lid on it?'

'Are you kidding me?' said the cowboy, sounding mildly irritated. 'Have you forgotten who he is? There's nothing he can't handle. This is small fry, and we've got people everywhere. Everything's going to be just fine.'

The two men then exchanged a conspiratorial look and clinked their bottles in what almost seemed like a celebratory salute. They then spent the next fifteen minutes or so talking about sports results and ranking the waitresses based on their looks until Paige returned with their steaks. All the while, Andrew remained immobile while looking down at his phone and listening to the conversation.

'Thanks, Sugar,' said the cowboy with a wink as she placed his meal in front of him. 'Looking good.'

Paige said nothing as she placed the other plate in front of the mohawk guy. As she was leaning forward, the cowboy quickly reached behind her and gave her a smack on her rear.

'Hey!' she said, swiftly recoiling from the table with a furious look.

Andrew instantly felt the impulse to intervene, but he restrained himself. The last thing he needed after having barely set foot in the town was to end up in a jail cell like Barton.

'Oh, don't be like that, Paige,' said the mohawk guy calmly. 'We like you, that's all.'

'Keep your damn hands to yourself,' said Paige angrily as she spun on her heels and strode back towards the far end of the diner.

'So, any word from the team?' said the cowboy, his voice now hushed and serious as he leaned forward.

'They got back a few hours ago,' replied the mohawk guy in similarly muted tones as he mirrored his companion. 'They're doing their debrief right now.'

'Mission complete?' asked the cowboy.

'Well,' grinned the mohawk guy. 'Let's just say Altamirano's pretty young wife is back on the market. Shame we're not allowed to take trophies.'

'Bonuses for everyone coming up,' said the cowboy contentedly, raising his beer bottle off the table and extending his arm across to his friend.

'Fuck yeah,' said the mohawk guy, clinking his own bottle against it. 'Man, I can't believe I wasted so much fucking time working for Uncle Sam. Risking my ass for peanuts all over the world when there are jobs like this around.'

'Well,' said the cowboy, taking a swig and smacking his lips. 'You can thank the general for that. If it wasn't for him, we might both be working night shifts as security guards or some other shitty damn job. He's a fucking hero in my book. A real patriot.'

'Damn straight,' said the mohawk guy. 'I can't wait for the big one. Set things straight.'

'A fresh start,' said the cowboy, raising his bottle again. 'It's what this country needs. And way overdue, by my reckoning.'

'Amen to that,' said the mohawk guy.

Over the following twenty minutes or so, the two men spoke little as they finished their meals and emptied their beer bottles. Then the cowboy waived for Paige to come over to settle the bill. A few moments later, Donna approached instead and placed their bill on the table.

'So, who's picking this up?' she said.

'Well, this ain't no date,' said the cowboy with a grin as he pulled a wallet full of cash from a back pocket, 'so I guess we're splitting it.'

The mohawk guy did the same, and both men left a couple of large banknotes in a pile in the middle of the table, clearly out of reach of Donna's hands.

'You can keep the change,' said the mohawk guy. 'Maybe go buy yourself some nice underwear or something.'

Donna, now looking very uncomfortable, shot Andrew a brief glance. He had been leaning back for several minutes, looking vacantly out of the window while still listening to the conversation, but now he had turned his head slightly to make eye contact with her. She saw him looking at her and gave a quick shake of the head before returning her gaze to the two men and producing what was obviously a fake smile.

She said nothing and took a step towards the table, leaning forward and reaching across to pick up the money. Suddenly, the cowboy scooted sideways a bit, reached over with an arm and grabbed her behind with a large hand as the other slipped around her waist. Closing his hand around one of her cheeks, he held her there for several seconds as she tried to move away. The mohawk guy was grinning and clearly enjoying the show.

'Stop it!' said Donna loudly as she struggled in vain to get free.

'Oh, don't be like that,' said the cowboy as he grinned up at her while pulling her closer. 'I know you like it.'

Andrew could no longer sit idly by and watch the disturbing scene play out. As much as he wanted to keep a low profile, he also knew that he would be unable to sit there and watch as the men abused Donna Cooper. And by the looks of it, whether it was due to indifference or for fear of getting involved, no one else in the diner looked like they were prepared to intervene. That left only him if anyone was going to stop what was happening.

He quickly picked the earphone from his ear, slid out of his booth and moved up next to Donna while assessing the physical strength of the bald cowboy. Andrew was of slightly above average height, and he was as fit and muscular as he had ever been, but the cowboy was still somewhat bigger and bulkier than him. However, Andrew also possessed a combination of strength and agility that the cowboy could almost certainly not match. Finally, and most importantly, he had the element of surprise. The cowboy no doubt thought that Andrew was just some wannabe white knight, but he could never have guessed that he was actually dealing with a highly trained special forces operator. If the two men were used to being big fish in a small pond, which they undoubtedly were, then Andrew was a shark from the deep sea, and they had no idea what they were up against.

Without a word, Andrew gripped the cowboy's right wrist and pulled his hand off Donna's rear. As he did so, he used his other hand to grab the man's palm, pulling it slightly towards himself and then suddenly pushing back against it and twisting the entire hand violently at an unnatural angle into a painful wristlock. The result was instantaneous. The cowboy yelled out in pain as Andrew raised the trapped hand and applied even more pressure. This caused the cowboy to lean forward until he was almost resting his torso on the table in an effort to reduce the pain. The whole thing had taken only a couple of seconds, but it allowed Donna to tear herself free of the cowboy's grip. She took several quick steps backwards while gawping at the violent scene playing out in front of her.

As she got out of the way, the mohawk guy scrambled up and out of his seat to launch himself at Andrew. As he did so, beer bottles toppled over, and cutlery clinked to the floor. At this point, the cowboy was in such intense pain that he was moaning loudly and slapping his other hand on the table in a sign of surrender, and Andrew had such firm control over his entire hulking body that he only needed one hand to maintain the wristlock.

As the mohawk guy moved up and came towards him, Andrew used his free hand to deliver a lightning-quick but hard curving strike to the side of the man's neck, which impacted perfectly on the man's vagus nerve. This nerve, which is one of the largest in the human body, runs down the side of the neck and controls several bodily functions, including swallowing and speech, but it is also involved in seizures.

When the strike landed, the mohawk guy's entire body immediately spasmed briefly, after which his mouth opened involuntarily, and he slumped back down onto the seat while clutching his throat and gasping for breath. In a standup fight between Andrew and what were probably two well-trained ex-soldiers, he would almost certainly have lost. But because they hadn't seen him coming and because they had underestimated him badly, he had been able to dominate both of them with minimal force.

'Are you two clowns done here?' he said calmly, barely breaking a sweat despite the situation.

When there was no reply, he returned to gripping the cowboy's wrist with both hands and began twisting it to the point where even he was surprised that something didn't snap. The cowboy groaned and grunted as he slapped the table some more while his body involuntarily attempted to twist and contort itself into a position that might relieve the debilitating pain shooting through his arm.

'Yes, goddamn it!' he yelled almost breathlessly. 'We're done. We're done, OK? Jesus Christ, just let go of my hand!'

'And you?' Andrew said evenly, fixing the mohawk guy who was still clutching his throat as his mouth worked like a caught fish and whose watering eyes were now glaring dumfounded up at his assailant.

'Done,' he croaked, releasing his throat and raising both hands to show his palms. 'We're done, you crazy motherfucker. Alright? You win.'

'Good,' said Andrew with a nod, maintaining the pressure on the bald cowboy's wrist and looking down at him. 'Here's what's about to happen. When I let go of Curly here, you two are going to walk out of this place with no fuss, and then you're going to get the hell out of here and never come back. Do you understand?'

'Yes, goddamn it,' wheezed the cowboy, beads of sweat running off his clean-shaven scalp. 'Whatever you say, alright? We're leaving.'

'And I have your word on this?' said Andrew. 'I am told that sort of thing means something around here.'

'You have our word,' panted the mohawk guy. 'Now let him go.'

Andrew released the wristlock and took a step back as Donna moved to stand slightly behind him and off to one side.

'Now, get out of here,' he said. 'And don't show your faces in here again.'

The cowboy gripped his contorted wrist with his other hand, flexing his fingers and wrist and grimacing with pain as he scowled up at Andrew. He snatched his hat off the table, and then the two men slid out of the booth and made their way towards the exit like two beaten dogs with their tails between their legs while the other customers looked on in stunned silence. One or two of them eyed Andrew suspiciously with a look that said 'You're in trouble now'.

'Wow,' said Donna, astonished, placing her hands on her hips as the unhappy duo exited the diner. 'Talk about biting off more than you can chew.'

'Who are those two guys?' said Andrew calmly.

'Local boys,' said Donna, looking out of the window as the two men scrambled up into their pickup truck. 'Travis Tatum and Cody Thornton. Tatum is the cowboy impersonator. They are two of the guys I told you about earlier. The ones from the ranch.'

'Tatum and Thornton,' mused Andrew. 'What exactly do they do out there at that ranch?'

'I really don't know,' said Donna as the throaty engine of the Chevrolet Silverado roared to life and the truck backed out aggressively from the parking space before tearing down the street with its tyres squealing angrily.

'Listen,' she continued. 'I really don't want any trouble with those people from the ranch. They're bad news, OK?'

'I'm sorry,' said Andrew, glancing at her. 'I didn't want to cause any problems for you. But I just couldn't sit there and let those two goons treat this place like they own it.'

'Well, I do appreciate that,' said Donna, giving him a quick smile. 'But sometimes it's just better to let things slide, you know? No one wants to mess with those guys.'

'Right,' nodded Andrew. 'I understand. I am sorry if I created a mess here. But I don't think those two will be coming back.'

'That's alright,' said Donna. 'Don't worry about it. You're certainly welcome back here any time. Next meal is on the house.'

'Thank you,' said Andrew. 'Anyway, I think I should get going and leave you to it.'

He walked back to his table and picked up his phone and his earbud. He then realised that the phone had been recording the whole thing and that it might come in handy as proof of what really happened in case the local police were to get involved. Hopefully, they had better things to do than spend time on a minor altercation in a diner.

'Take care,' he said with a gentle smile as he passed Donna on his way out. 'I really enjoyed the burger.'

'My pleasure,' smiled Donna faintly. 'I hope to see you in here again. Good luck finding your friend.'

FIVE

The next morning, Andrew awoke to find that he had slept surprisingly well on the basic but comfortable queen-sized bed in his room. There had been no noise from the few other guests that were staying at the motel, and traffic on the country road outside dwindled to almost nothing during the night. He got out of bed just after eight o'clock and walked over to open the front door a crack for some fresh air. The sun was up and casting a warm light over the flat desert terrain that stretched away into the distance from the town, and it made the small leaves on a handful of old elm trees dotted around the motel grounds sway in the gentle breeze and glow a bright and pleasant green.

He took a deep breath of the cool, invigorating morning air and left the door open while he got dressed. He picked out a dark blue shirt and a pair of khaki slacks from his limited supply of spare clothes, and a few minutes later, he was walking across the yard to the parking lot where his black rental car was waiting. He decided to skip breakfast since he was still full from the large meal he had consumed the night before. Instead, he was going to go straight to the sheriff's office and try to get some answers about Barton. He assumed that the man Donna had mentioned being detained was his old friend.

It was a quiet morning, and the only sounds were of a few birds chirping and the gravel crunching under his boots as he walked. Just as he was extracting the key fob from his trouser pocket and was about to press the button to unlock the Jeep, he thought he heard something very familiar. He stopped and listened, cocking his head and turning it slightly to try to pick out the sound. For a moment, he thought he caught it again, but then it was gone. He could have sworn it was the sound of helicopter rotors and the distant whine of at least one turboshaft engine. He turned his head to the other side to try to catch it again as he gazed out over the desert, but it had now gone. Or perhaps he had imagined it.

Suddenly he spotted a tiny black shape moving low over the far horizon, and then the very faint warbling and thudding noise of distant rotor blades washed over him in long undulating waves. He narrowed his eyes to peer at the aircraft in the far distance towards the south. He couldn't match the silhouette with anything he was familiar with, and the sound seemed subtly different from anything he had heard before. It sounded almost as if it was a twin-rotor aircraft. After a few moments, he lost sight of the chopper behind some trees lining the country road in front of the motel, and then it was quiet again. Could this be connected to what Donna had called the Stonewall Ranch? It would fit with the idea that it was some sort of private military contractor, although most of those did not have serious aviation hardware such as military helicopters. He unlocked the car and climbed up behind the wheel, put it in gear and drove out onto the road to make his way towards the centre of town.

A few minutes later, he arrived on Revelation's tree-lined central square, where the sheriff's office was located. It looked clean, quaint and attractive in the morning light, and with its 18th-century design, the limestone building was a throwback to a time several centuries earlier when the state of Texas was just being settled. He could see that the front door was open, and there was movement inside. Andrew parked up, exited the vehicle, took off his sunglasses and went inside. He was greeted by a tall and gangly desk sergeant wearing a sand-coloured uniform with rank insignia and the logo of the Revelation Sheriff's Office stitched onto its chest. The man looked up at him from under a light-coloured wide-brimmed hat as he entered.

'Good morning,' said Andrew as he approached the desk while placing his sunglasses in the front pocket of his shirt.

'It sure is,' said the sergeant, whose name was Fuller, according to the plastic nametag on the front of his shirt. 'Good morning, sir. What can I do for you?'

'My name is Sterling,' said Andrew. 'I'd like to speak to Sheriff Hogan if possible. Is he in?'

'Chief Hogan is in,' said Fuller hesitantly. 'But I'm gonna have to ask you to tell me what this is about. The chief's a busy man.'

'I am here about my friend Eddie Barton,' said Andrew. 'I received a message from him saying he was locked up here in this town accused of a double homicide. I am here to give him any assistance I can.'

Fuller's face immediately changed from relaxed and friendly to suspicious. Then he grabbed a pen and a notepad and placed his hand on the pad, ready to write.

'And you said you're a friend?' asked Fuller. 'Not a lawyer?'

'That's right,' said Andrew. 'Is Barton here?'

'And your name is Sterling, is that correct?' said Fuller.

'Yes,' nodded Andrew. 'Like the currency. So, can I see Sheriff Hogan? I've travelled a long way to be here today.'

'If you'd like to take a seat over there,' said Fuller, gesturing at three metal chairs by one of the walls in the lobby. 'I'm going to go and ask the chief about this.'

'Alright. Thank you,' said Andrew, taking a step back from the front desk. 'I prefer to stand.'

'I'll be right back,' said Fuller as he tore off the slip from the notepad and made his way to a corridor that looked to be stretching to the back of the building.

While Fuller walked back along the corridor to Sheriff Hogan's office somewhere in the back, Andrew walked over towards the three chairs. In a corner of the room was a large cactus plant in an earth-coloured terra cotta pot. The plant's long bristling needles looked like icepicks, and it appeared decidedly unsafe for a public space like this. Why anyone would decide to place such a hazard here, Andrew couldn't imagine, except perhaps that it was in keeping with the old building's exterior. It occurred to him that this town had probably started out with just one or two similar 17th-century structures just like it surrounded by flat high desert terrain that had been dotted with cacti like this one.

On the wall above the three chairs hung a framed reproduction of a painting. It depicted a small church-like mansion with a tall, stone-block façade rising up towards a scalloped roof. The central ridge of the building was placed above a colonnaded single-arched doorway. On either side of the door were a couple of small windows, and on top of the roof was a flagpole with the Lone Star Flag fluttering in the wind. Underneath the painting was a small brass plaque reading 'The Alamo - 1836'. Andrew's history of Texas was somewhat patchy, to say the least, but he seemed to remember that the Alamo was in the city of San Antonio and that it had been the scene of a famous siege during the Texas Revolution. However, the exact details of the event escaped him.

After less than a minute of waiting, Sergeant Fuller returned, and Andrew turned around to face him.

'If you'll follow me?' said Fuller. 'I'll take you to the chief.'

Sheriff Hogan was leaning back in his chair with his hands on the armrests as Fuller showed Andrew into the small and somewhat cluttered office. As Andrew entered, Hogan looked up but did not get to his feet.

Instead, he remained behind his dark wooden desk and regarded his visitor silently.

He was an overweight man in his mid-fifties with a heavy paunch, and he looked permanently slouched with his shoulders sloping down from his neck towards his arms. He had a chubby face with jowly cheeks and a rosy complexion that was partly hidden behind a fuzzy grey beard with a large patch of white on the tip of his chin. Small pale-blue close-set eyes peered out from under a cream-coloured Stetson hat. His white police shirt bore the stars and stripes on one shoulder and the county police insignia on the left, and on his breast pocket was affixed a bronze police star. The white shirt had slightly discoloured patches around his armpits, and there was some sort of reddish food stain on one of the sleeves.

'My name is Andrew Sterling,' said Andrew as he entered. 'Thank you very much for seeing me. You're Sheriff Hogan?'

The sheriff nodded and gestured to the empty chair opposite the desk while Fuller closed the door behind Andrew.

'That's right,' said Hogan in a lazy Texas drawl as he pushed the brim of his hat up a bit and leaned forward to study his visitor. 'I am Elijah Hogan, and I am the sheriff in this here town. What can I do you for? Fuller tells me you're here about a friend of yours?'

'That's right,' said Andrew as he sat down. 'Eddie Barton. He was apparently detained here several days ago. Do you still have him?'

Hogan regarded Andrew silently for a drawn-out moment before smacking his lips and leaning back once more, looking like he was considering how to address the situation. Then he took a breath and held it for a beat before letting it out and speaking.

'Mr Sterling,' he said reasonably. 'We did indeed detain Mr Barton after he killed two people right in our town. Shot them dead in an alley behind a place called the High Jinx Tavern. But before I answer any more of your questions, you need to tell me what's going on here. Who are you exactly, if you don't mind my asking? And what have you come here for?'

'Fair enough,' said Andrew, deciding to keep things vague for now. 'I am a former colleague of Barton's. We served together in the British Army a long time ago. I'm simply here because he reached out to me and said he was in trouble. He needed help.'

'Well,' said the chief, raising his eyebrows. 'He's in trouble, alright. That's for damn sure. Murdering two people in an alley? That's not the sort of folks we want in this town. But I am not sure how you think you might be able to help him. See, we have something called due process here in America. And that goes for the great state of Texas too. You can't just come in here and start messing with that. Things are gonna happen the way they need to happen. According to the law, see?'

'I understand,' said Andrew. 'Still. He could do with someone to look out for him. He didn't seem like he was in a good place when he got in touch.'

'Well, shit, I don't blame him,' said Hogan. 'It's not looking good for him. It's an open-and-shut case, if you ask me. Your buddy did it, and he's going away for a long time. In fact, he might just get the chair.'

Andrew levelled a cool look at the sheriff and held his gaze until the sheriff averted his eyes.

'Listen,' said Hogan, scratching his beard and giving a shrug. 'I'm just telling it like it is. I ain't gonna sit here and blow smoke up your ass. Ain't nobody gonna benefit from that. Your friend is in a serious pickle. So, the best thing you can do for him now, as far as I'm concerned, is to find the most expensive lawyer you can afford.'

Andrew looked at the sheriff for a moment, on the one hand disliking the casualness with which he was discussing his friend's plight, and on the other hand, having some sympathy for the chief of police in this small and seemingly idyllic town being less than enamoured with having a double murder happen.

'I appreciate the advice,' he finally said. 'But I ask you again. Do you still have Barton detained?'

'Nope,' said Hogan with a sigh, taking off his hat and placing it on the desk to reveal a tousled head of grey, curly hair. 'He ain't here no more. He was only in here for a few hours, and then he was handed over to a state trooper who took him back to Sweetwater.'

'So, is that where he is now?' asked Andrew.

'I assume so,' said Hogan with a shrug. 'If things go by the book, he's gonna be arraigned in front of a judge at the Nolan Country Courthouse. And then he'll be charged with double homicide. Sorry to be so blunt, Mr Sterling, but that's how things work around here. And I don't imagine there's a whole lot you can do for him until then.'

'Do you know where he is being held?' said Andrew.

'I do not,' said Hogan. 'Not my business. Frankly, I am just glad to see the back of him. But I can give you a number for the Nolan County DA. They might be able to help you.'

Hogan opened a desk drawer and rummaged around for a few seconds before pulling out a business card which he handed to Andrew. It had the official seal of the Nolan County District Attorney's office, and it included a number for the Assistant DA, who was a Mr Bremmer.

'Give Assistant DA Bremmer a call,' said Hogan. 'He might be able to help you.'

'Thanks,' said Andrew, tucking the card into a shirt pocket. 'I will do that. I don't suppose you'd be able to share any forensic evidence you may have found? Or any evidence from the alley?'

'Hell no,' said Hogan, shaking his head with half a smile playing on his lips. 'We can't divulge that sort of thing in the middle of an investigation. We picked up the spent casings and made sure to note everything that happened, but those things are kept between us at the DA's office.'

'I understand,' nodded Andrew. 'Do you mind if I briefly ask you about something else?'

'Sure,' shrugged Hogan, looking nothing like he was anywhere near as busy as Fuller had indicated. 'Shoot. If I have the answers, I'll be happy to give them to you.'

'I have been told there's a private military contractor in this area,' said Andrew, as Hogan looked at him impassively while he spoke. 'It's supposedly located on something called Stonewall Ranch. Do you know anything about that?'

'Of course,' said Hogan, giving Andrew a quizzical look. 'Everybody does. Stonewall Ranch is about five miles out of town. It's a pretty big employer around here.'

'What do they do, exactly?' asked Andrew. 'I mean, what sort of services do they offer?'

'I'm sure I have no idea,' smiled Hogan, seemingly quite content not to know much about the ranch. 'But it sure seems there's a lot of money in that line of work, and the general has brought a lot of business to this town. A lot of business.'

'The general?' said Andrew.

'General John McKinnon,' nodded Hogan, looking like he was used to everyone knowing exactly who the man was. 'U.S. Army, retired. It's his outfit. It's called Ironclad Tactical Solutions. Been a real boon for this town, let me tell you. Lots of his guys come here and spend their money, and they're paid pretty well by the looks of it.'

'I see,' said Andrew. 'And Barton was working there too?'

'I believe so,' said Hogan. 'And as far as I know, those two guys he shot were also Ironclad employees. Which makes the situation a damn mess. But I don't know what that whole thing was about or what sort of quarrel they might have had with each other. Like I said, it's all up to the Nolan County DA from here on in. All we did was collect the evidence from the alley where it happened, and then we handed it over. That's the end of it, as far as I'm concerned.'

'But you took Barton in on the night in question, right?' said Andrew. 'He was here in this building?'

'That's right,' said Hogan. 'But like I said. That was only for a few hours.'

'Who were the arresting officers?' asked Andrew.

Hogan looked up at the ceiling in a show of trying to remember.

'I believe that was Deputy Turnbull and Deputy Cooper,' said Hogan, indicating past the office door. 'They put him in cuffs and brought him back here. Locked him in one of those holding cells you might have seen on the way down here.'

'Any chance I could speak to them?' asked Andrew.

Just then, the office door suddenly burst open, and Sergeant Fuller stuck his head inside, looking agitated.

'Chief?' he said with a dark look on his face. 'Sorry to barge in like this. It's about Billy Ray.'

Sheriff Hogan turned to look at the sergeant for a moment, his eyes narrowing slightly, before he spoke.

'Yeah?' he said slowly. 'Well, spit it out, Fuller. What about him?'

'They found him, Chief,' said the sergeant, looking cowed.

Hogan didn't move for several long moments but simply gazed at Fuller, who was standing motionless with only his head inside the office. Then a grim look spread over Hogan's face, and with half a shake of the head and his lips pressed together, he briefly closed his eyes. Then he let out a deep sigh and looked over at Andrew.

'Mr Sterling,' he finally said, slowly picking up his Stetson and wedging it onto his head. 'I am very sorry. I have some urgent business to attend to, so I am going to have to ask you to leave.'

'Of course,' nodded Andrew, clearly sensing the gravity of the situation. 'Not a problem.'

'But rest assured,' continued Hogan. 'We'll do everything we can to get to the bottom of this thing.'

'Can we speak again?' said Andrew. 'I have a few more questions.'

'Sure,' said Hogan, looking distracted as he rose out of his chair and got to his feet. 'Maybe come by again tomorrow. Now, if you'll excuse me.'

And with that, Hogan pushed past Andrew into the corridor and disappeared around a corner. Seconds later, what sounded like a backdoor opened and then slammed shut. Fuller motioned for Andrew to follow him and began walking back to the front desk area.

'What was that all about?' said Andrew as the two men returned to the lobby.

'I am afraid I can't say,' said Fuller. 'Internal police business.'

'Fair enough,' said Andrew, holding up his hands briefly and showing his palms. 'I understand. Thanks for your help today.'

'You're welcome, sir,' said Fuller, returning to the front desk as Andrew walked back outside to his car.

As he got back in and placed his hands on the Jeep's large steering wheel, he stared absentmindedly out through the windscreen at nothing in particular. It was now mid-morning, and the sun was rapidly warming the car's interior and him with it as he pondered what he had just learned. He had got quite a few answers, but it also seemed that there were now a lot more questions. Where exactly was Barton? How had he ended up killing two of what appeared to have been his own colleagues? And precisely what was going on at Stonewall Ranch?

He pulled the card with the number for the Nolan Country Assistant DA's office and punched it into his phone. After a couple of rings, the curt voice of what sounded like a middle-aged man came on the line.

'Bremmer,' he said, sounding as if he was in a hurry.

'Mr Bremmer,' said Andrew. 'My name is Sterling. I was given your number by Sheriff Elijah Hogan in Revelation. I am looking for someone called Eddie Barton. He was arrested a couple of nights ago and brought to Sweetwater. Can you help me with that?'

There was a long pause before Bremmer spoke again.

'I'd love to help you, Mr Sterling,' Bremmer finally said. 'But I'm afraid I can't at the moment. The person in question has not yet been arraigned in front of a judge. And I am not at liberty to tell you when that might be or even where he is.'

'I see,' said Andrew. 'So, there's no way for me to contact him?'

'That's right,' said Bremmer. 'The only thing I can tell you right now is that he is being held at a secure facility and that he has elected to represent himself in court.'

'What?' said Andrew, furrowing his brow. 'He wants to represent himself? I find that hard to believe.'

'Well,' said Bremmer. 'That's how it is.'

'Listen,' said Andrew. 'Barton and I are old friends, and I love him like a brother, but there is no way he would ever choose to act as his own lawyer. He's a good guy, but he is not what anyone would call a well-read man. He just wouldn't do that.'

'I don't know what to tell you,' said Bremmer with a disinterested yawn. 'That's what it says right here on his file. I have yet to meet this guy, but I can only go by what the state troopers have filed. So, I am afraid I can't help you any more than that. Now, if you'll excuse me, I have a meeting in thirty seconds.'

'Alright,' said Andrew. 'Thanks for your time.'

'No problem,' said Bremmer, and then the call was disconnected.

Staring out of the windscreen, Andrew briefly considered driving to Sweetwater to see Bremmer in person, but he quickly found himself giving up on the idea. It was bound to be a waste of time. Bremmer had already made it clear that he was unable to provide any more information. And even if Barton was being held somewhere in a Nolan County police facility, Andrew would be unable to locate him, much less speak to him. Whatever had happened to his friend, and whatever had been the reason for his incarceration, the answers lay somewhere here in Revelation and not in some municipal building in Sweetwater. If it was true that the two men who Barton had killed were also from the ranch, then the answers had to lie there.

As Andrew placed the phone back in his pocket, he spotted a police cruiser with Sheriff Hogan behind the wheel come out of what he assumed was a courtyard behind the sheriff's office building. The cruiser pulled onto Main Street, turned right and sped down the road. For a brief moment, Andrew struggled to resist the urge to follow, but then he decided against it.

Stalking the chief of police probably wasn't the best way to get on his good side. Hogan might be a quirky character, but he was probably still Andrew's best shot at getting to the bottom of what had happened to Barton both before and after the night his friend had called him and left that haunting message. So, instead of giving chase, Andrew started the engine and pulled out onto Main Street. He was suddenly feeling hungry again, so he decided to head to Donna's Diner to have a late breakfast.

SIX

2500 kilometres northeast of Revelation at the huge sprawling John F. Kennedy International Airport, the widebody Air France Airbus A350 from Paris touched down amid loud squeals and white puffs of smoke from its eight wheels as the main landing gear made contact with the surface of the runway. After taxiing for a few minutes, the transatlantic journey for its 440 passengers came to an end as it parked up on its designated apron at Terminal 1's Gate 2 near the Air France lounge. As its four giant Rolls-Royce turbofan engines spun down to idle and were then switched off, the disembarkation bridges began extending to line up with the aircraft's two front exits on its left side.

Inside the comfortable first-class cabin, Jean-Pascal Mokri got up from his seat and stepped out into the aisle to fetch his single piece of hand luggage from the overhead compartment. The Lebanese financier had spent much of the flight asleep, safe in the knowledge that the plan he had been asked to carry out was progressing as intended, although various minor tasks still remained.

Mokri was a short man in his mid-fifties with a dark complexion, narrow brown eyes and a pair of thick, black eyebrows. His round head was bald with close-cropped greying hair at the sides, and he wore a pair of slim rectangular glasses with thin black rims. After having travelled from Lebanon to JFK in one go during the past twenty-four hours, he now had a short salt-and-pepper stubble that he was dying to get rid of at the earliest opportunity once he had checked into his upmarket hotel in central Manhattan. He was wearing Italian designer shoes and an expensive dark navy suit with an open white shirt, and his gold cufflinks were made in the likeness of ancient Babylonian coins showing a powerful lion.

Originally from a long line of market traders in Beirut, Mokri had left his chaotic homeland behind and headed for France to obtain a degree in finance at the Université Paris Dauphine. He had then worked at various prestigious investment banks in the French capital and decided to buy an apartment in the 1st arrondissement and live there permanently. After a couple of decades in the corporate world, he had eventually set up his own business catering to other Lebanese high-net-worth individuals who had made France their home.

Using his extensive network of contacts in Beirut and Paris, as well as a rapidly evolving shady reputation, he had then developed an agile and profitable private wealth management business. Its clients included politicians, financiers, industrialists and various former Lebanese army officers who were keen to keep their financial affairs and personal fortunes firmly behind a veil of secrecy.

It was through an acquaintance in the latter group of clients that he had one day been contacted by a financial advisor from New York who represented an American client. The client had a significant fortune, although not nearly as large as those Mokri's was used to managing. However, the man had been able to introduce Mokri to an entirely new type of financial dealings involving the funding of international arms trades. After a long career in the U.S. Army, the client had leveraged his connections in the weapons manufacturing industry to facilitate deals with various unsavoury customers around the world, and with the help of Mokri's financing, it had created significant fortunes for them both.

Now, however, after many years of working together, things had changed up a gear. The two men had devised a new plan that would make all of their previous ventures look like a cake stall at a summer fair. This was the reason why Mokri had come to New York. He was to personally oversee the groundwork for the operation, and there were plenty of pieces that had to fall into place. He had to set up new companies and trading accounts, line up stock brokers, and also make sure to wine and dine several key officials inside Wall Street's various regulatory bodies in an attempt to gain leverage over them. This was going to be fun.

He adjusted his suit and made his way along the aisle to exit the aircraft and head for immigration. When he stepped up to the female immigration officer sitting behind a pane of glass, he produced his most winning smile and handed over his passport. The seemingly unimpressed uniformed woman took it, opened it and glanced up at the recent arrival. She then scanned the passport and checked its stamps. Finally, she looked up at him again.

'How long do you intend to stay in the United States, Mr Mokri?' she asked.

'About a week,' said Mokri. 'If all goes well.'

'Business or pleasure?' she asked.

'Well, hopefully, a bit of both,' said Mokri while attempting a knowing smile, but the female officer's expression remained deadpan as she gazed at him with one eyebrow raised a fraction of an inch.

'Will you be remaining in New York State or be travelling onwards, sir?' she asked evenly.

'I will be in Manhattan the whole time,' said Mokri. 'I have a very busy schedule here.'

The officer leafed through the passport one more time and took another look at him before nodding and then re-checking something on her computer monitor.

'Alright, Mr Mokri,' she finally said, sounding wholly disinterested as she handed the passport back to him. 'Welcome to the United States. Enjoy your stay.'

'Thank you,' smiled Mokri. 'I'm sure I will.'

As he walked away and headed for the taxi stands outside the terminal, Mokri reflected on the many attacks carried out around the world by his fellow Lebanese countrymen through Islamist groups such as Hezbollah in their attempts to weaken and humiliate the United States. Most of them would have given an arm and a leg to simply swan through U.S. Customs the way he was now doing.

What none of them could seem to understand was that America's immense power did not come from its military, even if that was by far the largest and most powerful in the world. Its power came from its highly dynamic and irrepressible economy and financial system, which, aside from backing the world's reserve currency, produced about a quarter of the entire planet's economic output. Blowing up an American warship in spectacular fashion in the Persian Gulf or downing a high-tech surveillance drone over some godforsaken desert in the Middle East might seem like a great propaganda win. But in the grand scheme of things, it was utterly pointless. If America was ever to be brought to its knees, something much more ambitious would have to be engineered. Something that would hit the country where it really hurt, such as its stock market. There was no greater threat to the United States and to the smug self-assurance of its ignorant citizens than the prospect of a stock market crash.

Mokri's true motivation for taking part in the American client's grand design was mainly financial, and if everything worked out as planned, the rewards would surely be enormous. But watching the great United States choke on its own financial system would be an added bonus, and one that he would thoroughly enjoy. It was a peculiar thing that he should find himself working with this particular man to cause such a calamity for what was known across the Middle East as 'The Great Satan', but grand ambition sometimes makes for strange bedfellows.

As the midday sun shone over a bustling New York City, Mokri walked briskly to the row of yellow taxi cabs, got into the backseat of the one at the front of the line, and told the driver to head for Wall Street.

★   ★   ★

When Andrew arrived back at Donna's Diner, it was just before noon, and the place was already busy with plenty of lunchtime customers who were ordering everything from scrambled eggs with bacon, chicken wings, grilled cheese sandwiches and old-fashioned hot dogs. The business was clearly doing a roaring trade at this time of day, and Andrew couldn't help but smile as he entered the bustling establishment. He liked Donna, and he admired the young woman for her stoicism in the face of attempted bullying and abuse. As an entrepreneur in the small town of Revelation, she had clearly done well for herself, and as far as he could make out, she deserved every last bit of her success.

As she spotted him walk in, her face lit up, and she quickly came over to greet him.

'Howdy,' she said brightly. 'Didn't expect to see you back here so soon.'

'I was hungry again,' he smiled. 'And I couldn't think of a better place to go than here.'

'That's very kind,' she said, returning his smile. 'I'm afraid your booth from last night is taken, but you can sit over here at the bar counter.'

She gestured towards a couple of empty barstools by the long counter running almost the length of the diner.

'Sounds good,' said Andrew. 'Could I have one of those grilled chicken club sandwiches? I spotted it on the menu last night and thought it looked really good.'

'Good?' smiled Donna with a wink. 'That thing is famous around here. Take a seat. I'll be right back. Same beer?'

'Yes, please,' said Andrew as he sat down on a bar stool.

'Coming right up,' said Donna as she disappeared around the end of the bar and into the kitchen, where two chefs could be glimpsed through a cutout busily frying and cooking meals for the diner's patrons.

Andrew shifted and made himself comfortable while discreetly looking around the diner. Almost every seat was taken, and the jukebox was playing another classic 1950s song, this time by Johnny Cash. Glancing at the booths and along the bar counter, he saw families, store workers from elsewhere on Main Street on their lunch break, and a couple of men who might be truck drivers stopping over in the small town for a bite to eat at what appeared to be a famous eatery.

Two seats along on the other side of a young woman sipping a coffee and eating a doughnut, Andrew spotted a familiar face from the evening before, recognising the man as the one Donna addressed as 'Mayor'. The silver-haired man was wearing another slightly darker tweed suit, and he had just picked up a large burger from his plate and was about to sink his teeth into it when his phone rang from inside his jacket pocket. His shoulders slumped with disappointment, and he reluctantly placed the burger back on the plate and extracted the phone.

'Arlan Meeks here,' he said casually, before sitting up noticeably more straight on his bar stool as whoever was on the line spoke to him. 'Well, hello General. It's a pleasure to hear from you again. Oh, and thank you again for your latest campaign contribution. Very generous of you. All received and logged at the town hall, of course. I do appreciate it. How might I be of service today?'

Holding the phone in place next to his ear using his right shoulder, Mayor Meeks wiped his fingers with a napkin as he listened, nodding and grunting a couple of times before he spoke again.

'Well, certainly,' he said, gripping the phone with his right hand, clearly making an effort to sound serious and official the way one might expect from a town mayor. 'If you would like to come see me at my office this afternoon, then I'd be more than willing to try to move things along with the town planning department. I'm sure we can all come to some arrangement given your stature in this town.'

There was another brief pause during which Meeks listened intently, and then his eyebrows crept up slowly and his face took on a look of mild surprise.

'Oh,' he eventually said. 'Uhm, well, I don't see why not. I guess I can come out to see you. I suppose it's all the same. What time would suit you best? Alright then. Three o'clock it is. I'll look forward to it. Bye now.'

Meeks ended the call and sat for a moment looking down at his phone. Then he placed it inside his jacket pocket, checked the time on his gold wristwatch and took a swig from his canned Dr Pepper soft drink before biting into his burger. As he did so, he gave a faint moan of pleasure.

'Damn,' he said as he chewed. 'So good.'

As the mayor looked up and glanced to his side, he caught Andrew looking at him from a couple of metres away. Being on the other side of the young woman sipping coffee and thus outside of normal conversation range, he instead lifted his Dr Pepper in a friendly salute, and Andrew returned the greeting with a smile and a polite nod. This was clearly a friendly town, at least on the surface, but Andrew couldn't help feeling that there was a lot more going on beneath the surface than met the eye. And it all seemed to revolve around the mysterious general and the PMC he was running from Stonewall Ranch. If Andrew was going to get any answers about what happened to Barton, he would almost certainly need to pay the ranch a visit.

'Here you go,' said Donna as she reappeared on the other side of the counter and placed a bottle of chilled Blood & Honey along with a plate of delicious-looking grilled chicken sandwiches in front of him.

'Thanks,' said Andrew. 'Looks great.'

'You're welcome,' smiled Donna, and turned to head back towards the kitchen.

Just then, the waitress named Paige appeared next to her, holding a phone in an outstretched hand.

'Donna,' she said, her face a picture of concern as she offered her phone to her boss. 'It's for you. They tried to reach you, but you didn't pick up, so they called me instead.'

'Oh, my battery died this morning,' said Donna, taking the phone from Paige's trembling hand with a puzzled look on her face. 'What's going on, Paige?'

'You'd better speak to them,' said Paige, shooting a brief self-conscious glance in Andrew's direction. 'It's... about your brother.'

Donna reached out and took the phone from Paige's hand, brought it slowly up to her ear, and turned her back towards her customers.

'Hello. This is Donna Cooper,' she said, and then she began walking towards the kitchen and the diner's staff area at the back of the building.

Andrew did not hear her say anything more as she disappeared from view, but he noted that Paige was standing as if frozen to the spot for a long moment, about a metre away. She was looking down at her shoes with her hands clasped tightly in front of her. Her eyes were closed and her forehead was creased by deep furrows, as if she were trying to shut out what was about to happen.

Suddenly, a piercing wail came from the kitchen. It contained such raw pain and anguish that it sent an icy shiver down Andrew's spine and immediately brought the entire diner to a juddering halt. All chatter ceased in an instant, and everyone stopped what they were doing and turned to look towards the back of the diner. The only sound left was of the jukebox blithely continuing to play one of its 1950s classics, but even that suddenly seemed to sound distant and hollow.

As Andrew and the stunned locals watched, Donna suddenly reappeared and rushed past her colleagues and customers without seeming to notice them. Her face was contorted into a mask of pain and distress, and she looked nothing like the cheerful young woman Andrew had talked to just minutes earlier. She headed straight for the door, and once outside, she ran towards a small metallic-red coupe parked in one of the two staff parking bays in front of the diner. On the way, she fumbled with her car keys and dropped them so she had to stop, backtrack and pick them up before finally getting into her car and racing off.

Deeply unsettled by what he had just witnessed, Andrew turned back to look at Paige. She had not moved from her spot behind the counter and was staring vacantly out of the window towards the street. Still clutching her hands, her knuckles had turned white, her lips were trembling, and there were tears tracing a wet path down her cheeks.

'Paige,' he said in a hushed, gentle voice. 'Paige. What's going on?'

The waitress said nothing for a moment, but then her watery eyes shifted slowly and trance-like to look at Andrew. When she spoke again, her words hit Andrew like a blow to the chest and instantly made him realise that he was about to be drawn into something that was much bigger than the disappearance of Eddie Barton.

'Her brother,' she whispered. 'He's dead. Billy Ray's dead.'

SEVEN

Later that afternoon, Andrew decided to take a drive around the small town to familiarise himself with the place, and everything he saw confirmed what he had already concluded. Revelation was a quiet, comfortable and relatively well-off place to live, and it seemed in many ways to exist inside a bubble where time seemed to have stood still, or at least done its best to only inch forward over the past several decades.

He then headed out into the desert to have a look at Stonewall Ranch for himself. The ranch was clearly well known to the town's residents, even if they appeared not to know exactly what went on there, and Paige had been kind enough to provide him with directions. As it turned out, it was very easy to find since it was located at the end of a set of long and virtually straight country roads cutting through flat, parched plains that were sprinkled with small dry bushes and tufts of pale yellow grass. However, the ranch was not exactly anywhere near the town itself. In fact, by the time he reached it, Revelation had disappeared into the far distance, and he could no longer even see the town's church spires or the top of the town hall tower.

Judging by the tall, barbed wire fencing that ran along the road for miles before he arrived at its gates, the ranch had been built on a huge plot in the middle of the otherwise almost featureless terrain. When he arrived, he saw a long tree-lined dirt track stretch away from the country road towards a group of buildings in the distance. However, access to the ranch was barred by a set of tall metal gates, above which was an arch that had the weathered skull of a horned bull mounted on it.

Andrew stopped the car, killed the engine and got out. The clear blue sky seemed huge overhead, and a warm breeze swept across the arid terrain making the grass whisper gently in the wind, but the air felt clean and fresh. Up above, he spotted a couple of graceful predators circling, and they looked to be either falcons or hawks riding the updrafts and looking for prey in the dry undergrowth.

He walked across the gravel to the gate to discover that it was locked tight by a remotely operated locking system, and there was no way to contact whoever was in charge of allowing people in. He looked around and spotted two small cameras mounted on short sections of brickwork on either side of the gate. It was impossible to tell if they were active, but despite seemingly being the only person around for miles, he had the distinct sensation of being watched. On one of the sections of brickwork was a brass plaque that was roughly one metre long, and etched into its surface was the name 'Ironclad Tactical Solutions'. He was definitely in the right place.

He walked a few metres to one side to get a clear view of the terrain in front of him on the other side of the barbed wire fence, and that was when he noticed a low hum emanating from it. The fence was electrified, but there was no sign of any cattle anywhere. In other words, the electrified fence was not there to keep livestock in but to keep unwanted visitors out. Peering through the fence and along the treelined dirt track, he could make out what appeared to be a large compound nestled amongst a dozen much taller trees roughly a kilometre away. It looked like a sprawling complex of various types of buildings with a particularly large mansion at its centre. Its pitched slate roofs were just visible above the pale green canopies of the surrounding trees, and he could also make out several chimneys sticking up. However, there was no visible movement anywhere, and no discernible sounds came from the compound until suddenly a familiar noise rose up.

At first, he could only make out the high-pitched whine of turboshaft engines, but that was then quickly followed by the unmistakable noise of rotor blades spinning up. Seconds later, a large black tilt-rotor aircraft with two oversized engines rose up from behind the compound, and Andrew knew instantly that this was the aircraft he had seen early that morning. It resembled the U.S. Navy's Osprey VTOL aircraft that he himself had been transported on during operations in Afghanistan, but it was clearly quite different. It was larger yet sleeker and much faster-looking.

It rose to an altitude of roughly a hundred metres, and then its two engines gradually swivelled on their mounts to point forward, after which it began accelerating out across the plains. It picked up speed surprisingly quickly, and within seconds it was racing low across the flat terrain, turning slightly to one side and away from him to what he estimated was a southerly heading. As it moved, Andrew noticed that there were barely any reflections from the sun coming off it, and if it was anything like the advanced military aircraft he suspected it to be, then it was almost certainly painted with a radar-absorbent stealth coating that would allow it to penetrate past enemy anti-aircraft defences. Less than a minute later, it had disappeared into the distance, and the undulating sound of its two rotors had faded into nothing.

As he stood there, he wasn't sure what he had expected to find when he decided to drive out to the mysterious Stonewall Ranch. However, seeing the large sprawling compound for himself and watching what was unquestionably a very expensive piece of military aviation hardware take off left no doubt in his mind that whatever was going on at that ranch was serious business. And if Barton had somehow run afoul of its owner, the enigmatic General John McKinnon, then he might have had very good reasons to run and possibly even good reasons to kill.

On that note, Andrew decided to get into his car and drive back to Revelation to pay a visit to the High Jinx Tavern. He had to examine the murder scene for himself, and he also wanted to see the bar where his friend had been cornered and had then seemingly inexplicably ended up taking the lives of two of his colleagues. Before heading back to town, however, he drove further along the country road to see if there was a way to drive around the ranch's estate and get a sense of its true size. After several more kilometres, he noticed that the barbed wire fence cut away from the road and stretched for as long as the eye could see. But there was no road that would allow him to follow it. However, he also noticed that there was what appeared to be a well-worn dirt track running next to the fence on the inside of its entire perimeter. This could only mean that the tall fence around the ranch was not just for show and that patrol vehicles were moving along the perimeter's dirt track on a regular basis. Clearly, McKinnon's people were making sure that the fence was intact and that no one came in uninvited.

As he approached the gate to the ranch once more on his way back to town, Andrew spotted a car moving along the tree-lined dirt track from the compound. He slowed down so that the car would reach the end of the track before he got to the gate, and soon he found himself driving back towards Revelation behind a silver sedan. As they approached the town itself, they came to a railway crossing where the barriers were just being lowered.

Andrew used the opportunity to pull alongside the sedan and glance down inside it. The driver was an elderly man in a tweed suit, smoking a pipe. It was Arlan Meeks. The mayor had clearly come good on his promise to visit McKinnon that afternoon, and after everything he had seen and heard in his short time in

Revelation, Andrew began to get the distinct sense that the general was probably the most powerful man in town, including the sheriff and the mayor.

After the long freight train had passed and the barriers had been raised, Andrew accelerated past the sedan and headed for the address he had found for the High Jinx Tavern. The sun was now low in the sky, and when he arrived, it was with some trepidation that he pulled into the parking lot in front of the bar. It was located on a road off Main Street near the edge of town, and it was set back by about twenty metres. In front of it were parked several motorcycles and a couple of cars. To the right of the building, he could see the alley that led to the back of the tavern. The place where Barton had been cornered like an animal and then lashed out, killing two men. Andrew decided to go there first, so he parked the Jeep, got out and headed straight there. As he did so, there were several other people arriving, and a couple of groups of young men and women stood outside smoking and talking as he walked past. It all seemed perfectly calm and normal, and there was nothing to suggest that two men had recently been killed just a few metres away. But then, life had to go on despite the grisly events of a couple of nights ago.

As he turned the corner and began walking along the alley, an eerie feeling wrapped itself around him, and his eyes immediately began scanning for signs of the recent violent events. There was no doubt that Sheriff Hogan was correct in saying that the police had already searched the area for criminal evidence, but it was worth a shot for Andrew to examine the murder scene himself.

Dusk was now rapidly closing in, and the automatic light above the door to the interior had already come on. At the end of the alley were three large plastic garbage containers with hinged lids, and there were various bits of waste and detritus piled up along the wall near the door. As he approached it, he noticed that there was a patch of fresh light-coloured dirt on the ground directly in front of it, almost as if someone had attempted to cover over something. He used his boot to scrape the top layer off, and beneath it was a much darker area of compacted soil that seemed slightly moist.

Opposite the door was a sturdy wooden fence to the adjacent property, and Andrew spotted a small area on a wooden post that appeared to have been dug out or removed. Lowering himself onto his haunches and picking at it with his fingers, it was clear that there was a neat circular hole at the centre where a bullet had entered. The area around it had clearly been dug out by the police to recover the bullet as evidence.

Looking back over his shoulder to the door, he noticed a small black camera mounted just under the light. If the camera had been working on the night of the incident, Andrew needed to get his hands on the recording, one way or another. He walked back over to the door and gripped the door handle. It was locked from the inside, and he noticed that the lock was new and shiny, and some of the doorframe seemed to have been replaced by a fresh unpainted piece of timber. Looking around one final time and deciding that there was nothing more for him to find, he headed back up the alley towards the street, around the corner of the building, and went inside through the tavern's main entrance.

It was still early, and the tavern was not yet very busy. There were perhaps fifteen people inside. Only two of them were sitting at the bar, and there were a handful of other patrons scattered at some of the tables. Melancholy country music was filling the space, and the clacks of billiard balls came from a pool table off to one side where two young women wearing jeans and loose flannel shirts were playing and drinking beer out of bottles. Behind the bar counter were two barmaids busying themselves with polishing glasses and stocking up bottles in the fridges ahead of the evening to come. So far, so normal.

Walking towards the bar while familiarising himself with the interior layout and trying to imagine what might have happened here a few days earlier, Andrew headed for an empty bar stool and sat down. On the wall behind the bar was a TV that was set to one of the major news networks. No one seemed to be paying attention to it, but it was loud enough for Andrew to be able to hear the female news anchor speaking. She was a woman in her mid-thirties with androgynous facial features, unnaturally glossy blond hair and perfect makeup. She was wearing a turquoise business suit and pearl earrings, and her accent had a slight New York twang to it. Behind her and to her right was displayed a large map of Central America and one of its smaller nations outlined in red. There was also a black dot to indicate the location the news segment was about. As Andrew sat down and waited to be served, he glanced up at the screen and listened to the turquoise apparition.

'*...took place in the embattled Central American country where political violence, assassinations and kidnappings have become increasingly widespread over the past decade. Last night, the CEO of the country's largest oil exploration company PetroDorado was killed in his own home, along with his entire security detail and at least one member of his housekeeping staff. Luckily, his family was out of town, but the scene discovered later that morning is said to have been truly shocking. Let's go now to our local affiliate Esteban Rodriquez from CTN News for the latest on this story. Esteban, what more can you tell us?*'

The image cut to a young man in a suit standing outside a set of tall wrought iron gates, behind which an avenue stretched off into the distance through what looked like a tropical forest. Holding an oversized microphone with his network's logo wrapped around it, he launched into a wordy rundown of everything the local police had released so far, which amounted to precious little beyond what the anchor had already relayed. This didn't stop him from weaving speculation and conjecture with rumour and hearsay to provide several more minutes of what in the end amounted to little more than lurid entertainment at the expense of the dead CEO and his bereaved family.

As Andrew watched and listened, one of the barmaids came over and greeted him with a smile. Aside from her black uniform, she was sporting short and spikey blond hair with the ends dyed pink, and she had a small silver stud on one side of her nose.

'Hey buddy,' she said as she came over. 'What can I get you?'

'I'd like a beer,' said Andrew. 'Do you stock Blood and Honey?'

'Sure do,' she replied, turning to reach for a bottle in one of the glass-fronted fridges behind her.

'My new favourite,' he smiled.

'Yup,' she said. 'A lot of guys like that one. You don't sound like you're from around here. Europe?'

'Yes,' said Andrew. 'The UK. I'm Andrew.'

'Nice to meet you,' she said, placing the beer in front of him and briefly inspecting his clothes. 'I'm Zoe. Excuse me a second.'

She left to serve another customer, and Andrew looked back up at the TV, where the glossy blonde was now back. She was just finishing a segment on the president's upcoming State of the Union address to the Congress in Washington D.C., which had been delayed for several weeks because of multiple overseas military confrontations involving U.S. troops, some of which had resulted in significant casualties. This, in turn, had led to urgent efforts on the part of the president and the administration to secure domestic congressional support for another military excursion abroad, as well as extensive efforts to travel to the involved countries to mobilise support for armed intervention.

In a matter of days, the supposed leader of the free world would spend about two hours telling congressmen, senators and TV cameras about all the ways in which his particular administration was now doing a much better job solving all problems, foreign and domestic, than his predecessors and future would-be rivals. This was despite what everyone could see around them, which was that an ever-increasing number of serious problems seemed to go unresolved, and the bubble of politicians in the capital was perceived to exist further and further away from their electorate. As the news anchor pointed out, the president would no doubt be announcing several large initiatives to fix said problems, but those sorts of things rarely had the desired effect, and they sometimes made things a lot worse. Like a firefighter putting out flames with a flamethrower. The anchor then smoothly transitioned into talking about how the president would deal with increasing tensions with Iran, whose allies in Lebanon and the Arabian Peninsula had become ever more emboldened, and whose activities were yet again threatening to spill over into open conflict across the Middle East.

As Andrew watched, he realised that he had lost track of the number of times he had heard this type of news story in one form or another. Next year, it would probably be a different set of belligerents, and in ten years, it would most likely have reverted back to this exact same scenario once again. It seemed like a never-ending cycle of strife and violence, which in some respects was merely the depressingly predictable result of the hangover of empire mixed with fervent fundamentalist religion. Just another day on Planet Earth. He decided to tear himself away from pondering the state of the world and focus on more immediate concerns, and just then, Zoe came back.

'Sorry about that,' she said apologetically. 'So, are you here on business?'

'Not exactly,' said Andrew, taking a swig of the beer. 'In fact, I was wondering if you might be able to help me with something.'

'Alright,' she shrugged. 'I'll certainly try.'

'A couple of nights ago,' said Andrew, 'there was an incident in the alley behind this place.'

'No shit!' she exclaimed with a barely suppressed chortle. 'An incident. That's one way of putting it. One of our regulars killed two of our other regulars. Fucking crazy.'

'Well,' continued Andrew. 'The man they say did it is an old friend of mine, and I am trying to find out what happened. Can you tell me if anyone here talked to him that night?'

'Over there,' said Zoe, turning to jerk her head at a tall and slim colleague with long straight black hair done up in a ponytail. 'That's Charlene. She talked to him just before it all went to hell. Want me to get her for you?'

'If you wouldn't mind,' said Andrew.

'Sure,' said Zoe, giving him a quick nod.

She turned and walked across to the other side of the bar to whisper something in Charlene's ear. The two young women glanced furtively in Andrew's direction, and Charlene then nodded and came over to where he was sitting.

'Andrew, was it?' she said. 'You're here about your friend?'

'That's correct,' said Andrew. 'I would really appreciate it if you could tell me what you saw that night.'

Charlene raised her eyebrows slightly and looked up at the ceiling with a sigh, as if she were trying to recall the course of events. Then she leaned forward, placed her elbows on the bar counter and spoke in a low voice.

'Listen, I don't want to get drawn into any of this, alright?' she said meaningfully. 'I've already told the police all I know. But since you're Eddie's buddy, and I always thought he was a good guy, I'll tell you what I know, OK?'

'Thank you,' said Andrew.

'Alright,' she said. 'Eddie came in here looking all sweaty and a little out of it. He's usually pretty easy-going, but he seemed real tense, and he kept looking towards the entrance. Like someone was after him. He sat down just over there.'

She gestured to a bar stool a couple of metres away, just on the other side of a wooden support pillar, and Andrew turned his head to look. The empty bar stool was more or less out of sight from the tavern's entrance, and it was only a few quick strides from what appeared to be a door to the back of the building. Good old Eddie. Always covering his bases.

'I talked to him for a bit as I served him a beer,' continued Charlene, 'and he said something about some sort of problem out at the ranch.'

'Stonewall Ranch,' observed Andrew.

'That's right,' nodded Charlene, as if everyone in town knew exactly what that meant. 'Now, he didn't tell me anything else, and the next thing I know, he's running out the backdoor with two of his former colleagues after him. I'm used to seeing them both in here, and I never really liked the look of them. But they looked real mean that night. Like a couple of sharks coming for Eddie. Like they were going to hurt him real bad. Anyway, all three of them disappeared out the back, and shortly after that, we heard the shots. Then the police arrived and closed the whole place down. And that's basically all I know.'

Andrew took another swig of his beer and pondered what he had heard as he turned his head to try to picture the scene described by Charlene.

'Do you have CCTV cameras in here?' he asked, turning back to face Charlene.

'Sure,' she said. 'Of course. We get our share of brawling from time to time, but never anything like this.'

'I spotted one above the door in the alley,' said Andrew. 'Is that also active?'

'It should be,' shrugged Charlene.

'Do you still have the recordings from that night?' he said.

'I think so,' said Charlene. 'As I understand it, the police took a copy of them as evidence, but the originals should still be on our computer system.'

'And who has access to them?' he asked.

'Well, it's only supposed to be the manager,' said Charlene, 'but the files are sitting right there on the system. I could show them to you if you want. I'm not supposed to, but with you being Eddie's friend and all.'

'I would be very grateful,' said Andrew. 'If I am going to have a chance at helping him, I need to understand exactly what happened here.'

'Alright,' said Charlene. 'Come this way.'

She led him through the door to the back that said 'Staff Only' and into a small office. It had an old computer sitting on a desk along with a few piles of paper, and a paper-based rota system was printed on a large sheet of A3 that was hanging on a wall. In general, it seemed haphazard and disorganised. Moving like she used the computer on a regular basis, Charlene sat down behind the desk and pulled the keyboard towards herself. Then she gripped the mouse, and within seconds, she looked up and nodded at Andrew.

'Here,' she said, as he moved to stand behind her looking down at the screen. 'This is the footage from the inside just before Eddie arrived. There's no sound. But trust me, you won't need it to work out what's happening.'

Andrew watched as the footage played, and a shiver ran down his spine as he recognised the unmistakable stocky form of his friend entering the tavern and moving to the bar. He was wearing cargo shorts and a short-sleeved shirt, and he looked as tanned as Andrew had ever seen him. But this wasn't the old Barton that he knew. From the uncharacteristically tense way his friend moved and kept looking towards the entrance, there was no doubt that he was feeling on edge.

'And that's me and him talking,' said Charlene, as the recording played on for several more seconds showing Barton sitting down, being served and drinking from his bottle while eyeing the door. 'Now watch this. Here they come.'

The camera showed two burly men enter and head straight for Barton, almost as if they knew he was in there and where to find him. Barton immediately got up and headed for the back of the building. Slowly at first, but then running through the door and bolting down the corridor where he disappeared from view. The two large men tore through the crowd, shoving people out of the way as they raced after him.

'OK,' said Charlene, pushing her chair back a bit and getting ready to get up. 'I'm going to switch to the camera in the alley now. I've watched this once already, and I wish I never had. It's pretty bad. But feel free to watch it yourself.'

She stepped aside and walked to the other side of the desk where she could no longer see the screen, and Andrew took her place in front of the computer. Charlene had already switched to the camera in the alley and found the timestamp where Barton had just emerged. The image was frozen just as the door sprung open and his friend was barging through it out into the alley. Andrew gripped the mouse and clicked the Play button. As the recording resumed, Barton lurched forward and tripped, falling onto the ground and rolling once. Almost immediately, his two pursuers bolted through the doorway and began to circle like the sharks Charlene had described them as.

One of them drew a gun, and Barton moved with impressive speed to get inside the gun arc. After a struggle, there was a bright flash from the muzzle of the weapon, and the other man crashed to the ground. Barton and the gunman tripped and rolled around in a furious struggle for control of the gun, but then Barton seemed to get the upper hand. Bringing the weapon close to the other man's face, the attacker grimaced, and then his head jerked back as the gun fired again and parts of his brain were sprayed onto the ground next to his head. Barton rolled onto his back, and almost immediately thereafter, the alley was lit up by what Andrew assumed were the headlights of police vehicles. Then followed the arrest, and Barton was led away in handcuffs, seemingly cooperating fully with the uniformed officers and making no attempt to speak or resist. Studying the grainy image for his body language and facial expressions as this last chapter in the story played out, Andrew thought Barton looked utterly exhausted, but there was something else as well. He looked almost relieved.

Andrew stopped the recording and leaned back while still staring at the screen, which now showed an empty alley except for the two dead bodies lying in pools of blood. Charlene turned to face him, realising that the recording had come to an end.

'Well?' she said. 'Find anything?'

'I'm not sure yet,' said Andrew. 'Can we swap back to the inside again? I want to have a look at something. Are there any other cameras in there?'

'Yes,' said Charlene, moving to stand next to Andrew as she leaned forward placing one hand on the desk and gripping the mouse with the other. 'There's another camera angle that I can show you. Here it is.'

The screen now showed the interior of the tavern from a different angle moments before Barton walked in. The camera was pointed at the pool table, but it covered much of the rest of the tavern, including half of the bar counter. Once more, Andrew watched Barton move to sit at the counter and engage in conversation with Charlene. Leaning forward, Andrew stopped the recording and peered intently at the screen. Behind Barton, sitting in relative darkness inside a small booth, was a man who appeared to be on his phone. He was a scrawny-looking character with tousled hair and stubble, and he was wearing dark jeans and a dark green t-shirt. His face was partially lit up by the phone screen, and he was clearly leaning forward and looking in Barton's direction with his small, beady eyes. He then drew back for a moment while continuing the call, and then he leaned forward again to look at Barton once more and gave a nod. Then he ended the call and slipped the phone into a pocket.

'Who is that?' asked Andrew, pointing. 'And is it just me, or does he seem to be looking straight at Eddie?'

'Oh shit,' said Charlene. 'I didn't spot that before. That's Doug. Doug Madden. He's kind of a weirdo.'

'Is he local?' asked Andrew.

'Yes,' said Charlene. 'He lives in a small trailer park in a disused gravel quarry on the outskirts of town. Bit of a loner and a grifter. Deals drugs and moonshine. I wouldn't trust him any further than I could throw him. But you're right. He looks like he's watching Eddie and talking to someone about him.'

'Any idea who might be on the other end of that call?' said Andrew. 'It looks like Madden was directing those two goons straight to where Eddie was.'

'Looks like it,' said Charlene, peering at the screen as Andrew replayed the footage. 'And no. I don't know who he could have been talking to. But I guess it doesn't take Sherlock Holmes to work it out. Madden is known for doing odd jobs for the people at Stonewall Ranch, so if they were really here to kill him, then I guess Madden helped them find him.'

'Madden led them straight to him,' said Andrew darkly, giving a small shake of the head.

'That little bastard,' said Charlene, frowning as she switched back to a live shot of the alley where it was now dark.

'Tell me something, Charlene,' said Andrew, fixing her with a look. 'Where do I find Doug Madden?'

EIGHT

General John McKinnon was sitting at his desk in his office on the first floor of the main building at Stonewall Ranch. He was a well-built man with a neck like a bulldog, a square jaw and thin lips, steely blue eyes set in a weathered face, and a military-style crew cut that he had sported since his teens. Despite now being in his early sixties, he was still lean and strong as an ox, thanks to the punishing exercise regime he put himself through every morning. He also took pride in being able to compete with the best of his employees on his private shooting range using a variety of the latest and most advanced weaponry he was able to acquire.

The large office was in keeping with the rest of the main mansion on the ranch with its high ceilings and exposed wooden beams that were painted black. The rendered walls were white and the bottom half was clad in dark brown wood panels. Across a floor made of wide varnished floorboards lay several large and expensive rugs. The soft lighting came from two enormous silver chandeliers and a handful of wall lights casting a soft glow up onto the walls and the ceiling. His desk was old and made of mahogany, and he was sitting in a plush leather office chair.

Wearing dark army-green slacks, black polished boots and a crisp white t-shirt over his wide muscular chest, McKinnon was reading an update from his in-house intelligence unit, which was located in a separate room in the mansion. The unit was made up of a handful of highly skilled former military intelligence specialists whom McKinnon had hired to join Ironclad Tactical Solutions shortly after setting up the venture.

Born and bred in West Texas near the town of Fort Stockton, McKinnon had joined the Marine Corps straight out of high school, and he had quickly proven to be a natural soldier. On account of his physical fitness, sharp intellect and extensive experience in a range of flashpoints across the globe, he rose through the ranks of the Marine Corps. He then spent just under a decade serving as a team leader in Delta Force and then as commander of that branch. After almost three decades in the special operations community, he was appointed deputy commander of the Joint Special Operations Command, also known as JSOC. This organisation is responsible for training all of the various special forces in the United States military, as well as planning and executing special operations missions across the globe, the most famous of which have been those of SEAL Team Six.

It was now roughly five years since McKinnon had retired, and he had soon grown bored of the speaking circuit, and a strange lack of purpose had crept into his life. At the same time, he had felt a rising frustration watching the ineffectiveness and ineptitude of the self-serving politicians in Washington D.C. These people were not true American patriots. In fact, they were anything but. As far as McKinnon could see, they were busy selling out the country to foreign interests left, right and centre at the expense of the people of the United States of America.

McKinnon was a keen student of history, and he saw in himself a spiritual successor to the great men of the fight for independence from the British. He also had an unusual claim to fame in that he believed himself to be a direct descendant of one of the heroes of the American Civil War. This latter point had served as part of his motivation for what he believed the future had to look like, as well as the steps that needed to be taken in order to create that future.

Eventually deciding that the entire system was even more corrupt and broken than he had always known it to be, he had decided to strike out on his own and employ his experience and expertise by setting up a private military corporation based at his Texas ranch. Hiring some of the best and most experienced special operators he had come into contact with during his career, as well as several others that came highly recommended, he had been able to offer those men pay packages that were orders of magnitude better than what they had been making while serving Uncle Sam.

Keen to make sure that his men felt appreciated and that they were as effective as they could possibly be, he had set up a management structure that mirrored units like the SEAL teams. This included every member of his organisation having their own personal 'cage'. These were room-sized repositories set up inside an underground ops centre, and they were made out of metal netting and contained every conceivable weapon and tool that each individual member wanted. Nothing was off-limits, and no expense was spared. All that mattered was that they all had exactly the equipment they wanted in order to make them the best operators they could possibly be. In the SEAL teams, this ability to get any weapon they asked for was known colloquially as the 'Golden Ticket'. At Stonewall Ranch, it was just business as usual.

For the first many months of running Ironclad Tactical Solutions, McKinnon had spent time touring some of the most dysfunctional countries in the world. Here he had offered his services to whoever was prepared to pay the most, signing deals with warlords and dictators to provide local training, physical asset protection or direct-action services such as the elimination of potential political rivals. With a total staff of around forty people, including the intelligence unit, his support staff and round-the-clock guards at Stonewall Ranch, Ironclad now required serious cashflow for its continued operation, and this was why the fees demanded by the PMC from its clients were as high as they were.

McKinnon's best men, grouped together in a unit called the Nightcrawlers, had now coalesced into one of the best special operations units he had seen in his time in the military, and their combined skillsets had proven highly effective during the various special missions that Ironclad had undertaken since its inception. In hand-picking his operators from the various branches of the U.S. special forces community to join Ironclad, McKinnon had approached the most capable and loyal men he knew. But he had also selected them based on something else. In order for his grand plan to work, he needed men who saw themselves as true and uncompromising patriots, and who shared his belief that the current government in Washington D.C. was broken beyond repair and needed to be entirely remade, even by force if necessary. Men who would not shy away from actions that most people might deem to be an attack on the United States Constitution, and that could be argued to fall under the definition of treason.

As it turned out, there was no shortage of such men. Men who had once believed in duty and sacrifice, and who still saw themselves as defenders of their country but who had lost faith in the system. The best operators were also the most experienced, and virtually all of them had firsthand experience of how self-serving policymakers in the White House and in Congress had sent them off to risk their lives for dubious causes and then promptly turned their backs on them if they were killed, captured or badly injured.

It was a permanent and indelible stain on the United States military that never seemed to be addressed or even acknowledged, and for which there could be no forgiveness. These former soldiers were all angry and disillusioned, and they were more than willing to rally around McKinnon in his endeavour to offer them some sort of redress. To right the wrongs of the past and ensure a different future by delivering a single but furious hammer blow to the elites in Washington. But before this blow could be dealt, several other pieces of the intricate puzzle had to fall into place, and McKinnon was working away methodically to ensure that would happen.

The latest Nightcrawler mission had just been completed successfully by a team led by former SEAL master chief Cormac. McKinnon considered him to be one of his best and most loyal men, and the mission had gone about as well as he could have hoped. Working on behalf of a local rival energy company, the team had eliminated the CEO of PetroDorado inside his home at his sprawling woodland estate. The next morning, once the local stock exchange had opened, the rival company had then swooped in using hidden off-shore corporate entities to buy up a majority stake in PetroDorado as the stock plummeted on the news of the CEO's violent demise. The price crash had been amplified by news outlets and social media platforms suddenly and mysteriously being flooded with what appeared to be credible reports that Altamirano had been killed by a drug cartel that he had entered into business with, and who he now supposedly owed a lot of money.

The entire operation had gone perfectly, and through his financial intermediary, Jean-Pascal Mokri, McKinnon had even made a tidy profit himself by riding the sudden panic in the market using a variety of sophisticated financial instruments that were beyond his ability to understand, but which Mokri had set up well in advance of the hit on Altamirano's estate. Once again, his partnership with the Lebanese financial alchemist had borne ample fruit.

Sitting in front of his huge computer screen full of multi-coloured stock price charts, trade analysis and stockbroker reports, McKinnon watched as his personal account was credited with the proceeds from his trades. Then came a brief message from Mokri himself via an encrypted messaging service asking if McKinnon was available for a call. The former general replied to the message, and after a couple of minutes, his secure phone rang, and he picked it up immediately.

'Mokri here,' said the voice on the phone with an accent containing elements of French and Arabic.

'Jean-Pascal,' said McKinnon, drawing out the vowels in his Texas drawl. 'Nice to hear from you. How's it going in the Big Apple?'

'Very well,' replied Mokri. 'As you may have seen, the payment for the Altamirano job has hit our account.'

'Yes, I saw that,' said McKinnon. 'What do you say we lock in the profits on the PetroDorado options trades? We don't want to get greedy, right?'

'I agree,' said Mokri. 'I will see to it that the positions are unwound as soon as possible and the funds disbursed into the designated Swiss accounts.'

'Alright,' said McKinnon. 'Good work, Mokri. You're a hell of a wiz with these things. Anyway, how are the preparations for the next step in our plan going? We only get one shot at this.'

'I have had meetings with our designated prime brokerage firms and money market fund managers,' replied Mokri, 'and I have been assured that everything will be set up and ready within twenty-four hours.'

'Excellent,' said McKinnon. 'That's what I like to hear.'

'Is everything going as planned at the ranch?' asked Mokri.

'Everything's going fine,' said McKinnon. 'We're already on the clock for Operation Leverage. It will kick off as scheduled later tonight. The boys are en route to Galveston as we speak. If everything goes as planned, we'll be good to go on the big one. Our ops centre is monitoring the port right now and prepping for the mission. I'll keep you posted once we have the gold.'

'Excellent news,' said Mokri. 'Thank you. And good luck.'

'Hell, we don't need luck,' said McKinnon dryly with an almost dismissive self-assuredness that only a career at the top of America's special forces command could have given him. 'What we need are guns, bullets and a vision for the future. And we have all three.'

*   *   *

It was half past eight in the evening when Andrew drove his Jeep south and out of town. The air was still warm, and he had the driver's side window rolled down to get some fresh air as he drove. Just as Charlene had indicated, there was an old rusty water tower by the road leading out towards the desert, and next to it ran a narrow dirt track. It extended for about half a mile to the east, after which it curved down and out of view into a large disused gravel pit.

Inside was what appeared to be a small trailer park with a handful of makeshift homes made of old shipping containers elevated a couple of feet off the ground onto large grey breeze blocks.

As Andrew crested the lip of the abandoned quarry and drove down into it along a smooth incline, it became clear that only one of the dwellings was inhabited, and according to Charlene, this was where Doug Madden lived. The other ramshackle homes in the quarry were evidently vacant and derelict, judging by their missing doors and broken windows behind which torn curtains moved gently in the warm evening breeze. The one converted shipping container that looked to be occupied had light coming out of the windows, and there was an old rusty-looking flatbed pickup truck parked next to it.

As Andrew pulled up and stopped the car around twenty metres away from it, he noticed that the door had been left open. Outside was a firepit where a small wood fire was crackling, and a few metres away was an old oil barrel inside which something was burning and producing a fair amount of smoke. When he turned off the engine, he heard country music emanating from the improvised home, but he neither saw nor heard any sign of its occupants.

He exited the car and began walking across the rough gravel towards the front door, and as he did so, he noticed the distinct sweet smell of cannabis wafting through the air. When he was about ten metres from the door, there was a sudden rustle inside the home, and it seemed to shift marginally on its supports as someone moved around inside.

With no word of warning, a man wearing jeans, a Hawaiian t-shirt and holding a sawn-off shotgun emerged in the doorway. His eyes locked onto the trespasser, and he descended the two wooden steps down onto the ground. He was a skinny man in his thirties with short tousled hair, but the unhealthy, colourless pallor of his face, combined with his beady eyes and the deep wrinkles across his forehead gave the impression of a man at least two decades older. This was the man Andrew had seen in the security camera footage from the High Jinx Tavern. This was Doug Madden. Seeming groggy and slightly unsteady on his feet, he advanced towards Andrew and raised the weapon.

'Hold it right there, Mister,' he said, slurring his words in the telltale sign of having consumed significant amounts of alcohol. 'This here is private property. State your business or you're gonna have a real bad day, ya hear me?'

Andrew was around three metres from Madden when he stopped walking and raised his hands slowly to about chest height to show his palms.

'I'm sure it is,' he said calmly. 'But I doubt that it's your property. Are you Doug?'

'What's it to you?' said Madden, taking another couple of steps forward while keeping the shotgun pointed straight at Andrew.

'I'm just here to ask you some questions,' said Andrew, remaining immobile and keeping his hands raised so as not to unsettle the shotgun-wielding weed connoisseur.

'Questions?' said Madden. 'What about?'

'About something that happened in Revelation a few days ago,' said Andrew. 'Behind the High Jinx Tavern.'

Madden's eyes immediately narrowed and darted towards the Jeep and then back to Andrew.

'I had nothing to do with any of that,' said Madden nervously. 'Who wants to know, anyway?'

'I am just a concerned citizen,' said Andrew reasonably.

'Bull-shit,' said Madden, the shotgun trembling slightly in his hands as he took another step forward. 'You ain't even from around here. I can tell from the way you talk.'

Madden's brain was clearly pickled by too much whiskey and too many joints, and it was obvious to Andrew that he was having trouble focusing his mind as well as his eyes. Keeping the shotgun trained on Andrew, he took another half step towards the trespasser while seeming to examine his face. He was now about one metre away.

'You ain't one of them government types, are you?' he said suspiciously, tilting his head and moving it slightly to one side while peering intently at Andrew as if that might help him answer his own question.

'No,' said Andrew. 'I'm not.'

'Cuz those feds are everywhere, man,' said Madden with a conspiratorial look. 'You can't be too careful.'

'Oh, I agree,' said Andrew, deciding to play along with Madden's apparent paranoia. 'In fact, they're probably watching right now.'

'What do you mean?' Madden said,, looking both puzzled and wary.

'Right this very minute,' said Andrew. 'I'm sure one of them is watching you right here in this place.'

'What in the hell are you talking about?' said Madden, now more agitated as he looked around suspiciously as if there might be a bunch of federal agents hiding up on the edge of the quarry.

Slowly and watched intently by the gun-wielding pothead, Andrew raised his gaze to the sky. Then he proceeded to extend his right index finger and point straight upwards towards the stars.

'You really think those spy satellites they launch are only watching the Russians and the Chinese?' he said.

Following Andre's gaze, Madden's eyes widened as the realisation slowly sank in and exploded in the vacuous cave of his brain like a bright emergency flare.

'Holy shit,' he whispered slowly.

With lightning speed, catching Madden completely off guard, Andrew's right hand shot out, gripped the barrel of the shotgun and snatched it out of Madden's limb grip. Before the hapless gunman had a chance to react, Andrew had flipped the weapon around and was now holding it firmly in his hands and pointing it back at him. Andrew cracked it open and glanced down into the breech. Then he pressed his lips together and looked back up at Madden with one eyebrow raised.

'Seriously,' he said with a small shake of the head. 'If you're going to point a gun at someone, at least make sure it's loaded.'

With a gormless expression, Madden hesitated for a moment, but then he spun on his heels and began sprinting towards the door to his home. Whether he had another weapon inside was difficult to tell, but

Andrew couldn't take that chance. He dropped the shotgun and immediately gave chase, catching up with Madden just as he reached the open doorway. Barging into him with a rough rugby tackle, the two men crashed against the doorframe and then onto the floor of the improvised trailer home, where Madden let out a cry of pain.

'My rib!' he yelled in a shrill voice. 'You broke my damn rib.'

Andrew got onto one knee, grabbed Madden roughly by his shoulders and pinned him against the floor of the messy and pungent home. While still groaning, Madden quickly reached down to a trouser pocket and extracted a switchblade knife which he immediately flicked open. With a roar and a furious grimace, he brought the blade up towards Andrew's face, but Andrew managed to parry it, grip Madden's wrist and force the weapon from his hand. It fell to the floor, and then he used his grip on Madden's arm to twist it around to his back and force the man onto his front. Grabbing Madden by his greasy hair, Andrew then lifted his head a couple of inches from the floor and smacked it down into the floor. The carpet softened the blow, but not enough to prevent Madden's nose from breaking with a wet crunch. Madden screamed in pain and kept on wailing as Andrew pinned him in place.

'Damn it, Doug!' Andrew shouted angrily. 'Will you stop being an idiot? I just want answers to some simple questions, alright?'

'OK, OK!' yelled Madden, sounding scared as blood oozed from his mangled nose. 'I'll tell you what I know. Jesus Christ, you fucking psychopath!'

Andrew rolled him over onto his back once more and placed the tip of the knife on his throat.

'Now,' he snarled. 'No more tricks. Understand?'

Madden grimaced, barring his blood-coated teeth as he nodded furiously.

'Alright, man,' he said, his eyes looking terrified. 'You win. OK? No more tricks. I promise.'

'You know who Eddie Barton is, correct?' Andrew said icily, his face mere inches from Madden's.

'Yes, I do,' nodded Madden, now eager to be compliant. 'He's one of McKinnon's men.'

Andrew's eyes bored into Madden's, and he knew that the pothead was telling the truth. A truth that unsettled Andrew deeply. If Barton really was working for McKinnon, this whole thing had all the potential to become very complicated and very dangerous.

'You mean General John McKinnon?' said Andrew. 'Ironclad Tactical Solutions at Stonewall Ranch.'

'That's right,' said Madden.

'What's going on out at that ranch?' said Andrew. 'When I ask people about it, no one knows anything, but everyone seems to be treating this McKinnon character like he's some sort of local king.'

'What the fuck do I know?,' said Madden pleadingly. 'They don't tell me shit! All I know is those boys have got more cash than hardly anyone else in this damn town. Whatever it is they do out there, they're into some serious shit. And you'd have to be a damn fool to cross the general. Everybody knows that.'

'So, Ironclad is some sort of PMC?' said Andrew.

'That's right,' winced Madden. 'Bunch of ex-military types gone private. But I don't know anything more than that.'

'Alright,' said Andrew. 'Listen. I know you were in the High Jinx Tavern the night Barton killed those two guys. I saw you on their security cameras.'

'OK,' said Madden hesitantly, eyeing Andrew suspiciously at the mention of cameras. 'Yes, I was there.'

'Did someone pay you to follow Barton?' said Andrew. 'Were you hired to find him?'

'Yes,' said Madden. 'By a man called Cormac. I do odd jobs for him around town. Information. Errands. That sort of thing.'

'Cormac,' Andrew repeated. 'Tell me about him.'

'He works for McKinnon,' said Madden. 'He's a cold-hearted son of a bitch. A real hard-ass. You don't mess with him, you understand? If you cross him, he's gonna come after you until you're six feet under. I didn't have a choice, man. He told me to keep an eye out for Barton. So I did. It wasn't even that hard. The High Jinx is where most of those guys do their drinking, so I just went in there and waited. That's all. I swear.'

'Why were those two men chasing him?' asked Andrew. 'What the hell was going on that could end up with Barton killing both of them?'

'On my mother's grave, I don't know,' said Madden pleadingly. 'All I know is that Barton pissed off McKinnon pretty bad, but I have no idea how. You have to believe me, man. I'm just a fucking errand boy, alright? They would never tell me anything about what's going on out there. And trust me, I don't want to know. I'm telling you the truth! I don't have a clue what the damn problem was between them. If I had known this would end with murder, I would have stayed the hell away from it.'

'And Barton?' said Andrew. 'Do you know anything about what happened to him?'

'He got booked and taken to the sheriff's office,' said Madden. 'That's all I know. Please, man. Let me go. I've told you everything.'

Andrew had heard enough. After listening to the self-pitying verbal diarrhoea of the bloodied man on the floor in front of him, he did not doubt that what he was saying was the truth. Madden was just a messenger, and the good guys don't kill messengers.

'I believe you,' said Andrew, removing the knife blade from Madden's throat and getting to his feet.

'Alright,' he continued, taking a step back but still pinning Madden down with a hard stare. 'Here's what's going to happen. You're going to get in that truck of yours and leave town for a couple of weeks. I don't imagine anyone is going to miss you much, and I want you to lay low and not communicate with anyone. Especially not anyone from Stonewall Ranch. I don't want you telling anyone about me. And if I find out that you have, I will come for you, and I will find you. Is that clear?'

'Yes, sir,' moaned Madden, slowly sitting up while touching his nose and running a hand across the right side of his chest.

'Now,' said Andrew, now more amicably, folding up the knife and putting it in his pocket. 'Where can I buy some drugs? Coke or heroin. Maybe some meth.'

'What?' said Madden incredulously, peering up at Andrew with a dumbfounded look.

'You heard me,' said Andrew evenly. 'Who sells drugs in this town? Even a picturesque little place like this has a seedy underbelly somewhere. Right?'

'Well, sure,' said Madden uncertainly. 'I know of a guy.'

'Good,' said Andrew. 'Tell me where I can find him.'

NINE

At around ten o'clock that evening, Andrew rolled into the parking lot of a disused petrol station on the edge of town, not far from the old water tower. Given everything that he had seen and heard, and being unable to shake the feeling that asking questions about Barton, McKinnon and Stonewall Ranch was invariably going to lead to some sort of run-in with the general's men, Andrew was now in no doubt that it was a question of time before he was going to need a gun. Gun laws in America are famously lax compared with almost all other countries in the world, but that didn't mean that anyone could just walk into a local gun store and buy one, especially not someone like him who was a visiting foreign national. What he needed was a different source.

The old petrol station's main building and garage looked weatherworn and dilapidated, and several windows were broken or missing. The pumps had been removed a long time ago, and only the rust-stained concrete foundations were still there. Inside what had once been the garage and workshop was parked a mustard-coloured sedan, and standing by its trunk were two men smoking cigarettes and listening to the pumping trance music emanating from inside the vehicle. At first glance, they both looked to be in their late twenties or perhaps early thirties, and it was clear that they were running a temporary shop from the trunk of their car, casually poisoning and ruining the lives of the local youth with their toxic wares.

They were both wearing jeans, trainers and loose checkered shirts, and the taller of the two had black hair parted at the centre in a curtain hairstyle. His face was lean and pock-marked, and his eyes were small and shifty. His shorter but much stockier companion had light blond hair shaved almost down to his scalp, and he had a leather jacket slung casually over his right shoulder.

As Andrew drove up slowly, stopped the car and turned off the engine, a scrawny youngster on a small motorbike shook hands with the curtain-haired man, started the engine and drove off noisily while giving Andrew a wary look. Curtains stuffed what appeared to be a couple of banknotes into his pocket and took a long puff of his cigarette while looking in Andrew's direction through narrow eyes, clearly expecting another customer.

Stepping out of the Jeep and walking casually towards the two, Andrew noticed that they both straightened themselves up to their full height and puffed out their chests. The blond guy, who was clearly the muscle of the operation, dropped his jacket on the trunk and folded one of his meaty hands around a fist made with the other. The aim was clearly to intimidate, and Andrew played along by raising one hand uncertainly and greeting them in a halting tone of voice.

'Good evening, boys,' he said. 'I need a hit. Can you help me?'

Curtains took a slow step forward, and Blondie followed suit. As the latter did so, he lazily pulled up the left side of his shirt and pushed it back down behind the pistol that was tucked into his jeans, putting the weapon on clear display in a show of force. It was an old semiautomatic 9mm Beretta M9, but it looked well-maintained, and old guns could be lethal even in the hands of novices. Blondie then folded his stocky arms across his chest and tilted his head to one side while gazing coolly down his nose at the prospective customer.

'You new in town?' said Curtains in a tinny voice, narrowing his eyes. 'You don't look familiar.'

'Yes,' said Andrew. 'I'm just here for a few days. But I am going to hit the town tonight, and I want to get juiced. So, are you selling?'

Curtains produced a chuckle and gave Blondie a sidelong glance.

'Well, that depends,' he said with a wry smile. 'This ain't no charity, you know. You got cash?'

'Of course,' said Andrew, digging into a pocket and producing a thick wad of all the dollar bills he had brought with him from the currency exchange at Dallas-Fort Worth International Airport.

Curtains ogled the money for a beat while he subconsciously licked his lips in anticipation of a quick score.

'Well,' he said. 'I ain't ever seen you before, but I know you ain't no cop on account of your accent. Are you British or something?'

'Yes, I am,' nodded Andrew, feigning the impatience of being able to sense the drug he craved yet having it tantalisingly out of reach. 'But my money is one hundred percent American. So, are we doing business or not?'

'Well, will you listen to this guy?' chuckled Curtains somewhat mockingly, glancing at his companion who gave a derisive snort. 'He sure seems strung out right about now. Guess we'd better get down to business.'

'Yes,' said Andrew. 'Let's just get a move on.'

'Alright then,' shrugged Curtains and stepped back to the car. 'Come over this way and have a gander.'

While Andrew followed Curtains, Blondie took a slow step back and let his bulky arms hang loose by his sides. Still seeming suspicious, he then stepped over next to the back of the car while keeping a distance of about a metre. Curtains popped open the trunk and gestured to its contents which were laid out in neat piles on a blanket. There were small plastic sachets of cocaine, dark packets of marijuana, and a few other things that Andrew thought might be crystal meth and ketamine.

'Take your pick,' said Curtains. 'We've got what you need.'

Still holding his wad of cash in his left hand, Andrew leaned forward and looked down into the trunk, scratching his chin with his right hand in apparent anticipation of finally getting his hands on his favourite Class A drug.

'I'm an old-fashioned kind of guy,' he said. 'Give a bag of coke.'

'Sure thing,' said Curtains and reached inside to extract a small bag containing the white powder which he offered to Andrew. 'That'll be $500.'

'Right,' said Andrew, picking off five banknotes with the face of Benjamin Franklin printed on them. 'Here you go.'

He handed Curtains the banknotes and stuffed the bag of coke into his trouser pocket. As he did so, Curtains and Blondie exchanged a quick look, and Andrew sensed that some unspoken agreement had just passed between them. This was the opportunity he had been waiting for. As he had expected, greed was about to get the better of them and make them take their eye off the ball.

'On second thought,' said Curtains slowly as a shifty smile played on his lips and Blondie placed his right hand on the grip of his pistol. 'I think we'll make that $1000. You look like you can afford it.'

Andrew made a show of hesitating, shifting his gaze uncertainly from Curtains to Blondie and back again, and then he nodded and swallowed.

'Listen, guys,' he sighed in a defeated tone of voice. 'I don't want any trouble, OK? Why don't you just take all of it? You're right. I can afford it.'

'Well, ain't that just real nice of him?' said Curtains as he glanced at Blondie with a smirk.

Andrew took half a step towards Curtains and held out the wad of cash, and as the pock-faced drug dealer reached for it, he knew that both of the two men now had their eyes firmly locked on the money. As soon as

Curtains' right hand closed around the thick folded stack of dollar bills, Andrew made his move.

With blistering speed and power, he stepped to the side and jabbed Blondie hard in the throat with his right hand. The man's eyes widened in panic as he staggered back a step and felt his larynx collapse, and he involuntarily brought both hands up towards his throat and made a tight croaking noise. In less than a second, Andrew had snatched the pistol from his belt, racked the slide and pointed the gun straight at the face of a stunned Curtains, whose lips moved but who made no sound as he watched the tables turn in the blink of an eye.

Andrew took a step back to create some more distance between himself and the two drug dealers. With one bullet already in the chamber, he quickly released the magazine, pulled it out to see that it had another eight rounds in it, and then he slammed it back in.

'Alright,' he said. 'The fun is over, boys. I am taking this gun. I am also going to need my money back and any spare ammo you have for this gun.'

With his mouth open in a gormless expression, Curtains was slowly recovering his composure, but he had dropped the cash on the ground, and his hands had both moved up next to his head as he stared terrified at the muzzle of the gun now pointing at his face. Blondie wheezed and rubbed his throat as he regained the ability to breathe, and with his eyes watering and a pained grimace on his face, he began nodding.

'OK, man!' Curtains exclaimed, kicking the wad of cash over to Andrew, who picked it up without taking the gun off the drug dealer. 'Just relax, alright? Take your money and the damn gun. Just leave us alone now.'

'Don't forget the ammo,' said Andrew calmly, after which Blondie reached inside the trunk for a small box of fifty 9mm Parabellum bullets which he tossed over by Andrew's feet.

'Now, do you have a lighter?' asked Andrew.

'Sure,' said Curtains, confused. 'What the hell for?'

'Pick up your drugs in that blanket,' said Andrew. 'Drop it on the ground and set fire to it. And stop selling your shit in this town.'

'Dude! That stuff is worth like ten grand or more!' protested Curtains.

Andrew shifted his aim slightly to one side and fired the gun. The loud report of the Beretta gave both men a jolt, and they involuntarily ducked down and cowered. The bullet punched through the back window of the car and exploded out through the windscreen, leaving a large and barely transparent spiderweb of cracks in both. As the shot reverberated across the open terrain, the only other sound was the spent brass cartridge landing and bouncing twice on the ground at Andrew's feet.

'The next one goes in your kneecap,' he said icily. 'Now, do what I said.'

'Alright!' yelled Curtains. 'Jesus Christ!'

He turned around and frantically scooped all of the drugs into the centre of the blanket. He then lifted it out of the trunk and tossed it on the dusty ground. He flipped open a Zippo lighter and lit the blanket on fire. The flames quickly spread to engulf the drug stash, which burned with an unusual and pungent chemical smell mixed with the distinct pong of cannabis.

'There!' said Curtains, looking utterly defeated. 'You happy now?'

'Happier than when I arrived,' said Andrew, flicking the gun towards the car. 'Now get the hell out of here. And don't come back, do you hear me? I don't want to have to waste my time on you two amateurs again.'

'Whatever you say, man,' said Curtains, shuffling back inside the garage on the driver's side of the car while Blondie moved to the passenger side. 'Whatever you say,'

The two hapless dealers slammed the doors and the engine sprang to life. As Andrew stepped aside while keeping the gun on the vehicle, it backed out, drove across the forecourt, and onto the road, where it sped off into the distance away from town. As Andrew had suspected, the two men were not locals, choosing like most criminals to ply their trade far away from their own homes. As the car disappeared into the distance, Andrew picked up the box of ammo and slipped it into a side pocket of his trousers. He flicked the Beretta's safety on and walked back to the Jeep, and then he drove back to the motel with his newly acquired firearm.

TEN

It was approaching midnight on the coast of Southeast Texas, and the weather was shaping up to be perfect for the operation. There was barely any wind, the full moon was partly obscured by several high-altitude cloud layers, and a thick mist was covering the marshy area around Pier 39 in the Port of Galveston, where the U.S. Navy transport ship USNS Charles Drew was about twenty minutes from docking. Escorted by the Arleigh Burke-class destroyer USS Kidd, it had set out three days earlier from Port Newark in New Jersey, and its cargo had originated inside the triangular fort-like eleven-storey building on 33 Liberty Street in the heart of New York City's financial district.

This address in Lower Manhattan was the home of the Federal Reserve Bank of New York, which was second in the world only to the United States Bullion Depository at Fort Knox in Kentucky with regards to the amount of gold bullion held in its vaults. In order to ensure the proper functioning of the U.S. monetary system, and in an effort to disperse some of the gold reserves held in New York, it had been decided that several hundred of the standard so-called 'Good Delivery' gold bars were to be shipped to the Texas Bullion Depository in Leander, just north of the city of Austin. Here they would be stored alongside other gold and precious metal bars deposited there by both state and federal government institutions as well as private corporations.

With each bar weighing 400 ounces, or roughly 12.5 kilos, the entire shipment from New York came in at just over three metric tonnes, which in turn equated to a value of roughly 190 million US dollars. A sum like that would enable the financing of some serious military ventures, but it could also be employed in different ways. Ways that General McKinnon and Jean-Pascal Mokri had spent months planning and preparing for, and which were now on the cusp of being realised. Operation Leverage had finally received the green light, and the Nightcrawlers were moving in.

Launching in a small black dinghy from a fishing boat five kilometres out to sea, Cormac, Knox, Willis, and Tyler were wearing tactical vests over black wetsuits and carrying a full weapons kit as they made their way through the mist and the darkness towards the coast of the northern tip of Galveston Island, where the sprawling port complex was located. The signal to commence the operation had come from an inside source working for the port authority, and it had been sent when a scheduled convoy of government vehicles had been approaching the outer perimeter, moving through the checkpoint and heading for Pier 39.

The unmarked convoy consisted of two armoured transport trucks, two black sedans with four armed FBI agents in each, and one M939 troop carrier truck bringing twelve soldiers from the Texas Army National Guard based at Camp Mabry in Austin. The task of the National Guardsmen, along with the eight federal agents, was to ensure the safety of the gold bullion after it was taken off the transport ship and loaded onto the armoured trucks for the journey to the Texas Bullion Depository in Leander. The trip from Galveston to the depository through the south Texas countryside was scheduled to take just under four hours, and the FBI and National Guard escort were going to be following the gold all the way to its final destination.

Moving gold bullion by ship from New York to Texas was an unusual type of transport by any standards, but the powers that be had decided that carrying the valuable cargo by sea would be safer and much less conspicuous than driving a vulnerable and highly visible convoy halfway across the United States. What those same people did not know was that the existence and timing of the intended low-key operation had been uncovered by a small team of hackers who had infiltrated the New York Federal Reserve Bank's computer networks many months earlier, looking for just this type of opportunity.

With that information in hand, McKinnon's team had then devised a plan to hijack the transport and spirit the gold away. The ultimate purpose was to melt down the gold bars, create new and smaller bars, and then sell those at a large discount to intermediaries in order to shift them quickly and quietly through a black-market distribution network. These intermediaries would of course become responsible for the headache of dispersing the precious metal into the real economy, most likely through numerous avenues over a number of years in order for it to remain untraceable, but that would not be McKinnon's problem. For him, Operation Leverage presented an opportunity to build up enough collateral to be able to move ahead with the next step in his grand plan. Selling the gold to a shady accomplice at a discount would naturally reduce his profits significantly, but if he ended up walking away with a clean 100 million dollars, then that would be more than enough for what he had in mind.

The reasons that McKinnon had decided to use a gold transport to raise the needed funds for his plan were twofold. Firstly, gold was easy to melt and sell. Even if it was in standard gold bullion form with imprinted markings, those traces would disappear once the bars were melted down, thereby erasing any trace of its provenance. Secondly, hijacking a transport was infinitely less difficult than trying to break into Fort Knox or the Federal Reserve Bank of New York.

Had the bullion transport taken place on land, either by truck or rail car, McKinnon would still have attempted a hijacking. However, upon finding out that the shipment was to be carried by sea for the vast majority of the journey, he had decided to use that fact to his advantage and employ his team's unique skillsets as former SEAL team and Delta Force operators. Boarding hostile vessels on the ocean or in a port was a major part of their training, and a covert approach to their target from the sea was as normal to them as driving to the supermarket was for the average person. Between hitting the transport ship on the open sea while it was protected by a U.S. Navy destroyer and waiting until it had docked in Galveston and was in the middle of off-loading its cargo, the latter option was clearly preferable, and so this was what the Nightcrawlers were going to attempt. An assault on a heavily guarded ship inside a port was by no means going to be easy, and they would need to employ significant levels of force, but it was preferable to attempting a highly risky boarding operation at sea.

As their dinghy skimmed smoothly across the black water towards the port, it cut through the dense mist that cloaked their approach, slowing down gradually as it went. Its low-noise electric outboard motor made barely a sound as it propelled them towards their target, and with the team lying low inside the dinghy, the risk of being detected from the shore was minimal.

When they were about five hundred metres from the USNS Charles Drew, team leader Cormac cut the engine and gave the signal for his men to fit their rebreathers. These high-tech, military-grade closed-circuit underwater breathing apparatuses were matte black and looked vaguely like small plastic backpacks, and they worked on a very simple principle. When humans inhale and then exhale, their lungs are typically only able to absorb and metabolise about 5% of the available oxygen content. A rebreather re-cycles the exhaled air and continuously tops it up with oxygen from a pressurised supply canister. In addition, the rebreather is fitted with a carbon dioxide scrubber that removes the harmful CO_2. These two effects allow a rebreather to function and provide breathable air for up to three hours without having to be topped up. However, the more substantial advantage in covert special operations was that the rebreathers created no bubbles when the operators exhaled. This, in turn, allowed them to remain hidden for a long time until they decided to surface.

Without a word, Knox, Willis and Tyler donned their flippers and masks and then ran through a final weapons check. They then shoved the soft rubber bite-grip mouthpieces into their mouths and activated the rebreathers. Upon checking that their oxygen supply was functioning properly, they each gave a thumbs up. With a simple hand signal, Cormac sent them over the side, and all three operators slipped quietly into the water and were gone. He then readied his own equipment and followed suit, but before he left the dinghy, he punctured it in several places with his combat knife. The small vessel quickly began deflating, and within seconds, the outboard motor was dragging it down beneath the surface towards the bottom. They were committed now. The only way to get back to the ranch was to push forward and complete the mission.

Swimming at a depth of about five metres, Cormac led the men towards the military cargo ship using a green phosphor compass to maintain his bearing. Roughly twelve minutes later, the team stopped as the keel of the ship became visible overhead, less than ten metres away. Above the shimmering surface, they could also see the bright floodlights on the pier that lit up the ship and the surrounding area and cast moving shards of faint light into the water.

Up on the pier, ten of the National Guardsmen, who were all armed with standard-issue automatic M16 rifles, had created a wide cordon around the ship and the two armoured transports that were now parked next to it. The remaining two were escorting four of the FBI agents wearing dark suits up along the gangway from the pier onto the ship. Here they were met by part of the ship's crew, and two of them were then shown to the bridge while the other two were taken into one of the compartments in the hold where the gold bullion was located. Those agents would inspect the shipment, verify that it was all there, and then give the go-ahead for it to be lifted by crane from the hold onto the pier. From there, the gold would be loaded into the armoured transports, and the vehicle convoy would then make its way through the night back to Austin and the depository in Leander.

Underneath the oily black surface of the water, the Nightcrawler team swam right up to the hull of the cargo ship near its stern. On Cormac's signal, they took off their flippers and unclipped the straps on their rebreathers. They then drifted slowly upwards until they broke the surface in complete silence. Taking off their wetsuit hoods and masks and attaching them to the rebreathers along with their flippers, they released the now superfluous bundles of hardware and let them sink to the bottom of the silty harbour.

Knox opened a large black nylon bag attached to his belt and extracted a set of powerful fist-sized suction cups. While the rest of the team waited silently next to him, he attached the first one to the ship's smooth-painted exterior, used it to pull himself out of the water, and then attached another one about a metre further up the hull. By the third suction cup, he was able to use the first one as a foothold, and in this way, he quickly began scaling the side of the ship, creating an improvised climbing ladder for his teammates.

With their black compact suppressed Heckler & Koch 416D assault rifles and their remaining equipment strapped to their bodies, Cormac, Willis and Tyler followed suit. Within a couple of minutes, the quartet had slipped over the railing onto the main deck next to the superstructure and were lining up next to a door and getting ready to enter. Flicking the safety catches off, and with Cormac taking the lead, the four men moved smoothly and quietly inside. The metal interior was painted a light grey, and there was a low mechanical hum emanating from somewhere. The air was stuffy and humid, and it smelled vaguely of engine oil.

The team had studied the layout of the ship carefully, so they knew exactly where to go and what to expect every time they turned a corner or pushed up a stairwell to the level above. They barely made a sound as they advanced up through the levels of the superstructure towards the ship's bridge. When they were two levels below their target, the black-clad and heavily armed team was moving quietly through a narrow and dimly lit corridor when an enlisted sailor came out from a small room and spotted them. Stunned by what he saw, he just froze and gawped. Without a word, Cormac raised his suppressed assault rifle, aimed and fired twice. The weapon produced two clicks and two muffled puffs in quick succession, and the bullets clipped the sailor in the head, causing him to crumple to the floor like a ragdoll.

Without slowing down, the team pushed swiftly forward, stepped over the sailor's dead body, and began ascending the final stairwell towards their target. At the top of the stairs was a narrow hallway, and on one side of it was a closed door with a small porthole at the top, beyond which was the bridge. With a quick set of hand gestures, Cormac ordered Willis and Tyler to move low to the opposite side of the doorway while he and Knox lined up next to the door handle and prepared to enter. Once Willis and Tyler were in place, he gave the signal, opened the door and pushed through.

Fanning out through the interior of the bridge like a wave of lethal smoke, the team moved inside, their suppressed weapons firing repeatedly as they cut down the two FBI agents and then the entire uniformed crew, including the captain. No one inside had time to fight back as the quartet swept mercilessly through the space, aiming for headshots and firing in brief sets of twos and threes, leaving no one alive. It was all over in less than ten seconds, and when they were done, eight men lay dead in pools of blood.

'Clear,' whispered Cormac in a husky voice as the last of their victims slumped lifelessly onto the floor of the bridge. 'Willis, get set up.'

'Roger that,' said Willis, moving swiftly to the starboard side, where he opened a door that led out to the bridge wing.

A narrow walkway wrapped around the entire exterior of the bridge, and Willis used it to climb up onto the top of the superstructure while remaining out of view of the FBI agents and National Guardsmen down on the pier below. Moving to the centre of the large flat space, he opened a small watertight bag and extracted a black box roughly the size of a small toaster, extending its folding antenna. He powered it up and initialised the remote switch, which he slipped into one of his pockets.

Crawling to the edge of the superstructure, he then unclipped his compact SR-25 sniper rifle, flicked open the bipod legs and moved it into place. Lying prone with only the muzzle of the suppressed barrel sticking out over the edge of the superstructure, he then activated his throat mike.

'In position,' he whispered. 'Jammer is hot and ready to go.'

'Copy that,' replied Cormac, who was still on the bridge. 'Wait for my signal.'

He and Knox had now stripped off their wetsuits and donned the shirts and dark suits of the dead FBI agents. Tyler had put on the uniform of one of the dead crewmen, whose clothes did not have any obvious bloodstains. Due to the bulk of the three operators, the disguises only just fitted them, but no one would notice unless they came up close.

'Moving to the cargo hold,' said Cormac, gesturing for Knox and Tyler to follow him.

'Affirmative,' whispered Willis. 'I have overwatch position. Everything is nominal on the pier. You're good to go.'

With Willis lining up his sniper rifle on the National Guardsmen and the FBI agents below, the remaining trio left the bridge the way they had entered and began making their way swiftly down the stairwell with their main weapons concealed inside Knox's black nylon bag. Tucked into their belts under their stolen clothes were suppressed 9mm Glock 19 pistols. Using the memorised layout of the ship, they proceeded down below the main deck and pushed forward towards the cargo section. The bullion had been carried in the compartment closest to the superstructure, and the large hatches above it had now been opened in preparation for the gold to be lifted out by crane. The bullion was sitting on three steel pallets weighing around one metric tonne each, and when Cormac, Knox and Tyler reached the sturdy metal doorway leading into the cargo compartment, they stopped and held their position for a moment.

Cormac leaned briefly past the doorframe to catch a glimpse of the first of the three pallets being lifted up and out of the hold by a crane operated from the pier. Standing in a huddle around the pallets were the four FBI agents that had boarded the ship, along with the armed two-man National Guard escort. Everyone was looking relaxed as they watched the pallet being raised from the floor up into the air. It turned and swayed slightly as the steel cable stretched under the immense weight, but within a few seconds, it had been lifted out and placed securely on the pier where most of the other National Guardsmen began loading it into the armoured trucks. Soon, the crane was lifting the second pallet out, and everything seemed to be going according to plan.

While waiting for the crane to return for the third pallet, Cormac suddenly heard footsteps further along the dark metal corridor that ran alongside the cargo compartments. Cormac performed a quick hand signal, and all three operators hugged the wall to remain in the shadows while pulling out their pistols. Up ahead, two crewmen were walking along the corridor from the stern of the ship. As they passed under successive overhead lamps, their faces were lit up by cold white light. Both of them looked to be in their early twenties. They were walking purposefully without talking, and as they drew nearer, Cormac signalled silently to his two companions. Almost instantly, their suppressed guns clicked and popped, and a handful of 9mm bullets tore along the narrow corridor to find their mark. Both young men fell to the floor without uttering a sound, and then it was quiet again.

By now, the third pallet was being lifted out of the cargo compartment, and the FBI agents were standing in the light that spilled down into the compartment from the outside, their necks craned back to watch the final pallet leave the hold. As soon as the pallet had disappeared from view, Cormac, Knox and Tyler walked through the doorway and strode swiftly towards the group of six men inside the compartment. The group was about fifteen metres away, and as they turned to head for the doorway, they spotted the newly arrived trio.

Wearing their disguises bought them several seconds, and as they drew closer, Cormac raised a hand and called out.

'Alright, gentlemen,' he said casually. 'We're all done here. Time to get moving.'

Momentarily confused by the sudden appearance of what at first glance looked like two federal agents and a ship's crewman, the four FBI agents inside the compartment merely turned and looked at the new arrivals. However, Cormac noticed that the two National Guardsmen immediately gripped their M16s tighter, and their posture seemed to grow tense.

'Hold on,' said the lead agent suddenly, sounding perplexed. 'You guys were meant to wait on the pier.'

Moving swiftly now and closing the distance to the group, Cormac and his two companions waited until they were close enough to guarantee successful kills.

'Wait,' said the lead agent, as it suddenly dawned on him that the three approaching men were not familiar to him. 'Stop right there!'

All four agents reached inside their jackets for their weapons at almost the same time, and sensing the tension and confusion, the National Guardsmen were bringing up their rifles, but by then it was too late. While still walking forward, Cormac, Knox and Tyler whipped out their pistols and brought them up. In a furious flurry of suppressed gunfire that seemed coordinated at a subconscious level, the three highly trained and experienced special forces operators worked seamlessly as a unit to drop the National Guardsmen with headshots within the first second of the firefight. They then shifted their weapons to the FBI agents, who never even got a shot off before they too were cut down by a barrage of 9mm bullets that tore into them, making them spin and fall as spatters of blood filled the air while their weapons clattered uselessly to the floor of the cargo compartment.

'All clear,' said Cormac as the trio moved swiftly to stand in the middle of the scatter of dead bodies, making sure that all of their targets were dead. 'Willis, what's your status?'

'Last batch being loaded into the armoured trucks now,' said the prone sniper from the top of the superstructure via the mike in his headset. 'No one heard anything. I think we're good.'

'Copy that,' said Cormac. 'Time to fire up the jammer.'

'Roger,' said Willis. 'Jammer is active.'

Without any visible change to the small black unit with the antenna, it immediately flooded almost the entire electromagnetic spectrum with high-intensity noise that would overwhelm radio transceivers, including mobile phones and the encrypted personal radios that the FBI agents were carrying as part of their standard equipment. From one moment to the next, an area with a radius of roughly half a kilometre became a radio wave dead zone where no communication was possible except on the single narrow bandwidth that had been selected for the Nightcrawler team's own communications equipment. The convoy was now completely cut off from the rest of the world, and they would no longer be able to call for reinforcements. However, it was a question of time before one of them would notice that their comms equipment had failed, so the team had to move fast.

'Keep watching them,' said Cormac, as the trio retrieved their main assault weapons from Knox's black nylon bag. 'Moving out.'

While the National Guardsmen and the remaining four FBI agents oversaw the final gold bars being loaded into the armoured trucks, the trio of former special operators moved swiftly out of the ship's cargo compartment, which had now been turned into a slaughterhouse. They proceeded quickly up the stairs to the main deck, where they crept over to the railing on the port side, watched over by Willis who was still lying prone on top of the superstructure.

'Willis, are you all set?' asked Cormac.

'Ready to rock and roll,' came the answer from Willis, who now had one of the FBI agents directly in his optical sights while also knowing which target to switch to next.

'Send it,' said Cormac coolly.

Willis fired, and the standard 7.62 NATO round punched out of the barrel of the suppressed SR-25 sniper rifle and slammed into the side of the head of one of the agents. The agent's head exploded in a cloud of gore, and Willis immediately shifted his aim and fired again less than a second later. The second bullet slammed into the torso of one of the other agents, and he slumped to the ground almost at the same time as his colleague next to him. At that moment, Cormac, Knox and Tyler emerged from behind the railing and brought their assault rifles to bear on the remaining agents and the hapless National Guardsmen.

The pier instantly turned into bloody chaos, with National Guardsmen attempting to return fire while the FBI agents sprinted for cover behind one of the armoured trucks. Loud rifle reports from the M16s reverberated through the night air and bounced off the ship and the surrounding buildings, and muzzle flashes lit up the pier as the National Guardsmen let rip with long bursts of fully automatic fire. However, these were not highly trained soldiers, and their shots went wide of their well-concealed targets. One by one, the ten soldiers fell to the ground, except for one of them, who managed to scramble behind the armoured vehicle to join the two FBI agents.

As the gunfire stopped, one of the agents could be heard shouting desperately into his radio and trying in vain to contact his commander at FBI headquarters in northern Austin, some 300 kilometres away. The surviving three men were now cowering behind one of the armoured trucks, and there was no way for Cormac and his two companions to hit them. They were also keenly aware that they could not run the risk of damaging the tyres on the armoured vehicles.

'Willis,' he said into his mike. 'Do you have a clear shot?'

'That's a negative,' said Willis calmly. 'No shot.'

'Keep on them,' said Cormac. 'We're moving down.'

Cormac led the two other men to where the gangway from the pier reached the ship's railing, and the trio then began descending the sloping walkway towards the pier. Suddenly, there was a burst of M16 gunfire coming from the armoured truck, and bullets dinged into the ship's hull just above their heads. All three men returned fire, but by then, the National Guardsman had pulled back. Seizing the opportunity, the three operators then sprinted down the gangway and began moving towards the armoured truck. At that moment, they heard Willis open fire from the top of the superstructure.

'They're taking off,' came Willis' voice, sounding urgent.

Then there was the sound of running feet on the concrete surface of the pier, and then another shot rang out. It was followed by a shrill scream from somewhere on the other side of the truck, and then they heard the sound of someone crashing to the ground.

As the trio of operators rounded the truck with their weapons up and ready to engage, they just had time to see the two FBI agents disappear through a door into a small administrative building just as Willis fired again. The bullet smacked into the concrete wall next to the doorframe, making a large puff of dust explode from the wall. Then the door slammed shut. About ten metres away on the ground was the last remaining National Guardsman, writhing in pain. He had been hit in the leg, and blood was oozing out. When he saw the three operators, he attempted to bring up his weapon again, but Tyler let a burst of three bullets fly. The projectiles punched into the man's body, making it jerk several times, and then he lay still. Without breaking their stride, the trio moved swiftly past the dead soldier and took up positions on either side of the door to the administrative building.

'Willis, do you see anything?' asked Cormac.

'Negative,' said Willis. 'The lights are off, so I can't see inside. But I don't think there's another exit.'

'Like fish in a barrel,' said Knox matter-of-factly, slapping a fresh mag into the magazine well of his assault rifle.

'We can't let them walk,' said Cormac coolly. 'Tyler, you're up.'

'Roger,' said Tyler, moving up to the door and fixing a small directional breaching charge before moving aside again. 'Ready.'

The three men stood well back from the door, and then Cormac gave Tyler a nod.

'Fire in the hole!' said Tyler, clacking off the explosive charge.

With a bright flash and a deafening crack, the breaching charge ripped apart the door and flung its remains inside the building in a shower of splinters and debris. Inside, the two FBI agents had taken up defensive positions behind furniture while making a last attempt to call for help. When the explosion happened, they were blown back from their cover and knocked over onto the floor. With loud ringing in their ears, they attempted to get back onto their feet and bring their weapons to bear, but by then the Nightcrawler team was inside. They never stood a chance.

In a repeat of the takedown on the ship's bridge less than half an hour earlier, the trio flooded inside, fanned out and took down both agents without missing a shot. Going down in a hail of bullets, the agents' bodies slumped lifelessly to the ground as the smoke inside the room began to dissipate.

'All clear,' called Cormac. 'Coming out.'

'Roger that,' said Willis from his perch. 'Packing up and coming down.'

He got to his feet, collapsed his sniper rifle's bipod and slung it over his shoulder. Then he moved to pick up the electronic jammer and hurl it off the superstructure into the harbour's black water where it disappeared with a splash. He then climbed off the roof and made his way back down through the superstructure, along the deck and down the gangway. By the time he joined the rest of the team, they had closed up the armoured trucks that now contained gold bullion worth almost two hundred million dollars. Cormac got behind the wheel of one of them, and Knox entered the passenger seat next to him. Willis got in the driver's seat of the other truck alongside Tyler. Before they set off, Cormac switched radio frequencies and spoke into his mike.

'Echo 1,' he said, stroking his moustache. 'This is Voodoo 1. How copy?'

There was a brief pause and the sound of some static, but then a voice came back.

'We copy you, Lima Charlie,' it said.

The voice belonged to the pilot of the V-280 Valor aircraft that was now banking north having held its position about ten kilometres south of the coast of Galveston for the past fifteen minutes. His name was Reese, and both he and his co-pilot Irvine were former members of the 160th Special Operations Aviation Regiment, or SOAR, stationed at Fort Campbell in Kentucky. The regiment functioned as a glorified taxi service to the various special forces branches of the U.S. military, but its pilots were anything but taxi drivers. They were some of the best aviators anywhere in the U.S. military, and they were renowned for pulling off daring and seemingly impossible insertions and extractions in all kinds of terrain and weather conditions, often under enemy fire.

'We are moving to exfil,' said Cormac. 'ETA at designated LZ. Four minutes.'

'Copy. Four minutes,' said Reese. 'Echo 1, out.'

Cormac then swapped encrypted radio channels again and spoke once more.

'Alamo, this is Voodoo 1,' he said. 'Assets acquired. We're en route to the LZ.'

'Roger that, Voodoo 1,' came General McKinnon's gravelly Texas drawl. 'Good work, boys. Now get your asses out of there and get to that LZ.'

'Moving,' said Cormac. 'Voodoo 1, out.'

Cormac started the armoured truck's engine, and Willis quickly followed suit. The two heavy vehicles then drove fast along the pier, out through the perimeter of the port area and east along Harborside Drive. After about a minute, they joined the 3-kilometre-long Seawall Boulevard that was straight as a ruler and that led out through empty marshland to the isolated Fort San Jacinto Historic Point. Their secluded destination on the sandy northeastern tip of Galveston Island was a popular spot for day-trippers. However, the main reason it had been chosen as an exfiltration landing zone was the fact that the straight road leading out to it turned into a fifty-metre-wide parking area at the end. This was the perfect amount of space for the V-280 Valor to perform a vertical landing, after which the transfer of the gold bars onto the aircraft could be completed.

As the two armoured trucks, each laden with one-and-a-half tonnes of gold bullion, roared along the dark empty boulevard, the V-280 was tearing through the air towards the coastline at low altitude and heading straight for the Galveston Bay Estuary. Flying just a few metres above the top of the shallow waves of the Mexican Gulf, it quickly closed the distance to shore and came around in a wide left turn that bled off almost all of its speed as it approached the parking lot. As its two huge rotors tilted from facing forward to facing straight up, the aircraft became more like a helicopter than a conventional aeroplane. Amid a whirlwind of air and bits of sand and debris, it glided across the beach and prepared to set down on the parking lot just as the two trucks arrived.

'This is Echo 1,' Reese called out over the radio. 'We've got a problem. There's a car here. It looks like there's someone inside.'

Near the centre of the parking lot was a yellow sedan sitting in one of the bays, and a faint light was emanating from inside. As the headlights of the two trucks swept over it, it became clear that there were two people sitting inside in the front seats.

'I've got this,' said Cormac.

Flooring the accelerator, he gripped the steering wheel tight and headed straight for the vehicle. As the heavy armoured truck barreled towards the small vehicle, Cormac bared his teeth and glanced at Knox with a ferocious look.

'Hang on!' he shouted. 'Brace for impact.'

When the truck crashed into the driver's side of the sedan, the smaller and much lighter vehicle was shunted violently sideways in a shower of glass as all of its windows exploded and shattered into thousands of tiny pieces. The armoured truck barely lost speed as it powered forward, thrusting the sedan sideways and off the parking lot. Cormac hit the brakes and came to a halt, and Knox immediately opened the passenger side door and got out. Advancing towards the mangled vehicle, he brought up his HK-416D and moved around to the driver's side. The entire side of the car was folded in, and behind the bent wheel was the grotesquely deformed and bloodied body of a man. Knox continued circling around to the passenger side where the door opened and a young woman spilled out onto the ground. Her face was covered in blood, and she was clutching her side where her shirt was soaked in red. As she saw Knox, she held up her hand.

'Please help me,' she pleaded. 'I'm hurt.'

Knox pulled the trigger once, and a bullet slammed into her forehead. She instantly flopped down onto the ground.

'Area secure,' Knox said into his mike.

'Roger that,' said Reese. 'Setting her down.'

Hovering over the parking lot and turning the V-280 to face out to sea, Reese set the aircraft down. The downwash from the two spinning rotors created a maelstrom of wind and debris as the landing gear touched the tarmac, but then the engines were spooled down and the chaos abated. The aircraft's rear hatch was opened, and Irvine appeared in the opening, waving for the two trucks to approach. Cormac backed his truck up to the loading ramp, and the four operators, helped by Irvine, then began carrying the gold bars from the truck into the aircraft, where they were placed on six steel pallets with wheels that were in the locked position.

Unloading the truck took several minutes. With roughly 1,500 kilos of gold to move and each man carrying roughly 50 kilos per trip in their special heavy-duty carbon-fibre bags, each of them had to make about five or six trips. Then the process was repeated with the second armoured truck. Once they were both empty, the team was sweating profusely, and they all slumped down into the jump seats mounted along the inside of the aircraft cabin. As they strapped themselves in, Irvine hit the button to close the rear hatch and made his way forward to the cockpit, while Reese spun up the engines again in preparation for takeoff.

Seconds later, the V-280 lifted off and began accelerating out over the water just a few metres above the waves. Keeping low like this and utilising the aircraft's stealth characteristics, neither civilian nor military radar systems would be able to pick it up and track it. Banking slightly, it headed almost due south and kept on the heading for several kilometres until the coastline was no longer visible. Then it performed close to a 90-degree turn and headed west. By now it was travelling at just under 500 kilometres per hour, and it maintained its course for about fifteen minutes until it made another right turn back towards the Texas coast. As it tore over the beach of the uninhabited Aransas National Wildlife Refuge, Reese used his night vision goggles to fly nap-of-the-earth and hug the terrain at an altitude that in any other context would have seemed suicidally low. However, for someone like Reese, this was just another day at the office.

The target destination was an isolated spot in the green forested hills of Uvalde County near the tiny town of Utopia, some 310 kilometres to the northwest. The trip took just over 35 minutes, and when the V-280 flared out again and set down in the small clearing that had been selected for the transaction, three large trucks and a black SUV with tinted windows were waiting for them. In front of the SUV stood a portly middle-aged man wearing an expensive pin-striped suit and sporting thinning grey hair that was smoothed back over his head. This was McKinnon's fence, who would take the gold off his hands and spend the next several years melting it down and then quietly feeding it into the real economy again without anyone being any the wiser. He was a precious metals dealer by the name of Georgio Christopoulos, and he was one of Jean-Pascal Mokri's old business partners from before he began working with McKinnon.

As the V-280 touched down and the rear hatch was opened, Christopoulos stepped towards the aircraft and raised a hand in greeting, the downdraft making his suit flap in the wind. The shiny suit appeared particularly out of place in a forest in the middle of the night, but his wide toothy smile said that he was ready and able to complete the deal.

Covered by his three heavily armed companions, Cormac stepped down the ramp and shook hands with the Greek merchant. After a quick conversation, Cormac then flipped open a laptop and showed it to Christopoulos. The fence tapped in a ten-digit code and supplied his fingerprint using an inbuilt scanner, and after a few seconds, Cormac confirmed that the payment had gone through and that it had hit the designated Swiss account. Cormac then signalled for the three steel pallets to be rolled off the aircraft, and Christopoulos' men exited their vehicles and prepared to load the gold bullion into their own transports. Cormac and his team didn't wait around for this to be completed, but instead moved back inside the aircraft and took off. Another 45 minutes and 340 kilometres later, the V-280 touched down dead centre on the landing pad at Stonewall Ranch, and its large engines spun down for the final time. Mission completed.

ELEVEN

Andrew awoke in his motel room the next morning with a gnawing sense that there was a lot more to Revelation than met the eye, and that it all revolved around Ironclad Tactical Solutions. His run-in with Doug Madden had made it clear that somehow Barton had got on the wrong side of his employer, General McKinnon, but he found it difficult to imagine what might have caused it to end the way it did. The only thing that was certain was that there were things going on at Stonewall Ranch that had somehow caused Barton to run, and Andrew needed to find out what those were. However, he would first need a way inside, and short of sneaking in under cover of darkness, the best approach at this point would probably be to enlist the help of someone else. Someone like Sheriff Hogan, if he could convince him to help.

Andrew walked outside, climbed into the Jeep and drove back towards the centre of town. It was shaping up to be another sunny day, and by the time he parked in front of the sheriff's office, the air was already pleasant and warm.

'Morning, Sergeant Fuller,' he said, greeting the desk sergeant with a wave.

'Mr Sterling,' said Fuller, looking up from under his hat. 'What can I do for you?'

'Could I speak to Sheriff Hogan again, please?' replied Andrew. 'Our meeting yesterday was cut short.'

'Chief Hogan ain't in this morning,' said Fuller. 'He's gone to attend an important meeting.'

'I see,' said Andrew. 'Who is he meeting with?'

Fuller gave a small shake of the head and produced a wry smile.

'I can't tell you that,' he said.

'I guess that means he went out to Stonewall Ranch to see General McKinnon,' said Andrew, deciding to roll the dice and see what happened.

Fuller's reaction was instant, and it told Andrew everything he needed to know. The sergeant's back suddenly straightened noticeably, and his eyes narrowed with obvious suspicion. Then he looked down and began uselessly shuffling some papers around on the desk.

'Like I said,' he finally mumbled. 'I can't tell you.'

'Right,' said Andrew breezily. 'Do you know when he will be back?'

'No,' said Fuller. 'I don't. But I can let him know you were here. If you give me your number, I can give you a call when he gets back.'

'Maybe I'll just sit over in one of those chairs and wait for him,' said Andrew, glancing over his shoulder towards the two metal chairs under the reproduction of the painting of the Alamo. 'I don't mind waiting. But it was just a small thing I was going to ask him.'

'Yeah?' Fuller said hesitantly, seemingly not thrilled at the prospect of having an audience watch him for several hours until Hogan returned. 'What was it?'

'I was wondering if I could have a quick look at the cell that Eddie Barton was held in when he was here?' said Andrew.

'What for?' asked Fuller, puzzled.

'Barton is a diabetic,' Andrew lied. 'If he doesn't take his medicine, he could get very ill. He always keeps his medicine on his person, but I think he might have left it in the cell. I want to make sure that hasn't happened. Wouldn't look too good on you guys if he was moved out of this building without the medicine he needs, right? That might end up in a lawsuit.'

Fuller seemed to consider this unpleasant prospect for a few moments, and then he nodded and gestured towards an open doorway.

'Alright,' he finally said. 'Come with me. I'll take you to his cell.'

Andrew followed Fuller through the doorway and down a corridor to a locked door. Fuller opened it with a large key and led Andrew through to another short and wide corridor with three small cells on one side. Walking to the other end, Fuller stopped and pushed the unlocked door to the last cell open.

'Here it is,' he said. 'Have at it.'

While Fuller waited outside, Andrew walked into the cell and began looking around. It only took him a few seconds to spot the familiar dog tags dangling on a short metal chain from one of the slats under the top bunk. Making sure to stand so that Fuller could not see what he was doing, Andrew reached for them and cupped them into his hand. A quick glance at them before he shoved them in his pocket confirmed what he already knew. These were Barton's tags, and as he looked down at them lying in the palm of his hand, a cold shiver ran down his spine. He knew that Barton would never have parted with them voluntarily, so the only way they would have been left behind was if Barton had been moved by force.

Andrew was no expert on U.S. law enforcement procedures, but he felt sure that Barton would have been allowed to take all of his personal belongings with him if he had been moved to a jail in Nolan County the way Hogan had described. The fact that the tags were still here meant that Barton was taken against his will in a manner that had prevented him from bringing one of his most prized personal possessions with him. In other words, when Hogan said that Barton had been moved to Nolan County by state troopers, he had been lying. It was the only explanation. But why would he do that?

'So,' said Andrew casually as he made a show of inspecting the chair in the room. 'Who is Billy Ray? I heard you mention him the other day.'

'Well, he was a deputy here,' said Fuller reluctantly, as if he did not want to talk about it. 'I'm not allowed to tell you anything more than that.'

'Was?' said Andrew, stepping to one side so he could look straight at the sergeant.

'He's dead now,' said Fuller, looking uncomfortable. 'He killed himself.'

'Shit,' said Andrew, as his thoughts drifted towards Donna and her heart-rending reaction in the diner when she had learned of her brother's death. 'That's awful.'

'Yeah,' said Fuller quietly, staring at his shoes with his hands on his hips. 'It's a damn mess, to be honest. But I really can't say any more, OK? The whole thing is still under investigation.'

'He was Donna Cooper's older brother, right?' said Andrew gently. 'I guess that would have made him Deputy Billy Ray Cooper.'

'That's right,' said Fuller, shifting uncomfortably on his feet and appearing weighed down by the subject. 'He was. Listen, are you all done here? I really need to get back to work.'

'Yes,' said Andrew with a shrug and a last look around the cell. 'There is nothing here. I guess I was wrong. He must have taken the medicine with him after all. Thanks though.'

'No problem,' said Fuller, turning to leave. 'Let me take you back out.'

The two men returned to the front desk just as Sheriff Hogan appeared in the doorway. He was wearing his usual white shirt and beige trousers, and he waddled slightly as he walked inside, puffing from apparently already feeling the heat. As Andrew stepped forward to offer his hand, he detected a faint smell of alcohol on the chief's breath.

'Sheriff Hogan,' he said amicably. 'Fuller here has just very kindly allowed me to see Barton's cell. I was looking for his diabetes medicine, but it wasn't there.'

Hogan's warm damp hand gripped Andrew's, and his eyes shot sideways to fix Fuller with a brief stare. Then he nodded and broke into a forced smile as he returned his gaze to Andrew.

'I see,' said Hogan, and shrugged. 'Well. Fuller's a nice guy. That's why he's in charge of this desk here. Anything else we can do for you today?'

'When I was last here,' said Andrew. 'Before we were interrupted, I was asking if I could speak to the two arresting officers. Deputies Turnbull and Cooper, if I remember correctly.'

'Well,' said Hogan, sucking his teeth and tilting his head to one side. 'Sadly, Cooper's no longer with us. And Turnbull has gone out to visit family in California somewhere. I'm not sure where he is.'

'I see,' said Andrew. 'Can you tell me what happened to Deputy Cooper?'

'Well, I could,' said Hogan, 'but I am not going to. See, this is internal police business as far as we're concerned. And we don't need anybody poking their nose into this thing. It's messy enough as it is.'

'I understand,' said Andrew. 'It's just that Cooper seems to have taken his own life at a time that coincides with my friend being in this building.'

'Well,' shrugged Hogan as he scratched his beard. 'You just said it. It's a coincidence.'

'Right,' said Andrew. 'Perhaps it is. Anyway, since you're an important man in this town, I was wondering if you might be able to introduce me to General McKinnon?'

Hogan looked at Andrew for a long moment, as if trying to decide whether the man in front of him was being serious.

'Really?' he finally said. 'You'd like to meet him?'

'Yes,' said Andrew. 'He seems like a great man, and I thought maybe with my background in UK special forces, he and I might get on.'

At the mention of special forces, Hogan looked Andrew up and down with a certain level of respect before settling on his eyes again.

'Right,' Hogan said in a slow, drawn-out manner. 'Special forces, huh?'

'SAS,' said Andrew. 'Same as Barton.'

'Well,' said Hogan after pondering the request for a moment. 'McKinnon was with the special forces, on top of being a great patriot. But the thing is. You don't just drive out there without an invitation or someone having vouched for you. You're likely to get your ass shot off. You see, we take the idea of private property real serious here in Texas.'

'I think I understand,' nodded Andrew. 'In my country, we like to say that an Englishman's home is his castle. So, in a way, we feel the same way, except we don't have guns.'

Hogan's left eyebrow crept upwards over a couple of seconds as he regarded Andrew dubiously for a long moment before speaking.

'No guns,' he finally said ponderously, clearly trying to picture the absurd idea in his mind. 'And how does that work, exactly?'

'It's a good question,' said Andrew. 'I guess if the bad guys don't have guns, then no one else needs them either.'

'Bad guys always have guns,' said Hogan flatly, as if Andrew had just asserted that in the UK, two plus two makes three. 'Anyway, you could be right. Maybe

220 The Lone Star Conspiracy

McKinnon would like to meet you. I could try giving him a call and see what he says. He'll listen to me.'

'I would really appreciate that,' said Andrew. 'Thanks a lot.'

'Hey. No problem,' said Hogan. 'We're a friendly bunch in this town. Give me your number, and I'll get back to you.'

Andrew scribbled his mobile phone number on a sticky note from Fuller's desk and handed it to Hogan.

'I'm ready any time he is,' he said.

'Alright,' said Hogan, glancing down at the number on the small piece of paper. 'I'll let you know how it goes.'

'Thanks again,' said Andrew, shaking the sheriff's hand once more before turning to leave the building. 'I'll wait to hear from you.'

As Andrew began walking back out into the sunshine, he heard Hogan's voice behind him, at which point he stopped and glanced over his shoulder.

'A piece of advice, Mr Sterling,' Hogan said. 'I understand you and Eddie Barton were friends, but be careful you don't go poking your nose where it don't belong. People around here don't really like that.'

'Thanks for the suggestion,' said Andrew as he resumed walking out. 'I will keep that in mind.'

Less than an hour later, as Andrew was perusing the various shops on Main Street looking for some more clothes for what was becoming an extended stay in Revelation, his phone rang.

'Mr. Sterling,' said the familiar voice. 'This is Chief Hogan. I've just talked to McKinnon, and it turns out the general is really keen to see you. Who'd have thunk it? It seems like word has gotten around about you already.'

'Good,' said Andrew. 'I thought that might be the case. When can I meet him?'

'Well,' said Hogan. 'If you come back to my office in about twenty minutes, I can take you out there. You can drive your own car, and I'll drive ahead of you and show you the way.'

'That's very kind of you,' said Andrew.

'Well, we do take pride in our southern hospitality,' said Hogan. 'And I don't mind helping the general.'

'Great,' said Andrew. 'I'll see you shortly.'

Twelve

During the drive from the sheriff's office to Stonewall Ranch, Sheriff Hogan, who was in his police cruiser, made an obvious effort to drive below the speed limit and indicate well in advance of making turns, clearly keen to make sure that Andrew's Jeep stayed on his tail. Andrew already knew the way, but he wasn't going to let Hogan know that. As they left town and made their way across the flat, open terrain of the high desert, Andrew checked his newly acquired Beretta M9 to make sure that the magazine was full, and then he tucked it into his belt under his shirt. He did not expect to need it, but it was better to be safe than sorry.

When the two vehicles pulled up in front of the gates to McKinnon's ranch, they immediately unlocked and swung open as if by magic to allow the visitors to enter. Driving along the gravelled, tree-lined avenue towards the main compound of the ranch, Andrew peered out of the windscreen. Up ahead, the main mansion protruded up above the tops of the surrounding trees, and as they drew nearer, he spotted a checkpoint set up just before the avenue reached the compound. It was manned by two men dressed in dark shirts, desert-camo tactical vests, light-coloured cargo trousers and black leather boots, and they each cradled an assault rifle in front of them. Wearing dark sunglasses and sporting short crewcuts, Andrew had seen these types hundreds of times before in places like Iraq and Afghanistan. They were unmistakably private military contractors, also known as mercenaries for hire.

When Hogan stopped his car in front of a lowered boom by a small guardhouse, one of the armed men approached his police cruiser, and after a brief and amicable-looking conversation, the armed man waived the two vehicles through. Behind the guard, Andrew could see several more similarly clad and equipped men walking around the compound in pairs. It seemed to be the case that McKinnon was indeed operating a PMC from the ranch and that security inside the compound itself was a high priority. All told, he could see around ten guards walking the premises, and he reckoned that there would be a similar number that he couldn't see. A sizeable force for such a seemingly peaceful and pleasant spot in the middle of the arid and unpopulated Texas countryside. Clearly, McKinnon did not consider his PMC enterprise to be something that was entirely without risk to his own safety.

The main mansion was large and imposing with a huge front door, its many tall windows betraying the presence of rooms inside that had very high ceilings.

It looked to have been built not too long ago in the vaguely Germanic so-called Hill Country architectural style that was unique to Texas and which used limestone blocks on the exterior walls, dark high-pitched slate roofs and ample amounts of visible wood and metal to give it a rustic and rugged look.

Hogan and Andrew followed the curving gravel path that led around a circular and perfectly manicured lawn in front of the mansion. The lawn had a ring of burgeoning and colourful flowerbeds around its circumference, and its centre was adorned with an elaborate multi-tiered water fountain. Hogan parked his cruiser near the wide flaring stairway to the main door, and Andrew pulled up next to him. As the sheriff got out of his car, a tall lean man who appeared to be in his forties wearing a light grey pinstriped suit and a black tie came down the steps to meet him. Unlike seemingly all of the guards in the compound, he was clean-shaven and carried himself like someone who was more used to spending his time in boardrooms and upmarket hotels than dusty ranches in the high desert. When he spoke, he sounded considerably more metropolitan than anyone else Andrew had met so far during his visit to the Lone Star State.

'Chief Hogan,' said the man cordially as Andrew stepped out of his Jeep and began walking towards the two others. 'Welcome back.'

'It's good to be back, Roy,' said Hogan, turning to Andrew. 'Mr Sterling, this here is Roy Cobb. He's the manager of the estate. I guess you could call him General McKinnon's right-hand man here at the ranch. Ain't that right, Roy?'

'Something like that,' smiled Cobb affably as he extended a slender hand to Andrew. 'Welcome to Stonewall Ranch. 'The general is ready to see you.'

'Thank you,' said Andrew, giving Cobb's soft hand a firm squeeze and noticing how it yielded in his grip.

Cobb gave every impression of being a pencil-pushing administrator of McKinnon's sprawling estate, but as the two men shook hands, he noticed a slight bulge under the left side of Cobb's suit jacket, and then he spotted the telltale leather strap keeping the pistol holster in place. It seemed that everyone at the ranch was carrying a firearm. Or perhaps it was just that everyone in Texas did.

'Follow me, gentlemen,' said Cobb. 'I'll take you to him.'

Cobb led Andrew and Hogan up the steps to a large lobby with a set of two wide sweeping staircases leading up through the house to the floor above, and on both sides of the expansive room were large doorways leading into various dining rooms and sitting rooms with plush furniture and enormous rugs on the floor. All of the walls were rough rendered plaster painted off-white, and the ceilings were supported by thick wooden beams painted black.

Cobb took them straight ahead through a set of double doors that led to what looked to be a large function room. It had a varnished hardwood floor and was sparsely furnished, and on one side of the room was a series of tall windows providing an unobstructed view out over a large immaculate-looking garden complex on the other side of the mansion. He then turned right until he reached a set of stairs going down to what had to be a basement level underneath the mansion. The staircase stretched down at least one full storey before it emerged into a hallway with a dark blue carpet and soft lighting spilling over walls adorned with black textured wallpaper. As they descended, Andrew could hear music emanating from somewhere below.

Soon, he found himself escorted into what could only be described as a large tastefully lit bar area that would have seemed more appropriate in an expensive modern hotel in the middle of a major city. There was a long bar seemingly stocked with every possible drink anyone could desire, and it was manned by two attractive young women in skimpy black clothes. There was a small dancefloor and several pinball machines lined up by one of the walls, and there were several plush, curved booths inside which sat groups of burly and bearded musclebound men having drinks. They were all very obviously ex-military types.

As the trio entered, the talk amongst the men ceased, and all eyes turned to the stranger who had accompanied Cobb and Hogan into the basement. Even the two women behind the bar seemed to stop what they were doing to inspect the newcomer. Clearly, this place did not often receive new visitors. Andrew glanced at the women and noticed that one of them seemed to regard him with more than just idle curiosity. There was a vague look of puzzlement in her eyes. It was as if she felt there was something familiar about him.

'It's alright,' said Cobb calmly, addressing the burly men as the trio walked across the room towards an empty booth. 'This gentleman is here to see the general.'

Still eyeing Andrew suspiciously, the men slowly reverted back to talking and drinking, but one of them kept tracking him with his eyes. He was a giant of a man who seemed slightly older than most of the others, and he sported a shaved head and a large black moustache. Next to him were two other men that Andrew recognised from Donna's Diner. One of them was wearing a cowboy hat, and the other had a mohawk hairstyle. Tatum and Thornton. The two men who had accosted Donna until Andrew had intervened. That incident had clearly created some bad blood, and as Andrew glanced at them, the animosity was palpable from the way they eyeballed him, and they both looked as if they would like a chance to get even.

Cobb gestured for Andrew to sit down on the curving seat inside the empty booth, and Hogan slid onto the seat opposite him.

'I'll get one of the girls to get you a couple of drinks,' said Cobb. 'The general should be here in a minute.'

Then he strode across the floor to the bar where he sat down on one of the barstools and had a quick word with one of the young women. She was petite, pretty and slender. Her shoulder-length blond hair was glossy and wavy, and she was wearing a short black skirt and a shiny black silk shirt.

'Don't mind them,' said Hogan quietly as he leaned forward as much as his ample pouch would allow, shooting a furtive glance towards the men in the other booths. 'This here is their den, see? And they're not really used to strangers.'

'I'm not worried about them,' said Andrew calmly. 'I am sure they only ever do exactly what McKinnon tells them to do in this place. They are like a bunch of dogs on a tight lead. All bark and no bite.'

'True enough,' nodded Hogan sagely. 'Still. Try not to ruffle any more feathers. I heard about what happened at the diner. All I'm saying is, you don't want to make enemies around here.'

'Got it,' said Andrew with a nod, wondering why Hogan was so keen to avoid him making waves.

'So, where are you staying in Revelation?' Hogan said casually. 'Our town has a couple of real nice hotels just off Main Street. I could put in a word for you and get you a good price.'

'Thanks, but I'm in Mike's Motel,' said Andrew. 'On the edge of town.'

Just then, the young blond woman arrived with two tumblers that were three-quarters full of whiskey, and she placed them in front of the two men.

'Mike's Motel?' scoffed Hogan. 'You can do a lot better than that around here.'

'Well, it's perfectly comfortable,' said Andrew. 'I don't need anything fancy.'

'Triple Cask Bourbon,' smiled the blonde with a soft and pleasant voice. 'Best one we have.'

'Thanks, Sugar,' said Hogan, giving her a wink.

'Are you British?' she asked, her blue eyes meeting Andrew's as she produced a timid smile.

'Yes, I am,' said Andrew. 'London.'

'London,' she said, sounding intrigued. 'Oh, I always wanted to go there.'

'Alright now,' said Hogan, raising his right hand off the table as if to caution the young woman. 'Me and Mr Sterling here were just talking.'

'Sorry, Chief,' said the blonde, retreating back towards the bar while Hogan allowed his eyes to sweep greedily down over her body as she turned and walked away.

Andrew picked up the tumbler, lifted it briefly to salute the distracted sheriff, and then he put it to his lips. The young woman had been correct. It was one of the best whiskeys he had ever tasted. As he savoured the sharp tang of the dark, golden liquid, he watched as the blonde picked up a tray full of drinks prepared by her colleague. She carried it over to the nearest booth and began picking the drinks off the tray and placing them on the table in front of the men. Once finished, she turned to walk away, but at that moment, a lean-faced man with a black ponytail reached out and gave her a slap on her rear, resulting in leering hoots and laughter from the other men. Her head whipped around and she gave him a look of mock indignation, shooting him what appeared to be good-natured daggers. However, as soon as she turned away to walk back to the bar, Andrew spotted some very different emotions flashing across her face. It was revulsion, exasperation and barely repressed anger in equal measure. It was clear that she did not appreciate the crude advances of McKinnon's men, but she was likely tolerating them so as not to lose her next paycheck.

Suddenly, a figure appeared in the doorway leading upstairs, and the atmosphere in the room changed immediately. The men in the booths went quiet, and they seemed to tense up, almost as if they were ready to jump up and stand to attention. The man was tall and powerfully built, but he was significantly older than the others. He was wearing a pressed dark army-green shirt with an open collar and a pair of black trousers. His face was leathery with deep creases on his forehead, and in the corners of his eyes, he sported a short crewcut. As he strode purposefully towards Andrew and Hogan, his left hand made a quick gesture to his men.

'At ease, boys,' he said in a gravelly voice. 'Carry on.'

As the men settled back down and continued their drinking and talking, Hogan got up and shuffled swiftly aside to let the general take his seat in the booth across from Andrew. Barely acknowledging the sheriff, General McKinnon sat down and regarded Andrew for a moment. Then he stuck a big hand across the table in greeting. Andrew took it in his and received a short, hard squeeze for his trouble.

'Welcome to Stonewall Ranch,' said McKinnon, leaning back in his seat and regarding Andrew across the table.

'Thanks for seeing me,' said Andrew. 'I appreciate it. I won't take too much of your time.'

'That's no problem,' said McKinnon. 'I am always interested to meet fellow special operations soldiers from other countries. I've heard good things about the SAS. Never worked with you boys myself when I was in the teams, but I hear you're real hard-asses.'

'Some might say that,' nodded Andrew with a slight smile.

'That'll be all, Chief,' said McKinnon, glancing up at Hogan with a nod. 'Thanks for coming out. Mr Sterling and I are going to have a talk.'

'Right,' said Hogan with obvious deference. 'I should probably be getting back to the office myself. Ya'll have a nice day.'

He tipped his hat at Andrew and gave McKinnon a quick nod, and then he turned around and walked back to the stairwell where he disappeared. McKinnon picked up Hogan's tumbler and emptied it in one gulp. Then he winced and smiled as the alcohol burned his insides.

'Damn, that's good,' he said, licking his lips as he slammed the tumbler down on the table and turned to wave for the blond barmaid to refill it. 'The finest damn Bourbon money can buy. Made right here in Texas.'

'It's pretty good,' said Andrew, watching the general and getting the distinct impression that in this realm, McKinnon was the equivalent of an omnipotent king.

'So,' said McKinnon, leaning forward and resting his elbows on the table. 'You say you were a friend of Eddie Barton?'

An icy shiver immediately ran down Andrew's spine as he noticed the use of the past tense about his friend. Looking into McKinnon's hard eyes, he suddenly found himself fearing the worst for Barton. However, he decided to let it slide and hope that McKinnon hadn't noticed himself. At that moment, the blonde returned and topped up both of their tumblers. As she gave Andrew his refill, she glanced at him for a moment, but when he looked up at her, she quickly broke into a friendly smile and returned her gaze to the tumbler.

'Thanks, Darling,' said McKinnon as she stepped away and returned to the bar.

'Barton and I were both in the 22nd Special Air Services regiment,' Andrew explained, taking another sip of his whiskey. 'Spent a few years together in B Squadron.'

'See much action?' asked McKinnon probingly as he raised his tumbler to his lips and regarded Andrew across its edge.

'A fair bit,' shrugged Andrew. 'It was a busy time. But I guess you might have gathered that from Barton's CV when you hired him.'

McKinnon nodded pensively as he slowly swirled the whiskey inside the tumbler and took another sip.

'Yup,' said McKinnon. 'We do take vetting pretty seriously around here whenever we hire new people. Gotta make sure they are who they say they are. You'd be surprised at how many frauds are out there. And we run new prospects through a number of tests before we offer them a contract. Weapons handling. Tactics. Driving. All that type of stuff. And Eddie was pretty good, if I remember correctly. You see that big guy behind me with the moustache? That's Cormac. He's in charge of making sure the new hires are up to scratch. Said your boy Eddie was one of the best he had ever seen.'

'I'm sure that's true,' said Andrew, the past tense once again ringing as loudly as Big Ben at noon inside his head. 'What do you know about the night he was arrested?'

'No more than you do, I suspect,' said McKinnon casually. 'Got into a brawl with two of my other guys. There was a kerfuffle. Someone had a gun, and Eddie shot and killed them both. Damn shame for it to happen that way. But that is just how it goes sometimes. My men are thoroughbreds. Natural-born warriors. And when they get some alcohol into their blood, well, sometimes things get messy. Ain't no surprise, really.'

'You don't seem too upset about it,' said Andrew, raising an eyebrow slightly.

'Like I said,' shrugged McKinnon. 'It's a shame that it went the way it did. But I ain't gonna sit here and cry about it. I have lost a lot of good men under my command, and this was a stupid way for it to happen, but the only thing you can do is try to learn from it and move forward. Ain't no sense in lingering on it.'

'Any idea what it was all about?' said Andrew. 'How could it end the way it did?'

'I really can't say,' shrugged McKinnon. 'Could be something to do with a girl. Or maybe Eddie owed them some money, and things got out of hand. I have no idea. But it's all bygones now, as far as I'm concerned.'

'Right,' said Andrew pensively. 'So, what sort of work was Barton involved in?'

'Like most of our guys, he started out doing corporate close protection jobs in Dallas,' said McKinnon. 'Then later on, he took part in providing some of our overseas services. I obviously can't tell you exactly what that was all about, but I am sure you can work it out.'

'I probably can,' nodded Andrew. 'Anyway, Hogan gave me a number for the Nolan County DA's office, and I talked to a guy there named Bremmer. He wasn't very forthcoming. He couldn't even tell me where Barton is right now.'

'Well,' said McKinnon. 'The wheels of justice sometimes turn slowly. But I am sure they will get there in the end.'

Andrew emptied his tumbler, leaned back in his seat and allowed his gaze to wander around the basement for a moment. The décor was more downtown nightclub than country ranch, and it was obvious that no expense had been spared in making this a cosy hangout for McKinnon's men. Andrew knew better than anyone how important it was to be able to either relax or blow off steam between missions, but this level of comfort was in a whole different league from anything he had ever experienced.

'It's a nice place you have here,' said Andrew. 'Not what you would expect to find out in the high desert.'

'Gotta keep the men happy,' said McKinnon, following Andrew's gaze around the room for a moment. 'They work hard, and they need to feel appreciated. Lot of egos in the special operations community, as I am sure you know already. So, we do what we can to keep the boys content. But you're right. I guess you wouldn't expect to find a place like this out here in the desert.'

'It's a beautiful part of the country,' said Andrew. 'I like the huge flat terrain, even if it is pretty stark and dry.'

'You just nailed it,' said McKinnon with a grin and a nod. 'That right there is called the settler spirit. A man sees a wide open plain like that, and he starts to feel the urge to tame it growing inside his chest. And then he wants to keep moving forward and claim the land for civilisation.'

'That's very poetic,' said Andrew, keen to stroke the general's ego.

'Are you familiar with the idea of manifest destiny?' said McKinnon.

'Can't say I am,' said Andrew.

'I thought that might be the case,' said McKinnon. 'I guess you English types don't know much about our history, which is ironic considering how this country started in the first place. But anyway. Let me educate you.'

McKinnon refilled his tumbler and downed half of it. Then he turned slightly in his seat to look across the room.

'You see that picture frame on the wall over there?' he said, pointing to a large gold frame containing a black background with white text. 'That's a quote from 1845 by a newspaper editor called John O'Sullivan. It was after Texas had joined the United States. He wrote about "the fulfilment of our manifest destiny to overspread the continent allotted by Providence for the free development of our yearly multiplying millions." Isn't that a beautiful quote? What it says is that the United States was given to us by God and that it is our destiny to settle this whole continent in order to allow our people to live free and multiply.'

'I see,' nodded Andrew pensively. 'I suppose that worked out pretty much as he thought it would.'

'Damn straight,' said McKinnon. 'Because of the spirit embodied in that quote, this nation is the greatest nation that has ever existed on the face of the earth. And we oughta make damn sure it stays that way.'

'I am sure the Chinese have something to say about that,' said Andrew, producing a wry smile.

'Let those bastards come,' said McKinnon, giving a dismissive wave with his hand. 'We can deal with them too. But that may be a topic for another time.'

'You're probably right,' said Andrew. 'Tell me, why is this place called Stonewall Ranch? Wasn't there someone by that name in the American Civil War?'

'Right again,' said McKinnon, jabbing an index finger towards Andrew and producing a satisfied nod. 'Indeed there was. General Thomas J. Jackson, also known as 'Stonewall' Jackson. Probably the most famous general in the Confederacy after Robert E. Lee. A true patriot, and as it happens, my direct ancestor.'

'Really?' said Andrew.

'That's right,' nodded McKinnon emphatically. 'See, I come from a military family, and my granddaddy used to tell me stories about our family's past. So, several years back, I hired one of those genealogy companies to trace my ancestry back to the Civil War. And they traced my line all the way back to the middle of the 1830s using public records, DNA analysis and whatnot, and wouldn't you know it? I am a descendant of the great man himself.'

'That's interesting,' said Andrew, looking impressed as he nodded slowly. 'Stonewall Jackson.'

'And let me tell you,' said McKinnon, narrowing his eyes as he leaned forward. 'I can often feel the connection with him across time. That bond. Almost as if he was right here speaking to me. He was a great patriot, and so am I. He gave his life to defend the freedoms that the men of the thirteen colonies fought and died for, and I too would lay down my life to protect this country against tyranny. Against all enemies, foreign or domestic.'

'A worthy cause,' said Andrew, sensing that the general was getting into his stride and keen to learn as much about him as he could.

'I'll drink to that,' said McKinnon, raising his glass. 'Anyway, do you consider yourself a scholar, Mr Sterling?'

'Depends on what you mean by that word,' said Andrew.

'Well, I obviously don't mean a religious scholar,' McKinnon said. 'And by the way, I would never use that word about someone who has only ever read one damn book. No, I'm talking about history. The history of this great nation, to be exact.'

'I can't say that I am,' replied Andrew. 'Are you referring to anything in particular?'

'I am referring to the Constitution of the United States,' said McKinnon, with the air of someone who had just placed a Royal Flush on the Poker table. 'Specifically, the 2nd Amendment.'

'That's the right to bear arms, isn't it?' said Andrew.

'Damn straight!' said McKinnon, slapping the table with his hand. 'And why do you suppose that right is enshrined in our very constitution?'

'Why don't you tell me?' Andrew smiled affably, having a pretty good idea about where this was going.

'It's got nothing to do with people being able to protect themselves from intruders,' said McKinnon. 'Although that is a very useful thing to be able to do. And it ain't because we're afraid of getting invaded by the Russians or the Chinese. The 2nd Amendment is there so that the free people of these United States can rise up against the tyranny of our own government, should that ever become necessary.'

'I see,' said Andrew. 'And do you think that it might become necessary one day?'

McKinnon scoffed as if the answer was blindingly obvious to anyone with eyes in their head.

'I don't think things have ever been as bad as they are right now,' said McKinnon ruefully. 'Washington is a damn cesspit, if you ask me. None of those politicians are working for the American people anymore. They're all in it for themselves. Lobbyists and special interests have taken over Congress and the White House, and the country is coming apart at the seams. It's plain for anyone to see. And at some point, things are going to come to a head. This simply can't go on, and I personally think it is about time for the people to rise up.'

'Do you think this could lead to another civil war?' asked Andrew.

'To tell you the honest truth,' shrugged McKinnon. 'I wouldn't rule anything out at this point. I have studied the Civil War in great detail, and I can see a lot of parallels lining up at the moment. And a lot of folks here in Texas feel it more strongly than most. See, you may not know this, but the Lone Star State was born out of a desire for independence even before it became part of the United States. That desire was what led its people to break away from Mexico in 1836, and for their new state to be fought over by the Mexicans and the Union a decade later. This desire for freedom and independence still runs deep here, and we don't much like it when people in Washinton try to tell us how to live our lives.'

'So, I suppose that's why Texas sided with the Confederacy during the Civil War?' observed Andrew.

'That's exactly right,' said McKinnon, his southern drawl stronger than ever. 'Most people think the Civil War was fought because of a disagreement about the morality of keeping slaves. But I am here to tell you that that is total horseshit. It couldn't be any further from the truth. It is oversimplified and it deliberately misrepresents the issue just to make the southerners look bad, and make the northerners feel good about themselves. And don't forget that it was the northerners who wrote the history books, so they were always going to end up being biased. Do you really think that all those tens of thousands of Southerners who fought and died in that war did so because they wanted to own slaves? That's just plain crazy. What kind of man would lay down his own life just so he can keep owning a few slaves? No one in their right mind would do that. It's all total crap.'

Andrew sat back impassively and let the general rant on. If nothing else, listening to him was instructive, and it allowed Andrew to get the measure of the man that Barton had worked for and eventually run afoul of.

'The Civil War was not about slavery,' continued McKinnon dismissively as the blond barmaid came back to refill their glasses, and this time McKinnon grabbed the bottle from her and placed it next to himself. 'The issue of slavery was incidental to the motivation of those men fighting and dying. In their hearts, what they were fighting for was not the right to own slaves but the right to be free. Free from the taxes and tyranny of an overbearing government in a far-off city that was trying to impose its will and its values on all of those folks. Just like during the American Revolution. The rallying cry 'Live free or die' actually meant something to them, just like it did to their forefathers during their struggle against you British.'

Once again, Andrew ignored the jibe and kept listening.

'That freedom,' McKinnon went on, 'had been dreamed of in the Declaration of Independence in 1776, then fought for and promised to them by this nation's constitution in 1789. And let me tell you, in 1861, they weren't about to let it be taken away from them by that agitator Abraham Lincoln and his cronies up in Washington D.C.'

McKinnon paused for another drink while Andrew waited patiently for him to go on.

'On top of that,' he said, 'they were also fighting for their economic survival. You see, in the South at that time, almost the entire economy was based on tobacco and cotton farms. And slaves were a necessity to keep those farms running. It had been that way ever since the first English colonies were established in Virginia at the start of the 17th century. Now, President Lincoln's 13th Amendment, which proposed to free the slaves across America, would have wiped out the entire economy of the South from one day to the next. It would have caused the utter ruin of the southern states, so secession from the Union was the only way for the people of the South to avoid that catastrophe and preserve their way of life. That's what began in November of 1860, when South Carolina declared its secession. And pretty soon, another six states including Texas followed to form the Confederate States of America. So, you see, the Civil War was only ever about freedom.'

'Freedom for white people,' said Andrew evenly. 'What about freedom for black people? For the slaves? Am I pretty sure there were several million slaves in the Confederacy when the Civil War began, right?'

'That's right,' said McKinnon, 'and I am pretty sure they were a lot better off there than they would have been back where they came from.'

'You mean back in Africa,' said Andrew, not quite able to fathom what McKinnon had just said.

'That's right,' said McKinnon resolutely, seemingly unaware or indifferent to how he sounded.

'Well,' said Andrew, reluctant to be drawn into a debate about race relations. 'I think it is safe to say that the Civil War didn't exactly solve the issue of race in this country.'

'Sure didn't,' said McKinnon. 'Anyway, just so you know. Here in the South, many of us don't like to call it the Civil War. We prefer to call it the Northern War of Aggression. After all, we didn't invade them. They invaded us. The Confederacy was a sovereign nation, so when the Union marched its troops into our states, it became a foreign invader. As simple as that. A tyrant trying to take away our liberties. And any right-thinking man would have taken up arms against them.'

'A sovereign nation?' said Andrew sceptically. 'Doesn't being a sovereign nation require recognition of statehood by other nations? I am pretty sure that no other country ever recognised the Confederacy. Not even my country, which was probably the most likely to do so because of all the cotton it imported from the South.'

'So, now you're a historian and a legal expert?' said McKinnon, clearly riled by talking to someone who didn't always agree with him. 'And an expert in international law, no less.'

'No,' said Andrew calmly. 'I don't need to be an expert. I just need to know what actually happened. But anyway, all of this begs a very simple question. If faced with the prospect of tyranny, do the ends justify the means? Would anything be off-limits in pursuit of the freedom you seem to be talking about?'

'That is indeed the question,' nodded McKinnon musingly. 'That's very perceptive of you. Tell me, have you ever heard of the Dahlgren Affair?'

'No, I haven't,' said Andrew. 'Is this also to do with the Civil War?'

'Yup,' said McKinnon. 'Not a lot of people seem to know about this event, but I believe it is very instructive when thinking about those greater issues of justification for actions taken in defence of freedom. See, in 1864, a Union Colonel by the name of Ulric

Dahlgren and a group of soldiers were on their way to mount an attack on Richmond. They were hoping to burn down the city and free some Northern prisoners, but they also had written orders to find and assassinate President Jefferson Davis. Can you believe that? Of course, when the attack failed, those orders were found on Dahlgren's body. Proof that the North was prepared to kill a duly elected president.'

'He was the president of the Confederacy,' said Andrew, 'which, as I said earlier, wasn't a recognised nation at the time. So, you could argue that he wasn't actually the president.'

McKinnon produced an incredulous chortle and gave a shake of the head as he stared across the table at Andrew.

'He was the President of the Confederacy of the United States,' he said with ill-concealed acrimony, 'including this very state that you're sitting in right this moment. The point is this. If the Union could justify assassinating the president of the Confederacy, then surely so could the Confederacy justify killing Abraham Lincoln. Don't forget, the Union was the aggressor. The South was only defending itself.'

'So, you think the assassination of Lincoln was justified?' said Andrew. 'What was the name of the guy? Booth or something?'

'John Wilkes Booth was a hero of the South,' said McKinnon passionately. 'Only bad thing I have to say about that young man is that he was a couple of years late in doing what he did. Do you know what he said after he shot Lincoln and jumped down onto the stage of that theatre?'

'No,' said Andrew. 'Why don't you tell me?'

'He said "I have done it! The South is avenged!",'
said McKinnon. 'Now that's a real patriot right there.'

'To be perfectly honest,' said Andrew, 'he sounds
like a lunatic.'

'Listen, Mr Sterling,' McKinnon sighed with a
frown and what appeared to be rising anger. 'I liked
you when you and I first sat down at this table, but
now I am starting to feel like you're abusing my
hospitality. I allowed you to come out here to my
ranch, and I offered you my valuable time. But now
here you are arguing with me about things you don't
understand. And that just ain't good manners.'

'Well, everyone is entitled to their own opinions,'
shrugged Andrew. 'But they're not entitled to their
own facts. And I simply disagree with you about what
the facts are.'

'Alright, listen,' said McKinnon, slowly raising
himself out of his seat and placing his hands on the
table as he leaned forward. 'I ain't here to debate
history with you. You're English, so I suppose you
won't ever be able to really understand any of this. I
think it's time we brought this meeting to an end. I've
got work to do. So, why don't you head on back to
that motel of yours, and then you can be on your way
to wherever it is you're going. We're done here.'

'Fine by me,' said Andrew, emptying his tumbler
and placing it back down on the table. 'Thanks for the
whiskey.'

'Cobb will see you out,' said McKinnon, turning to
snap his fingers at the estate manager, who
immediately slid off his bar stool and came over. 'Mr
Cobb. Mr Sterling here is leaving. Please escort him to
his car.'

'Yes, sir,' nodded Cobb, gesturing for Andrew to follow him.

'I appreciate your time,' said Andrew as he got up from his seat.

'You take care now,' said McKinnon, fixing Andrew with a cold look that made his words sound more like a threat than anything else.

As Cobb led Andrew towards the staircase leading back up to the ground floor of the mansion, McKinnon's men eyed him all the way. When he glanced across the room to the bar, he caught the blond waitress regarding him with a peculiar look that almost seemed like recognition, as if she had seen him before and was trying to recall where. But Andrew knew that he had never seen her before in his life.

Once back outside, Cobb stopped at the top of the steps to the front door and gave Andrew a polite nod.

'Have a nice day, Mr Sterling,' he said with a thin smile.

'Thanks,' said Andrew, putting his sunglasses on and heading down the steps to his Jeep. 'You too.'

As he drove out of the compound, surrounded by scowling armed mercenaries, and continued back along the tree-lined avenue to the country road, he pondered his meeting with McKinnon. The general was clearly a proud Texan and military man whose mind was steeped in a somewhat revanchist history and the idea of courageous frontier men bravely defending themselves and their freedom from an overbearing central power out on the East Coast. While this was probably just par for the course in many parts of Texas, Andrew couldn't help but feel that these ideas burned particularly intensely in McKinnon's mind.

Without intending to, Andrew had also managed to rub the general the wrong way. But that had ended up being a revealing turn of events in itself. He was not too concerned about it since he wasn't expecting to ever get another invitation to Stonewall Ranch. And he couldn't imagine having a constructive conversation with McKinnon about anything at this point.

However, the most significant outcome of the meeting was that McKinnon had kept referring to Barton in the past tense. This could just be because Barton was no longer at the ranch and that he was on his way to stand trial for double homicide. However, Andrew couldn't shake the feeling that there was more to it than that. Then again, Assistant DA Bremmer had told him that Barton was being kept somewhere in Nolan County, but what if that wasn't true? Andrew shook his head and decided that he couldn't allow himself to think like that. He had to believe that Barton was still alive, and it was now his job to try to uncover the circumstances of what had happened to him and why.

Driving back towards Revelation, he decided that he needed to speak to Donna Cooper. Her brother Billy Ray had been one of the arresting officers on the night Barton was taken into custody, and his suicide had happened mere days after Barton's arrest. This was suspicious, to say the least. And with the way Andrew had seen Sheriff Hogan behaving in front of General McKinnon, it was clear that the general had some sort of hold over law enforcement in

Revelation. The bottom line was that nothing to do with the sheriff's office's investigation of the double murder or the suicide could be taken at face value. Andrew had to find out for himself.

★ ★ ★

'What do you want me to do about that guy?' said Cobb as McKinnon joined him on the front step.

In the distance at the far end of the dusty tree-lined avenue, the Jeep was passing through the gates and joining the country road leading back to Revelation.

'I want you to keep a close eye on him,' said McKinnon as he watched the Jeep disappear off in the distance. 'He's trouble. Got a real uppity attitude about him. And I think he's gonna keep digging to find out more about Eddie Barton. We can't have that, you hear? We can't have someone like that snooping around. Especially not now when we're getting ready to up the ante.'

'I understand,' said Cobb. 'I'll have one of our guys follow him. And if he gets too close? If he really starts digging?'

'Well,' said MacKinnon solemnly as he placed a powerful hand on Cobb's shoulder and gave it a quick pat. 'Then you'll know what to do.'

THIRTEEN

When Andrew swung by to have a late lunch, the owner of Donna's Diner was nowhere to be found. After eating a meal consisting of a steak, some fries and a beer, he then had a brief conversation with Paige, during which he managed to persuade her to provide him with Donna's home address. The waitress was able to sense the sincerity in Andrew's claim to want to help, and it was obvious to him that she was deeply concerned about the wellbeing of her boss after the devastating news about her brother's apparent suicide.

'I still can't believe it,' she said, looking stunned as she reflected on what had happened. 'I just never thought he would be the type of person to do such a thing. He always seemed so happy and carefree, and everyone around here liked him. At least as far as I know. It doesn't make any sense.'

'I'll go and visit Donna now,' said Andrew. 'Offer her any help I can.'

'Please tell her that we miss her here,' said Paige. 'It's just not the same without her.'

'I'll make sure to do that,' said Andrew. 'Take care.'

Ten minutes later, he parked the Jeep outside a modest but characterful and well-maintained house on a quiet residential street not far from the town centre. The street was lined on both sides with large ash trees, and their light green leaves fluttered gently in the breeze. On both sides were neat-looking houses sitting on trimmed lawns behind low white picket fences. Everything looked pleasant and prosperous, and as Andrew stepped out of the car into the warm midday sun, he spotted a few children riding bicycles a few houses down.

Donna's home was a one-storey wooden bungalow built in a somewhat modernist architectural style with large windows, clean lines and ninety-degree angles everywhere. Around the edges of the lawn were small circular flowerbeds with lavender, marigolds and dahlia flowers. There was also a drive with room for a single car, and her metallic-red coupe was parked there. It was quite evident that the diner had provided Donna with a comfortable life, but as Andrew pulled the handbrake and got out, he knew that what he was going to find inside the house was someone to whom those things meant very little at this moment.

He walked up the driveway to the front door and gently used the knocker. As he took a step back and waited, he steeled himself for what was bound to become a difficult conversation. But the truth was that he needed Donna's help to try to discover what had happened to Barton. And perhaps he would be able to help her in turn.

When Donna Cooper opened the door, Andrew was momentarily taken aback by the sight of the petite young woman. She looked nothing like her cheerful and radiant former self from the day before. Her eyes were sunken and red, as if she had been crying when Andrew knocked, and her skin appeared to have turned several shades paler and more ashen. She was now wearing light blue jeans and a purple long-sleeved blouse. When she saw him, it seemed to take her a moment to realise who he was and where she knew him from. Then her expression turned to one of puzzlement, but she still managed to produce a weak smile as she greeted him.

'Oh, hello,' she said, her voice sounding thin and papery. 'Andrew, right?'

'Yes,' said Andrew. 'Paige was kind enough to let me have your address. I'm sorry to turn up like this, but I think we might be able to help each other.'

'With what?' she asked, producing a brief sniff.

'Remember I told you that I was looking for my friend?' he said. 'Well, it turns out he has been arrested for double murder.'

'That was him?' asked Donna, looking shocked.

'Apparently, said Andrew. 'I don't know exactly what is going on, and I am struggling to make sense of it. But something definitely isn't right about this whole thing, and I think that somehow it involves your brother. So, please let me ask you a simple question, and I apologise in advance if it sounds insensitive. Is there any part of you that thinks that perhaps your brother did not take his own life?'

This was a make-or-break moment. Donna would have every right to yell at him to get off her property and then slam the door in his face, but that was not what happened. Instead, her eyes moved quickly across his face as if searching for something, and then she took half a step forward and glanced down the street, first to one side and then the other.

'You'd better come inside,' she said quietly, stepping back into the small hallway and gesturing for him to follow. 'If we're going to talk about this, I don't want anyone listening in.'

The interior was cosy and welcoming, with creams and off-whites dominating the colour scheme. It was sparsely but tastefully decorated, the furniture was simple and comfortable-looking, and Donna had added a splash of primary colours provided by a selection of cushions and impressionist paintings on the walls. The wood flooring was a rich brown, and its varnished surface gave it a slight sheen. Everything looked neat and tidy, and it was very obvious that every room had a subtle woman's touch.

As they stepped into the living room, which had a small wood burner and a TV, Andrew saw that there was a half-empty tea mug on a coffee table, and next to where Donna had been sitting on one of the two sofas was an open photo album. She closed the white French blinds on the windows facing the street and gestured to the other sofa.

'Please have a seat,' she said before shooting him a self-conscious smile. 'Wow, I must have said those words a million times in my life over at the diner.'

'Paige says she misses you,' said Andrew as he sat down on the other sofa. 'She says the diner isn't the same without you.'

'That's nice of her,' said Donna, clearly touched. 'Can I get you anything? Tea or coffee. I've got some beers in the fridge.'

'I wouldn't mind a beer,' said Andrew. 'As long as it isn't non-alcoholic. That stuff should be outlawed.'

Donna found herself producing a small laugh, and she looked much better for it.

'One beer coming up,' she said, giving a brief nod and disappearing into the kitchen at the back of the house.

Glancing to his side, Andrew spotted a framed photo sitting on one of the shelves in a white-painted bookcase. He didn't have to inspect it for more than a couple of seconds to know exactly who he was looking at. This was a picture of Donna's brother. Deputy Billy Ray Cooper. He was wearing a cream Stetson hat and a crisp khaki-coloured police shirt with insignia on the shoulders and the 'Sheriff's Office' metal badge on the left side of his chest. The likeness to his sister was obvious. He was good-looking with the same wide, easy smile as Donna, and his friendly eyes spoke of an open and sunny disposition that would have suited the role of deputy in a small town like Revelation perfectly. Standing there in the warm Texas sun in front of a police cruiser and seemingly smiling at someone off-camera, he looked the image of a young man who had found his calling and who was glad to get up in the morning and go to work doing what he loved.

'He looked happy,' said Andrew, as Donna returned with the beer.

'He was,' said Donna weakly, handing the drink to him before sitting down on her sofa. 'Nothing ever really got to him. He was so good at seeing the bright side of things. Always finding a silver lining, no matter how dark everything seemed. I've lost count of the number of times he was my shoulder to cry on when things weren't going well for me. And he always managed to give me these little pieces of good advice that just made so much sense. I keep thinking I'm going to see him again, but I know that will never happen now.'

As she spoke, Andrew could hear her beginning to choke up, and her lower lip trembled as her eyes welled up with tears, likely for the umpteenth time that day.

'I guess you two were close,' said Andrew.

'Yes,' she said. 'After our parents died in a car crash when we were young, we had to band together to get through it. And we've stayed close ever since.'

Donna's words resonated powerfully with Andrew, who had himself lost his own parents in similar circumstances when he was a boy, and he immediately felt a bond of empathy and shared experience with the young woman in front of him.

'I still remember him as a kid,' she continued. 'I looked up to him like you wouldn't believe. He could do no wrong. He was only eight or ten years old when he announced that when he grew up, he was going to serve his country. And I believed him. Even then, I knew he meant what he said. He wanted to join the Marines, but he was rejected on medical grounds. Colour blindness. So, he joined the police force here in our home town instead. Never looked back.'

'So, he enjoyed his work?' said Andrew.

'Sure did,' said Donna. 'He loved being out there serving the community. He liked the job, but he and Sheriff Hogan never really got along too well. Billy Ray thought Hogan was less interested in upholding the law and more interested in playing nice with local business people who would support his next run for sheriff. Billy Ray's moral compass was always pointing due north, and he was always right in what he said.'

Donna looked up at the ceiling, and her eyes welled up as she spoke.

'Now that he's gone,' she said faintly, her voice almost breaking. 'I just feel kinda lost.'

'I'm very sorry about what happened,' said Andrew. 'Do you have any reason to believe that there might have been foul play involved in Billy Ray's death?'

Donna lifted her eyes from her tea mug and looked straight at Andrew for several silent moments. Then she took a breath before speaking.

'What I am about to tell you can't leave this house, OK?' she finally said, suddenly looking more serious and intense than Andrew had thought her capable of.

'You can trust me,' said Andrew earnestly. 'I think we both feel that there are things going on in this town that aren't quite the way they should be.'

'You're right,' said Donna. 'People don't like to say it out loud, but General McKinnon and his men have poisoned this town. He practically owns the police and the mayor and whoever else he needs to keep control of, and his guys behave as if they own the place.'

'And your brother?' asked Andrew gently. 'How does he fit into all of this?'

'Billy Ray was an idealist,' said Donna with a sad sigh. 'He always believed that if good people did good things, then eventually everything would turn out alright with the world. Unfortunately, most people don't seem to look at it that way.'

'That's an admirable quality,' said Andrew. 'You're right, though. Most people are a lot more cynical than that. But without people like your brother in this world, I guess the rest of us wouldn't stand much of a chance of making it a better place.'

'That's very nice of you to say,' said Donna. 'That's how I always saw him too. But when he started to work for Sheriff Hogan, I sensed that he wasn't quite his usual self anymore. After a few months, it was like he grew concerned about something. But he never told me what it was.'

'What do you think it was about?' said Andrew.

'I'm thinking he discovered that Hogan was taking money from McKinnon to look the other way,' said Donna. 'I am convinced that McKinnon is doing stuff out at his ranch that he doesn't want anyone to know about. And I think Hogan is taking bribes to help keep everything a secret.'

'Any idea about precisely what Billy Ray might have discovered?' said Andrew.

'No,' said Donna. 'All I have to go on is the fact that McKinnon seems to have raised half an army out there, and judging from how they're spending it, his people must be paid crazy amounts of money. It all just seems weird. Something ain't right. What about your friend? How is he involved in this?'

'I am not sure exactly,' said Andrew, 'except that he joined McKinnon's crew sometime last year.'

'Was he really the one who shot those two men behind the High Jinx Tavern?' said Donna.

'Yes,' said Andrew, images of the scene of the double homicide filling his mind. 'I saw the security camera footage.'

He then went on to convey his understanding of the course of events on the night of Barton's arrest, and he also told Donna about his conversations with Sheriff Hogan and Assistant DA Bremmer.

'The night it happened, he phoned me and asked for my help,' he continued. 'He didn't tell me any details, although, of course, I found out once I got here. But I am still in the dark about why he was chased by those two colleagues of his and why he ended up killing them. It was completely out of character, so he must have felt extremely threatened.'

'Do you think they were trying to kill him all along?' said Donna. 'Was that why they were chasing him?'

'It seems that way,' said Andrew. 'Although over what, I really can't guess. McKinnon tried to convince me that it might have been over a woman or some money, but Barton was never that petty. I just can't imagine that would have been enough for things to spin out of control the way they clearly did. But I discovered something strange at the sheriff's office.'

'Really?' she said. 'What?'

'I convinced Sergeant Fuller to show me Barton's holding cell,' said Andrew. 'And I found his military dog tags. Now, I know for a fact that Barton would never leave those behind voluntarily. There's no other explanation for this than that Barton was removed from that cell by force, and the state troopers would not do that to him for no reason. Only if he resisted being moved to Sweetwater, and I just can't imagine that happening. He just wasn't that kind of guy. Now, I know that Bremmer told me that Barton had been moved to the Nolan County jail, but I am beginning to wonder if that is actually true. And when I spoke to General McKinnon, he kept referring to Barton in the past tense. It all adds up to the feeling that what I have been told is simply not the way things really are.'

'That all sure does seem very strange,' said Donna. 'Same as my brother's supposed suicide.'

'So, you don't really think he ended his own life?' said Andrew.

'Hell no,' scoffed Donna with a grimace that was a mix of pain and derision. 'Not a chance. I know that's what Hogan and his boys claim happened, but there is no way Billy Ray would ever take his own life. If there was something going on that was so bad that he would ever even think about doing such a thing, he would have come to me first. I just know it. My brother did *not* kill himself.'

'So, what exactly are they saying happened?' said Andrew.

'They said he shot himself inside his living room,' said Donna quietly, her gaze dropping to her hands, which lay clasped in her lap. 'Used his police sidearm, apparently. They told me that they won't allow me inside his apartment because it would be too upsetting, and they say the whole place is still cordoned off for forensics. But I don't think I want to go there anyway. I don't think I could bear being in that place again.'

'What about the coroner?' asked Andrew. 'Surely there's a report we can get our hands on.'

'Are you kidding me?' said Donna. 'The coroner is Josiah Hogan. He's Sheriff Hogan's younger brother, and he'll cover for the sheriff all day long. No use going to him.'

Andrew gave a bitter shake of the head and took a sip of his beer.

'So, if Billy Ray didn't take his own life,' he said gently, 'who do you think killed him? And why?'

'I think McKinnon is behind it somehow,' said Donna darkly. 'Billy Ray must have seen or heard something that he wasn't supposed to see, and they killed him for it. Pure and simple. Thinking back to the last couple of days, it did seem like something might have been really weighing on his mind. But I have no idea what. He never said he was concerned about anything in particular. And anyway, he was always trying to protect me from worrying too much.'

'As far as you know, was Billy Ray working that evening?' said Andrew. 'Hogan told me that he was there when Barton was booked in.'

'He would have been,' said Donna. 'They take turns manning the sheriff's office during late hours, and he would have been on duty that night.'

'So, maybe he saw something,' said Andrew. 'If Barton was taken away by someone other than the state troopers the way Hogan tells it, would Billy Ray have objected?'

'Absolutely,' said Donna. 'No question about that.'

'If McKinnon's men were out to get Barton,' said Andrew, 'they might have arranged with Hogan to pick him up from the holding cell after his arrest. Clean and simple.'

'But they can't just do that,' said Donna with a frown.

'That's exactly right,' said Andrew. 'And if Billy Ray was there to see it, he would have said something. Maybe he even tried to stop them. And that might have been enough.'

'Enough for them to kill him to make sure that he didn't talk,' said Donna, looking at Andrew wide-eyed as the scenario played out in her mind. 'To hide what they did.'

'It's obviously all just my speculation at this point,' said Andrew.

'But it sounds like something that could actually have happened,' said Donna. 'I think we might be on to something here.'

'Well, I have to tell you,' said Andrew. 'After everything I have seen and heard in this town in the short time that I have been here, it seems to me that under the wholesome small-town veneer of this place, there are some dark things lurking. I don't know what yet, but I intend to find out. It's the only way to discover what happened to my friend.'

'You're not wrong,' said Donna. 'This town. It can't go on like this. For as long as McKinnon is here, he'll have a hold over Sheriff Hogan and everyone else. And for as long as that's the case, this place will be drowning in corruption and violence.'

'I am sure you're right about Hogan,' said Andrew. 'When I first met him, he said all the right things about doing his best to investigate what happened the night Barton was arrested. But from the way he talked, he just didn't seem like he was genuinely interested. And when I asked about your brother, he was dismissive and told me it was internal police business. That was the end of that. And I hate to say this, but I really didn't get the sense that he was very upset about it. In fact, he didn't even seem surprised, and that just came across all wrong to me. And then, when he took me to Stonewall Ranch, he behaved like McKinnon's lapdog.'

'You went out to the ranch?' said Donna.

'Yes,' said Andrew. 'I had a little talk with McKinnon. 'He's every bit the force of nature that people seem to treat him as, but he's not quite there, in my opinion. Anyway, Hogan escorted me out there, and he became a compliant little puppy in McKinnon's presence. It was pathetic to watch, to be honest.'

Donna gave a slight shake of the head and pressed her lips together.

'Hogan is just bad news,' she finally said as a determined and ominous look slowly spread across her normally pleasant face. 'A spineless SOB. And if he had anything to do with Billy Ray's death, I will find out, and I will rain hell down upon his head. Same with General McKinnon.'

'You know these are very serious people,' said Andrew, fearing that Donna might be considering embarking on some sort of one-woman vigilante mission. 'Especially McKinnon. That ranch is like a fortress. And he runs a company that is in the business of selling violent solutions to problems. He is also dangerously deluded about this country's history and his own place in it. He thinks that he is descended from Stonewall Jackson, which might be the case. But he also seems to think that the country is crying out for a radical change of course, and I wouldn't be surprised if he believes that it is his destiny to lead that change. Men like him are very unpredictable, and that makes them dangerous.'

'I don't care,' said Donna quietly. 'I will make this right if it is the last thing I do.'

'Do you have anyone who can help you?' asked Andrew.

'I do,' said Donna with a brief nod. 'Uncle Emmett. Our mother's older brother. He raised us for a time after our parents passed away. Lives on a small homestead a few miles north of town. Rears cattle out there. If I asked him for help, he'd be there in a heartbeat.'

'I assume he already knows about Billy Ray's death,' said Andrew.

'Yes,' replied Donna. 'We spoke on the phone last night. As you can imagine, he's as upset as I am.'

'What can you tell me about him?' said Andrew. 'Why do you think he might be able to help?'

'Because he's got a good heart,' said Donna. 'And he ain't afraid of no one. He's not exactly a spring chicken anymore, but he used to be an Army Ranger, and he is still as strong as an ox working the land out there. The only thing is, there's some bad blood between Emmett and Sheriff Hogan, so it might get complicated.'

'What does that mean exactly?' said Andrew. 'What happened?'

After a brief pause during which Donna tilted her head slightly to one side and gazed out of the window while wringing her hands, she eventually spoke again.

'Uncle Emmett has a history with the law,' she said. 'Something that Hogan never misses a chance to remind him of.'

'Jail time?' asked Andrew.

'Yes,' said Donna, 'but it was never what Hogan always tries to make it out to be. You see, back when Hogan was just a deputy, Emmett was in a bar in town, and a female friend of his from high school was being harassed by some drunken dude. He was a nasty piece of work, and his hands were all over her, trying to pin her against the wall. Emmett saw this happen and walked over with a billiard cue and gave the guy a real hiding. Beat him black and blue and broke his wrist, if I remember correctly. Emmett was sentenced to two weeks in jail for GBH, and then another week for telling the judge he'd do it all over if he ever saw something like that happen right in front of him again.'

'I see,' said Andrew, raising an eyebrow and finding himself producing a thin smile. 'I think I like the sound of him already.'

'He's a good man,' said Donna. 'Quick-tempered, sure. But his heart is in the right place, and I am proud to call him my uncle.'

'Sounds like he might be someone we can ask to lend a hand if we need it,' said Andrew.

'Oh, we sure can,' said Donna. 'He would never let me down.'

'Good,' said Andrew, leaning forward on the sofa and clasping his hands in front of himself. 'Listen.

Can you tell me where Billy Ray's apartment is? Since we can't trust the police in this town, I'd like to go and have a look at it myself.'

'Well, sure,' said Donna with a puzzled look. 'But it's all cordoned off. No one is allowed in there.'

'Just because something isn't allowed doesn't mean it isn't possible,' said Andrew with a meaningful look. 'But I don't want to get you involved in this, so if I go there, it will be my own choice and have nothing to do with you. As far as anyone is concerned, you have no idea what I am up to, alright? There's just too much at stake for you. Your business. Your safety. Let me give this a shot and see what I can find.'

'Alright,' said Donna. 'But it's not without risk for you either. They could come down on you real hard if they catch you.'

'I can handle myself,' said Andrew.

'Why are you doing this?' she asked, sitting back on her sofa and regarding him for a moment. 'Why are you helping me?'

'Because it is the only way to get to the truth,' said Andrew. 'And besides, it's the right thing to do. If your brother was murdered and I am able to do something to help uncover the truth, then I won't just stand by and let those people get away with it. It also happens to be the best chance of digging into what happened to my friend.'

'Alright,' said Donna, reaching for a pen and a notepad on which she scribbled an address. 'Andrew, I really appreciate this, but just don't get yourself into any trouble. Things can take a sinister turn around here pretty quick, as I'm sure you've already worked out.'

'I'll be fine,' said Andrew. 'You and I need to get to the bottom of this thing, so we need to work together.'

FOURTEEN

In anticipation of paying Billy Ray's apartment a visit that evening, Andrew decided to catch a couple of hours of sleep. He drove back to the motel, had a shower and a change of clothes, and then he lay down on the bed with the TV on. After a few minutes, he muted the sound, picked up his phone, and hit the speed dial.

'Hi Andrew,' said Fiona. 'Are you OK?'

'Yes, I am fine,' he said. 'You?'

'Fine,' she replied. 'You'll be glad to know it's been another rainy day in London. How's it going over there?'

Andrew proceeded to provide Fiona with a quick summary of what had happened since his arrival in Revelation, leaving out the incident with the two drug dealers since he didn't want her to worry.

'Listen,' he then said. 'I met with this former army general who seems to practically run things around here. General John McKinnon. The guy has a real messiah complex and an ego the size of Trafalgar Square. Anyway, he told me that he is the direct descendent of none other than General Thomas 'Stonewall' Jackson. You know of him, right?'

'Of course,' said Fiona. 'Confederate general. Major hero of the South. He got ambushed and killed by his own men in a case of mistaken identity, if I remember correctly.'

'Really?' said Andrew. 'I didn't know that. The general seemed to leave that out.'

'Well, it's probably not how they like to remember him in Texas,' said Fiona, and Andrew could hear a smile playing on her lips.

'Right,' said Andrew. 'Anyway, is there a way for you to find out for me whether McKinnon is telling the truth about this or whether he just made it up to try to impress people?'

'It's not exactly my area of expertise,' said Fiona. 'But let me think about it. I am sure I know someone who can find out pretty easily. I would be very surprised if Stonewall Jackson's lineage isn't mapped out in great detail. I imagine that his descendants are probably proud of their relation to him.'

'That's what I was thinking too,' said Andrew. 'I already feel like I have the measure of the man, but if this thing about Jackson turns out to be untrue, then I'll know for sure what sort of person he is.'

'OK,' said Fiona. 'Leave it with me. I'll get back to you. You're not picking a fight with this guy, are you?'

'I'll try not to,' said Andrew. 'But I may need to apply a bit of pressure to get to the bottom of what happened to Barton.'

'Just be careful,' said Fiona. 'I want you back here in one piece.'

'Don't worry,' he said. 'I'm always careful.'

*   *   *

He woke up three hours later to see the golden afternoon sunlight cut through the motel room's large single window and inch its way slowly across the opposite wall as the sun sank towards the horizon. He sat up and swung his legs out onto the floor, rubbing his eyes and giving a yawn. The jetlag was still playing havoc with his circadian rhythm, and sleeping at odd hours of the day didn't exactly help. However, it was important that he be at the top of his game that evening. After all, he was planning to break a police cordon and enter a possible murder scene.

After splashing some water on his face and drinking a can of Coke from the minibar, he left the motel room and climbed up behind the wheel of the Jeep. As he pulled out onto the road and headed for the centre of town, he glanced up into the rearview mirror and noticed a small silver car leave the parking lot and head in the same direction. About ten minutes later, he parked in a bay on Main Street and watched as the car drove past, but he couldn't see the driver. After about a hundred metres, it made a left turn and disappeared from sight.

I'm becoming paranoid, he thought to himself with a small shake of the head.

He left the Jeep and began walking along the pavement until he reached one of the outfitter stores. Heading for the clothes section, he quickly found what he was looking for. A pair of black cargo pants and a matching shirt, as well as a small black baseball cap. He also picked up a hunting knife that came in a sturdy, dark brown leather sheath. He then walked over to the gun section and got himself another box of 9mm ammo for the Beretta M9. Finally, he picked out a small and slim black backpack. Paying with cash, he slung the backpack containing his purchases over his shoulder and left the store.

Spotting a bar on the other side of the street, he crossed over and entered. He needed to kill a few hours until it got dark, and this was as good a place as any. The establishment was called The Remington, and it turned out to be a country & western bar with live music. There was a bar counter on one side of the space and a handful of tables and chairs placed opposite it, and at the back of the long room was a small stage where a man and a woman were playing cover songs. She was playing an acoustic guitar and singing into a microphone, and he had a flat steel-stringed guitar lying on his lap.

Andrew walked up to the bar, bought himself another bottle of Blood & Honey, and sat down at a small table for two by the window where he could watch the world go by outside. He placed the backpack under the table and took his first swig of the beer. As he sat there and looked out at what on the surface appeared to be the epitome of idyllic small-town America, he wondered how many of the people out there realised just how shady the town really was. Perhaps it was common knowledge, and people just chose to ignore it as long as it didn't impact them. That was most likely what the majority would do, but it was exactly that sort of indifference and lethargy that allowed people like McKinnon to exert influence on men like Hogan and possibly also the mayor, Arlan Meeks.

Reflecting on how Donna had spoken about her brother's idealism, Andrew was reminded of a famous quote. *"The only thing necessary for evil to triumph in the world is that good men do nothing."* That quote seemed apt for the town of Revelation, and according to Donna, that sentiment appeared to have been an important part of Billy Ray's character. Andrew could still remember the first time he read those words, and they had resonated with him as strongly as they would probably have done with Billy Ray. The origin of the quote seemed to be uncertain, but as far as he knew, it had often been attributed to the 18th-century Irish statesman and member of Parliament, Edmund Burke, who was critical of the British Crown's actions towards the American colonies. Strange how those words would come into his mind at this time and in this place.

As the country music duo played, Andrew was pondering the quote and gazing absentmindedly out of the window when the door to the street opened and a young woman entered. She was wearing blue jeans, white trainers with no socks, a pink T-shirt and a white baseball cap emblazoned with the orange bull logo of the American football club, the Texas Longhorns. Her blond hair was tied back in a high ponytail that stuck out through the back of the cap. Moving with obvious intent, she headed straight for Andrew's table and placed a slender hand on the back of the chair opposite him.

'Can I join you?' she asked as Andrew glanced up at her face, which was partly hidden under the baseball cap.

'I guess so,' he said hesitantly, wondering why she was being so friendly.

'Perfect! Scarlett,' she said, reaching across the table to offer him her hand and meeting his gaze for the first time.

'Hello, Perfect Scarlett,' Andrew smiled as they shook, and he suddenly realised that he recognised her. 'Don't I know you from somewhere? I feel like I've seen you before.'

'Stonewall Ranch,' said Scarlett. 'Barmaid. Black outfit. I served you and Hogan whiskey.'

'Right,' said Andrew, sitting back and regarding her for a moment. 'You look different.'

'I know,' she smiled with a shake of the head. 'Cobb makes us wear those short black skirts and tight-fitting shirts. It's either that or you're no longer on the payroll.'

'Cobb,' said Andrew. 'Yes, he seemed like a less than trustworthy character, if you don't mind my saying so.'

'Oh, I don't mind,' said Scarlett. 'None of the girls like him. He's got the eyes of a snake. I don't think there's anything McKinnon could ask of him that he wouldn't do.'

'How did you find me?' said Andrew. 'I'm assuming this isn't just a chance encounter.'

Scarlett gave a self-conscious chuckle and took off her cap and hairband to let her blond, wavy hair spill down onto her shoulders.

'That's right,' she said. 'It's not. I heard you talking to Hogan, and you told him you were staying at Mike's Motel. So, I just parked up there and waited. Followed you into town. And here I am.'

'That was you in the silver car?' asked Andrew.

'That obvious, huh?' she asked, sucking her teeth.

'I'm afraid so,' said Andrew. 'What can I do for you?'

'I know who you are,' said Scarlett with an earnest look as she lowered her voice and leaned forward slightly across the table.

'Really?' said Andrew, briefly glancing out through the window and then scanning the bar's interior once more. 'Who am I, then?'

'You're Andrew Sterling,' she said, looking him straight in the eye. 'Eddie Barton's friend from back in the day. You're with the SAS. He talked about you, and he once showed me a picture of you two together on an operation.'

Andrew levelled a guarded gaze at Scarlett for a long moment, but there was nothing in her eyes that spoke of anything but honesty and sincerity.

'Just how well do you know Barton?' he said, slightly taken aback by what she had just told him.

'As well as anyone can, I guess,' said Scarlett, now more subdued. 'We're... involved. But we obviously haven't told anyone. I would have gotten fired for sure, and Eddie might have gotten disciplined or something. Fraternising with co-workers at the ranch is totally off-limits. General McKinnon runs that place like a military base.'

'You're aware of what happened behind the High Jinx Tavern?' asked Andrew.

'I know what they *say* happened,' said Scarlett. 'But I am not sure I believe it.'

'Well, you should,' said Andrew reluctantly. 'I hate to be the one to tell you this, but Barton killed those two men. I saw the security tapes myself.'

Scarlett's mouth fell slightly open, and her eyes suddenly looked fearful. Then she folded her hands on the table and cleared her throat as she took a moment to compose herself. Sitting up straight in her chair and taking a quick breath, she gave a nod and met Andrew's gaze again.

'I see,' she finally said, using an index finger to swipe a lock of hair from her face, fixing it behind her ear. 'Well. There must have been some reason for him to do that. Listen, I know he is ex-military. Special forces, right? So, I am sure he has done things that I probably wouldn't want to know about. But a cold-blooded killer, he is not.'

'I know,' said Andrew. 'It was evident from the video that he was just defending himself. And I thought it was clear that he tried to de-escalate the situation. But then one of the men pulled a gun, and things went south very quickly from there.'

Andrew proceeded to tell Scarlett about his talks with Hogan, Bremmer and McKinnon, and it was obvious from her face that she was as sceptical as he was about whether any of what those men had said was true. He then also relayed his and Donna Cooper's suspicions about the death of Billy Ray.

'These people just can't be trusted,' Scarlett said. 'They're all in cahoots.'

'That's my conclusion as well,' said Andrew.

'Do you think Eddie is alright?' she said, now sounding genuinely concerned.

'I'm not sure anymore,' said Andrew darkly. 'That's the honest answer. If they were prepared to kill Billy Ray, then I have no doubt that they would get rid of Barton in a heartbeat. But I still don't know what this whole thing is all about.'

'Shit,' said Scarlett bitterly, her face now lined with worry as she hesitated for a moment before speaking again. 'There's something else I should tell you.'

'What?' said Andrew, leaning forward and wrapping one hand around the fist of the other.

'The day before Eddie was arrested,' she said quietly, 'I overheard McKinnon order Cormac to "*solve the problem*" just as they were coming out of the general's office upstairs. I didn't think anything of it at the time because McKinnon is constantly issuing orders to his men. But somehow, that just sounded so ominous. Like something bad was about to happen. And then, within hours, Eddie is in jail, accused of a double homicide. Surely that can't be a coincidence.'

'No,' said Andrew pensively as another piece of the jigsaw puzzle fell into place. 'It's difficult not to make a connection there. If only there was a way to locate Barton. I would drive to Nolan County right now, but I don't feel like getting arrested for breaking into a jail. And that definitely won't help. I also need to find out what happened to Billy Ray.'

'I'm really concerned about Eddie now,' said Scarlett, her blue eyes welling up slightly as she bit her lower lip nervously.

'I understand,' said Andrew, placing a hand gently on hers. 'Try not to worry. The fact is, we don't know anything for sure yet. The best thing you can do right now is carry on as normal. I intend to do whatever it takes to get to the bottom of this whole thing.'

*　　　*　　　*

Pete Murphy exited the Dollar General store on 69th Street, roughly three kilometres from the Port of Galveston where he worked as a security guard. He had held the job for almost a decade, and unlike a lot of his colleagues working for the port, he was more than happy to take the night shifts. Hardly anything ever happened during the night, and if there was ever any activity, it was usually scheduled well in advance. This allowed him to read books or play online poker games on his phone against opponents from all over the world. Murphy wasn't the sort of person to brag, but he had squirrelled away a half-decent amount of winnings in a local savings and loans association. One day, he was going to retire, buy a boat, and then spend his time crisscrossing the Caribbean and enjoying life on the golden beaches of its many islands.

As the doors slid open and he walked out into the parking lot, he was clutching a yellow plastic bag with the shop's name emblazoned across it in blue. The bag was full of various household items that he had put down on a list during the previous couple of weeks, and today he had gone to get them all and bring them back to where he lived.

He was forty-three years old with a short beard and a receding hairline, and he was now some way off his prime as far as physical fitness went. He lived happily by himself in a small house on Sycamore Drive just a stone's throw from the store, and his only companion there was a fuzzy Pomeranian named Bandit, on account of his propensity to steal food from the fridge whenever Murphy turned his back.

Walking along Sycamore Drive carrying the plastic bag, Murphy contemplated what had happened a couple of nights earlier. Sitting in his guard house, he had heard the barrage of gunshots coming from Pier 39 shortly after the convoy had entered, and he had broken into a cold sweat when he realised the part he had played in the mayhem. By accepting the four-figure offer put forward by the man who had approached him in his usual drinking hole several weeks earlier, Murphy had become an accomplice to what turned out to be an orgy of violence.

When he took the money, he had never imagined that something like that could happen. The man had simply asked him to send an empty text message from a burner phone to a specified number as soon as the convoy approached the outer perimeter of the port. A voice at the back of Murphy's head had attempted to remind him that if something appeared too good to be true, it almost certainly was. However, after being presented with a packed envelope bursting with $100 bills, he had soon found a way to quell that voice. Opportunities like this practically never came his way, so he had thrown caution to the wind and walked home with the cash burning a hole in his pocket.

The very next day, the FBI had come knocking, and he had told them everything that had happened that night, including hiding inside his guardhouse as the two armoured trucks roared up the road and raced out of the port complex heading east. The two federal agents appeared to have accepted his story, and Murphy had found no trouble channelling his anxiety about the whole situation into nervous energy presented as post-traumatic stress resulting from being within a hair's breadth of a run-in with mass killers. Since the agents had turned up, he had heard nothing more from them, and he allowed himself to believe that this would be the end of it.

When he thought about exactly how he had earned this unexpected windfall, he felt sick to his stomach about it. However, what was done was done. Running off to the FBI and admitting his role in what had happened that night served no purpose whatsoever now. It wasn't going to bring back those national guardsmen and FBI agents, and it could end up landing him in prison for a very long time. Better to keep quiet and go on as normal, and then hope that no evidence was ever recovered.

Arriving at his house, Murphy walked up the driveway to the front door. Fishing out his key from a trouser pocket, he unlocked the door and stepped inside.

'Yo! Bandit!' he called cheerfully. 'I'm back. I got you something from the store.'

Any other day, Bandit would have been coming at him like a missile from his wooden dog bed at the back of the house. But not today. Murphy closed the front door, stepped into the hallway and put the plastic bag down on a chair.

'Hey, Bandit!' he called. 'Are you asleep, buddy?'

Murphy stood there listening for a few seconds, and then he moved towards the back of the house. His face had now grown concerned, but when he stepped through the doorway to the kitchen, it was as if his stomach was falling through the floor, and he suddenly felt nauseous. The white tiles on the kitchen floor were smeared with blood, and at the far end of the room was Bandit curled up in his bed. Except that this was not the dog that Murphy was used to seeing. The pet's head had been severed and was lying a few inches from the rest of his body. Only then did Murphy notice that the backdoor had been forced open. The lock had been wrenched apart, and the thin French blinds that hung on the back of it were swaying almost imperceptibly in the breeze coming in from the outside.

With his head still spinning from the sight of the gratuitous violence against his beloved pet, Murphy took another couple of steps towards the dog bed. Suddenly, a large figure wearing a balaclava burst from the utility cupboard behind him. He wrapped his left arm around Murphy's neck, and a fraction of a second later, the security guard caught a glimpse of a large combat knife moving out and around in front of him. Before his assailant could complete the move and plunge the blade into his chest, Murphy managed to bring his arms up to block the blow. The knife sliced through his right lower arm, and he cried out, more from shock at the sight of his skewered limb than from the pain that had barely had time to register in his brain yet.

His attacker yanked the knife back out amidst a spray of blood that spattered onto the floor and the white kitchen cabinets. Now fighting for his life and grimacing from the effort, Murphy gripped the attacker's knife arm and held it firmly away from himself. Then he pushed his attacker backwards, and the balaclava-clad man seemed to almost lose his footing as the two men crashed into the wall next to a cupboard. The glass-covered photo frames hanging there shattered as they fell onto the floor while the two men continued to struggle for control of the knife.

To Murphy's horror, the powerful attacker's left arm now also gripped the hilt of the knife, and slowly but surely, the razor-sharp blade began to move closer to Murphy's chest. Grimacing, and with spittle flying from his mouth as he wheezed and groaned with his desperate effort, Murphy tried to push the knife away, but it was no use. The attacker was simply too strong, and Murphy's right arm was rapidly becoming weaker.

When the tip of the blade touched his shirt just above his heart, he found himself producing a thin, pleading groan. In response, the attacker suddenly seemed to mobilise even more force, and as the blade slid into his chest all the way to the hilt, Murphy's eyes went wide, and he gasped at the sensation of the cold steel entering his body. With the blade having severed arteries and sliced into his heart and left lung, his body froze in terror as the realisation of his impending death suddenly paralysed him. With a liquid gurgling noise and a shallow cough that sent blood dripping off his lips, his body gradually went limp until it was only held up by the arms and the blade of the assailant. The powerful intruder slowly released his grip and let the body of the security guard slide to the floor, where his dead eyes stared vacantly in the direction of his decapitated dog.

Tyler reached up and pulled his balaclava off his head, and then he adjusted his short ponytail. He used Murphy's clothes to wipe the blood from his combat knife before sheathing it, and then he crossed the room to the backdoor, outside of which he had placed a small holdall. Emptying the two 1-litre bottles of diesel fuel around the house took only a few moments, and then he used some towels he found in a cupboard to create a place to start the fire. He placed the towels in a puddle of diesel on the floor and lit them. A few seconds later, the towels were burning, but unlike with petrol, it would be about a minute before the fire became hot enough to finally ignite the diesel.

Tyler slipped out of the backdoor and donned a cap, pulling it down low in front of his face. With his head down and his hands dug deep into the pockets of his jacket, he joined the pavement and began walking down the street. After about a hundred metres, the engine of a car fitted with phoney numberplates parked by the side of the road suddenly sprang to life, and its headlights came on. Tyler opened the door to the front passenger seat and got in. As the car sped down the street and drove off into the early evening, large yellow flames engulfed Pete Murphy's kitchen, and soon the entire house was ablaze.

FIFTEEN

Late that evening, Andrew stopped the Jeep by the side of a narrow street in what had once been an area of town with various industrial enterprises. He parked up and killed the engine about fifty metres from a small two-storey apartment building that had once been a cotton mill, but which had since been turned into four separate dwellings. One of those new apartments had belonged to Billy Ray Cooper, and it was located a roughly ten-minute walk from Main Street and the sheriff's office. This would have been very convenient for Donna's brother, and he could probably have got by without owning a car. However, a man without a car in Texas was like a cowboy without a revolver or a fireman without a firehose. It simply didn't happen.

Billy Ray's blue Chevrolet pickup truck was still parked outside the building, but it had police tape draped over it. It had apparently not yet been taken away for a thorough forensic analysis. Perhaps the police were so keen to treat this as an open-and-shut case that there was no real sense of urgency in getting it done.

Andrew waited a few moments, looking around and checking his mirrors to make sure that the street was abandoned, before stuffing the Beretta under his belt and exiting the vehicle. As he drew nearer to the apartment building, he could see that there were no lights in the windows of the top two apartments. Walking casually along the street, he then made his way to the front door and studied the intercom system. Just as Donna had said, Billy Ray had been in Apartment 3, and his name was still next to its button, so he pressed the button for Apartment 2, where he had noticed the lights were on. After a few seconds, the voice of what sounded like an older man came through the speaker.

'What?' it said gruffly.

'Sorry,' said Andrew, doing his best to emulate a Texas accent. 'Delivery for Apartment 3. He ain't answering. Can you let me in so I can put it outside his door?'

'Knock yourself out,' came the curt reply, and then the connection was terminated and the door buzzer growled.

Andrew pushed inside the lobby and walked up two flights of stairs to the door to Apartment 3, which had two strips of white and blue police tape fixed across it and an additional yellow strip stuck onto the floor saying, "Do not cross". He ignored the warnings and fished a small fold-up lockpicking set from his pocket. Selecting what he thought would be the appropriate pick, he began exploring the lock's tumblers. After a couple of minutes of trial and error, the lock made a satisfying metallic click, and he was able to open the door.

Ducking under the police tape and slipping inside, he closed the door silently behind him and stood in the hallway for a moment to make sure there was no sound of movement either inside the apartment or out in the stairwell. To his left was a spacious living room with three tall windows facing the street. Through the French blinds, he could see another old two-storey building on the other side of the street, but it appeared to be an abandoned industrial building since none of its ghostly old windows were lit up. Straight ahead was a kitchen, and next to it at the back were a bedroom and a bathroom, each with a window facing a courtyard behind the building.

Keeping the lights in the apartment turned off, Andrew stepped inside the living room, which was only dimly lit by the streetlights outside. As soon as he entered, he found himself stopping and staring at the disturbing scene in front of him. Placed with its back against the wall directly opposite the centre window was a beige three-person sofa, and behind it on the wall was a truly grisly sight. It was as if someone had thrown a cupful of paint onto the wall, creating a dark blemish that had then left rivulets running down towards the floor and onto the sofa's backrest, discolouring that too. In the centre of the blotch, whose edges spoke of it having been created by a forceful spray, was a small circular hole.

This was where Billy Ray had taken his own life using his police sidearm, if Hogan was to be believed. Andrew gazed at the gory display for a moment and stepped closer, noticing a large dark discoloured area on the seat of the sofa. Evidently, Billy Ray's head and body had slumped down and to the side after the shot that caused his death had been fired, and the sofa cushion had then absorbed a large amount of his blood.

Having seen the photo of a happy and smiling Billy Ray just hours earlier, Andrew was unsettled to now be standing in his living room and seeing firsthand the evidence of his gruesome death. But if anything, it also made him even more determined to find out the truth about it. By all accounts, Billy Ray had been a well-liked and idealistic young man, and his life had ended right here, and much too soon. Andrew walked to the far side of the living room to be able to view the scene from a different angle, but so far there was nothing to suggest that Billy Ray's death had happened any differently from what the police were claiming.

Eyeing the small hole in the wall where the bullet had entered, Andrew realised that it was not a brick wall, as might have been expected from an old former cotton mill. Instead, it was clear that it was a drywall separating the living room from the bedroom at the back. This meant that the bullet would have travelled through both sets of plasterboard and ended up somewhere in the bedroom. In fact, having witnessed firearms tests to demonstrate the potential risk of friendly fire inside small confined spaces, Andrew had seen standard 9mm rounds go through as much as twelve sheets of plasterboard. In other words, if someone was firing a 9mm handgun inside a house that had been constructed in this way, there was at least a theoretical risk of hitting a fellow operator who was as many as six rooms away.

He exited the living room for the hallway and walked into the bedroom. Unlike the small and neat entry hole in the living room, the wall in the bedroom had a ragged exit hole the size of a large coin where the bullet and small fragments of plasterboard had exploded out through the drywall and into the bedroom. The solid wooden bedframe seemed to have finally stopped the bullet, because whoever had examined the apartment after Billy Ray's death had cut away a sizeable piece of the frame, including the bullet, presumably to take them away as forensic evidence.

Lowering himself onto his haunches next to the ned, Andrew noticed that the missing section was only about twenty centimetres from the floor. Turning his head to look at the hole in the wall, it was clear that it was located significantly higher up, but not quite as high as the entry hole in the living room. The bottom line was that the shot that killed Billy Ray had been fired downward at an angle that appeared unnaturally steep.

Moving back into the living room, it was very obvious that Andrew had been correct in his assertion. With his shadow falling onto the sofa, Andrew placed himself directly in front of the sofa while facing the wall, the way he imagined a potential killer might have stood. He raised his arm to simulate firing a shot at a person sitting there. The bullet would have entered Billy Ray's head at the top of his forehead and punched through the wall behind him several centimetres lower. This went against every suicide with a firearm that he had ever heard of. In almost all other cases, the person turning a gun on themselves would either bring it up to their temple on one side of their head and fire horizontally into their own brain, or they would place the gun under their chin or in their mouth before pulling the trigger. In both of the latter cases, the bullet would travel almost vertically up into their brain and exit their skull to hit the ceiling. In Billy Ray's case, none of those things had happened.

Andrew lowered his arm and clenched his jaw. In order for the scene in front of him to make sense in the context of a suicide, Donna's brother would have had to bring the gun up in front of his head, turn it around and then point it slightly downward before finally pushing the trigger away from himself. For someone like Billy Ray, who would have been significantly more proficient at using a firearm than most people, this seemed like an extremely unlikely thing for him to have done. People who decided to take their own lives usually wanted to make sure they got it right the first time, and this seemed to Andrew to be one of the least likely ways of ensuring success. In other words, Billy Ray's death was almost certainly not a suicide.

With a sharp crack, the window glass directly behind Andrew suddenly shattered, and the unmistakable sound of a high-calibre bullet zipped past his head and slammed into the wall in front of him. Punching through the plasterboard, it made a fist-sized hole and tore an even bigger hole in the drywall in the bedroom. As pieces of shattered glass clattered onto the floor, Andrew spun, ducked and threw himself to one side, and an instant later another bullet punched through the broken window pane and made another hole in the wall as dust and debris from the chewed-up plasterboard filled the air. Then another bullet smacked into the wall, and then another.

However, there was no rifle report at all, which meant that the shooter's weapon was fitted with a high-quality suppressor. In addition, the rate of fire was so high that the incoming projectiles could only have been fired from a military-grade semi-automatic sniper rifle. Whoever was firing was a well-trained shooter using some serious hardware. However, even a proficient marksman sometimes misses his target, and standing in front of the sofa, Andrew had felt the high-pressure wake as the first bullet tore through the air just a few centimetres from his head.

He scrambled underneath the window to get into cover and away from the parts of the room that the attacker could hit. For all he knew, the shooter had a night vision scope fitted to his weapon, which meant that he would be able to see the apartment's interior as clear as day even now with all of the lights turned off.

Ripping the Beretta from his belt, Andrew yanked back the slide and steeled himself for a brief moment. Then he swivelled and raised himself enough to be able to point the gun out of the shattered window towards the abandoned factory building across the street. He immediately fired a handful of rounds at different windows in quick succession and then ducked back down into cover. He wasn't expecting to hit anything, but it was clear that his attacker was either holed up inside the factory or lying prone in a concealed position on its roof, and perhaps Andrew could make the shooter give away his position.

For a few seconds, the firing stopped, and Andrew risked re-emerging to release another burst of rounds. He quickly pulled back into cover, and a split second later, another sniper bullet smacked into the window frame mere inches from his head. The wood exploded in a shower of splinters uncomfortably close to Andrew's head.

Scrambling through shards of glass across the floor in a prone position, Andrew then crabbed his way out into the hallway as more bullets smacked into the apartment through window frames, whose glass panes had now shattered completely. The shooter must have somehow seen the movement because another bullet slammed into a wooden doorframe and tore a chunk of wood out of it which splintered and flew across the hallway.

Staying low and moving as fast as he could, he made his way into the kitchen. Its walls were clad with tiles, so the risk of a bullet punching through what was now four or six sheets of plasterboards as well as a kitchen tile was now low. Or so he hoped. Getting to his feet, he opened the window to the courtyard and was about to climb up onto the kitchen counter and out of the window to the fire escape. Then he spotted a portable fan sitting on the counter and had an idea.

He snatched a hand towel from a peg and jammed it into a wall-mounted cupboard door so that it hung in front of the fan, blocking a pendant light. Then he hit the light switch and also switched the fan on, engaging the automatic swivel mechanism. As the fan swivelled from side to side, it moved the towel, which in turn gave the illusion of movement inside the kitchen to anyone looking into the building from the outside. This would hopefully buy him a bit more time for what he planned to do next.

He mounted the kitchen counter, opened the window and dropped down onto the top flight of the external metal fire escape staircase where he immediately began heading down. Above him, he could hear the telltale sound of projectiles smacking into drywall and timber supports, and there was even the sound of tiles shattering and falling onto the kitchen floor. The shooter clearly still believed that Andrew was in there, so at least for now his plan had worked. But for how much longer? Eventually, the shooter would recognise the pattern in the movement of light and realise that he had been tricked, and then he would probably pack up and leave in a hurry.

Andrew descended the stairs as fast as he could and made it down into the courtyard. Then he headed for the exit which led to a narrow side street from which he was able to emerge out of view of the shooter. With his weapon drawn, he crossed the street to the abandoned factory building and climbed over a fence to a courtyard similar to the one he had just left. As had been the case with Billy Ray's apartment building, the abandoned factory had an old fire escape fixed to the rear of the building. Andrew could no longer hear the sound of shots, but it was unclear whether the shooter had stopped firing or whether Andrew was simply out of range to be able to hear.

He moved swiftly but quietly to the fire escape and began climbing it two careful steps at a time. The element of surprise was going to be all-important, and he couldn't afford to make even the smallest amount of noise. Moving cautiously, he looked through the dusty windows to the empty factory floors as he went up, and there was no sign of the shooter inside.

After about a minute, he reached the top of the staircase from which he was able to climb up onto the flat roof where he now thought the shooter had to be positioned. Hauling himself up and over the raised edge of the roof, he immediately spotted the man lying prone on the other side behind what looked to be a U.S. military standard-issue M110 semi-automatic sniper rifle that was resting on a bipod.

It was no wonder that the bullets slamming into Billy Ray's apartment had done as much damage as they had. With a weapon like that firing standard 7.62 NATO rounds, even in its suppressed configuration, the bullets would be leaving the rifle's muzzle at about 2,500 kilometres per hour and delivering devastating amounts of kinetic energy on impact.

The prone man was wearing dark clothing and a black baseball cap worn backwards, and he was lying almost perfectly still about twenty metres away. However, Andrew could see the suppressed barrel of the rifle moving ever so slightly from one side to the other as the sniper attempted to reacquire his target through the night vision scope mounted on top of the weapon.

Without making a sound, Andrew got to his feet, raised his weapon and advanced silently towards his would-be killer in a semi-crouched combat stance.

When he was about halfway there, he stopped and aimed. From this distance, he could easily have put a bullet in the back of the shooter's head, but he needed this man alive. He needed answers.

'Hands! Right now!' he shouted in a commanding voice that would have caused almost anyone else to comply immediately.

Without even a moment's hesitation, the shooter released his grip on the sniper rifle and rolled quickly to one side onto his back while pulling a suppressed pistol from a shoulder holster. He then immediately opened fire, releasing a flurry of shots that forced Andrew to throw himself into cover behind an old brick chimney stack next to him. The bullets peppered the chimney, sending small chunks of brick and dust exploding from it, and Andrew only just managed to get fully into cover behind it.

The barrage of projectiles was coming in so fast that Andrew lost track of the number of rounds fired. However, waiting for the shooter to run dry was not an option. He had to find a way to immobilise him quickly without killing him. He decided that attempting to shoot him in the legs was probably his best option, so when the firing stopped, he readied himself for a couple of seconds, and then he emerged from behind the chimney stack with his weapon up.

As he looked across to the edge of the roof, he only just caught the man disappearing over the edge of the building and out of sight. As far as Andrew remembered, there was no safe way down to the street below at the front of the building, so unless the shooter had grown wings, he appeared to have been prepared to risk a two-storey fall to the pavement in order to get away from his pursuer.

Still with his weapon raised, Andrew advanced towards the spot where the shooter had been lying, and that was when he spotted the black metal grappling hook that was gripping the inside edge of the roof. It had a grey nylon rope attached to it, and the rope trailed over the edge and down along the side of the building. The sniper rifle was still there, but if the shooter was any kind of professional, he would have been wearing gloves in order to leave no fingerprints.

Cautiously stepping up near the edge and peering down in case the shooter was waiting for him, Andrew spotted the man running along the near side of the street away from the centre of town. After about thirty metres, he hopped onto a motorcycle that was parked in the shadows where a streetlight had gone dark. Realising what was about to happen, Andrew raised his Beretta and aimed, but then decided against firing. A slight miss might accidentally kill the man, and he wasn't prepared to risk that.

'Shit!' he swore through gritted teeth, and then he bent down and gripped the rope.

With the nylon rope firmly in his hands, he swung himself out over the edge of the building and began rappelling down towards the street the way the shooter had done just seconds earlier. It took only a few seconds to get down, but when he was about halfway, he heard the motorcycle engine roar to life. He lowered himself another metre or so, and then he let go of the rope and let himself drop the final couple of metres to the pavement. He landed heavily, and pain shot up through his lower legs just as the motorcycle revved aggressively, swerved out into the street and took off.

Sprinting in the opposite direction, Andrew reached his Jeep about ten seconds later, tore open the door and flung himself inside behind the wheel. As soon as the engine started, he threw the car into gear. With its four-wheel-drive engaged, all of the Jeep's wide tyres squealed as they spun on the asphalt before gripping the road surface and propelling the car forward in a violent acceleration that almost caused him to sideswipe another parked vehicle. He managed to regain control of the car just as the motorbike's red taillight disappeared around a corner a little less than a hundred metres up ahead. Flooring the accelerator and waiting until the last second to slam the breaks, he then threw the Jeep into the corner and narrowly missed colliding with a lamppost as he continued his pursuit.

Soon they were approaching the edge of town, and Andrew knew that he would have to act fast to bring the chase to an end. If he allowed the motorbike to leave town and drive out onto the almost straight country roads surrounding Revelation, the bike's superior acceleration and straight-line speed would outmatch those of the Jeep. He pressed the button to roll the window down and stuck out a hand holding the Beretta. He fired a single shot at the bike's rear tyre, but it missed and ricocheted off the road right in front of the sniper. However, upon realising that he was now the one being shot at, the sniper began to swerve wildly as they left the last built-up section on the western edge of town where a road led further west into the high desert.

Andrew kept the accelerator pressed all the way to the floor, and the bike and the Jeep were now approaching 200 kilometres per hour. He kept firing round after round in the hope of making the shooter continue his swerving and thereby preventing him from accelerating away, and the plan worked, but it would not work for long. As soon as he ran out of bullets and needed to reload, the sniper would simply twist the bike's throttle all the way open and leave him behind. There was only one thing left to do. He had to put a bullet into the shooter's leg or somehow manage to disable the bike with a well-placed shot. He lined up the Jeep to drive in a perfectly straight line as it tore through the desert along the country road. At the same time, with only a couple of bullets left in the magazine and with the wind tearing at his hair and shirt, he aimed the Beretta as carefully as he could and gently squeezed the trigger until it broke.

The pistol fired, producing a loud report and a bright muzzle flash as the bullet left the gun barrel. The 9mm projectile caught up with the sniper's bike in a fraction of a second and ripped through the wide rear tyre, causing it to burst and tear itself to shreds almost instantly. As the explosion caused bits of shredded rubber to fly up into the air, the bike immediately began to swerve wildly out of control, and it was a miracle that it didn't throw the sniper off as it bucked and jolted. It was only the force of the angular momentum produced by its rapidly spinning wheels that allowed the sniper to keep it upright and maintain some measure of control. However, the chase was over and he knew it.

Slamming on the breaks amid a cloud of white smoke from the tyres, the sniper swerved to the right to try to get clear of his pursuer before he was rammed by the oncoming Jeep. However, the missing rear tyre had made the bike unstable and had changed its handling dramatically, but it was still travelling at well over a hundred kilometres per hour. When the sniper slammed the brakes, the rear wheel suddenly stepped out and spun the entire bike around, throwing the sniper off and up into the air as the bike then toppled over and slid across the blacktop in a shower of metallic sparks. The sniper, who was wearing only regular clothing, clipped the tarmac and instantly went into a violent spin as his body skidded across what was akin to a long cheesegrater made of asphalt. The bike spun off the road and caught a rock, sending it spinning and tumbling up into the air before it finally landed heavily and came to a stop inside a cloud of dust. The sniper continued rolling and spinning across the tarmac for another fifty metres or so, and by the time he finally came to a stop, his entire body had been stripped of most of his clothes and a disturbing amount of his skin. His head and face were missing large patches of hair and tissue, and blood was oozing from every part of his mangled and broken body.

Andrew pulled up alongside him, stopped the car and bolted out with his Beretta aimed squarely at the sniper's head. However, as he approached, a quick glance made it clear that the sniper was no longer a threat to anyone. The man was dying. That much was clear. Andrew probably only had a few moments left with him before he expired. If he was going to get any answers out of him, it had to happen right now.

Lowering himself onto one knee next to the bloodied sniper and leaning forward to look at his face, Andrew suddenly realised who he was looking at. Despite the large oozing patches of missing skin and hair that glistened in the Jeep's headlights, one feature was unmistakable now that his baseball cap had been ripped off. He had a black one-inch-long mohawk running the length of the top of his head. This was the man Donna had identified as Thornton at the diner. The man whose friend Tatum had grabbed Donna, and ended up embarrassing himself in front of a diner full of customers, including the mayor. Was his effort to kill Andrew a simple matter of revenge, or was he acting on orders from McKinnon? Or was it perhaps both?

'Thornton,' he said icily. 'Listen to me now. What happened to Eddie Barton?'

Thornton stared up at him as thin clouds of dust from the bike's wreckage remained hanging in the air and drifted off slowly across the terrain. His eyes were narrow slits, and Andrew could see significant internal bleeding in one of them.

'Why did McKinnon want him dead?' said Andrew, now raising his voice. 'What did he find out?'

Thornton's lips moved, but Andrew couldn't hear him. Grimacing from the pain, Thornton was clearly in a huge amount of agony, and he probably knew that he was dying, yet his eyes remained fixed on Andrew's.

'Speak!' Andrew shouted. 'I want answers!'

'You…' whispered Thornton almost inaudibly as blood dribbled from the side of his mouth. 'You'll…'

Andrew could barely make out the words. Placing the muzzle of the Beretta pointing straight down into Thornton's torn chest in order to make a point, Andrew leaned down to put his ear nearer his bleeding mouth. As the dying sniper spoke again, he bared his blood-covered teeth in a snarl.

'You'll be joining your dead buddy soon,' he whispered, and then he winked as a malevolent grin slowly spread across his bloodied and contorted face.

Andrew sat back up and looked dispassionately down at the dying man, whose mocking eyes remained locked on his. An instant later, a final shot rang out over the desert. Thornton's body spasmed violently once as the bullet ripped through his heart and embedded itself into the road, and then he lay still.

With the sound of the Jeep's engine idling about five metres behind him and the car's headlight bathing him and Thornton's corpse in bright white light, Andrew's head sank to his chest as he closed his eyes and produced a long, slow exhale. Having been the target of an assassination attempt, having then killed one of McKinnon's men, and having just discovered that his old friend Barton had been dead all this time, whether he liked it or not, one thing was undeniably clear. He was now at war.

SIXTEEN

Returning to the motel room well after midnight, Andrew briefly considered swapping rooms or finding alternative accommodation somewhere else, but he decided against it. McKinnon's tentacles seemed to reach out into every corner of the town, so if the general wanted to locate Andrew, he would be able to do it without any problems.

It was also likely that Andrew would have now bought himself some time. Before leaving the site of the bike crash and Thornton's corpse, Andrew had dragged the motorcycle and the dead sniper off the road and hid both behind some thick, low bushes. After working hard for fifteen minutes, he had covered Thornton's body with large heavy rocks to prevent it from becoming an obvious and conspicuous feasting site for vultures and other scavengers. He realised that both the bike and the corpse would be found eventually, but it was a big desert out there, and with a bit of luck, they would not be located for several days.

Before covering up Thornton's body, Andrew had noticed that the sniper seemed to carry no mobile phone or any other communications equipment. This meant that the success or failure of his mission to kill Andrew in Billy Ray's apartment had not been communicated to anyone else yet. In addition, no one knew about the pursuit that had ended in Thornton's death, and this would also work to Andrew's benefit, at least for a time.

Andrew lay down on the bed and was immediately reminded by his aching body of the frantic escape from the barrage of sniper fire, the long drop to the street below and the effort to move a large number of heavy stones in order to fully cover Thornton's body. Within minutes, he was asleep.

He awoke mid-morning to the sound of birdsong and an eighteen-wheeler truck roaring past from east to west on the country road outside. He blinked a couple of times and then sat up in bed as the memories of the violent events of the night before flooded back into his mind. After a shower and a shave, he was putting his clothes back on when his phone buzzed and wriggled around on top of the small varnished writing desk that was placed on one side of the motel room. It turned out to be Donna, so he answered the call immediately.

'Andy?' she said. 'Can you talk?'

'Sure,' said Andrew. 'Is everything alright? Are you still at home?'

'Yes,' said Donna, a hint of anxiety in her voice. 'I've decided to take a couple of days off to try to find my feet again. Paige is covering for me. She's amazing. Anyway, there's something I need to tell you.'

'Alright,' said Andrew, sitting down on the end of the bed. 'What is it?'

'Sergeant Fuller showed up early this morning,' she said. 'He came to hand me a cardboard box full of Billy Ray's personal items that were left inside his desk at the sheriff's office. He didn't really say much. Just handed me the box, offered his condolences and left. Anyway, I want to show you something. Can you come by later?'

'Sure,' said Andrew, deciding to wait to tell her about the previous evening. 'I can be there in about an hour. I just need to grab myself some breakfast somewhere.'

'OK,' said Donna. 'If you head over to the diner, there's a free meal waiting for you. Just tell Paige I sent you. It's the least I can do.'

'Thanks. I might just do that,' said Andrew. 'I'll come to you straight after.'

'Great,' she said. 'See you soon.'

Just before midday, Andrew parked up next to the curb in front of Donna's house and walked up to knock on the door. When she opened, she looked marginally better than the last time he had seen her. Perhaps the prospect of a visit from a friendly soul did her some good. Her eyes looked clearer, and she was wearing dark blue jeans and a short-sleeved light blue and white checkered shirt.

'Come on inside,' she said, stepping aside to let him enter. 'I'll get you a beer.'

'No thanks,' smiled Andrew as he stepped inside the living room and sat down on the sofa in the same spot as during his previous visit. 'If I could just have a glass of water, please?'

'Sure,' she replied, and went into the kitchen.

Inside the living room on the coffee table was an open cardboard box roughly the size of a shoebox. As Andrew sat down and Donna returned with the glass of water, he peered inside and saw a slim wallet with a few credit cards, a couple of personalised ballpoint pens, some banknotes, a packet of chewing gum and a membership card to a local gym. However, the most noteworthy item was a mobile phone.

'Thanks,' said Andrew as he took the glass and pointed at the box. 'This was Billy Ray's personal phone?'

'That's right,' nodded Donna, sitting down on the sofa opposite him. 'Apparently, he left it at the station.'

'That seems odd,' said Andrew. 'Why would he do that? Wouldn't he bring it with him when he left the sheriff's office?'

'Exactly,' said Donna, reaching inside the box, scooping the phone up into her hand and switching it on. 'But there's more. All of his personal messages have been deleted. Emails. Text messages. Everything. Even his browsing history is gone. It's like the phone has been wiped clean of anything that might provide clues to what he was doing.'

'Hogan,' said Andrew. 'Why would he do that?'

'That's the question,' said Donna. 'Now, I am sure that if I asked him, he'd say that there were messages in there pertaining to official police business and that they could not be allowed to be released and so on and so forth. But that's just hokum. I swear, Hogan was involved in this somehow, and he is trying to hide it.'

'I think you may be right,' said Andrew.

'But,' said Donna, raising her left index finger as her right thumb moved across the phone's screen. 'When Billy Ray first got the job as a deputy, I was worried about his safety, so I made him install a hidden tracking app. It basically uses mobile phone networks to log its location at all times, and it can show its movement on a map. Look here.'

Donna got up from her seat and shifted over to sit next to Andrew with the phone in the palm of her hand.

'Look at this,' she said, unhiding the app and opening it. 'Here's the log view showing all the dates for which there is location data, which is every single day since he took the job. And here is the map view, so if I select the date when your friend Barton was arrested, I can see exactly where Billy Ray was every minute of that day.'

She selected the date, tapped a menu icon, and then tapped a button to show a map of the area around Revelation overlaid with a thin blue line indicating the phone's location during that day. It began around noon at his home near the centre of town and proceeded to the sheriff's office. After several hours, it continued on to a number of locations around town, which would have been places that Billy Ray had visited during his working day. Late in the afternoon, it returned to the sheriff's office where it then remained until late that evening.

'This is where it gets weird,' said Donna, indicating to the last part of the blue line. 'Billy Ray would normally have walked home just before midnight, but he didn't do so on that day. Instead, it looks like he got into his police cruiser and drove out of town into the desert. And look at this. He drove along this main road towards the west, but then he veered off and went right out into the desert. Now, there might be a dirt track out there that he followed, but that still doesn't explain why he was even out there in the first place. Especially at that time of night when his shift had ended.'

'You're right,' said Andrew, examining the route shown on the map. 'That is strange. What's out there in that area?'

'Nothing, as far as I know,' said Donna. 'I can't imagine what could have possessed him to drive all the way out there so late. But he spent about ten minutes there. And now Hogan wants me to believe that my own brother then returned home and shot himself. It simply can't be right. I just don't believe any of it. Not for a second.'

'And you shouldn't,' said Andrew, 'because I am now convinced that Billy Ray was murdered, and I think there is plenty of evidence to back that up.'

Donna's mouth fell open as she looked at him, and a distressed expression began to spread across her face as tears welled up in her eyes.

'Who?' she said, faintly. 'Why?'

Andrew proceeded to recount the events of the previous evening, including the ambush in Billy Ray's apartment, Thornton's violent death and his last words.

'Thornton's dead?' said Donna, seemingly struggling to believe it.

'Very,' said Andrew.

'His buddy Tatum is gonna be really pissed,' said Donna, looking concerned. 'Those two go way back, apparently.'

'I don't mind,' said Andrew evenly. 'Thornton got what he deserved as far as I am concerned. Tatum can do his worst.'

'But why did they kill my brother?' she asked, her voice almost breaking.

'Wrong place. Wrong time,' said Andrew regretfully. 'Nothing more than that. I think he happened to be on duty when McKinnon's goons showed up and grabbed Barton. That was probably already bad enough, but then I think he followed them out into the desert, and that made them decide to take him out. After all, he was now a witness to what I think was a murder. I think they may have cornered him out there, brought him back to his apartment under the pretence of having a serious talk, and then they simply shot him and tried to make it look like a suicide. And Hogan was only too happy to oblige and play along.'

'So, you think Barton is dead too?' said Donna hesitantly.

'I wish it wasn't so,' said Andrew. 'But that is what it looks like to me at this point.'

'Oh god,' said Donna softly, closing her eyes and lowering her head. 'Those bastards. I can't believe they murdered Billy Ray and Barton. We have to do something. We can't let them get away with this.'

'I agree,' said Andrew. 'And we're not going to. But we obviously can't go to the sheriff, and I don't believe that involving the state troopers will help either. I am sure that this guy Bremmer is as bent as a butcher's hook and firmly on McKinnon's payroll. The only other option is the FBI, but that will be an uphill battle, to say the least. At this point, we only have some pretty speculative evidence from Billy Ray's apartment and an implied confession from a dead man that only I heard speak and who is currently buried under a bunch of rocks out in the desert. It won't be enough to move the needle on this. But what it will do is allow McKinnon and his cronies to mobilise against any effort by the FBI to actually investigate at some point.'

'And it will put a big target on both of our backs,' said Donna, 'if there ain't one there already.'

'Well,' said Andrew, rubbing his stubbled chin. 'I am hoping that I am the only one they will be after. But that's fine with me. I am coming for them anyway.'

Donna sat silently for a moment, looking pensive, and then she wiped a tear from her left eye and turned to face Andrew again.

'We should head out to my uncle Emmett's farm,' she said. 'We're going to need all the help we can get.'

'Alright,' said Andrew, nodding slowly. 'If that's what you think, then let's do that. But first, I want to retrace Billy Ray's route from the night he was killed. We need to see what's out there.'

★   ★   ★

It was early afternoon when Andrew and Donna left her house and got into his Jeep. With him behind the wheel, she was in the front passenger seat, cradling Billy Ray's phone in her hands while she directed him towards their destination. The tiny spot on the screen where her brother had appeared to stop for several minutes on the night of Barton's arrest. It took around five minutes to drive through town and then another twenty minutes along the westward country road until they reached the location where Billy Ray had taken a sudden turn north into the almost flat high desert. As Donna had suspected, there was a small dirt track there snaking away from the road through the arid terrain that was dotted with thousands of parched-looking bushes as far as the eye could see. The beginning of the track was so faint and covered with windblown dust and small dry twigs that it would have been nearly impossible to spot unless they had known where to look.

'This is it,' said Donna.

'OK,' said Andrew, slowing down and taking the four-wheel-drive Jeep off the road and onto the barely visible path through the bushes.

The track meandered through the low vegetation for more than a kilometre, and then it descended into a shallow dip in the landscape where there was a wreck of an old minivan. It was almost rusted through, and it was missing all of its windows. Judging by its design, it looked to be at least thirty years old, perhaps a lot more.

'What is this place?' said Andrew.

'No idea,' said Donna, looking down at her brother's phone, 'but this is close to the right spot.'

Near the van were the scattered remains of what had once been a firepit made from breezeblocks. Next to the pit were several empty beer bottles that were half-buried in the loose pale dirt and whose labels had long since disintegrated and disappeared under the harsh Texas sun. By the looks of it, this had once served as a hidden meeting spot for local youths keen to avoid the gaze of their elders on nights out sharing alcohol, cigarettes and stories. Perhaps some of those youths were now adults living and working nearby. Perhaps some were now part of McKinnon's crew at Stonewall Ranch.

'It looks like Billy Ray parked just over there by that large bush,' said Donna, pointing.

The two of them got out of the Jeep and walked towards the spot where Donna's brother appeared to have stopped his police cruiser on that tragic night. The tyre tracks in the dirt were those of a regular car like a sedan, so it seemed likely that her assertion was correct. Nearer to the rusting wreck were several more tyre tracks, and these appeared to have been left by heavier vehicles fitted with wide tyres with deep treads.

'Four-wheel drives,' said Andrew, looking at the tracks.

'Yup,' said Donna. 'Pickup trucks, most likely. Two of them.'

'There are footprints here,' said Andrew, walking cautiously towards the tracks while inspecting the ground ahead of him. 'They're going this way.'

They followed a set of faint footprints from what appeared to have been three or four people moving deeper in amongst the bushes. The prints continued for another fifty metres or so, and as they led Andrew and Donna around a large bush, the sight that met them caused both of them to stop dead in their tracks.

About five metres up ahead was a rectangular area on the ground where the soil had been visibly disturbed. The area was roughly the same length as a fully grown man, and next to it in a bush had been tossed an old weatherworn spade.

Suddenly feeling light-headed as a cold shiver ran down his spine, Andrew moved slowly towards the disturbed soil, one strangely detached step at a time. He knew what this was, but his brain seemed to refuse to believe what his eyes were telling him. Donna followed beside him and approached the area with her hands clasped in front of her mouth. As Andrew stepped closer, his eye caught something lying on the ground that produced a yellow glint as the afternoon sun reflected on its metal surface. It was a spent bullet casing. He bent down and picked it up, turning it over as he inspected it. It was a 9mm brass casing, and when he brought it up to his nose, he could still pick up a very faint scent of cordite. This had been fired only a few days ago.

'Oh no,' Donna whispered, shifting her gaze to the rectangle. 'Is this…?'

'I think so,' said Andrew bitterly. 'But I need to know for sure.'

He stepped over to the bush and pulled out the spade. As he did so, he noticed a dark stain on the wooden handle that appeared to have been made by some form of liquid. He began digging, steeling his mind for what he might find. One ominous spadeful at a time, he began to dig out the trench that appeared to have been made just a few days earlier. It didn't take long for him to sense that there was something just beneath where the tip of the spade had reached.

Tossing the tool aside, he fell to his knees and began scooping the sandy soil up and out of the trench, and suddenly his hands swept over something small and hard. He brushed some more soil aside and uncovered a couple of white plastic buttons attached to what appeared to be an army-green shirt.

With the hairs at the back of his neck standing on end, he then reached about thirty centimetres to one side and scooped away several handfuls of soil. After a few seconds, the pale face of a dead man emerged, and Andrew instantly felt the blood in his veins turn to ice.

The dead man's face was square with a slightly protruding jaw, and his eyes were closed. His skin was mottled and grey with an eerie translucent quality, and his hair and beard were short and blond. High on the left side of his forehead was the dark matted mess of hair and ripped skin that was the edge of an exit wound.

As the reality of what he was seeing cascaded into Andrew's mind like a deadly avalanche of darkness threatening to smother him alive, he felt the blood drain from his face, and he had to make a conscious effort to keep breathing.

'Eddie,' he whispered as he looked at his old friend's bloodied yet strangely peaceful-looking face.

'Oh no,' said Donna with a whimper, and then she lowered herself onto her knees and buried her face in her hands.

'Those fucking cowards,' said Andrew bitterly.

'I'm so sorry,' said Donna with a small sob. 'This is so awful.'

Still staring at his old friend's face, Andrew reached out, took her hand in his, and gave it a squeeze. Then he turned his head to look at her. An ominous darkness had swept across his face, and his eyes spoke of terrible and unstoppable vengeance.

'What's done is done,' he said icily. 'What matters now is what we do about it. Trust me. They will not get away with this.'

SEVENTEEN

Still reeling from the discovery of Barton's body buried in the Texas high desert, Andrew drove silently back towards Revelation with Donna by his side. It was now late in the afternoon, and the sun was beginning to set far away to the west across the desert. Inside him, a storm was brewing, and as they pulled up outside Donna's house, she clearly sensed the darkness that had enveloped his mind. When he stopped the car, his hands remained on the steering wheel, and his gaze was fixed straight ahead, staring unseeingly out into infinity.

Turning to face him, she placed a hand gently on his arm, and only then did he seem to awaken from his numbed stupor to look at her.

'Andrew,' she said softly. 'I would ask if you're OK, but I know you're not. What can I do?'

'Nothing,' said Andrew without much emotion. 'Except to stay safe. I'm going back to the motel. I need to think. Do you have a gun?'

'I do,' said Donna. 'Billy Ray taught me to shoot and gave me a Walther PDP. It's small and easy to use. I only ever shot it at the range, though.'

'That's fine,' said Andrew. 'It's the same principle. Just point and shoot until they stop moving. Don't let anyone come into your house. I don't care who they say they are. They need to stay well back from your front door, or you shoot them for trespassing, OK?'

'Got it,' nodded Donna. 'Do you really think I am in danger?'

'You and I have been digging around,' said Andrew. 'And we've discovered things that were meant to stay hidden. Things that no one was ever supposed to find out about. They already tried to take me out, so that puts you in the crosshairs as well.'

'Alright,' said Donna. 'I guess you're right. Will you keep in touch?'

'Of course,' said Andrew. 'I just need a bit of time to think things through. I'll call you soon.'

'OK,' she said. 'Take care of yourself.'

And with that, she opened the door, stepped out of the Jeep, and walked up to the front door of her house. He remained sitting in the car and watched her go. Stepping inside, she then gave a small wave and a weak smile before closing the door again, after which Andrew finally put the car into gear and drove off.

Picking up a takeaway meal on the way, he returned to the motel just as dusk fell. As he did so, he found himself checking his rearview mirror much more often than he would normally have done while also keeping tabs on any other vehicles and whether they appeared to be following him.

When he pulled into the parking lot and stepped out of the car, he was acutely aware of how he had slipped into old and deeply ingrained habits that usually only came to the fore on overseas deployments with the Regiment. Identifying the makes and models of other cars, memorising their number plates, noting whether there were other guests visible inside the motel reception and being alert to vehicles passing on the country road.

After locking the motel room door behind him, he grabbed a beer from the fridge and slumped into a lone armchair placed in the corner of the room. Deciding to try to watch some TV before going to bed, Andrew switched on the flatscreen mounted to the wall but kept it muted. Flicking aimlessly between channels while his mind relentlessly replayed the harrowing events of that evening, he realised that all of the news channels, both local and national, appeared to be covering the same story. He unmuted the sound.

A dozen national guardsmen and eight FBI agents had been killed during the violent hijacking of a gold transport in the Port of Galveston. The event had sent shockwaves through the city, and local police chiefs and heads of the National Guard and the local FBI office were being wheeled out in front of cameras to provide what little information they were prepared to share while looking suitably cowed and contrite about the apparent ease with which the criminals had been able to pull off such a major heist. There was no information about precisely how much gold had been taken or who the perpetrators might have been, but there was already rampant speculation that the incident had been carried out by foreign terrorists who were now about to use that very gold to finance further attacks on the United States and her allies.

Andrew watched impassively for a few minutes and then turned the TV off. The image of Barton's pale face wouldn't leave his mind, and he suspected that it would haunt him for the rest of his life, especially if he didn't manage to bring the killers to justice. Accepting that he was now being pulled into the mindset of a vigilante, it was becoming clear to him as he sat there that justice and vengeance in this case were one and the same thing. Whoever was responsible for Barton's murder was going to pay, and only he would be able to make them.

After eating half of his takeaway and finishing his beer, and with a cold clarity about what needed to happen next spreading through his mind, he finally laid down on the bed and fell asleep.

★   ★   ★

Several hours later, Stonewall Ranch was a hive of well-coordinated activity in preparation for the upcoming mission that was going to be decisive for the success or failure of General McKinnon's grand plan. The four most experienced members of the elite Nightcrawler team were standing in front of their cages near the ops centre in the secure part of the basement under Stonewall Ranch. They were wearing their black tactical gear, and each had their choice of weapons and equipment strapped to their bodies ready to head upstairs and board the V-280 Valor for the night mission.

As the team performed their final equipment checks, the double doors to the ops centre opened, and General McKinnon walked in, flanked by Cobb. The four operators immediately stood to attention as the general addressed them in his baritone voice.

'At ease, men,' he said. 'We're all set. Weather's perfect, and surveillance indicates that the facility is in nominal condition with respect to staffing and guards. I don't need to remind you of the risks on this one. Make sure you have all the equipment you're going to need.'

'Looking forward to getting rolling on this one, sir,' said Knox with a grin.

'Don't interrupt the general,' said Cormac gruffly, giving his number two a look.

'It's alright,' smiled McKinnon calmly, nodding at Knox and placing a hand on his shoulder. 'I appreciate a soldier who is keen to get out there and kick some ass.'

'How many guards?' asked Willis.

'Only six now,' said McKinnon. 'Two at the gate and four in the facility. Two of those are permanently stationed near the stairwell to the basement. If you are smooth and fast, this should all be a cakewalk.'

'I assume that we don't leave any loose ends this time,' said Tyler, removing a toothpick from his mouth. 'I don't mind tying those up if we need to, but apparently, the Galveston PD issued a BOLO on the vehicle we used for the hit on Murphy. We had to take it to the scrapyard and turn it into a cube.'

'That's right,' said McKinnon. 'This mission is too important to leave any witnesses. We can't allow anyone to talk. You need to clean house before you leave.'

'Roger that,' said Cormac.

'Everyone ready?' said McKinnon. 'This is the one that opens the way forward to the big day. So, don't screw it up.'

'We won't, sir,' said Cormac. 'Those guys won't know what hit them.'

'That's what I like to hear,' nodded McKinnon with a satisfied smile. 'Saddle up, boys. Chopper's waiting.'

Five minutes later, carrying a large black holdall each, the team boarded the V-280 where Reeves and Irvine were waiting in the cockpit for permission to take off and begin the roughly 800-kilometre trip that was scheduled to take just over two hours. The flight plan required Reeves to pilot the aircraft at a very low altitude west into New Mexico and then north through a rugged and sparsely populated area before crossing into Colorado and then heading for their final destination some 23 kilometres due east of the city of Pueblo.

The four operators strapped themselves in and settled in for the ride. As soon as the green light came on outside on the landing pad, the aircraft took off. It then tilted forward to immediately begin gaining speed, its sleek shape cutting through the air and accelerating rapidly as the twin tilt-rotors moved to their level flight positions and added even more forward thrust. Within seconds, it was tearing through the air and skimming across the high desert at more than 400 kilometres per hour.

Its inherent stealth characteristics would make it almost impossible for radar to pick up, and with

Reeves engaging its augmented flight control system, it was virtually invisible. The laser scanners mapped the terrain ahead several thousand times per second and built up a 3D image of what was coming, which was displayed inside the pilot's helmet. The autopilot would then continuously adjust the aircraft's pitch and altitude to keep it at a safe distance from the ground. The net result was that Reeves could fly the aircraft at almost maximum speed just a few metres above the ground, and its onboard systems would ensure that it never clipped trees or ridges and never crashed into anything. This level of nap-of-the-earth flying was impossible for a human pilot to achieve on his own, but an integrated system where the pilot's inputs were augmented by the terrain mapping computer meant that the aircraft could skim across even the most challenging terrain at full tilt and be completely safe from detection by any radar.

After almost two hours, the red lights inside the passenger cabin came on, and the quartet of former special forces operators got to their feet and prepared themselves for the insertion. This included packing their tight-fitting next-generation CBRN suits. Like their older and much bulkier predecessors, the suits were designed to protect the wearer from chemical, biological, radiological and nuclear agents, but unlike those now obsolete suits, these hugged the wearer and offered almost unimpeded movement even while carrying and operating firearms. They were made from several thin layers of special rubber-coated and metal-impregnated membranes, and they each came with a mask that could filter out toxins, pathogens and radioactive materials from the air. The team members were not expecting to need them, but in case of an accident during retrieval of the weapon, they would each be bringing one along for the mission, just in case.

The aircraft was only going to be on the ground for a few seconds, and unloading had to be done quickly so that the V-280 could take off again and relocate to a safe spot far away from built-up areas and busy highways. Parked inside the cargo bay were four ATVs. With their oversized tyres and motorcycle handlebars, they looked like standard all-terrain vehicles, but these were fitted with electric engines that made them almost completely silent even at high speeds. As the four men mounted their vehicles, they could feel the aircraft flaring out and breaking as it approached the designated landing spot. Then Reeves' voice came over their encrypted headsets.

'10 seconds,' he said calmly as the chopper's nose rose steeply and it rapidly bled off speed before rotating in the air and descending the final few metres.

Moments before touchdown, the rear cargo doors opened and the loading ramp was extended. When the wheels finally touched the ground, the ramp was fully extended and ready to be used. Without a moment's hesitation, Cormac and Knox drove their ATVs off the aircraft and out into the black night. Seconds later, Willis and Tyler followed. Almost immediately, the two powerful turboshaft engines growled loudly, and the aircraft lifted off into the night sky. Mere seconds later, everything was quiet again.

The terrain was open prairie and flat as a pancake, and there was hardly a tree for as far as the eye could see. The ground was covered by a scraggy carpet of long dry grass, and a few bushes were dotted here and there. Wearing their night vision goggles, the four men could watch the aircraft as it disappeared towards the hills to the north, and soon it was a tiny dot on the horizon. With Cormac taking the lead, the quartet headed south along a pre-planned route through a shallow, dried-up creek towards their target.

Just under two kilometres away across the open terrain of southern Colorado was the northern edge of the Pueblo Chemical Weapons Depot which covered an area of 24,000 acres of fenced-off and guarded federal land. The enormous area measured roughly seven by eight kilometres in size, and inside the fenced-off perimeter was a huge grid of dozens of roads, each with access to tens of small rectangular plots on which underground storage bunkers had been built for the U.S. Army's chemical weapons stockpile. At its maximum capacity during the height of the Cold War, the depot had just under two thousand active individual bunkers containing chemical weapons, mainly in the form of 155mm artillery shells fitted with mustard gas warheads.

Through a series of international disarmament agreements, primarily signed along with the former Soviet Union and subsequently with the Russian Federation, the United States had committed itself to the destruction of its chemical weapons stockpile on the understanding that the Russians would do the same. Much of that effort had taken place at a smaller and separate compound inside the depot called the Pueblo Chemical Agent Destruction Plant, and it had been working non-stop for years to make sure the United States lived up to its treaty obligations to rid itself of some of the most horrific weapons ever devised by mankind.

However, what only a small number of individuals inside the Pentagon and the military's top brass knew was that the Pueblo facility was still in possession of several batches of an extremely toxic experimental and now discontinued nerve agent that had been developed several decades earlier.

The agent had originally been intended for use on medium-range missiles to be fired into North Korea in case of a ground invasion of South Korea. If North Korea were to mobilise its reserves, its army would number close to one-and-a-half million soldiers, and it was thought that its military possessed around five thousand tanks as well as thousands of APCs and artillery pieces. Such a horde of invaders spilling across the DMZ into South Korea would be virtually impossible to stop without using weapons of mass destruction. In practice, this meant either nuclear or chemical weapons, but for fear of triggering a global nuclear exchange, the military doctrine that had been developed for South Korea's defence was the massive pre-emptive use of chemical weapons on troop concentrations inside North Korea before an invasion could get into full swing.

The chemical agent was based on a version of the exceptionally toxic VX nerve gas, and it had been named JSX after the mythical grim reaper of Korean mythology, *Joseung Saja*. The shells containing JSX had also been scheduled for destruction, but because they had been stored in a South Korean military facility for over ten years before being brought back to Colorado, a bureaucratic issue about their legal ownership status had developed between the United States and South Korea. This, in turn, meant that until this issue could be definitively resolved and a procedure for their destruction could be agreed upon, they remained sealed off inside a bunker underneath the main complex in Pueblo.

Through his extensive network of high-ranking current and former military top brass, General McKinnon had discovered this fact, and slowly over the next several months, a complex plan had crystallised inside his mind. One that included a dozen moving parts, including his elite Nightcrawler team and the involvement of Jean-Pascal Mokri. And if it worked out as he hoped, the United States would finally awaken from its apathetic slumber, and McKinnon's own life would become almost unrecognisable.

The chemical weapons destruction plant was located in the northeastern corner of the sprawling Pueblo Ordnance Depot. It consisted of four main structures, including the administrative building and the main processing hub, as well as about a dozen cylindrical storage tanks for water and various chemicals. A number of large pipes connected all of the various locations, making the whole site look vaguely like an oil refinery. The only way in or out was through a set of manned checkpoints on the southern edge of the depot near Colorado State Highway 96, which ran east to west through the state. The rest of the depot's almost thirty-kilometre-long perimeter was guarded by a tall fence topped with spools of razor wire and thermal cameras fitted every few hundred metres.

The destruction process for the artillery rounds was fully automated, and it entailed the extraction of explosive components followed by the washing out of the chemical agents. The resultant sludge was then sent through a bio-treatment plant that neutralised the chemical agent using microbes. Finally, the empty shells were heated to one thousand degrees in order to sterilise them before they were transported off-site to be melted down and recycled.

Having now completed the destruction of all of the U.S. military's mustard, sarin and VX gas stockpiles, the plant at Pueblo had almost completely wound down, and it was scheduled to be decommissioned and dismantled within a few years. All of the concrete storage bunkers on its vast area had already been emptied, and most of them had been broken up and removed from the site. The result of this was that the number of guards permanently on duty at the depot had been reduced from around thirty to just six since there was no longer much to protect. Only the destruction plant itself now retained any of the weapon stockpiles in the form of JSX, and since this fact was a closely guarded military secret, only a small number of guards were now deemed necessary to ensure the safety of the site.

This was exactly the sort of weak spot that McKinnon had learned to exploit during his time as deputy commander of JSOC. Had this been a similar facility inside Iran or Syria, he would have exploited precisely this same weakness and used exactly the same tactics to assault the depot. Using a small but hard-hitting team, the plan was for his men to get in, acquire the JSX, and then get out again in less than half an hour. After that, they were to make their way back to the V-280, and Reeves and Irvine would then transport them and the chemical agent back to Texas.

Wearing their black tactical clothing and night vision goggles and carrying weapons and the backpacks containing their CBRN suits, they drove the ATVs down into a dried-out creek that ran south from the insertion point. Providing cover and allowing them to proceed out of view of the depot's cameras, the creek meandered south for almost two kilometres, and at its closest point, it was just three hundred metres from the destruction plant's fenced-off perimeter.

Several options for disabling the cameras along the perimeter fence had been considered. Long-range sniper fire and using an explosive charge to cut the video feed to the control room had both been ruled out due to the unacceptable levels of noise it would create. In the end, the decision had been made to use a drone to carry a small EMP device to a nexus in the plant's internal power grid. The localised electromagnetic pulse would fry the electronic components in the nexus' control management systems and leave the entire plant in the dark. Not even the backup generators would be able to compensate. The team could then move in and leverage their advantage in carrying night vision equipment.

After stopping at the bottom of the dried-out creek, they quickly donned their CBRN suits but left their masks attached to their belts.

'Ready the drone,' said Cormac, after the team had left their ATVs behind and climbed to the top of the creek where they went prone in the grass.

Tyler opened his backpack and extracted a small quadcopter. He then unwrapped and attached the EMP device, which was about the size of a large beer can. Then he placed the assembly on the ground in front of him, activated the controller and completed a quick diagnostic routine.

'Drone's ready to go,' he said, after a few seconds.

'Hit it,' said Cormac.

The drone took off, and using the 1st-person view from its camera beamed back to his phone, Tyler guided the drone low across the tall grass towards the fence, almost exactly between two of the security cameras mounted atop the fence posts. When it was about ten metres from the fence, he guided the drone up above the razor wire, and after a couple of seconds, it dropped back down and raced low over the ground towards the facility. Roughly two hundred metres later, Tyler guided it skilfully between two buildings, under a set of large pipes and through a gap to the electric power supply nexus near the centre of the plant. After allowing the drone to hover for a few seconds while he gently rotated it to get his bearings, Tyler slowly manoeuvred it up to a metal box containing the control unit for the local grid. Setting the drone down on top of the box, he glanced over at Cormac who gave him a quick nod. Then he pressed the button for the detonator.

Inside the power nexus, the EMP device activated, instantly producing an extremely powerful burst of electromagnetic waves across a broad spectrum of frequencies. Travelling at the speed of light, the spherical burst tore through everything within a range of several hundred metres, continuously losing intensity at an exponential rate as it travelled away from the device. Eventually, it would become almost undetectable, and in their current location, the Nightcrawler team was in no danger of their electronic devices being adversely affected. However, within metres of the device, all electronic components were instantly fried, rendered permanently disabled, and good for nothing more than to be thrown on the scrap heap.

Watching from the edge of the creek, the team saw a single bright white flash near the power nexus, and then the entire facility fell into complete darkness. As soon as that happened, Cormac got to his feet and his team followed.

'Let's move,' he said, and then they hurried back down to mount their ATVs.

A few seconds later, they were racing across the relatively even ground directly towards the fence. As soon as they got there, Knox and Willis jumped off their ATVs and ran up to the fence. Each of them using a spray can containing liquid nitrogen, they then began marking a circular pattern on the fence that was large enough for an ATV to fit through. Tyler fastened a steel wire to his ATV and sprinted up to the fence where he used a hook to attach the wire to the centre of the marked area. After a few seconds, the liquid nitrogen had cooled the marked pattern of the metal fence to roughly minus two hundred degrees Celsius, at which temperature most metals become weak and brittle.

Tyler hurried back to his vehicle, and as soon as Knox and Willis turned to give him the thumbs-up, he twisted the throttle, and the ATV leapt forward. With a muffled ringing sound, the steel wire went taut, and the marked section of the fence was then ripped from its surrounding area, creating a large hole for the team to pass through. The entire thing had taken about half a minute. Still wearing their night vision goggles and led by Cormac, the team filed through the hole and began covering the final two hundred metres to the plant's main building at high speeds. At that moment, the confused guards and other personnel that had been plunged into darkness inside the plant were completely oblivious to what had happened and to the violence that was about to unfold.

After less than a minute, the team arrived at a back entrance near a raised loading bay, and they quickly dismounted their ATVs and donned their CBRN masks. Then they lined up on either side of the door with Tyler kneeling next to it fixing an adhesive breaching charge. On Cormac's signal, the charge ripped the door off its hinges amid an ear-splitting boom that sent it cartwheeling into the loading area beyond.

The four operators filed swiftly inside the dark building and switched on the green laser pointers mounted under the barrels of their weapons. Their military-grade NVGs turned the pitch-black space into a detailed view displayed in front of their eyes in shades of green, and upon seeing three workers who had been trapped in the darkness near a forklift, they immediately opened fire on them with their suppressed weapons. A hail of bullets smacked into the hapless workers, who never stood a chance.

The Nightcrawlers then headed straight for a wide set of double doors on the opposite side of the large open space. Having studied the plant's internal layout, which they had acquired through McKinnon's intelligence unit hacking the construction company for the blueprints, they knew exactly where they were going. They also knew which areas could potentially be used by the guards as chokepoints.

With speed and aggression that had been honed by thousands of hours spent in kill houses running drills on dummy targets, the men pushed across the loading area and through the double doors, ready to engage any threat they might encounter. On the other side was a corridor some ten metres long and three metres wide. At the opposite end of it was an open area with a service elevator and a stairwell. However, there was also a steel door next to it that led to another corridor connecting to the administrative building, and as the Nightcrawler team advanced towards the elevator, the steel door suddenly opened and two guards appeared holding torches. They were wearing dark grey uniforms with white badges showing the Pueblo Chemical Weapons Depot's logo, and they both carried sidearms in holsters attached to their belts.

As the guards entered the corridor, their torches allowed them to see the terrifying sight of a team of armed special operators wearing NCGs and CBRN suits and moving directly towards them with their weapons up. Before either of the two guards even had time to reach for their firearms, the Nightcrawlers cut them down with submachinegun fire. As the guards dropped heavily to the floor in a heap, the team continued forward without any loss of momentum, and with the elevator having no power, they headed for the stairs.

After a short descent down to the plant's only sub-level, they found themselves in a lobby with another elevator door and a steel-framed glass door leading to a room beyond which there were a large number of painted metal storage racks. In each of the racks were dozens of compartments holding large artillery shells that were packed with the lethal JSX agent and which were waiting to be destroyed as soon as the bureaucratic impasse with South Korea had been resolved.

Next to the large racks, there was also a separate and smaller polished steel rack that held a number of cylindrical glass containers that were roughly fifteen centimetres tall and five centimetres wide. Inside them was a clear liquid, and they looked about as innocuous as a collection of drinking glasses filled with water. However, the liquid inside them was one of the most toxic chemical compounds ever developed, and exposure to even a tiny amount of the diabolical neurotoxin would ensure a quick but exceptionally painful death. Altogether, there was enough JSX in this storage rack to kill hundreds of thousands of people if the entire contents of the bunker were to be spread as an aerosol in a densely populated area.

The Nightcrawlers, however, were not here to acquire such a large amount of the toxin. All they needed to retrieve were two cylinders. One, which would be the primary delivery vehicle, and then a second cylinder that would serve as a backup in case something went wrong with the primary container.

Advancing swiftly with a set plan in mind, the team moved across the floor to the glass door where Knox extracted a diamond-tipped glass cutter from his backpack. Dragging the metal tool down along the entire edge of the glass pane next to the polished steel frame, he sliced a groove into the glass, which then allowed him to kick the whole pane in. It came free inside the room and fell to the floor where it shattered into thousands of pieces. This wasn't exactly the most elegant solution or one that the team was used to using when breaching a locked door, but for obvious reasons, they could not risk using explosives in this case.

Stepping through the gap into the storage bunker while the rest of the team took up defensive positions in the lobby area on the other side, Willis entered the bunker and headed for the cylinders. Thousands of small shards of broken glass crunched beneath his boots as he walked across the concrete floor, and when he reached the rack, he pulled a black miniature plastic case from a small pack strapped to his chest. Flicking the lock open, he placed it on a metal table next to the rack. Inside, fixed to the case and its lid, were two sheets of firm polyethylene foam. Each sheet had two cutouts whose shape and size corresponded perfectly to the dimensions of the small JSX containers.

'Take it easy,' said Cormac from the other side of the door. 'You've got your suit on, and we have plenty of time. 'So just relax.'

'Affirmative,' said Willis as he took a deep breath and a bead of sweat ran down his face inside his mask. 'Here goes nothing.'

He reached for the nearest cylinder, extracted it from its slot and placed it gently inside the first foam cutout. Then he repeated the exercise and secured the second cylinder.

'Got'em both,' he said with obvious relief as he closed the plastic case, snapped the lock, and placed the case back inside the pack on his chest.

'Good work,' said Cormac. 'Now, let's get the hell out of here.'

With Cormac in the lead, the team began moving back up the stairs when suddenly all of the lights came on. Momentarily disorientated by their NVGs being overloaded and displaying nothing but bright uniform green, the team ripped off their goggles and pushed upstairs.

'What the fuck is going on?' said Knox. 'They're not supposed to have power for at least another hour.'

'Must be some sort of shielded backup system,' said Cormac. 'Time to improvise. We need to clear the administrative building and shut down the whole system. On me.'

When the quartet arrived back up on the ground floor, they moved through the steel door and advanced along the corridor towards the door to the administrative building beyond. Pushing through it to arrive inside a large open-plan office, they were met almost instantly with gunfire from two guards taking cover behind an improvised barricade made from office furniture. Instead of taking cover, all four operators immediately opened fire and peppered the barricade with fully automatic fire from their submachine guns. The barrage of gunfire ripped through the furniture, shredding wood and fabric and felling both of the guards, who dropped lifeless to the floor. Knox moved swiftly to where they had fallen and shot them both in the head just to make sure.

Willis had been hit once during the exchange of fire, and the bullet had punctured his CBRN suit. However, the ballistic vest that they all wore underneath had stopped the projectile and absorbed most of the impact. He was going to end up with a large purple bruise, but it was infinitely better than the alternative.

'Everybody alright?' said Cormac, glancing at Willis.

'No hits,' said Knox.

'Same here,' said Tyler. 'Those guys can't shoot for shit.'

'All good,' said Willis, wincing. 'Vest stopped it.'

'OK,' said Cormac. 'Let's hit the control room.'

The team moved to the other side of the office, passed through an open doorway and along a corridor to a security centre packed with monitors that were normally showing live split-screen footage from all of the many security cameras spread throughout the depot. Now, however, most of them were merely displaying white noise, except for a handful of internal cameras that seemed to have survived the EMP blast. One of those cameras appeared to be mounted above the doorway immediately behind the team because they suddenly realised that a small square on one of the screens was showing a live image of themselves. Acting on instinct, Cormac turned, raised his weapon and fired once. The square on the screen now also displayed only white noise.

'We need to shut this whole damn thing down and leave nothing behind,' he said.

Suddenly, Willis gasped and buckled to his knees. Then he toppled over and began to produce violent choking noises. Watched by his stunned teammates, he groaned loudly and reached up to rip his mask off.

'Motherfucker,' swore Cormac as he looked down at Willis and suddenly realised what had happened. 'The bullet clipped the case. It must have broken one of the cylinders. Everybody out!'

Without a word, and with a panicked Willis looking up at them from the floor, the two others left the security centre while Cormac reached down to open the pack still strapped to Willis's chest and extract the black plastic case. As he had feared, the bullet that had been stopped by his colleague's ballistic vest had first punched through the pack holding the plastic case, shattering one of the cylinders containing the JSX. Soon after, the vapours would have crept through the small puncture in his CBRN suit and come into contact with his skin. The nerve agent was now travelling through Willis' body, causing a severe and irreversible neurotoxic reaction.

Willis was gasping painfully for air, and white foam was forming around his mouth as he tried in vain to speak. The veins on his forehead were pushed out, and his bloodshot eyes looked as if they were about to pop out of his head. As Cormac took a step back from his dying teammate, he opened the cracked case, removed the remaining intact cylinder, and tossed the case onto the floor behind Willis. Then he backed up and glanced over his shoulder.

Willis was now writhing on the floor, choking on his own foamy saliva, his skin was blistering at a terrifying rate, and he was in such agony that he was on the verge of passing out. His body then began to convulse in violent spasms that would soon cause him to break his own spine. Then would come the massive internal bleeding and the eventual shutdown of his heart, lungs and brain.

Cormac looked on with a bitter expression for a couple of seconds, and he knew exactly which way this was going. Clenching his jaw and producing a deep sigh inside his mask, he then pulled his suppressed SIG Sauer P320 pistol from its holster, pointed it at his team member's head and pulled the trigger. The bullet slammed into Willis' head and blew out the back of his skull, and almost instantly the former special operator went limp, except for a few remaining muscle spasms in his legs and neck.

'Thermite,' Cormac called, and without hesitation, Knox and Tyler extracted an M14 TH3 thermite grenade from their belts.

Cormac did the same, and all three men then pulled the pins and tossed the incendiary devices inside the security centre.

'So long, brother,' said Cormac darkly. 'I'll see you on the other side.'

Then he slammed the door shut and began moving away from the door. When the thermite grenades ignited, they didn't produce a large explosion. Instead, their contents of iron oxide and aluminium powder began to ignite and mix, which resulted in a powerful exothermic reaction. The TH3 grenades were not intended for use against infantry or other soft targets but instead had been designed to disable military materiel. Creating intense heat upwards of 2,500 degrees Celsius, they produced a molten metallic blob that was capable of melting right through an engine block or the breech of an artillery piece.

Soon after the three grenades had ignited, the security centre and all of the equipment set up inside it caught fire. Within minutes, that fire would erase all trace of the Nightcrawlers having been there, and they would also consume Willis's corpse, leaving no trace of him ever having been there. The small room quickly filled with thick smoke and blindingly bright light as the temperature soared and everything inside it ignited.

The remaining trio of operators retreated to the open-plan office where Cormac stopped to give the only order he could give at this moment.

'Decon!' he shouted from behind his mask.

Knox and Tyler immediately extracted several orange-coloured spray cans from their backpacks containing a highly effective VX-negating chemical compound. Without a word, the two men began spraying the remaining JSX glass cylinder that Cormac was now holding in his gloved hand. Once completed, they sprayed their team leader's entire CBRN suit and then proceeded to repeat the exercise on each other. This was far from an ideal way of removing the highly toxic nerve agent, but if done properly, the chemical compound in the cans would completely break down the VX agent and make it safe for them to eventually take off their suits.

'Echo 1. This is Voodoo 1,' said Cormac. 'Exfil. I say again. Exfil. Our ETA at the LZ is six minutes.'

Almost immediately, Reeves came back over the radio, and the three team members could hear the cockpit noise in the background.

'Voodoo 1, this is Echo 1,' he said. 'Good copy. Extraction in six minutes.'

Then Cormac swapped channels and spoke again.

'Alamo, this is Voodoo 1,' he said. 'Jackpot. I repeat. Jackpot. Over.'

'Copy jackpot,' said McKinnon.

'Voodoo 3 is down,' Cormac then said. 'We had to leave him. We are now RTB.'

After a brief pause, McKinnon's baritone voice came back, and the general sounded grave but calm.

'Voodoo 1. I copy your last,' he said sombrely after a brief pause. 'Come on home, boys.'

EIGHTEEN

Two hours after his final communication with the Nightcrawler team, McKinnon watched from his first-floor office as the V-280 landed on the pad at Stonewall Ranch. When the engines had spun down and the rear cargo hold doors opened, only three men walked out. Cormac, followed by Knox and Tyler, and he could tell from the way they carried themselves that the loss of their brother weighed heavily on them.

McKinnon clenched his jaw, reminding himself that in wars, people die. What mattered was that the team had completed the mission, and the final piece of the grand plan could now be placed on the board. Just one final step to go, and they would all be making history. He was about to head down to meet the men when there was a familiar knock on the door, and Cobb appeared.

'Sir,' he said, looking concerned. 'I think we've got a problem.'

'I know,' said McKinnon slightly irritably. 'I was the one who talked to Cormac, remember?'

'Yes, sir,' said Cobb. 'But that's not what I meant. There's something else.'

'What?' said McKinnon, turning to face his number two.

'Thornton has gone AWOL,' said Cobb. 'I told him to shadow the Brit and step in if he started digging, and I haven't heard from him since last night. He called in to say that he was following Sterling, who looked like he was heading for Cooper's apartment. Not a word since. Something's not right.'

McKinnon tilted his head slightly to one side and narrowed his eyes.

'I'm starting to feel like we have a rat in the house,' he said in a slow drawl as he gave Cobb a dark look and then sucked his teeth. 'I need you to get on this, Cobb.'

'I'll get some of the guys together,' Cobb said.

'Yeah,' said McKinnon broodingly. 'You do that. I am losing patience with that son of a bitch. We've got to take him out before he does some real damage. We can't afford any hiccups this late in the game. Do you understand?'

'Yes, sir,' said Cobb. 'I'll take care of it.'

★   ★   ★

The next morning, Andrew awoke with a knot in his stomach as he realised that he was going to have to tell Scarlett what he and Donna had discovered out in the desert the previous evening. She clearly had strong feelings for Barton, and Andrew couldn't help the sense that, with her good-natured and sparkly personality, Scarlett would have been a very good match for his friend. Perhaps someone for him to finally settle down with after a fast-paced and often chaotic life. But now none of that was going to happen.

Andrew was getting dressed when there was a knock on the door. The sheer curtains were drawn, allowing him to see out, but they made it difficult for anyone outside to see in, especially when it was a sunny day like today. He grabbed his Beretta and moved silently to stand close to the bed's headboard, and this allowed him to peer out through the window and see who was there. It was the young man from the motel's reception.

Tucking the pistol into the small of his back and pulling his shirt down over it, he walked to the door and opened it.

'Morning, sir,' said the desk clerk, extending a hand in which he was holding an envelope with Andrew's name handwritten across the front. 'This came for you. It was shoved under the door to the reception. I guess whoever delivered it wasn't sure which room you were in.'

'Thanks,' said Andrew, taking the envelope and looking at it. 'Any idea who it is from?'

'Nope,' said the youth. 'Our cameras don't work.'

'That's reassuring,' said Andrew, looking at the young man with a raised eyebrow.

'Hey, like I said, man,' said the youth, shrugging as he began to walk back towards the reception. 'I only work here. Have a nice day.'

Andrew closed the door and sat down on the bed. He ripped open the envelope, pulled out a small folded sheet of paper and read the short message.

"Please meet me at the football stadium at noon. It's important. Scarlett."

Andrew looked at the note and re-read it. He hadn't noticed a football stadium, but then he hadn't yet explored all of Revelation. After a quick online search, he discovered that the stadium was on the northern edge of town. It was near what used to be the local train station before it had been shut down, as had happened in so many other small towns across the central and western United States over the past half-century. Judging by the handful of pictures he could find of it, it was relatively small with a limited capacity in the stands, but it was probably about the right size for a town like this.

As he inspected the images, a message from Fiona arrived on his phone asking if he could speak, and he called her back immediately.

'Hey, Sweetie,' he said. 'How are you?'

'Good,' she said brightly. 'I've found out something interesting about your General McKinnon. Are you alright? You sound a bit down.'

'Well, I'd be lying if I said yes, unfortunately,' he sighed.

'What do you mean?' she said.

Leaving out the most gory details, he then went on to tell her about his grisly find in the shallow grave in the desert, and about how he was now about to go and break the news to Barton's girlfriend.

'Oh no,' Fiona said, faintly. 'I'm so sorry. I know you two went back a long way. Are you OK?'

'I will be, once this is settled,' said Andrew.

'Andrew,' she said, suddenly serious. 'I know you. You're not going to let this lie, are you? You're going to get yourself involved.'

'I have to,' he said, closing his eyes and rubbing his forehead. 'What happened here can't be allowed to stand.'

'But what about the police?' she asked.

'Not a chance,' he said bitterly. 'They're as bent as a boomerang. 'Either I do this, or it won't get done.'

'Alright,' said Fiona after a brief pause. 'I believe you. Just promise me you will be really careful. This whole situation sounds like it has all the potential to blow up like a landmine if you take a wrong step.'

Andrew was tempted to tell her just how accurate her metaphor was, but he refrained. There was no sense in making her too worried by telling her just how much danger he might end up putting himself in. But the reality was that he simply had no choice. This was something he had to do because no one else would.

'I'll be careful,' he said. 'I want to see you again soon. Please just trust me when I say that I need to do this.'

'I trust you,' Fiona said.

'What was it you needed to tell me?' he asked.

'Oh,' she said. 'This McKinnon character. I managed to pull a favour from someone who happens to know a professor of modern American history at Georgetown University in Washington D.C. She has written several papers on the political leanings of the descendants of important historical figures from the American Civil War. It turns out that people's political views are a lot more captive to their family history than they might think. Anyway, she was able to provide the complete history and family tree of Thomas 'Stonewall' Jackson's descendants, and General McKinnon doesn't show up anywhere.'

'So, he made it all up?' said Andrew.

'Either that or whoever looked into it for him made a mistake,' she said. 'Or maybe they just told him what he wanted to hear.'

'Well, he seemed very enamoured with the idea,' said Andrew. 'It's part of his whole spiel about patriotism, honour and duty. That sort of thing. I suspect he has decided to believe it, regardless of what the facts might be. And I am sure it makes his men respect him even more.'

'You're probably right,' said Fiona. 'If they're all a bunch of Confederacy-loving revanchists, then this would be a great hook for General McKinnon to cultivate loyalty towards himself.'

'Exactly,' said Andrew. 'Thanks for this, Fiona. I appreciate it.'

'That's no problem,' she said softly. 'Whatever you need. Just... come home safe, OK?'

'I will,' he said, hoping he wasn't about to make a liar of himself. 'This will all be over soon.'

★   ★   ★

At five minutes to noon, Andrew parked his Jeep in the modest local football stadium's parking lot on the outskirts of town. Aside from his vehicle, the parking lot was completely empty. On the way from the motel, he had done his best to make sure he wasn't being followed, and there had been no sign of anyone tailing him. However, this didn't make him feel much better since he was slowly coming to the uncomfortable conclusion that General McKinnon seemed to have eyes and ears everywhere in Revelation.

When he got out of the car and looked around, all was quiet. He proceeded to walk towards the tiered white-painted wooden stands that wrapped around the football field, heading for a gap in the stands that allowed free access to the 120-yard-long playing field. Stepping onto the field near the central 50-yard line that divided the two halves, he spotted Scarlett sitting on the opposite stand under the large, black electronic scoreboard. She was wearing light-coloured jeans, trainers and a white t-shirt, as well as her Longhorns cap over her blond hair. When she saw him, she gave him a quick wave. Walking across the pitch towards her, Andrew began to feel weighed down by what he would now have to tell her.

'Hi Andy,' she said.

As he walked silently up the aisle of the tiered stand and sat down heavily next to her, his body language and demeanour must have given his mood away, because she gave him a puzzled look.

'What's going on?' she said. 'What's wrong?'

Mustering what mental fortitude he could while also trying as much as possible to control his own emotions about what had happened, he then went on to tell Scarlett why she would never see Eddie Barton again. He conveyed as much detail as he felt was necessary to allow her to understand what had happened, but kept enough back to make sure she wouldn't end up tortured by mental images of Barton's last moments far into the future.

Her reaction was nothing more and nothing less than what he would have expected from anyone else in her position. Shock, despair and anger, followed by a desire to curl up and disappear from the world. As she eventually buried her head in her hands and sobbed quietly, he put an arm gently around her and just sat there silently with her for several minutes, allowing her to begin to process the harrowing news.

'Do you think he knew?' she finally asked, her voice weak, almost like a whisper. 'That they were going to kill him?'

'I really don't know,' said Andrew bitterly. 'It's possible. I mean, why else take him out into the desert like that. What I'm trying to say is that he might have known what was coming.'

'I hope they didn't make him dig his own grave,' she said faintly, shaking her head and closing her eyes. 'That would be so awful and callous.'

Andrew said nothing, but despite hoping that he was wrong, he suspected that this was probably exactly what had happened.

'We're not going to let them get away with this,' he eventually said with cold determination in his voice. 'We'll make sure of that.'

'How?' Scarlett asked, looking up at him with red tearful eyes.

'I assume you know Donna Cooper?' said Andrew.

'Of course,' she said. 'Everybody knows Donna. Wait, are you saying...?'

Andrew nodded as he watched the puzzle pieces fall into place inside Scarlett's mind.

'Are you saying those bastards killed Billy Ray too?' she said, aghast.

'It looks like Billy Ray followed them out into the desert,' Andrew said. 'Probably saw the whole thing. And they killed him for it.'

'Oh God,' Scarlett breathed. 'They're animals.'

'Donna and I are working to find out exactly what happened and who did what,' said Andrew. 'And when we do, we're going to make things right. No police. No Hogan. No state troopers. Nothing. We're going to put an end to McKinnon and his rabid dogs.'

'If you did,' said Scarlett, 'it would be the best thing that had happened to this town for a long time.'

'We'll definitely try,' said Andrew. 'But we'll need as much help as we can get. Donna told me that her uncle Emmett might be able to provide some assistance. We're going to go and meet him later today.'

'I've met Emmett,' said Scarlett. 'He's no fool. And he ain't no pushover either. You really don't want to end up on the wrong side of him.'

'Good,' said Andrew. 'I'm glad to hear it. Things might get rough. In fact, I am sure they will. But I think I have a plan that could work. Anyway, why did you want to meet up? You said it was important.'

Scarlett nodded and turned her eyes up towards the sky as if trying to focus her mind after the shock and pain of being told about Barton's death. She reached into the back pocket of her jeans and produced a small, black foldable smartphone.

'This is Eddie's phone,' she said, before correcting herself and looking downcast. 'I mean, this was Eddie's phone. I found it inside his personal bunk room out at the ranch. I snuck in there when no one was looking. All the Tier 1 operators have a room like that, and they are pretty cosy. It's a private space for them to chill out and sleep. Anyway, they had cleared out the whole place, including all of his personal items, but this had fallen down the back of a storage trunk sitting by a wall.'

'How did you manage to find it?' asked Andrew.

'I tried calling him,' she said. 'He didn't pick up, but then I realised that I could hear it ringing from out in the bar. Some silly recording of a dog barking. I'd recognise that stupid sound anywhere. I walked into the corridor with the bunk rooms on one side, and that's when I knew that it was still inside his room.'

She flipped it open, powered it on and handed it to Andrew.

'I can't get in, though,' she said. 'It's protected by a password.'

Andrew took the phone in his hands, holding it quietly for a moment while reflecting on how until just a few days ago this had been Barton's phone. The display was black, except for a horizontal box urging him to enter a password. Beneath it was a circle with a stylised image of a fingerprint inside it. The latter option would also unlock the phone, but Andrew couldn't stomach the idea of driving back out to the desert to dig up his dead friend one more time.

'Any ideas?' asked Scarlett.

Andrew shook his head as he pondered what Barton might have picked as his password, but nothing came to mind. As he did so, the display eventually timed out and switched itself off again.

'Did you say the ringtone was a barking dog?' he asked.

'Yes,' said Scarlett. 'You want to hear it?'

She extracted a small pink smartphone from her pocket and swiped her way to her contacts. Then she called Barton's phone. When it came alive again and the sound of a dog barking began emanating from its tiny speaker, Andrew suddenly felt as if a portal through time and space had opened behind him and that he was being pulled backwards through it. Back to a place where the sound of that particular dog fit in perfectly. The FOB in Mali. This was the bark of Asbo, the German Shepherd that Barton had taken under his wing all those years ago. Barton had evidently kept the recording of the dog's bark and used it as his ringtone.

'I know what the password is,' he said as he began typing. 'It's the name of a dog Barton made friends with. He was a little rascal, but Barton loved him.'

When he had finished typing, the password screen disappeared, and a display full of Barton's various apps sprang into view.

'Wow,' said Scarlett, leaning over to look. 'That all looks normal. I don't think this has been tampered with.'

'There has got to be something here,' said Andrew. 'Something that can give us some answers. If Barton had things playing on his mind, I am sure he would have written something down. He was a lot more thoughtful than most people gave him credit for.'

'I know,' said Scarlett softly. 'Try his files. Pictures. Voice notes. That might give us something.'

Andrew tapped the 'Files' icon, and a menu of items appeared. He selected images, and together, he and Scarlett went through all of them over the course of several minutes. Most of them were scenery shots from various places in the high desert. It was clear that Barton had enjoyed hiking on his own. There were also several shots of various weapons laid out at a shooting range that looked to be somewhere at the Stonewall Ranch. Then there were photos of him with some of the other ex-military operators from the ranch, including one in which Andrew recognised the Viking and the guy with the neck tattoo that Barton had ended up killing in the alley behind the High Jinx Tavern. Another image showed him inside a different bar in a group that included both Tatum and Thornton. Thornton was now lying dead under a mound of rocks, but Tatum was still out there, most likely having put two and two together and now eager for revenge. Everyone in the photo was grinning and raising pitchers of beer. Seeing his dead friend smiling alongside the two men who might well have been responsible for his death made Andrew sick to his stomach, but he decided to keep it to himself for now.

'See if there are any hidden folders,' said Scarlett.

Andrew tapped a small menu in the top right and unchecked the 'Hide folders' option, and immediately a new folder appeared. It was named 'Pete Tong'.

'Who is Pete?' said Scarlett.

'It's not a person,' said Andrew, looking down at the folder icon. 'Pete Tong is slang for 'wrong'. It's a UK thing. Don't try to make sense of it. Anyway, he clearly put something in here that he thought was messed up somehow. Let's have a look.'

He tapped the icon, and the folder opened to reveal a single video file titled 'Scarlett'. Its thumbnail was an image of Barton's face with his mouth half open, as if he were in the middle of speaking. Andrew and Scarlett looked briefly at each other.

'Are you ready for this?' he asked her.

'Yes,' she nodded bravely. 'I want to know. I need to know.'

'Alright,' said Andrew. 'Let's see what this is about.'

He pressed 'Play', and the video began playing. It showed Barton inside what Andrew assumed was his bunk room at the ranch, and Andrew felt a shiver run down his spine as he saw his friend's face and heard his voice. Wearing a black t-shirt and a short-trimmed blond beard, he was sitting on his bed, cradling the phone in both hands as he made the recording, and his face looked troubled and tired. When he began speaking, his voice was low and quiet. He sounded uncharacteristically uneasy, and his Yorkshire dialect had now taken on a slight American twang.

'Hey Babe. I really hope I won't ever have to send this message. But if you're seeing this, then I guess things have gone tits up. I'm not sure how to say this, but I think I'm in trouble here. Let me try to explain. I've told you that I am in McKinnon's group of Tier 1 operators. We've been doing all kinds of stuff all over the world, and some of it I'm not proud of. But I figured it was time for me to finally make some serious money, and as you know, McKinnon pays his operators well.

Anyway, I thought I was just going to coast along for a few years, and then maybe you and I could retire somewhere quiet and enjoy life, but I've got to tell you now, I need to get out. I can't be a part of what McKinnon is planning, and I am starting to think that the man's not all there. He's clearly suffering from delusions of grandeur. And as you know better than anyone, he has hired a whole bunch of racist redneck conspiracy theorists who seem to loathe what they think is the Deep State. They all believe that Congress and the President have abandoned them and that the country is heading for self-destruction unless true patriots like them step up and act.

Now, I thought that this was all BS and that they were just grandstanding, but I was wrong. They fucking mean it, and McKinnon has convinced them that the only solution here is a clean slate. Some sort of shock to the system that will finally make the politicians realise why they are in Washington. I don't know what it is, but there are some missions coming up that I just can't justify to myself. In a couple of days, McKinnon wants us to hit a gold bullion transport in the Port of Galveston, and the plan is to leave no one alive. And there's another one lined up for something up in Colorado. Some sort of military installation. And then there is what he calls "the big one".

Again, I don't know what that means exactly, but Cobb and Cormac seem to know, and I've overheard them talking about it using words like "the attack" and talking about some sort of device. Whatever it is, it's fucking crazy, and I won't do it. So, I need to find a way out of this damn mess. But I can't just walk away. With what I know, they won't let me leave just like that. I need some sort of leverage to make sure McKinnon leaves me the hell alone when I break it to him. I am still trying to work out how to spin this. Anyway, I've been babbling on enough now. And if you see this, then please get hold of the police or the FBI. I might be alright, but I might not be. I'm hoping for the best. And I hope to see you again soon. Bye.'

The recording ended, and Andrew and Scarlett both sat in stunned silence for several moments as they tried to take in what Barton had said. Andrew was also reminded of the news stories about the hit in Galveston. Next to him, Scarlett sniffed as a single glistening tear moved slowly down her cheek.

'I guess he was never able to send that message,' said Andrew as he turned to look at her. 'Are you OK?'

Scarlett nodded bravely and sniffed again, but said nothing in reply.

'This thing is much bigger and much worse than I thought,' said Andrew, returning his gaze to the phone. 'McKinnon was responsible for that hit on the Galveston gold transport. And from the sounds of it, he's planning some sort of attack on Washington D.C.'

'That thing in Colorado,' said Scarlett suddenly. 'That was McKinnon too.'

'What thing?' said Andrew. 'I haven't seen any news about that.'

'There was an attack on an army depot in Pueblo,' said Scarlett. 'Some kind of chemical weapons facility. Several dead guards and a big fire. The whole area is locked down.'

'Shit,' said Andrew, pondering the news for a moment. 'Were they after some kind of chemical weapon for their attack? Are they actually that crazy?'

Scarlett shook her head and pressed her lips together.

'Look,' she said. 'I have seen enough of McKinnon to think that he just might be prepared to do something like this. Working in his private bar, you overhear things. He's always going on about how the country is falling apart and how the politicians in Washington should all be lined up and shot at dawn. That type of thing. But I never thought he was actually going to try something like this.'

'Well,' said Andrew. 'For the moment, we only have Barton's words for it, and he's not here anymore. We can't go to the FBI with this, regardless of how serious it might sound. They're not going to take us seriously. Not for one minute. This is something we have to try to deal with ourselves, at least for now. Barton might have been right about the gold transport but wrong about an attack in Washington. We just don't know. But that doesn't change the fact that they killed him. And I want to make them pay. For Barton and for Billy Ray.'

'Alright,' said Scarlett. 'So, what are we going to do now?'

'I think you should go back to the ranch and behave as normal,' said Andrew. 'But try to listen out for conversations that can give us more information. Maybe even try to record it if you can. Eventually, we're going to need evidence if we want to involve the authorities.'

'OK,' said Scarlett, visibly steeling herself. 'I'll go back there.'

'But if you start to feel that you're not safe there,' said Andrew, 'then simply leave. Make up an excuse. And then I'll meet you in town. Alright?'

'Thank you,' said Scarlett, looking up at the sky. 'Let's swap numbers. And if there's anything I can do, then just call me, OK? I mean it.'

'I will keep that in mind,' said Andrew. 'I can already think of something I might need your help with.'

NINETEEN

Around mid-afternoon, Andrew picked Donna up from a bus stop close to Main Street. Beginning to realise the danger she might be in, she had asked for Andrew to avoid coming to her home for now, and she had instead walked to the bus stop and waited for him there. Once inside the car, she directed him out of town and north along a winding country road through some low hills towards Emmett Cooper's homestead. As they drove, Andrew recounted his meeting with Scarlett and told her about what they had found on Barton's phone.

'So, that's what they were trying to hide,' said Donna glumly, looking down at her hands which lay clasped in her lap. 'That's why they killed your friend, and that's why my brother was murdered. To cover everything up and prevent anyone from stopping what they're planning to do.'

'It seems that way,' said Andrew. 'With an operation of this scale, I don't imagine there's anything McKinnon isn't prepared to do to stop people from interfering.'

Gripping the steering wheel and gazing out through the windscreen at the sunbaked road ahead for a moment, he then gave a small shake of the head.

'I thought McKinnon was a bit eccentric when I first met him,' he eventually said, 'but now I realise how wrong I was. He's not just eccentric. He's completely out of his mind.'

'Yeah,' said Donna. 'I think the word you're looking for is 'batshit crazy'. A psychopath who doesn't care about anyone but himself. Makes me wonder how he managed to get his men to be so loyal.'

'Some men need someone to follow,' said Andrew. 'Someone to look up to and to try to emulate. They feel better in this world if they can believe that there's someone else who has all the answers and who knows what to do. So, for all the swagger and musclebound roughness of Stonewall Ranch, what you're really looking at is just a bunch of little boys with guns looking up to a slightly older boy with a gun. And when he says 'jump', they all jump. And if he tells them that they need to jump because they are serving a higher purpose, they jump even higher. It's been that way since the dawn of time. And I don't imagine that will ever change.'

'It's so pathetic,' said Donna in a voice laced with derision. 'And it's really scary that these men are so easy to manipulate.'

'I agree,' said Andrew. 'But that appears to be the nature of things. Anyway, I think that we might be able to exploit it somehow. You see, the thing about military organisations and PMCs like Ironclad Tactical is that they operate within very well-defined rules, and that makes them predictable. We should be able to use that against them.'

'Right,' said Donna, glancing at him. 'Well, that's definitely not my wheelhouse, so I will leave that part to you and Emmett. I think I told you he was an Army Ranger once upon a time. So, if you two can get inside the heads of McKinnon and his gang of thugs, then we might have a chance of doing something about them. Turn left up here by that mailbox.'

Donna pointed ahead to a rusty, domed rectangular red flag mailbox sitting on a leaning wooden post. It had no name or house number on it, but a small dirt track led away from it through the dry scrubland. In the distance about three hundred metres away, were a couple of buildings nestled amongst a cluster of low and parched-looking mesquite trees. As they drove nearer along the dusty track, it became apparent that the plot was surrounded by wire fencing and that a few heads of cattle and a handful of sheep were grazing inside a couple of enclosures.

Andrew parked under a tree about twenty metres from Emmett's house. It was a slightly ramshackle, single-storey farmhouse built from wood beams and rendered bricks. Its low-pitched and mildly uneven roof was clad with asphalt shingles, and it extended out over a raised porch that was held up by wide exposed wood beams, and it wrapped around the two sides of the house that faced south. Near the corner of the porch were a small wooden table and a rocking chair. Protruding from the roof directly over the unpainted front door was a gabled dormer with a small casement window, indicating that there was a modest, low-ceilinged room up under the roof. Hugging the exterior wall at one end of the structure was a stone chimney that extended above the roof's ridge, from which rose a thin column of grey smoke.

Next to the house was a dark brown barn with a lean-to facing away from it. It had a gambrel roof and a couple of small windows, and one of the large barn doors was slightly ajar. Behind the barn and off to one side was a smaller shed, and in front of it near a couple of oil barrels was parked a Ford pickup truck. Once upon a time, the truck appeared to have been white, but it was now almost covered in pale orange dust and dirt, especially around the wheel wells.

'Well,' said Donna. 'He's home.'

'Interesting place,' said Andrew as he killed the engine, and the two of them sat for a moment looking out of the windscreen. 'Rustic, is probably how a real estate agent would describe it.'

For the first time in days, Andrew heard Donna chuckle, and he found himself feeling a sense of relief. As if some of the dark clouds that had hung over them were perhaps beginning to lift. He glanced at her with a lopsided smile.

'Come on,' he said. 'Let's go meet your uncle.'

The two of them stepped out of the Jeep into the sun and began walking slowly towards the house across the dry compacted dirt. As they looked around, there was no sign of life anywhere, except for the cattle and the sheep. Andrew would have expected someone like Emmett to have a guard dog, but the only sound he could hear was the faint and regular metallic squeak of a small multi-bladed windmill sitting atop a metal tower about thirty metres behind the house.

'He might be in the barn,' said Donna, gesturing towards the open barn door. 'Let's have a look.'

Donna led the way into the relatively dark space whose floor was strewn with dry bits of hay, and whose many wooden rafters were adorned with a large collection of handheld farm tools, ropes and chains as well as various metal parts for engines, all organised according to some system that no doubt only made sense to Emmett. The air was dry and it smelled of dust and petroleum. In the middle of the barn was a small rusty tractor that appeared to be at least as old as Andrew and whose engine had been partially disassembled with its nuts and bolts and components lying in an oily metal tray on the floor next to it.

'Emmett's always busy fixing something,' said Donna as she stepped past the tractor towards the back of the barn.

Andrew ambled slowly inside with his hands in his pockets, looking around the space as a couple of birds fluttered from one rafter to another up under the roof.

'It's empty,' said Andrew. 'I guess he's not here.'

'Oh, I'm here alright,' came a deep and gruff voice from the barn door in an accent that was about as Texan as anything Andrew was ever going to hear. 'Don't move a damn muscle.'

Turning his head slightly to one side, Andrew could see the shadow of a large man stretching across the floor, and he appeared to be holding a stocky, short-barrelled weapon.

'Now, let me see those hands,' commanded the voice as Donna hurried back from the back of the barn. 'Drop the piece. I can see it under that shirt of yours. And don't you try nothing neither.'

Andrew said nothing as he raised his hands slowly above his head.

'Emmett, it's me!' called Donna, rushing forward. 'It's alright. This is Andrew. I brought him here.'

'Oh yeah?' said Emmett sceptically. 'What for? And who is he anyway?'

'He's a friend, Emmett,' she said, emerging from the back of the barn. 'Now lower the damn shotgun.'

After a brief pause, Donna's uncle did as she had asked, and Andrew slowly brought his hands back down to turn around and face their mercurial host.

Of average height but with a powerful and stocky build, Emmett looked to be about sixty years old. However, it was difficult to tell because of his leathery and weatherbeaten face. His neck was almost as thick as his thighs, and he had a strong wide jaw, a short and scraggy grey beard, and his narrow eyes had permanent wrinkles around them in a testament to him most likely having spent his entire life outside squinting under the glaring Texas sun. On his head was a grimy and heavily worn beige Stetson hat, and in his hands was a sawn-off shotgun.

'Hello, Mr Cooper,' said Andrew. 'My name is Andrew Sterling. Sorry to just walk inside your barn like this. We thought you might be in here.'

'Well, I wasn't,' said Emmett, adjusting his hat. 'And it's just Emmett. You're lucky I didn't blow you to kingdom come, son. What's going on here, Donna? Why is this man here?'

'It's about Billy Ray,' said Donna earnestly. 'Andrew has helped me look into it, and we're convinced he didn't take his own life.'

At that, Emmett narrowed his eyes even further for a moment, and then he broke open the breech of the shotgun and gave a brief nod.

'Damn straight, he didn't,' he said with an air of thinking himself vindicated. 'I never believed that for a second. Now, I think we best go inside. Follow me.'

Emmett led them across the yard to the main house and pushed through the front door. The interior was sparsely furnished, but despite the outdated décor, it looked much cleaner and tidier than Andrew had expected.

'Come on in and sit down,' said Emmett, gesturing to an unvarnished wooden dining table with four chairs arranged around it. 'I'll get us something to drink.'

Andrew and Donna sat down while Emmett went to rummage around in a cupboard, coming back with a bottle of whiskey and three tumblers.

'I apologise for pulling a gun on you,' said Emmett as he poured, filling all three tumblers to the brim.

'No problem,' said Andrew.

'I didn't recognise the car, see?' continued Emmett, setting the bottle down on the table and placing his hat next to it. 'And I ain't one for allowing trespassers onto my land. Some buckshot usually does the trick, although it's been a while since I've had to kick someone off my property. I guess I've got a reputation by now. Nobody comes around unless I ask them to, and I never do. Donna here comes to visit every so often, but that's about it.'

'Do you ever get lonely out here?' said Andrew, happy to engage in some small talk and get the measure of the man.

'Are you kidding me?' said Emmett with a chuckle. 'No, I like it out here by myself. Like a famous man once said, *"Hell is other people"*. I think that might have been Groucho Marx.'

'I'm pretty sure that was Jean-Paul Sartre,' smiled Donna. 'French philosopher.'

Emmett was raising his tumbler to his mouth when he stopped mid-motion and turned his head to look at her, creases slowly forming on his forehead.

'French, huh?' he said as if someone had just offered him a major insight into the workings of the universe, and then he shrugged. 'Well, I guess they ain't all bad.'

He then downed his drink, smacked his lips and poured himself another.

'My condolences about Billy Ray,' said Andrew sincerely.

'Yeah, he was a good boy,' said Emmett darkly after a long pause. 'Could have run for mayor, if you ask me. Would have won too. And the town ought to have been grateful. Damn waste of a fine young man.'

Donna looked pained as she lowered her gaze to her hands which were folded on the table in front of her. Emmett then leaned forward, reached across to her and closed his large calloused right hand gently around hers.

'I'm so sorry, Darling,' he said. 'It wasn't his time to go. And as you know, I never believed that he would have taken his own life. Not in a million years.'

'I know,' Donna nodded quietly.

'That's why we're here,' said Andrew. 'We don't believe it either. In fact, we're convinced that there was foul play involved.'

Emmett took another sip, placed the tumbler back on the table and leaned back in his chair. Then he folded his arms across his wide chest and looked at the two of them.

'Tell me everything,' he said.

Andrew and Donna then took turns explaining everything they had found out, including all the details about Billy Ray's apartment, the attack on Andrew, Eddie Barton's death and the video on his phone, McKinnon's apparent plans and Hogan's complicity in the whole thing. By the end of it, Emmett shifted in his seat and gave a slight shake of the head.

'I always said Elijah Hogan was a good-for-nothing son of a bitch,' said Emmett resolutely as he glanced at Donna. 'Didn't I always say that, Donna?'

'Yes, you sure did, Emmett,' she replied. 'More than once.'

'Damn right, I did,' said Emmett, sucking his teeth. 'That motherfucker. I even tried to talk Billy Ray out of joining the police and working for him. But Billy Ray wouldn't listen. He was stubborn, God rest his soul.'

'Donna told me there are some bad feelings between you and the sheriff,' said Andrew.

'Bad feelings,' grunted Emmett. 'You might call it that. I can't believe he was ever elected. But I guess if you can get McKinnon to pay for your campaign, then anything is possible in a place like this. And now, McKinnon owns his ass. Hogan will do whatever the general tells him to do. You better believe it.'

'I've had the pleasure of Hogan's company a couple of times myself,' said Andrew. 'He's slippery, and I think he is helping to cover up my friend's murder.'

'I don't doubt it for a minute,' said Emmett resolutely. 'Hogan talks a good game as sheriff, but that bastard is so full of shit, if you buried him in the ground, you could get the county to class him as a septic tank.'

'Well, he certainly appears to have sold out to McKinnon,' said Andrew. 'And it seems to me that McKinnon is dangerously deluded. The way he talks about the history of this country and that of his own family just seems detached from reality. Honestly, I think he is capable of just about anything, including what Barton seemed to be suggesting.'

'I couldn't agree more,' said Emmett, nodding. 'You've got his number, son. But there's a lot more to those two than meets the eye. A lot of history that goes back to before any of them two was even born.'

'What do you mean?' said Andrew as Donna glanced up to regard her uncle with a puzzled look.

'Well,' said Emmett. 'I've spent some time in the local town archives. And I found out some stuff that certain people would like everyone to forget about.'

'Like what?' said Donna.

'Like the fact that the granddaddies of both McKinnon and Hogan were Klansmen right here in Texas a long time ago,' Emmett said, downing another glass of whiskey.

'You mean the Ku Klux Clan?' said Andrew.

'Yup,' said Emmett. 'The one and only KKK.'

'You never told me any of that,' said Donna, looking surprised. 'Why not?'

'No sense digging up the past if you don't need to, I suppose,' said Emmett. 'But I found myself taking an interest in the history of this town, and that's when I came across a list of Klansmen that had the name Hogan on it. Didn't take long to verify precisely who that was. Not long after, I discovered the same about McKinnon. And wouldn't you know it, the name Meeks was on there too.'

'Meeks as well?' said Donna, her mouth falling open.

'That's right,' said Emmett. 'Their ancestors were all part of that merry band of thugs together.'

'So, those guys are not just working together out of convenience,' said Andrew as he leaned forward. 'They're not just scratching each other's backs. It goes much deeper than that.'

'That's right,' said Emmett. 'Their family ties go way back to a time when they were fighting side by side for a cause that many people today would like to pretend never existed. But it happened right here in Texas and across pretty much all of the southern states.'

'But wasn't it a pretty marginal movement?' said Andrew. 'I thought it was only ever on the fringes of politics.'

'Hell no!' Emmett exclaimed. 'Sure, the Klan started out small in the defeated South just after the Civil War. But then it grew in power until it had helped restore white rule in states like North Carolina, Tennessee, and Georgia. It had its day here in Texas too.'

'I'm not really familiar with the details of that history,' said Andrew. 'What do you mean by "restore white rule"?'

Emmett picked up the whiskey bottle and topped up their tumblers.

'After the American Civil War,' he said, 'the federal government initiated the so-called Reconstruction effort. The aim was to rebuild the economies of the South and to give civil rights to the black former slaves. So, in a state like North Carolina, for example, this meant that state power went to both black and white officials. Now, as you can imagine, a lot of white folks resented that, especially after having been humiliated in the Civil War by armies that also included black soldiers. So, groups like the Ku Klux Klan sprang up, and they started terrorising the black population.'

'That I do know about,' said Andrew.

'Oh, it gets a lot worse,' said Emmett. 'See, they basically did all they could to try to suppress black votes during the elections. They engaged in voter intimidation and a lot of violence that was often carried out at night with these assholes wearing their stupid white sheets just to scare people. Anyways, the Klan eventually helped the whites take back control of the state legislature of North Carolina by the late 1870s. And the same thing happened across much of the South. Then, over the following decades came what's known as the Jim Crow laws. These were a bunch of laws designed to marginalise and disenfranchise the black population, and laws were pushed through that introduced racial segregation throughout society. This went on for almost another century until the 1950s when those laws were finally dismantled.'

'I had no idea it was that organised,' said Andrew.

'Oh, you'd be surprised,' said Emmett, getting up from his seat and walking to a bookshelf where he extracted a book about the history of the United States. 'And it went right to the top of this country for many decades. Listen to this quote. "*The white men were roused by a mere instinct of self-preservation, until at last there had sprung into existence a great Ku Klux Klan. A veritable empire of the South to protect the southern country*".'

'That's nice,' said Donna sarcastically.

'But who do you think might have written those words?' said Emmett conspiratorially as he sat back down.

'Some kind of head of the Klan?' she said. 'One of those grand wizards, or whatever silly names they run around calling themselves.'

'Nope,' said Emmett. 'Those words are from a book called 'A History of The American People'. It was written in 1902 by Woodrow Wilson, eight years before he became the 28th president of the United States.'

'Are you serious?' said Donna. 'The president?'

'Absolutely,' said Emmett. 'There was a major revival of these kinds of attitudes at that time, and they were pretty mainstream in America back then. In 1925, there was a Ku Klux Klan march through Washington D.C., and thirty thousand Klansmen took part, all dressed up in white robes and carrying crosses. A whole bunch of them were senators and congressmen too. They even took off their hoods so everyone could see them. They weren't afraid of nothing, because they all knew that they could do whatever they wanted and get away with it.'

'That's crazy,' said Donna.

'If I am not mistaken,' said Emmet, 'there were something like four million members of the Klan at its peak. And that's just the actual members. Add to that all the sympathisers, and then you're suddenly talking about a huge part of the entire population. America may not look like it from the outside, but much of the resentment from that bitter time still courses through the veins of this nation. Officially, though, there are only a few thousand Klansmen left today. And they obviously ain't out in the open anymore. But their ideas live on.'

'I never realised it was that bad,' said Donna. 'I'm not sure we were taught any of this in school.'

'Like I told you,' said Emmett. 'Most people would like to forget about all of this. But the echoes of those bygone days still linger across these lands. Especially in a town like this.'

'It all sounds so similar to the way things have gone many times in the past,' said Andrew. 'Old grievances that breed resentment and violence in endless cycles. Sometimes I feel like history keeps repeating itself.'

'Actually, that's all a bunch of horseshit,' laughed Emmett good-naturedly, 'if you don't mind my saying so. I've heard people say that before, and I disagree. It ain't that history repeats itself. It's just that historians are having to say the same damn thing over and over again because people just won't fucking listen.'

At that, Donna couldn't help but smile as she sipped her whiskey.

'You could be right,' said Andrew, producing a half smile and a nod.

'Now,' said Emmett seriously. 'Returning from the past to the present. We've got to decide what to do about all of this. What can I do to help?'

TWENTY

Andrew, Donna and Emmett spent the next hour or so going over different options for how to approach the situation and how to try to recover evidence from Stonewall Ranch and put a stop to whatever General McKinnon was planning. At one point, Emmett was about to say something, but then he suddenly stopped himself mid-sentence, turned his head to one side and froze.

'I think we've got company,' he said, getting up from the table and walking towards a small window facing the front yard.

Andrew and Donna followed suit and peered out of another window. Outside, they could see two silver pickup trucks making their way along the dirt road towards the farmhouse. As they sped along, the sun glinted off their bodies, and clouds of pale dust swirled up behind them. They were going much too fast to be friendly visitors.

'Here comes trouble,' said Emmett, sounding tense but composed.

'No prizes for guessing who that is,' said Andrew flatly.

'Donna,' said Emmett. 'Take this.'

He handed Donna the sawn-off shotgun that he had placed leaning against the wall near the front door. Then he hurried to a gun cabinet under the wooden staircase leading to the room upstairs. He opened it, plucked a box of shotgun shells from a shelf and tossed it to her.

'You remember how to shoot one of those, right?' said Emmett. 'I showed you a long time ago.'

'Sure,' said Donna, looking mildly unsettled as she gazed down at the stubby weapon cradled in her hands. 'I haven't shot one of these things since, though.'

'Don't worry about it,' said Emmett, rummaging through the cabinet. 'It's like riding a bike. You never forget.'

'What about your pistol?' Andrew said as he pulled his Beretta from the small of his back and checked the magazine.

'I left it in the car,' said Donna, opening and closing the breech to check that the shotgun was loaded. 'This will have to do.'

Emmett pulled a large silver revolver from a shelf and pushed it into his trousers, and then he lifted a long, full-sized shotgun from a rack and broke open the breech. He then reached inside the gun cabinet again and opened a box of .45 ACP ammo, pouring the chunky shells into a trouser pocket. And then he repeated the exercise with a box of shotgun shells, using two of them to load the weapon.

'I'll head upstairs and try to get an angle on them through the window,' said Andrew, beginning to move.

'Good idea,' said Emmett. 'Donna, you stand by the door to the basement and cover the backdoor. I'll stay here and cover the front.'

'Got it,' said Donna, moving purposefully and seemingly without fear.

Outside, the two pickup trucks had come to a grinding halt on the compacted dirt inside a cloud of dust, and three men had stepped out of each of them. Peering down from his hidden vantage point behind the sheer white curtain of the open first-floor window, Andrew didn't recognise any of them. They were muscular and wearing cargo trousers, boots and t-shirts, and they were all carrying assault rifles.

After a few seconds, they had spread out in a semi-circle in front of the house, and without hesitation or a word of warning, they raised their weapons all at once and opened fire. Bullets tore through the windows and smacked into the front door where they splintered the wood and kept going inside the house. The barrage of lead also chewed up parts of the exterior wall and splintered Emmett's rocking chair. Soon, there was a cloud of dust and powdered brick drifting along the front porch. Within a few seconds, the automatic weapons ran dry, and when each of the attackers stopped firing to change magazines, the firing paused for a moment.

Inside the house, Emmett had dropped to the floor and rolled into cover behind the hearth of the open fireplace, and Donna was crouching inside the kitchen where she was shielded by two brick walls. Upstairs, Andrew had pulled back from the window to make sure he wasn't spotted. The only thing between him and the six assault rifles was the window and the wooden dormer. However, as the incoming fire ceased, he immediately realised that all of the bullets had been aimed at the ground floor. The attackers had clearly believed them all to be downstairs. This now offered him the element of surprise.

Moving up to stand out of sight behind the curtain, he raised his Beretta and took aim. The unsuppressed report of the 9mm pistol inside the small wooden room was deafening. An explosion of hot gas from the pistol's muzzle pushed at the curtain, and a fraction of a second later, the bullet tore through it and slammed into the forehead of his first target. The man went down where he stood, collapsing onto the dusty ground as his hands released their grip on his assault rifle.

Even as he fell, Andrew was already shifting his aim to the next target. He fired again, and another well-placed shot sent a bullet smacking audibly into the chest of another mercenary. The man was jolted backwards by the force of the impact, and his finger closed around the trigger of his weapon, squeezing off a long burst as he fell to the ground. The bullets stitched a path across the already mangled front door and continued up to the window above. One of them narrowly missed Andrew as it ripped through the curtain. A couple of seconds later, the four remaining mercenaries opened up on the window with their weapons now reloaded.

A torrent of lead burst through the dormer, and splinters of wood and shards of glass from the window exploded into the room where Andrew had now thrown himself back across the floor to the far wall where he hoped to be out of the line of fire. The storm of lead turned the air thick with dust and debris, but Andrew somehow managed to avoid being hit. However, this wouldn't last for long. Eventually, one of the bullets would cut through the right spot in the roof structure and find him. Worse still, the mercenaries might be armed with hand grenades, in which case it would all be over very soon.

Bracing himself for the familiar clonk of a grenade landing and rolling on a wooden floor, Andrew suddenly heard a thunderous boom from downstairs. There was a shrill scream from outside, followed by another boom, and then there was confused shouting and the sound of boots running on the dry soil. Emmett had now joined the fray with his shotgun, and from the sounds of it, he had managed to cut down at least one of the remaining attackers. Then followed the loud bark of his revolver, firing six times and sending six heavy .45 ACP rounds out of the front of the house.

Still lying on his back, Andrew reached for a fresh magazine and slotted it in, and then he risked moving cautiously towards the window to peer out. When he looked down through the shredded curtain, he saw the two men he had shot lying dead in pools of blood. Next to them was the body of a man whose left leg had been shot off at the knee and who had then taken a second hit from Emmett's shotgun to the chest. All three were as dead as could be. That left three more who had now scattered.

Andrew moved closer to the window to see if he could spot them, but nothing was moving outside.

'Are you alright up there?' came Emmett's raised voice.

'Yes, I'm OK,' called Andrew as he stepped back from the window. 'You?'

'I took one in the leg,' Emmett grunted. 'It's nothing, though. Donna, are you OK?'

'I'm fine,' said Donna, her voice sounding shaken. 'What do we do now?'

'Just stay there,' said Emmett. 'This ain't over yet.'

Still crouched low, Donna peeked out from the nook leading to the door to the basement, and she spotted Emmett in cover, pressed up against the side of the hearth. He was clutching his shotgun and fumbling with two new shells trying to reload it, and his left trouser leg was soaked in blood. Behind him was an open doorway where the front door had been, and smoke and dust hung in the air.

'Emmett, you need help!' she shouted.

'Nonsense,' he called back to her. 'I'm fine. Stay there.'

At that moment, Donna heard movement off to her side, and when she turned her head, she could just see boots through the gap under the backdoor. As she noticed the door handle beginning to move, she gripped the shotgun and turned to face the door. At almost the same time, the door suddenly burst open, and outside was one of the attackers with his weapon raised and ready to engage.

Donna fired first, and when she pulled both triggers at the same time, the sawn-off shotgun produced an ear-splitting boom as it sent two lots of steel balls ripping through the air and slamming into the mercenary's torso. An instant later, he was lifted off the ground and hurled backwards by about a metre, where his smoking and lifeless body thudded heavily onto the ground and lay still. He never knew what hit him. The recoil from the double-shot nearly ripped the shotgun from Donna's grasp, but she managed to hold on to it, and within a few seconds she had reloaded and was ready for anyone else attempting to enter through the back.

'Donna?' shouted Emmett.

'All good,' she yelled. 'I got him.'

'That's my girl,' said Emmett.

At that moment, Andrew came down the stairs and joined Emmett by the fireplace. Kneeling next to the former Army Ranger, he glanced down at his bloody leg while keeping his Beretta aimed squarely at the open doorway.

'Are you going to be alright?' he asked. 'You're losing blood.'

'I'll be fine,' said Emmett. 'As long as we finish this thing lickety-split.'

'I'm going to assume you mean fast,' said Andrew, getting back onto his feet and ripping a sleeve from his shirt. 'Tie this around your leg nice and tight. You two stay here. I'm going for the last two of those guys.'

'Be careful,' winced Emmett. 'We did good. It'd be a damn shame to fumble this thing now.'

'I will,' said Andrew, moving towards the backdoor. 'It's those two goons who need to worry now. I'll be right back.'

Passing Donna on his way, Andrew moved low and quietly to the backdoor and briefly peeked out to look both ways. He could see no movement in either direction, and straight ahead of him was just flat desert terrain stretching away from the house for miles. Wherever the two remaining mercenaries had gone, they were still somewhere on the property, and they were unlikely to give themselves up.

Moving in a crouched position as fast as he dared for fear of making too much noise, Andrew slipped out of the back door and moved to the corner of the house. He leaned out from cover to try to spot their attackers, but he could still see nothing. Eyeing the barn, he decided that they had most likely taken up a defensive position inside it.

With his Beretta held low and ready to engage, he moved swiftly to the small shed and stopped behind it to make sure he wasn't exposing himself to an ambush somewhere out in the open. At that moment, he heard movement inside the shed, and a split second later, a pistol shot rang out from inside it, and a bullet exploded out through a wooden plank about a foot from his face. Then another bullet burst out, tearing through another plank and sending splinters of wood flying through the air.

Andrew threw himself to the ground, rolled onto his back and opened fire from his prone position. Almost emptying the magazine, he quickly squeezed off thirteen of the fifteen shots in a pattern that would cut across virtually every inch of the shed's interior.

Just two rounds left. When he had finished firing, there was silence for a moment, but then he was rewarded with the dull thud of a heavy body slumping to the floor inside. Then he moved around to the front and ripped the door open. Inside was a bearded mercenary who looked like he had taken a bullet to the chest and one to the lower left side of his head. Lying next to him on the ground were the man's pistol and his assault rifle.

Wasting no time, Andrew picked up the assault rifle and stripped a magazine from the man's tactical vest. Slamming the fresh mag into the magazine well, he then pulled the charging handle to slot the first round into the firing chamber and flicked the fire selector to three-round bursts.

Still moving in a combat stance with his new weapon cradled low, Andrew advanced towards the barn and stopped outside to listen. He could hear movement inside and decided to roll the dice on a different approach. Moving to one of the oil barrels sitting on the ground outside, he crouched down into cover.

'Hey!' he shouted. 'All your buddies are dead. Do you want to join them, or do you want a chance to live?'

He had barely completed his sentence before a barrage of assault rifle fire erupted from inside the barn, bullets punching out through the wooden doors and bits of wood spinning through the air.

'I guess that's my answer,' he grunted to himself as he grimaced and pressed up against the steel barrel which also took several loud hits.

Once the burst of fire had abated, he decided to risk moving from his position. He inched silently to sit just underneath one of the small dusty windows and slowly raised himself up to peer inside. The window was half open to allow for ventilation inside, and he moved his head to be able to see through the gap. After a moment, he spotted movement at the back of the barn, but his view was blocked by several pillars and rafters. All he could see was the shadow of someone taking cover behind the tractor. However, he noticed that sitting on a rafter directly above the mercenary was a rusty metal toolbox. It was covered in dust, and he reckoned it probably contained old spare parts or tools that Emmett no longer used, but Andrew could think of one very good use for it.

Moving slowly and silently, he took a long step away from the window and thumbed the fire selector to single shot. Then he rose enough to raise the assault rifle and aim at the toolbox through the gap in the window. The loud report of the rifle reverberated through the half-empty barn, and the bullet slammed loudly into the toolbox. The kinetic energy of the copper-jacketed lead projectile was enough to cause the lid to fly open, knock the box off the rafter and send it and its contents spilling onto the mercenary below. As the tools and metal parts rained down on him, he yelped in pain as a couple of them hit and cut open the top of his head.

Immediately after seeing the toolbox go flying, Andrew began sprinting around the corner to the barn doors, and by the time the metal shower had come to an end and the tools and parts had clattered onto the floor, he was through the door and moving swiftly alongside the tractor. With less than a second to go before he reached the tractor's large rear wheel, he flipped the fire selector back to full auto, and then he rounded the corner to where the mercenary was. The man was down on one knee, steadying himself with one hand and holding the other to his head. His assault rifle was on the floor next to him. Still moving, Andrew brought up the weapon, aimed at the man's chest and pulled the trigger.

The metallic click as the weapon jammed sounded as loud to Andrew as a flashbang going off inside the cavernous space. Had the weapon fired, he would have sent a volley of lethal bullets into the mercenary's torso and instantly punched his ticket to the afterlife. As it was, he was now continuing forward under his own momentum holding an expensive piece of metal that was about as useless as a wooden club.

Seeing Andrew coming around to the back of the tractor with his weapon up, the mercenary had brought up his arms in a reflexive attempt to shield himself from the bullets, but he heard the click at the same time as Andrew and reacted almost immediately. Realising that he had been given one final chance to survive, the burly bearded man launched himself at Andrew with a roar and gripped the barrel of the jammed assault rifle. With gritted teeth, the man wrestled it to one side as he rugby-tackled his opponent, and the two men went sprawling onto the dusty floor.

When the two of them went down, the assault rifle fell to the floor, and the mercenary landed heavily on Andrew who ended up partially winded. Reaching for the Beretta at the small of his back, he managed to extract it, but the mercenary gripped his wrist with both hands. Andrew attempted to twist the pistol towards the man's face and then squeezed off a shot, but it missed. The man was now looming over him with a maniacal grin. Using every ounce of his strength and grimacing from the effort, Andrew attempted to twist the gun towards the mercenary, and when he thought the bullet would connect, he fired again. At the same moment, the man threw his head to one side, and when the pistol fired the final shot in its magazine, the bullet tore off most of the man's ear and left a scorch mark on the side of his face. He roared in pain as the blood began to trickle out of his mangled ear, and then he let go of Andrew's wrist with one hand and gripped his throat with the other.

Unable to breathe, Andrew managed to punch the mercenary hard in the gut twice, and the bearded man finally groaned and rolled off with surprising agility. Back on his feet, and with blood streaming down one side of his head, he spread his arms out to his sides like a crow and began circling Andrew with a hateful grin on his face.

'So, you're Barton's boyfriend,' he said mockingly. 'Well, this is the end of the line for you, pretty boy.'

Andrew ignored the taunt and allowed his eyes to sweep over his surroundings looking for anything he could use as a weapon. Hanging from a rafter behind the mercenary was a steel mattock with a wooden handle sporting a wide hoe on one side and a pickaxe on the other. On another rafter were a handsaw, a mallet and a set of woodworking chisels.

The mercenary evidently had the same idea, because he glanced to one side and immediately reached behind a support beam where a chainsaw was sitting on a table, out of Andrew's sight. As soon as he had grabbed the chainsaw, he yanked the chord, and the beast sprang to life with an aggressive growl. The man revved the engine and produced an even wider grin.

'You're fucked now,' he shouted over the noise of the chainsaw.

He then began advancing while revving the engine wildly as blue-grey smoke shot out of its exhaust. Andrew could see the hundreds of small steel teeth on the chain ripping around the blade in a blur as the mercenary came towards him. He began moving sideways to try to circle clear of the blade, and at the same time, his eyes darted this way and that, searching for something to use. He made a sudden rush for the mattock and tore it off the support beam just as the mercenary lunged with the chainsaw blade pushed out in front of him. The blade cut through the air uncomfortably close to Andrew's shoulder, but he managed to spin out of the way while holding on to the mattock.

Spinning the handheld farming tool around so that the pickaxe was pointing forward, he then held it low as the two men continued circling each other, each of them waiting for their opponent to miscalculate and make themselves vulnerable to an attack. Andrew feigned a swing but the mercenary didn't buy it. As the big man moved across the barn floor, he left a trail of blood, but it didn't seem to bother him in the slightest. He kept his eyes locked on Andrew's, trying to anticipate his moves and then immediately counter them.

The mercenary lunged again and tried to stab the spinning blade directly at Andrew. All it would take was for him to connect once with any part of Andrew's body, and the fight would be as good as over. As he thrust the lethal blade forward, Andrew moved slightly to one side and performed a rapid sideswipe with the mattock. The swing connected with the blade and broke it clean off the chainsaw halfway down. As the chain came off the broken blade, it immediately began flailing around in the air, and part of it flung backwards and tore across the mercenary's lower left arm before he could let go of the chainsaw and drop it on the floor. As blood spurted from the man's arm, the infernal machine clattered onto the floor where it landed on its side and kept idling impatiently.

With impressive speed, the mercenary leapt to one side and pulled the mallet from the support beam. It was a heavy-duty tool with a large and heavy steel head fixed to the end of a long wooden handle. The mercenary immediately swung the mallet up over his head and came at Andrew with a roundhouse-style attack. Instead of attempting to move out of the way, Andrew stepped inside the man's reach and slammed the head of the mattock straight at his chest. It connected hard, but only with the top of the head. The man was pushed backwards a step, and he lost his grip on the mallet which flew off into a dark and messy corner of the barn.

Realising that he was about to lose the fight, the mercenary gripped the mattock's wooden handle with both hands and pushed hard. This forced Andrew to try to resist the push, and that gave the man his opening. Instead of entering into a tug-of-war, he simply let go of the mattock and darted along one side of the tractor towards the back of the barn while Andrew had to stop himself from falling forward. It only bought the mercenary a couple of seconds, but it was enough for him to make it back to the spot behind the tractor where he had dropped his assault rifle earlier.

Andrew had been outplayed, and any second now the mercenary would re-emerge holding an assault rifle with a full magazine. Instead of scrambling for cover, which might buy him some time but would still end with him lying dead somewhere, he stepped out next to the tractor, gripped the mattock firmly and brought it up over his head as if he were preparing for a two-handed overhead axe throw.

Holding it there while tensing every muscle in his body like hundreds of coiled springs, he waited until he saw the first sliver of the mercenary's elbow as he came out from behind the back of the tractor holding the assault rifle. At that moment, Andrew took a long step forward to add momentum to his throw, and then he hurled the heavy mattock forward. As it cartwheeled through the air, the mercenary emerged fully from behind the tractor with a confident evil scowl holding the assault rifle, ready to open fire on his defenceless victim.

Spinning forward end over end, the mattock arrived with perfect timing to slam the pickaxe first into the chest of the mercenary, and its long steel spike buried itself all the way up to the handle, the force of the impact punching him off his feet. He fell onto his back with a heavy thud, the back of his head smacked audibly into the floor, and his hand released the assault rifle before he could fire a single shot. His body spasmed a couple of times in quick succession, and then he seemed to exhale one final time before he lay still.

Andrew bent forward and panted with his hands on his knees and his head lifted to look towards the dead mercenary.

'Fuck you,' he breathed.

He stood there for a few moments, catching his breath and drawing a sigh of relief that his gamble with the mattock had paid off. Immediately hearing Fiona's voice in his head asking him to be careful, he then decided that this event should be one that he might decide against telling her about when he got home. As he exited the barn and staggered towards the main house, Donna emerged, flanked by Emmett who was using his shotgun as a crutch. It appeared that the makeshift bandage had managed to stem the bleeding enough for him to be upright, and he had an arm wrapped over Donna's shoulder to help him walk. Donna's face looked blank as she gazed at the death and destruction in front of the house.

'You OK?' shouted Emmett.

'All good,' said Andrew, giving a thumbs up.

'We need to get Emmett to the hospital,' called Donna as she and Emmett came out of the house and joined Andrew in the front yard next to the dead mercenaries.

'I'll be fine,' protested Emmett irritably. 'It's a flesh wound. Nothing some whiskey and a bandage can't take care of.'

'No!' said Donna sternly. 'Damn it, Emmett. You listen to me, alright? Enough of this cowboy swagger of yours. I already lost a brother this week. I am not losing an uncle because he was stupid enough to bleed out when he could have been patched up. Now get in the damn car.'

Emmett glanced at Donna for a moment and then turned to look at Andrew who gave a shrug.

'Alright,' he finally relented. 'If you say so.'

'That's better,' said Donna, who suddenly looked taller and more forceful than just a few hours earlier.

After walking to Andrew's Jeep accompanied by Donna who was by his side propping him up, Emmett turned back to face his ruined house.

'Well, shit...' he said pensively after a few moments, placing his hands on his hips and looking at his shot-up farmhouse. 'This place is gonna need some work.'

Donna regarded the house for a long moment, and then she gave a small shake of the head and turned to Emmett with an uneasy look.

'This is a fine mess we've got ourselves into, ain't it Emmett?' she said.

'Well,' said Emmett. 'If it ain't, it'll do until the mess gets here. But I guess that's what insurance companies are for. It'll be nice to have those parasites pay *me* for a change.'

'Yes,' said Donna. 'It ain't really fit to live in for the time being.'

'Sure ain't,' said Emmett, wincing from the pain in his leg. 'I guess I won't be staying here until McKinnon has been put out of business for good. Otherwise, his dogs will just keep coming back for more.'

'Then let's end this,' said Andrew resolutely. 'Let's make sure that he is brought down once and for all. I have a plan that I think might work.'

'Alright, son,' said Emmett. 'Let's hear it.'

TWENTY-ONE

'WHAT?' roared McKinnon with a shocked and furious expression. 'All of them?'

He was sitting at his desk inside his office at Stonewall Ranch, glowering at Cobb who was standing in front of him looking browbeaten.

'Yes,' said Cobb. 'The last we heard from them was on their approach to the farm. Since then, nothing. So, I sent another team out there, and they found the place all shot up but abandoned. And our guys are lying dead all over the place. Shot to pieces. One of them even got killed with a pickaxe.'

'Jesus H. Christ,' said McKinnon ruefully. 'How the fuck can one dude, a waitress and a fucking pensioner take out an entire team of our guys? It just don't make no damn sense.'

'I'm not sure,' said Cobb, cowed. 'I haven't seen it for myself yet, but by the sounds of it, the three of them were holed up inside the house and set up an ambush there.'

'No shit?' exclaimed McKinnon, giving a shake of the head and producing a derisive chortle. 'And our boys just walked right into it. Un-fucking-believable.'

'Most of them got dropped right in front of the house,' said Cobb. 'One at the backdoor, one in a shed and one of them was found inside Emmett's old barn. That was the pickaxe guy. Looks like he was cornered in there and eventually taken out. He looked all kinds of messed up, apparently.'

'Well, where the hell are those three now?' said McKinnon, placing both hands palms down on the desk in front of him. 'Tell me we have a fix on them.'

'We're not sure, exactly,' said Cobb. 'I've told a couple of our guys to try to find out, and I've asked Hogan to tell his boys to be on the lookout for their vehicles. Nothing yet, though.'

'Figures…' grunted McKinnon scornfully.

Cobb stood silently watching his boss for a long moment as the general gazed vacantly out of the window with his eyes narrowed and his lips pressed tightly together. Eventually, he risked addressing him again.

'What do you want me to do, sir?' Cobb finally said with a cautious demeanour.

After a pause so long that Cobb ended up wondering if the general had even heard him, McKinnon finally replied. Slowly turning his head to direct his cold gaze at his 2nd in command, like a large artillery piece swivelling to fire at a new target, McKinnon shot Cobb a piercing look.

'I. Want. Them. Dead,' he said slowly, menace dripping off every word. 'I don't give a rat's ass how much firepower we have to bring to bear on this. I need this asshole removed from the face of the Earth.'

'I'll make it happen,' said Cobb, hoping that he would be able to deliver on his promise.

'You'd better,' said McKinnon as he rose from his desk. 'Maybe get somebody from out of town. Somebody who knows what the fuck they're doing. And how about setting up an ambush at Donna's house? Have people waiting where we think they might turn up.'

'I know a freelancer down in San Angelo,' said Cobb. 'A guy called Jim Marlow. He could probably be here in about an hour. Former SWAT team sniper gone private. Expensive but worth the money. Word is that he has never failed an assignment.'

'Alright. Sounds good,' said McKinnon, heading for the door. 'Whatever it takes and whatever it costs. I want this fucking problem solved.'

Walking past Cobb and out of the room without another word, McKinnon headed down to the ground floor and then further down into the basement. Here, he used a keycard to unlock a set of double doors that led to a wide corridor with black walls and soft lighting. He proceeded along the corridor past the door to the ops centre and the open doorway to the large preparations room where the Nightcrawler team had their cages. At the end of the corridor, he once again used his keycard to enter the dark ISR room.

In the military, the intelligence, surveillance, and reconnaissance units performed all the intelligence gathering required to pull off the often high-risk missions devised by JSOC to be carried out by teams from the Navy Seals or Delta Force. As soon as

McKinnon had established Ironclad Tactical Solutions, he had built a similar unit that operated from beneath his ranch, and he had hired some of the best people he had come into contact with during his time at JSOC. Not all of the candidates had shared his views on the state of the country and what might be required to fix it, but enough of them had done so to allow him to set up a highly capable internal intelligence unit for his PMC.

The ISR room was dark and spacious, and on virtually every inch of the walls were mounted large screens that showed satellite images or surveillance photos from various locations relevant to ongoing and upcoming Ironclad missions. On the largest central screen was a live feed from a high-altitude drone circling over a small settlement somewhere in Africa. Its camera had zoomed in on a small street where two technicals carrying several armed men had stopped.

As McKinnon entered the room and the door clicked shut behind him, its four occupants who were all wearing shirts and ties and who were sitting in front of their display banks looked up. One of them got to his feet and came over to meet the general. His name was Caleb Ryder, and he was heading up the ISR team. When McKinnon had entered, he had been in the middle of coordinating a mission to find and recover an army major in one of the unstable African countries where Ironclad had secured contracts.

'How are we doing?' said McKinnon, jerking his head at the large screen. 'How's the major?'

'We've secured the area and will be extracting him back to the capital soon,' said Ryder. 'He's taken a beating, but he'll live. All hostiles have been eliminated.'

'Very good,' nodded McKinnon. 'They'll love us for this. That should be enough to secure the next few contracts.'

'Absolutely,' said Ryder.

'Anyway,' said McKinnon. 'Did you manage to find that thing I asked you to look for?'

'I did,' said Ryder. 'I pulled in a favour from a pal in the British MoD. He owes me big time from way back when he and I were on a night out in London. I'm not going to bore you with the details, but without me, he would have ended up getting arrested, and his career would probably have been toast.'

'So, what did you find out?' said McKinnon slightly impatiently.

'Let me just get the report,' said Ryder, stepping back to his desk and picking up two sheets of paper that had been slotted inside a clear plastic folder.

He extracted the documents and handed them to McKinnon who immediately recognised the Ministry of Defence logo in the top left. It was dated two days earlier, and it contained a complete overview of the military career of one Andrew Sterling, including details about his time with the Special Air Services regiment. There was even a section listing significant covert missions that he had taken part in that had never been publicly acknowledged. It also included a psychological profile and a list of Sterling's various medals and commendations.

As McKinnon skimmed the printout of the MoD file, his eyebrows crept up, and he found himself nodding grudgingly in appreciation of the man's track record.

'Well, I'll be damned,' he finally said, still gazing down at the document. 'I guess that explains a thing or two. Looks like we've got ourselves an honest-to-god, grade-A hero.'

'It looks that way,' said Ryder. 'Do you want me to forward this to Cobb?'

'Yeah, you do that,' said McKinnon. 'He needs to appreciate what we're dealing with here. This guy's a nuisance, but he ain't no dope, that's for sure. Thank you, Ryder. That'll be all.'

'Yes, sir,' said Ryder, giving a respectful nod and returning to his desk.

'Son of a bitch,' McKinnon mumbled quietly to himself before closing the folder, turning around and heading for the door.

★   ★   ★

Jean-Pascal Mokri stepped out onto the pavement in front of the towering glass and steel skyscraper on Wall Street in Manhattan's financial district. He had just descended from the 29th floor, where he had completed a meeting with the brokerage firm selected to prepare and eventually execute the trading strategy that he and McKinnon had agreed on. It had taken weeks to finalise, and he was only in town to sign the documents, but there was now a plan in place that Mokri felt confident would work.

Using a range of different financial instruments, such as short positions on the S&P500, call options on high-volatility stocks and credit default swaps on vulnerable companies, they had now prepared a portfolio of tools that would maximise the impact of an uncontrolled and sudden fall in the markets. Using detailed analyses of the correlations between a multitude of different asset classes and financial instruments, the portfolio was now set up to exploit the fact that traditional risk management strategies break down during extreme market turmoil. This would result in a perfect storm of volatility, which he expected would net himself and McKinnon several billion dollars. Once all of the positions had been closed out and the profits locked in, the money would then immediately be transferred out of the country to various safe havens around the world.

As Mokri inhaled the warm, exhaust-laden air out on the street, he felt on top of the world. From humble beginnings in Lebanon, he was now about to be catapulted onto the Forbes Rich List along with General McKinnon if he ever decided to make his wealth public. Mokri pondered this for a moment. Perhaps he would lay low for a couple of years and then start donating money to charities and thereby ingratiate himself with politicians who could always be reliably counted on to flock around the reflected glory of major philanthropists. He might even consider doing so in his country of birth. Yes, it was largely still a bloody mess and in some respects barely a country, but he viewed it as buying an option on political influence down the line. He wouldn't even have to move there. After all, who would want to actually live in that shithole? Certainly not him.

As he stepped out to the curb, he hailed a taxi and got into the back, telling the driver to take him back up to his hotel near Central Park. As the yellow cab swung out onto Broadway and headed north through Lower Manhattan, he extracted his phone from his suit pocket and selected a number from its contact list. It rang twice before being picked up.

'Mokri,' said a gravelly voice. 'What's up?'

'General,' said Mokri. 'You'll be glad to hear that I have just completed my final meeting with the firm. They have set up a dedicated team to ensure that the trades are placed and executed on your signal. Everything's ready.'

'Excellent,' said McKinnon, sounding somewhat preoccupied. 'That's… Yeah, that's great.'

'Is everything alright?' said Mokri.

'Everything's fine,' said McKinnon. 'We've had a little bit of a hiccup here at the ranch, but everything is under control. We'll deal with it.'

'What sort of hiccup?' asked Mokri, puzzled.

He wasn't used to hearing the general sounding so distracted. In fact, he had never known him to be anything but like a laser in terms of his ability to focus on the job at hand. This was unusual, to say the least.

'Don't worry about it,' said McKinnon dismissively. 'We'll deal with it. All you have to do is make sure those boys on Wall Street jump when we say jump. Alright?'

'Of course,' said Mokri. 'They stand to make some serious fees on this, so I am sure we will have their full and undivided attention.'

'Great,' said McKinnon. 'Let me know about your movements in the next couple of days. I need to be able to reach you once things kick off, you understand?'

'I will make sure to do that,' said Mokri.

'Alright then,' said McKinnon. 'I've got to go. I'll talk to you soon.'

The call ended, and Mokri stared down at his phone. The entire exchange had been quite out of character for the usually calm and exceptionally self-confident former army general. Something was clearly on his mind. It was almost as if he was worried about something. Mokri pondered it for a while as he watched the seemingly endless rows of high-rise buildings roll past outside the window. Eventually, though, he dismissed it. There was no chance of McKinnon not coming through on this. There was simply too much to lose. Or rather, there were gains so extraordinarily massive on offer that McKinnon would move mountains to complete the final phase of the grand plan.

Mokri leaned back and thought ahead to later that evening, when he would treat himself to an evening of the best and most exclusive entertainment the Big Apple could offer. He had secured a membership at a private member's club that was as famous for its exquisite food and excellent cocktails as it was for its Russian hostesses. He wondered if Tatyana was still working there. If she was, perhaps he would present her with an offer she wouldn't be able to turn down. Mokri smiled to himself. Life was good, and the future was looking bright.

TWENTY-TWO

That evening, about an hour after sunset, Andrew headed back to the motel. He had decided to find somewhere else to sleep that night, and he even considered bedding down in his car somewhere out of sight. Either way, staying at the motel was no longer an option. First, however, he had to retrieve his passport from the room safe and make sure that nothing was left there that could be used to track him down.

Earlier, he had dropped Donna and Emmett at her house, and she had then driven her uncle to the hospital in Sweetwater using her own car. The plan was for Emmett to get patched up and for him to claim that the gunshot wound had been the result of the accidental discharge of a hunting rifle at his farm. Both Donna and Emmett seemed convinced that the hospital staff would accept that story without question. They swore that these things happened from time to time, and they were sure that the hospital would be more interested in the insurance policy and payment details anyway. The two of them would then stay in a hotel in Sweetwater overnight using false names.

When Andrew pulled into the parking lot at Mike's Motel, nothing seemed out of the ordinary. Quickly scouting the area from his vehicle, he parked in his usual spot and got out carrying the assault rifle from Emmett's farm wrapped inside a jacket. Once inside his room, he locked the door, drew the curtains of the single window facing the front and began clearing out the room and putting his limited number of possessions into his backpack.

After about ten minutes, he was ready to leave and walk over to the reception to settle the bill. But then he noticed that a large pickup truck was pulling into the parking lot outside, the bright cones from its headlights sweeping across the area. As he watched, the bulky truck drove along slowly and parked in a bay directly behind his Jeep. The vehicle was a grey Chevrolet Silverado with tinted windows, and only then did he realise where he had seen that truck before. It was the same truck that Tatum and Thornton had been driving when he first made their acquaintance inside Donna's Diner. With Thornton dead in the desert, this had to be Tatum behind the wheel, and even if he wasn't here under orders from McKinnon, he was no doubt keen to exact revenge for his friend.

Andrew turned off all of the lights, pulled the Beretta from the backpack, slotted in a fresh magazine and waited by the window where he peered out through a slim gap between the curtains. For several minutes, nothing happened. No one exited the pickup truck, and there was no visible movement inside the vehicle due to the heavy tint of its windows. Then the passenger door opened, and a man that Andrew did not recognise stepped out and headed for the reception. With his shaved head and black beard, he was broad and mean-looking, and he glanced around furtively as he walked along with his hands in his pockets. He did not carry himself like the other ex-military types that McKinnon had on his payroll. Instead, he had a decidedly shifty look to him, as if he would be more at home in a violent street gang than in a private military company. Perhaps this was one of Tatum's own pals roped in to help take Andrew down.

Tilting his head, Andrew was able to follow him with his eyes all the way to the reception, and once inside, the man had a brief conversation with the desk clerk. At one point, Andrew could have sworn that the clerk pointed in the direction of his room, but perhaps he was just imagining it. After a couple of minutes, the man re-emerged and walked back to the pickup truck, where he opened the door and got back in. Several more minutes passed with no movement at all, and Andrew concluded that whoever these men were, they were here for him, and they were now staking out his motel room in order to finish the job that their colleagues had started and failed to complete at Emmett's farm. Perhaps they were intending to wait until much later than night to then kick in the door and kill him in his bed, or perhaps they were waiting for reinforcements. Either way, Andrew wasn't minded to wait around and find out.

Looking across to his Jeep, he concluded that there was no way for him to reach his car safely. Similarly, an assault on the Chevrolet would be too high-risk since he had no idea precisely how many armed men might be inside. The only remaining option, which he knew was the right one but which still managed to rub him the wrong way, was to try to evade and slip away unnoticed. It felt cowardly, but the rational part of his brain told him to slap down his pride and do what was most likely to allow him to live another day. And then he could take the fight to them at some later stage on his own terms.

The only other way out of the room was through a small window next to the door to the bathroom. It looked just about big enough to allow him to squeeze through, but it was bolted shut from the inside, presumably to stop vandals or thieves from entering from the back of the building. If he was going to get through there, he would have to break it open. Outside, Andrew could see a small grove of mesquite trees whose stunted growth in the dry soil had made them appear more like large bushes. If he could get in among them unseen, he would then be able to cut a path through the grove and around the back of the motel to join the road closer to town. From there, he would have to improvise.

He walked into the bathroom and unscrewed the metal showerhead from the hose, and using that as an improvised tool, he managed to wrench open the metal brackets that kept the window closed. Pushing the window open and quickly scanning the outside, he tossed his backpack through along with the assault rifle, and then he climbed up and out. It was a tight fit, but he made it out, closed the window and was soon moving quietly through the grove carrying his possessions. As he skirted the perimeter of the motel's plot, he could see the Chevrolet still parked behind his Jeep, but he was now cloaked in darkness amongst the trees, and the car's occupants would be unable to see him.

After about ten minutes of cautious walking through bushes and tall grass, he had circled around the motel and continued across several large semi-open industrial plots, including a scrapyard and what appeared to be a farming equipment repair yard. When he finally reconnected with the road into town, he found himself at a business that appeared to only sell second-hand cars. Keeping to the rear of the main building, he quickly scanned the cars parked there. Then he located a door to the interior of the shop and kicked it open. Within a couple of minutes, he had found what he was looking for. Inside a flimsy wooden drawer that proved easy to break open, he discovered a collection of key fobs. Rummaging through them, he then extracted the one that had a Honda logo on it.

Back outside, he pressed the unlock button, and the four orange indicator lights on the dark grey Honda Ridgeline flashed twice as the mid-sized pickup truck produced a quick chirp. The car appeared to be perhaps five years old, and it looked unremarkable, which was exactly what Andrew was after. Climbing in behind the wheel, he was gratified to see that the fuel tank was almost full, and as he turned the ignition, the engine came to life and began purring under the hood.

With the headlights still off, he drove slowly out past the shop and across the forecourt onto the road, and only then did he turn on the lights. Driving at an inconspicuous speed, he weaved his way around the town centre along a residential road until he arrived at the attractive tree-lined street where Donna's house was located. Parking behind a car about one hundred metres short of her property, he switched off the engine and the headlights but remained in the car for about ten minutes. This was a particularly sleepy part of town, and during the time he sat there, only one car passed by, heading almost to the far end of the street before pulling into a driveway. Its occupant then exited the vehicle along with a dog, and the two of them disappeared inside a house. Then everything fell quiet again.

Racking the slide on the Beretta and shoving it into his trousers, Andrew opened the door and stepped out of the car. He walked along the pavement past neat houses with well-kept front lawns. Along the street were several vehicles sitting by the curb, including a black van parked under a tree roughly twenty metres further along from Donna's house. As he walked along, he eyed both it and several other vehicles, but there appeared to be no sign of any threats.

He eventually came to the house next to Donna's. It was another modest but well-maintained single-storey dwelling where no one seemed to be at home, so he cut across the lawn to the back garden and climbed over the fence between the two properties. Then he pulled out his gun and moved cautiously up to the backdoor of Donna's house. After a few moments of listening and peering inside through the windows and satisfying himself that no one was inside, he used the key she had given him to open the door.

His purpose for being here was to retrieve Billy Ray's phone, which Donna had left there before heading to Emmett's farm with Andrew earlier that day. Now, however, after the shootout at her uncle's property, it was almost certainly only a question of time before McKinnon's men ransacked the whole place in search of anything that might be used to find them. And if they happened to catch Donna there, then Andrew didn't even want to think about what those men might do to her. Having already killed her brother, he had no doubt that they would take pleasure in humiliating her before killing her too.

Moving straight to the shoebox containing Billy Ray's phone, which Donna had pushed under one side of the bed in her bedroom, Andrew picked it up and put it in his pocket. He then returned to the living room where Donna's photo albums were still lying open on the sofa. He peered out through the window to the street, looking for anything untoward, but everything was quiet. However, years of training and experience had made him hyper-aware of anything that might indicate a threat, and just as he stepped back from the window, he saw the black van move. Or rather, he noticed the almost imperceptible wobble of the reflection of a streetlight in the van's windscreen. The movement was slight, but it was just enough for him to notice, and it could only have been caused by movement inside the van.

Immediately pulling back and out of view, he then considered his options. If there was a hit squad waiting in the van, he wouldn't stand a chance if he went out through the front door. If instead he went out of the backdoor, he might be able to sneak away, but returning to his newly acquired pickup and the backpack and assault rifle lying inside it would be virtually impossible without being shot at. He had to find a way to determine if there really was an ambush waiting for him out there.

He went back into Donna's bedroom, opened her closets, and found a long dark coat and a hat. With the coat still on the hanger, he put it on a coat stand by the front door and placed the hat on top of it. He then opened the door slightly ajar and used his foot to push the improvised decoy in front of the opening so that it would be visible from the black van.

The sniper inside the vehicle immediately spotted the door open and the dark shape emerge. Using the rifle scope to adjust his aim through the small hatch in the side of the van, he then pulled the trigger on his suppressed Remington 700 compact sniper rifle, which was a small, high-accuracy weapon favoured by SWAT teams.

The sleek 7.62mm bullet exited the barrel at almost twice the speed of sound, and a split second later it punched through the coat and slammed into the brick wall behind it amid a puff of dust and a loud thwack. About a second later, another round tore through the coat and buried itself in the wall.

In the hope of fooling the sniper for a few more seconds, Andrew kicked the coat stand over and bolted for the back of the house. As he reached the backdoor, another shot cut through the coat that now lay draped over the coat stand in the hallway. It seemed as if the sniper had bought into the illusion and believed that he had fatally wounded his target and now only needed to finish the job.

Realising that he would only have a few seconds left before the sniper would realise that he had been tricked, Andrew barged out through the backdoor and ran to the corner of the house from where he could see the van. He flicked the safety on his Beretta to 'off', peeked around the corner and then lined up his shot. He could see the small hatch in the side of the van, but the sniper and his rifle were hidden inside, so it was impossible for him to determine what the sniper was aiming at. He had to act fast.

Pulling the trigger repeatedly while still trying to aim as much as possible between shots, Andrew fired six shots in rapid succession. The 9mm copper-jacketed bullets punched six neat holes in the bodywork of the van near the hatch. To his relief, this did not result in an immediate return of fire. Instead, the van rocked slightly from one side to the other as the sniper scrambled around inside, and a couple of seconds later, the glaring headlights came on and the engine roared to life. Immediately thereafter, the van swerved out into the street and took off.

Andrew ran out across the front lawn and fired another four shots as the vehicle accelerated away from him, but none of them appeared to do any damage to the van or its driver. He then sprinted back towards the Honda and threw himself in behind the wheel. As he started the engine, the van's taillights disappeared around a corner.

He wrenched the pickup truck into gear and floored the accelerator. The truck had a large and powerful engine under the hood, and with its four-wheel drive engaged, it accelerated quickly along the street. Within half a minute, Andrew had reached the corner where the van had disappeared out of sight, and as soon as he made the turn, he spotted it up ahead just as it was making a hard right. Punching the throttle once more, he tore along the street and threw the truck into the corner, narrowly missing a parked car. He was now less than fifty metres from the van, which looked wobbly and unstable at the speeds at which it was going. As it took another turn, it sideswiped a parked car whose alarm immediately began blaring.

After another left turn, Andrew decided to hang back until they had left the town's residential areas, but as soon as the van swerved onto a wider road leading south out towards the desert, Andrew floored the accelerator again and quickly caught up with the van. The driver shot through a red light at the last intersection before leaving town, and Andrew was forced to follow. Luckily, there were no other vehicles around. The chase now took them through a sparsely built-up area where the only buildings were a petrol station, a fenced-off electricity substation and a couple of warehouses. Along the road on one side were a number of evenly spaced trees.

With the memory of Thornton's demise still fresh in his mind, Andrew was keen to avoid having another valuable source of intelligence die on him before he could extract the information he needed. Instead of shooting at the driver again and risking killing him, he decided to attempt a PIT manoeuvre. The so-called Precision Immobilization Technique involved using the front of his own vehicle to nudge the back of the vehicle in front of him to one side. This offensive driving technique, which was part of standard SAS training, would cause the van's rear wheels to lose their grip on the road and the vehicle to then spin out of control and come to a stop. It worked reliably on smaller vehicles, but it was more difficult to pull off against a heavy van.

Increasing his speed and closing the distance to the van, he began to pull alongside it, but the driver spotted what he was doing and swerved away. However, the van was now almost on the verge, and since the pickup truck had a significant advantage in terms of engine power, Andrew just kept coming until the van had nowhere to go. He wrenched the wheel towards the van, and the front of the pickup smacked into the side of the van's rear, causing it to step out to the other side. As metal ground against metal and sparks flew, the van's rear wheels almost lost contact with the road, but then the driver regained control and attempted to accelerate away. As the distance between the two vehicles opened up to a few metres, Andrew could see smoke billowing out from the rear wheel where the impact had happened, and evidently, some of the van's bodywork was now making contact with the tyre.

This did not stop the driver from trying to flee, but his attempt at escaping the much more powerful pickup truck was futile, and Andrew was about to ram into the same spot again when suddenly the smoking rear tyre exploded. As the van raced along, the rear wheel began tearing itself to shreds, and soon its remaining parts were flailing violently against the wheel well and the van's bodywork. Andrew could see that the driver was struggling to control the vehicle, but because it had front-wheel drive, he just barely managed to avoid veering off the road and crashing. Soon, a shower of bright sparks sprayed out from the wheel hub, which was now making direct contact with the road.

Realising that the game was up, the driver suddenly swerved to the side and onto the verge where he slammed the brakes amid a huge billowing cloud of dust and came to a stop. Andrew barely had time to brake and get out of his pickup truck before the driver had bolted from the van and begun running out into the bushy, high desert terrain.

Andrew swung the pickup around so that its headlight illuminated the desert and the driver in a bright glare. Grabbing the assault rifle, he decided to ignore the driver for the moment and instead advanced towards the van with his weapon up, ready to engage. Moving swiftly around to the back of the vehicle, he tore open the doors and was prepared to either find the sniper dead from his Beretta fire or waiting for him inside with a gun. However, when he pulled the doors open with his fire selector set to full auto, he found a virtually empty rear compartment. The only things it contained were a Remington 700 and an improvised metal support on which the sniper would have rested his rifle as he aimed out through the small hatch. That was when it dawned on Andrew that the driver and the sniper were one and the same. This man worked solo, and by some miracle, he had avoided getting hit by any of the shots fired by Andrew's Beretta.

Andrew immediately swung the assault rifle around and acquired the running, lit-up sniper through the mounted scope. Keeping the cross-hairs on his attacker who was now about fifty metres away, he shouted as loudly as he could.

'Stop! Right now!' and then he aimed and fired.

The bullet slammed into a rock roughly five metres ahead of the fleeing sniper.

'Last chance!' shouted Andrew as the man lost his footing, stumbled and almost fell.

When Andrew fired again and the bullet split a rock next to him in two, the sniper finally got the message. There was simply no way for him to outrun the supersonic projectiles, and if Andrew had wanted to hit him, he could easily have done so. Realising the folly of his attempt to escape, he slowed down and came to a stop with his hands raised above his head. Through the scope, Andrew could see that he was panting heavily.

'Turn around and walk back towards me,' said Andrew.

The man immediately complied and began walking, his face screwed up as he moved across the ground with the pickup truck's glaring headlights shining directly at him. He understood that his only chance of staying alive now was to do exactly as he had been told. When he was about twenty minutes from the van, Andrew called out to him again.

'Drop any other weapons you have!' he shouted.

'I've got nothing else!' came the reply.

'Pull up your shirt and do a full turn,' said Andrew.

The sniper did as Andrew had asked, and it became clear that he had been telling the truth. Evidently expecting to be able to complete the hit at Donna's house with just the Remington, he carried no other weapons on him.

'Keep coming,' said Andrew as he used the strap on the assault rifle to sling it over his shoulder while whipping out the Beretta to aim at the sniper. 'All the way to me. Then turn around and get on your knees.'

The sniper, looking decidedly tense and dejected all at the same time, advanced slowly towards Andrew. He was wearing trainers, dark grey jeans and a black, tight-fitting long-sleeved t-shirt, and he appeared to be in his late thirties. His hair was short and dark, his face was clean-shaven, and if he had been put behind a shopping trolley in a supermarket, there wouldn't be a person on Earth who would have been able to guess that this man was a professional hitman. When he was about three metres away, Andrew called out to him.

'That's enough,' he said. 'On your knees.'

Without a word, the sniper slowly turned his back to Andrew and lowered himself onto his knees while keeping his hands above his head.

'Take off your belt,' commanded Andrew. 'Toss it back to me and put your hands behind your back.'

Once again, the sniper did as he had been told, and soon after, Andrew had tied the defeated man's wrists together. He did not resist or try to overwhelm Andrew. Instead, he appeared to be content with not ending up being shot dead, which struck Andrew as eminently sensible. Perhaps this man was someone he could talk to.

'What's your name?' Andrew said, stepping around to the front of the man with his Beretta still trained on him.

'Marlow,' said the man in a defeated tone of voice, keeping his head down. 'Jim Marlow. Hey man, thanks for not shooting me.'

'Well, I might change my mind,' said Andrew coldly. 'I am assuming you already know who I am.'

'Sterling, right?' said the man. 'Andrew Sterling. That's all I know about you. Just your name and what you look like. They sent me pictures.'

'Who did?' said Andrew.

'My handler,' said Marlow. 'The guy who gives me the jobs. He just calls himself the Fixer, but I don't know his real name. And I don't know who his client is. I have no idea who wants you dead.'

'I think I might,' said Andrew humourlessly.

'Look, man,' said Marlow. 'It's just a job, alright? It's nothing personal.'

'It's kind of difficult to think that way when you have 7.62 rounds coming at you,' said Andrew.

'You know your stuff,' said Marlow, glancing up at Andrew. 'Were you in the military?'

'The less you know, the better,' said Andrew. 'How are you paid?'

'Untraceable cash,' said Marlow.

'Were you paid upfront?' said Andrew.

'Half up front, half upon completion,' said Marlow. 'Standard setup. Handover in person at our usual location just outside San Angelo.'

'Alright. Listen, Marlow,' said Andrew. 'I am going to make you an offer, and you are free to decide if you want to take it. Alright?'

'Sure, man,' said Marlow, sounding eager to please. 'Whatever you want.'

'Here it is,' said Andrew. 'Either you call your handler right now and tell him that I am dead and you want the rest of your money, or I walk you out into the desert and put a bullet in the back of your head. So, what's it going to be?'

Marlow managed a small laugh at the lack of actual options available to him, and then he nodded.

'Alright,' he said. 'You've got me. My phone is in my back pocket.'

Ten minutes later, Marlow had completed the call to his handler and arranged for the payment of the remaining bounty. The handover of the cash was scheduled to take place two hours later in an abandoned warehouse on the western outskirts of the small city of San Angelo roughly forty minutes to the south. Andrew made Marlow bend the van's mangled bodywork away from the wheel well and then swap out its blown tyre for a spare. He then had Marlow walk him through the usual procedure for collecting his bounties. Finally, he made Marlow point to the warehouse shown on a satellite map on Andrew's phone.

'If you play your cards right,' said Andrew, 'I'll let you walk away from this alive. It's not you I am after. I'll even let you keep the money.'

'Thanks, man,' said Marlow.

'I'll be right behind you all the way to San Angelo,' said Andrew, 'so don't do anything stupid, OK?'

'Listen,' said Marlow calmly. 'I'm just happy to be alive, alright? I won't try anything. I swear.'

'Good,' said Andrew. 'Now, let's get moving.'

TWENTY-THREE

Almost two hours later, Andrew had taken up position in a dark spot on the other side of the open disused plot in the industrial area where the abandoned warehouse was located. The warehouse was about the size of a small house, and it was made from heavy corrugated metal that looked as if it had once been painted dark green, but that was now various shades of ochre, brown and red due to the rust that seemed to cover its entire exterior surface. It had an opening at one end that was big enough to fit a large van, and perched high on its gable was a floodlight that illuminated the surrounding area.

Sitting inside his pickup truck's passenger seat with the assault rifle resting on his lower arm as he gripped the wheel, Andrew was now tracking Marlow's van as it drove slowly along a narrow dirt track from the road towards the warehouse. Andrew could see the sniper clearly through his scope, and all he could do now was hope that the man valued his life sufficiently to refrain from alerting the handler to his presence.

Marlow continued on until he arrived at the warehouse. He then proceeded to drive his van through the opening and inside the warehouse where he stopped the vehicle. After a couple of seconds, he turned the engine off, and then the van's red taillights turned off. Watching the van from behind, Andrew could no longer see Marlow, but there was enough light spilling into the warehouse for him to be able to see that the sniper had remained inside the van.

According to Marlow, the handler would show up carrying the cash within a couple of minutes of him parking inside the warehouse. Andrew took a couple of deep breaths and steadied his aim in anticipation of the handler emerging. His intention was to place a non-fatal shot in one of the handler's legs and then squeeze as much information out of him as possible while Marlow made off with the money. Marlow would never work as a hitman again, but that was undoubtedly a good thing, even for Marlow. People like that, even the good ones, often had a short life expectancy.

As he watched, a car drove past on the main road cutting through the industrial estate, and for a moment Andrew thought that it might be the handler. But then it continued on and disappeared. Andrew leaned his head back into the side of the rifle to look at the van through the scope again, and in that instant, a huge explosion ripped through the warehouse, lifting its entire roof into the air amid a giant fireball. The van was completely enveloped in the bright flash, and the explosion seemed to have emanated from directly beneath it.

With a jolt, Andrew jerked his head away from the scope and stared in shock and disbelief at the fiery conflagration about two hundred metres in front of him on the other side of the disused plot. As a burning, roiling column of fire and smoke rose from where the warehouse had stood until a few seconds earlier, he could see the mangled wreck of the van thrown over onto its roof. Looking through the scope again, it was barely recognisable as a vehicle and looked more like a twisted collection of jagged pieces of burning metal put together in an attempt at flaming modern art. Marlow had stood no chance of surviving the blast, and it would become a challenge for any forensics team to find anything that might identify him, except perhaps his teeth, which could be held up against his dental record. Everything else would have been ripped apart and burned to a crisp.

Gazing incredulously at the inferno, Andrew decided to get away from the scene as quickly as possible. Soon, there would be a fleet of fire engines and police vehicles swarming all over the area, and he didn't relish the prospect of having to explain his presence or the two recently fired weapons in his vehicle. With his headlight still switched off, he pulled out onto the road and sped away. There was no reason for him to remain in San Angelo, and any chance of finding out who Marlow's handler had been working for was now gone for good. Whoever the handler was, he had clearly been instructed by his client to eliminate Marlow after the successful hit on Andrew. And this now gave Andrew a window of opportunity, because as far as anyone knew, he was already dead.

What he needed to do now was head back to Revelation and get Donna, Emmett and Scarlett together somewhere safe to come up with a plan. If he was to have a chance of discovering evidence of McKinnon's involvement in the deaths of Barton and Billy Ray, and if he was ever going to find out what the general was planning in Washington, then there was only one path ahead. One way or another, he would have to get inside Stonewall Ranch undetected.

★   ★   ★

Jean-Pacal Mokri was sitting in a plush purple velvet-covered booth at the private members club in Manhattan named Decadence. The club was one of the most exclusive venues in New York, and no expense had been spared on its décor. The floor was varnished wood laid in a herringbone pattern. The walls were clad with ornate dark wood panels, and soft diffuse lighting emanated from a series of golden wall lights. The ceiling was made from dark wood, and it was coffered with deep, square plaster sections illuminated by a soft purple glow coming from concealed lighting strips.

Wearing a grey pinstriped suit and a pink shirt with gold cufflinks, Mokri was sipping champagne and enjoying the company. It had turned out that Tatyana no longer worked there, so on either side of him was a blond scantily clad young woman from somewhere in Belorussia. He couldn't remember where exactly, and he wasn't too interested. What mattered was that they were both exceptionally attractive and friendly in that transactional way that he appreciated, and both were dressed in something that approximated clothing but which bordered on what could more accurately be called 'strips of fabric' or perhaps even just 'strings'.

In front of him was a bottle of Bollinger Special Cuvée champagne and a small silver cylinder from which he had just extracted an expensive handcrafted Cuban cigar worth more than the combined monthly wages of the two women.

As he sat there, he was reminded of the song 'New York' sung by Frank Sinatra and the lyrics, *"If you can make it there, you can make it anywhere."* And he really had made it. He was on top of the world, and things were only going to get better from now on. Once the plan had been carried out, the only limits to what he would be able to do would be set by his own imagination. And he could imagine a lot.

As he puffed on his cigar with one hand and placed the other on the thigh of the young woman next to him, a male waiter approached. He was wearing black trousers, a white shirt and a blue silk waistcoat with floral patterns that had a slight sheen under the soft lighting. He plucked an elaborately created cocktail from a silver tray and placed it in front of Mokri, and then he produced a small bow.

'This is on the house,' he said deferentially with a slight foreign accent that Mokri couldn't place. 'Our signature Grapefruit Negroni with Moroccan honey. Bitter yet sweet. We hope you'll enjoy it.'

Saying nothing, Mokri nodded appreciatively and sat forward to reach for the cocktail as the waiter returned to the bar. It was a rich amber colour, and a small corkscrew of orange peel had been delicately arranged on half of the circumference of the glass. Mokri, who liked being pampered, picked up the drink and put it to his lips. As he drank, he could taste the bitter tang mixed with the honey, and the combination was divine. Perhaps he should order two more of those for the young women. After all, he had been planning to take one of them with him back to his hotel, but why settle for one when he could have two?

Finishing the delicious cocktail, he placed the glass back on the table, leaned back and smiled to himself. He then reached into his suit jacket pocket to extract his phone. There was just time to do a quick check of the markets in order to get a fix on where the different positions included in his and McKinnon's trading strategy would be initiated.

He opened his preferred financial markets app, ran his eyes down the list of financial instruments and noted the price changes for that day. Everything was still within acceptable limits. All he was waiting for now was the go-ahead from McKinnon. As he used his thumb to work his way further down the list, he suddenly realised that he was having trouble focusing his eyes. He blinked a few times, but to no avail, and then he felt a sharp stab in his stomach. Placing the phone on the table, he sat up and winced as he took a deep breath. Something wasn't right. He began to sweat, and he could now feel his heart racing.

Getting up and pushing past the young startled woman to his right, he staggered out of the booth and walked unsteadily towards the restrooms. By the time he got there, he felt nauseous, and sweat was pouring from his face. Ignoring the other people in the restroom, he barged into a cubicle and slammed the door shut. Turning around and sitting down on the closed toilet seat, he ripped open the top buttons of his shirt and gasped for air. Then he felt his heart begin to flutter uncomfortably.

Inside his body, the digoxin was now spreading throughout his body, and as it made its way to his heart, it induced increasingly severe palpitations. In small doses, the prescription cardiac glycoside medicine was used to regulate conditions such as irregular heartbeats. However, the dose of the bitter-tasting chemical compound was strong enough to wreak havoc on Mokri's heart, and after another few seconds, he entered cardiac arrest.

Mokri felt it happen. It was as if a tight and painful cramp suddenly shot through his chest, like an icepick stabbing right through him. Then he felt as if a powerful hand suddenly closed around his heart and squeezed it hard, preventing it from beating, and his whole body spasmed involuntarily as it happened. With wide eyes that looked as if they were about to pop out of his head, his arms clawed at the walls of the cubicle as he tried to get to his feet, but it was as if his body had lost all power, and his ability to control it was fading fast. He opened his mouth to cry for help, but only a pathetic squeak passed his lips.

Slumping back down onto the toilet seat and grimacing wildly from the excruciating pain, he gripped the left side of his chest with both hands. As the veins on his neck and the sides of his head bulged, he slid from the toilet onto the floor, where his body began to convulse. Producing a wet guttural groan, Jean-Pascal Mokri eventually curled up into a foetal position and lay there trembling for several long moments. Then he suddenly stopped moving, and his whole body relaxed and slumped lifelessly to the floor.

★   ★   ★

After spending the night inside his car sleeping in a layby on the highway back from San Angelo, Andrew stopped for breakfast at a small roadside diner about twenty kilometres from the city. He then headed for a set of GPS coordinates that Donna had sent him. Her text message had indicated that Emmett had been successfully patched up and that his wound was already healing fast. He was taking powerful painkillers but apparently swore that he felt better than he had done in years.

Just after midday, Andrew drove his pickup truck off the main road to the west of Revelation and continued along a dirt track that cut through the rocky and slightly undulating terrain northwest of town. With the loaded Beretta lying on the passenger seat and the assault rifle placed within reach across the backseats behind him, he was in no mood to take chances. What had begun as an effort to assist a friend in need who had ended up in the custody of local police, had now descended into a violent struggle to uncover the truth about something much bigger than a single man. However, that man had been Andrew's old friend, and he was now lying dead in a shallow grave in the desert. Come hell or high water, Andrew was now involved in whatever this was, and he was determined to see it to the end.

In the distance, a range of barren hills rose up, and as he approached the GPS coordinates, the barely visible dirt track meandered through the parched landscape until it finally ended inside a gully in front of a light-coloured rockface. At the centre of the rocky rise was the entrance to what appeared to be an old mine, complete with heavy timber supports and a set of rickety-looking metal rails that extended into the darkness inside. The seemingly derelict mine would have looked completely abandoned had it not been for Donna's red coupe parked near the entrance. Next to it was a small silver hatchback that belonged to Scarlett. As Andrew parked next to the other two cars and turned off the engine, Donna, Emmett and Scarlett all emerged from the shade of the entrance. The women gave him a wave, and Emmett looked to be waddling slightly due to his injured leg, but he otherwise looked to be back to his normal self.

'Everything alright?' called Andrew as he stepped out of the vehicle and approached them.

'All good,' said Donna.

'We're fine,' said Scarlett.

'How are you, Emmet?' said Andrew, regarding the older man for a moment.

'Good as new,' said Emmett, putting out his large calloused hand to greet Andrew. 'It was just a scratch.'

'Interesting place,' said Andrew, looking around inside the gully. 'I'm assuming this is some sort of abandoned mine?'

'That's right,' said Emmett. 'But it was never on any maps. It never had a permit, you see. My old man told me about this place when I was a boy, and we rode out here a couple of times. He told me that a bunch of illegal miners went looking for silver here about a hundred years ago. Apparently, they never found any, and then the mine collapsed on them. The tunnel only goes in about fifty yards, and then there's just a wall of rock. The story goes that they all got trapped in there and died, and no one has ever tried to open it back up again. So, I guess they're still in there somewhere.'

'That's a bad way to go,' said Andrew, glancing in the direction of the dark entrance.

'I suppose that's true,' shrugged Emmett, 'but I guess that's what you get for being an opportunist like that. Anyway, how are you doing, son?'

'Well,' said Andrew, glancing at Donna. 'I managed to get Billy Ray's phone from Donna's house, but the hallway might need a bit of work.'

He proceeded to tell the two of them about the events in Revelation and then later in San Angelo the previous evening.

'Hot damn!' said Emmett, after Andrew had told them about the explosion that incinerated Marlow and any chance of discovering the identity of his paymaster. 'We're dealing with a bunch of certifiable psychos here, as if I needed any reminding. And there's definitely something very big about to go down.'

'Evidently so,' said Andrew, 'and they are prepared to do anything to prevent anyone from finding out what it is. But we can stop them. We just need to find a way to get inside Stonewall Ranch and locate the evidence we need. So, thank you for coming out here to meet me.'

'Pay it no mind,' said Emmett. 'Anyone with eyes in their heads can see that the police ain't gonna do nothin' about this whole thing. So, it's up to us now.'

'We all have good reasons to be here,' said Donna sombrely. 'Isn't that right, Scarlett?'

'Damn right,' said Scarlett with a steely look. 'Those bastards took someone near and dear to all of us, and they need to pay. Whatever it is they're cooking up out there at the ranch, we need to stop them if we can.'

'Amen to that,' nodded Emmett.

'Alright,' said Andrew, lowering himself onto one knee and drawing a rough outline of Stonewall Ranch in the dirt, using small rocks to indicate various buildings that he saw on his visit there. 'Let's make a plan then. I don't want any of you to be put in harm's way if we can avoid it, but I need to get inside McKinnon's office. And I am sure they also have some sort of operations room where they plan their missions. There's bound to be a tonne of evidence there if I can just find a way to get to it.'

'They do,' said Scarlett. 'I've never been inside, but it is down in the basement near the team rooms.'

'But listen,' said Emmett. 'They call it Stonewall Ranch, but they might as well have named it Fort Knox. Ain't nobody getting into that place undetected. Not without some serious skulduggery.'

'There's always a way,' said Andrew. 'Some weak spot that nobody has thought of. Something so mundane and trivial that no one has even considered it a vulnerability.'

'What about the cops?' said Scarlett. 'We need a way to stop Hogan and his deputies from showing up and ruining the whole thing. Isn't that the first thing we need to take care of?'

'I might be able to do something about that,' said Donna. 'If Hogan and his posse are called out to Stonewall Ranch, they'll need their police cruisers. But if they don't work, then they'll be stuck in town.'

'How are you fixing to do that?' said Emmett. 'How do you stop a bunch of cars from working?'

'Sugar,' said Donna. 'You pour sugar into the gas tanks, and pretty soon the engines stop working.'

'She's right,' said Andrew. 'If you put enough sugar into a fuel tank, it gets pulled into the combustion chambers, where it basically turns into sticky caramel, and then the whole engine block overheats and seizes up. Sabotage 101. It's simple but very effective.'

'But you'll need access to the back of the sheriff's office,' said Scarlett. 'How are you going to get in there without anyone seeing you?'

'I'll find a way,' said Donna. 'I only need a couple of minutes there alone. I'm sure I can pull it off.'

'Alright,' said Andrew. 'That could work. But you'd have to be really careful. Hogan is as crooked as they come, and some of his deputies might be too. Possibly Sergeant Fuller as well. This is not without risk.'

'I understand,' said Donna. 'But this is something I can definitely do.'

'Ok,' said Andrew. 'Just as long as you bring your gun.'

'Of course,' said Donna.

'I think I might have an idea for how to get you inside the ranch,' said Scarlett, looking pensively at the dirt map in front of them and then glancing up at Andrew.

'Alright,' said Andrew, turning to face her. 'Let's hear it.'

'They've got about fifty people working out there at any given time,' said Scarlett, 'and every few days, a large truck comes in bringing food and drinks for the catering staff to put into the refrigerators. I am sometimes asked to help out with that. If you could find a way to get inside the delivery truck, then you should be able to sneak out when they're not looking. I might be able to distract them for long enough.'

'That could work,' nodded Andrew. 'Are you able to draw me a sketch of the interior layout? Especially the basement level?'

'Sure,' said Scarlett. 'I don't have access to all of it, and I don't know what goes on in the different rooms, but I think I have seen enough of it to make a decent sketch.'

'Great,' said Andrew. 'That takes me inside. But if I am going to be able to gain access to McKinnon's office and then the basement level, we will need a major distraction of some kind. Something that will put the whole ranch on high alert.'

'Well,' said Emmett, pointing to a spot outside the ranch's perimeter. 'I could hole up here with a rifle and start taking potshots from outside the fence. That oughta scare'em plenty.'

'No doubt,' nodded Andrew, 'but it won't take them long to find you and pin you down, and then you'll have no way out of there. You probably won't make it out alive.'

'I agree,' said Donna, looking uneasy. 'It's too risky, Emmett. If they were prepared to kill Billy Ray, they wouldn't think twice about sending you to kingdom come. I'm just not OK with this.'

'Alright, fine,' said Emmet, holding up his hands. 'If that's how you feel. Let's come up with something else then.'

'How about driving a tractor through the fence right about here,' said Donna, pointing to a spot on the perimeter fence where the distance to the mansion was the shortest. 'You could put a brick on the accelerator and point it straight at the mansion. That would be sure to create havoc. They wouldn't be able to stop it with bullets, and by the time they realise that there is no one in the cab, it would be crashing through buildings and whatnot.'

'They could probably shoot out the tyres pretty easily,' said Andrew. 'I don't think it would make it to the mansion. But it just might cause enough trouble for them to let me move around unseen for a short time.'

'Hang on now,' said Emmett, holding up a hand. 'Wait a little old minute, Donna. You just got me to thinkin'. I reckon I've got an idea.'

'What?' said Donna.

'Now, this might sound totally crazy,' said Emmett. 'But I have an old friend who might be able to help us out here. Bill Scarborough. All I need to do is convince old Bill to lend me a piece of farming equipment that I don't even think he's using anymore. Damn thing is just collecting dust in his barn.'

'Farming equipment?' said Andrew.

'That's right,' said Emmett, a sly enigmatic smile spreading across his leathery face. 'And let me tell you, she's a beaut.'

Twenty-Four

After the war council by the abandoned silver mine had ended, Donna and Emmett drove off towards Bill Scarborough's farm about eight miles further north, and Scarlett returned to Stonewall Ranch to get ready for her shift. It was vital that she show up for work as usual and that no one suspected that she was now playing her part to get Andrew inside the ranch and then help bring the entire place down. Before leaving, she drew Andrew a map of the ranch interior and provided him with details of the Sweetwater catering company that serviced the ranch twice a week. All he had to do was to sneak onto the right delivery truck just before it left the packing warehouse. Because it was the same truck and driver making the run to the ranch every time, Scarlett also gave Andrew a description of the driver, which would allow him to identify and board the correct vehicle.

By late afternoon, with the sun at his back and moving lower towards the horizon, Andrew was headed east along Interstate Highway 20 towards Sweetwater. Scarlett had told him that, with an 8 p.m. arrival at the ranch, she reckoned the delivery truck would be leaving the warehouse roughly half an hour before that. The terrain this far north of Revelation was somewhat less arid, and on both sides of the highway, there were wide strips of green irrigated farmland where local farmers appeared to be growing corn and various types of feed grain. The landscape was almost completely flat, and when Andrew joined the I-20 cutting east in an almost perfectly straight line, he found himself among more cars than he had seen for days.

After about 10 kilometres, he was approaching the small city of Roscoe when he spotted a sign by the side of the road announcing the presence of a Sunoco Gas Station up ahead. Deciding that he needed both food and fuel, he peeled off and drove under the highway to pull in at the fuel station on the other side of the interstate. Parking next to a pump, he got out and filled up the tank while looking around the area. There were only a couple of other vehicles around, but as he glanced towards the underpass through which he had just arrived, he spotted a police cruiser turning and heading in his direction. He finished filling the tank and headed inside to pay and pick up some food. As he did so, the police cruiser pulled into the forecourt and parked next to another pump behind his pickup truck. As it did so, he saw that it had the words Texas Highway Patrol emblazoned along its side.

After paying, Andrew walked back outside to see a deputy wearing a dark blue uniform standing by the front of the cruiser and looking at the back of his pickup truck. Holding some sort of electronic PDA device in one hand, he was wearing a dark hat and aviator sunglasses, and by his hip were a pistol, a spare mag and a set of shiny steel handcuffs. For a moment, Andrew considered turning around and walking back inside, but then the deputy looked up and regarded him as he approached.

'Is this here your car, sir?' he asked casually.

'Yup,' Andrew lied.

'Hmm,' said the deputy as he looked back down at his PDA. 'It says here this car was reported stolen down in Revelation yesterday. Do you know anything about that?'

The deputy wore a name tag that read 'Deputy Harris', and as he spoke, his voice remained calm and friendly, but Andrew noticed that his right hand was now hovering near his service pistol. Once again, Andrew decided against doing anything rash and instead hoped that he would be able to talk his way out of the situation.

'That must be some sort of mistake,' said Andrew steadily. 'I've just come from Eunice over in New Mexico. This is my first day in Texas.'

'Really?' said Deputy Harris, sounding unconvinced before regarding Andrew for a moment. 'You ain't from around here, am I right?'

'No, sir,' said Andrew. 'I'm just passing through on my way to the East Coast.'

'East Coast, huh?' said Harris, appearing to ponder the idea of going there on purpose and then deciding that it sounded unlikely and perhaps even pointless. 'You got some ID, sir?'

'Not on me,' Andrew lied again since his passport and credit cards were in his back pocket.

'Are you carrying a firearm on your person?' said Harris.

'I am,' said Andrew calmly, keen to avoid making the deputy nervous. 'Do you want me to show you?'

'Yes, please, if you don't mind,' said Harris, his fingertips now touching his service pistol. 'You go ahead and do that real slow now. Molasses-like.'

Andrew slowly pulled up his shirt and turned around to show the deputy the Beretta sitting at the small of his back.

'I'm going to have to take that from you for now,' said Harris. 'Alright, sir?'

'OK,' said Andrew, not moving a muscle until he felt Harris fishing out the pistol and taking a step back.

'Alright now, I'm going to ask you to step over here and sit in the back of my cruiser for a minute,' said Harris. 'I need to run your plate again and then call the sheriff in Revelation. We need to clear this up.'

Andrew turned around to look at him for a moment, considering one final time whether to try to resist and get out of there, but once again, he decided against it. It was likely to end in bloodshed, and the last thing he needed right now was to end up killing or injuring a state trooper. He would have to go along with the trooper's request and then try to play for time and wait for an opportunity to disappear.

'Fine,' he shrugged. 'Not a problem.'

With his right hand now placed on the grip of his pistol, Deputy Harris opened the rear passenger door for Andrew who climbed inside. Harris then closed the door and reached inside the front for his radio. After a brief conversation that Andrew struggled to hear from inside the back of the vehicle, Harris clipped the mike back onto the radio and climbed inside. He then started the engine and turned his head to speak to Andrew through the metal wire mesh.

'OK, sir,' he said, putting the cruiser into gear. 'We're just going to park out of the way and then wait here until this is all cleared up.'

'What do you mean by cleared up?' said Andrew.

'If you'll just kindly sit back and wait for about fifteen minutes, sir?' said Harris. 'Thank you.'

Harris drove slowly to the far side of the forecourt where he parked the cruiser, turned off the engine and stepped out, closing the door behind him. Then he leaned back against the front of the hood, adjusted his hat and folded his arms across his chest.

Inside the back of the police cruiser, Andrew was considering his options. If he couldn't manage to get out of there soon, he would miss his window to sneak inside the delivery truck in Sweetwater. And it would be a question of time before the deputy found the assault rifle inside the Honda, and then he would likely be in a lot more trouble than simply having driven a stolen car. He looked around the back of the cruiser, but unsurprisingly, there was nothing that would allow him an opportunity to escape.

Twenty minutes later, during which time Harris had barely moved a muscle except for turning his head to look at passing cars and tipping his hat once to greet someone, another police cruiser entered the forecourt and parked up. Unlike the vehicle he was in, this one looked only too familiar and had the word 'Sheriff' emblazoned down its side. Sitting inside at the wheel was Sergeant Fuller.

Shit, thought Andrew. *This is not good.*

Glancing occasionally in Andrew's direction, Harris and Fuller spoke for a couple of minutes, after which Harris came over and opened the door with his right hand resting on his pistol. He handed Fuller the Beretta, and the sergeant then circled around near the back of the cruiser where he extracted his own pistol from its holster.

'Sir, I'm gonna hand you over to Sergeant Fuller here,' said Harris. 'It seems you have some unfinished business down in Revelation. Please step out of the vehicle.'

Saying nothing, Andrew got out of the car and levelled a cold gaze at Fuller who gestured towards his own cruiser as Harris slipped a pair of handcuffs on Andrew's wrists.

'Fuller,' said Andrew evenly, eyeing the sergeant. 'Listen to me. I know what happened to my friend. I know what happened to Cooper. Are you really prepared to be a part of this thing?'

'Just doing my job,' shrugged Fuller, opening the rear passenger door. 'Now, please get inside, sir.'

Realising the futility of trying to talk to Sergeant Fuller, Andrew got into the back of the cruiser, and the deputy then slammed the door shut. After another few words with Harris, Fuller got into the front seat and set off for Revelation.

★   ★   ★

Andrew attempted to get through to Fuller a couple more times during the drive back to Revelation, but Fuller simply ignored him and turned on the radio. To Andrew, sitting handcuffed in the back of a police cruiser in rural Texas while listening to country music was certainly a novel experience, but not exactly a welcome one. His mind was racing, trying to anticipate what would happen next and how he could get out of his predicament. It was likely that Fuller would bring him back to the sheriff's office where Hogan would then hold him in a jail cell for stealing a car and probably a whole host of other trumped-up charges. Andrew might even end up making district attorney Bremmer's acquaintance in Sweetwater and then getting a firsthand look at the inside of the Nolan County jail.

When Sergeant Fuller drove his police cruiser into Revelation, he picked the same route that Andrew had driven on his first day in town. However, instead of continuing on towards the centre of town and the sheriff's office, he took a right turn along a road that cut through the outskirts and passed a Home Depot store, a trailer park and a water treatment facility.

'Where are we going?' Andrew said, leaning forward in his seat to get Fuller's attention.

As on the previous occasions, Fuller ignored him and turned down a street towards a small complex of dilapidated warehouse buildings that were arranged in a horseshoe shape. From the looks of the buildings and their loading bays, it appeared to have been part of some sort of logistics company. It was sitting behind a chain-linked fence, but the gate was open and there appeared to be no one there. Perhaps the company had gone out of business.

Fuller drove through the gates and parked near one of the loading bays. He turned the engine off, stepped out, pulled his gun from its holster and opened the door for Andrew to exit.

'Get out,' he said. 'And don't try anything.'

'Wouldn't dream of it,' said Andrew coolly.

Walking behind Andrew with his pistol pointing at his back, Fuller led him up a ramp and into a small section of the warehouse. The space was empty except for a few stacks of wooden pallets and a rusty-looking forklift. Fuller directed Andrew to stand in the middle of the space, facing the outside.

'What now?' said Andrew.

'Now we wait,' said Fuller, standing off to one side with his pistol still pointing at his handcuffed detainee.

As it turned out, they didn't have to wait long, because only a few minutes later, Andrew heard the sound of a car engine, and then he saw Sheriff Hogan's police cruiser park next to Fuller's. Shortly thereafter, the overweight sheriff entered the warehouse, taking his hat off and wiping sweat from his brow before placing it back on his head and waddling towards the two others.

'Nice to see you again,' said Andrew, as he levelled his gaze at the sheriff.

'I wish I could say likewise,' said Hogan wearily, pulling up the belt in his trousers lest his large paunch push them off his hips.

'So, is this your idea of justice here in Revelation?' said Andrew, looking around the warehouse. 'I thought you said you like to do things by the book?'

'That's real cute,' said Hogan with a small shake of the head as he regarded Andrew for a moment.

'You're going down, you know,' said Hogan flatly. 'And when you're down, there ain't no getting back up. Not for you. Not as long as I'm the sheriff in this town.'

'From what I hear,' said Andrew. 'The only reason you're sheriff is because McKinnon paid for it to happen. You'd be nothing without him. That's what people say, anyway.'

Hogan stopped in front of Andrew, lowered his head and placed his hands on his hips while staring down at the concrete floor for a long moment before speaking again.

'Goddamn it,' he finally said with a bitter sigh. 'Why'd you have to come here and make trouble for everybody? Why couldn't you just keep your damn nose out of our business?'

'An old friend asked me for help,' said Andrew. 'I couldn't let him down.'

'Well, that's mighty noble of you,' said Hogan, nodding sagely but with a strange look of regret on his face. 'Even for a Limey like you. Still, the fact remains. You've caused all kinds of problems for people in this here town. You really shouldn't have done that. And now this whole thing is out of my hands.'

'What do you mean?' said Andrew, but then he heard the sound of a vehicle arriving, and it sounded like a large pickup truck.

'You'll see,' said Hogan, stepping over next to Fuller.

When three large bearded men walked inside the warehouse wearing leather shoulder holsters with pistols, Andrew immediately recognised one of them. It was Travis Tatum, the Stetson-wearing wingman of the recently deceased Cody Thornton. When he spotted Andrew, he pulled his pistol out and racked the slide, and then a vicious leer spread across his face.

'Well, looky here,' he said mockingly. 'If it ain't that damn Brit again. When they told me, I wasn't sure if I believed them, but here you are again. In the flesh. Nice job, Hogan.'

'Just get him out of here,' said Hogan, sounding uneasy. 'You boys do what you need to do. I don't want nothin' to do with it, and I don't want to know anything about it.'

'Relax, old man,' said Tatum, turning to Hogan and giving him a wink. 'You're already knee-deep. What, with Billy Ray and all? But as long as you do as the general tells you, everything will be just fine. Don't you worry.'

'We're headed back to the office now,' said Hogan, signalling for Fuller to follow him as he started walking. 'Like I said. No need to tell us how this ends. As far as we're concerned, this never happened.'

'That's what I like to hear,' said Tatum, returning his gaze to Andrew as the two cops began leaving the warehouse for their police cruisers. 'Nice to see you again, Sterling. If that's your real name. Not that I care.'

'It is,' said Andrew, doing his best to appear calm while his mind was racing to find a way to turn the tables on the three goons.

On his way out, Fuller walked over to Tatum and handed him Andrew's Beretta, and then he followed Hogan out to the cruisers.

'Right,' said Tatum slowly, as Hogan and Fuller disappeared, his expression hardening as he gestured to the two men by his side. 'Say hello to my two buddies, Curtis and Buck.'

Curtis was tall and broad with a full beard, and he was wearing cowboy boots, jeans and a blue and green checkered flannel shirt. Buck was shorter but equally bulky, and he was wearing a camo t-shirt, black cargo trousers and boots.

'Trust me, these two gentlemen have been keen to meet you ever since we found Thornton where you left him,' said Tatum. 'And I must admit, I've been looking forward to seeing you again myself. Curtis, make sure he ain't carrying anything else.'

'Oh,' said Andrew, raising an eyebrow as Curtis approached and began patting him down for weapons. 'So you found him? Was it the vultures that gave it away?'

'Smartass,' said Tatum icily. 'Let's see how long that lasts.'

'Just these,' said Curtis, giving Andrew's passport, credit cards and phone to Tatum.

'Shit,' chuckled Tatum. 'Hogan and Fuller really did a piss-poor job of searching him. Man, that Hogan ain't the sharpest knife in the drawer. In fact, he's an idiot. But as McKinnon likes to say, he's *our* idiot.

Anyway, the general will be keen to see what's on here.'

He held up Andrew's phone next to his head and waggled it from side to side while looking at his prisoner. Then he put it in his trouser pocket and opened Andrew's passport.

'Andrew Sterling,' he said musingly. 'Supposed to be some sort of hero soldier. SAS, just like his dead friend. You don't much look like that right now, if you don't mind me saying so.'

Andrew said nothing but kept his gaze levelled impassively at Tatum.

'Right,' Tatum finally said, closing the passport. 'Get him into the car, boys. We're going back out into the desert. Have ourselves some fun.'

TWENTY-FIVE

The pickup truck trundled along the faint dirt track into the high desert. The sun had just set beyond the hills to the west, and the sky was worthy of a painting with its long, high-altitude wisps of pink clouds framed against a pale steel blue sky. As the truck moved through the dusk, its powerful headlights lit up the almost barren terrain in front of it as the vehicle rocked and bounced slightly as it moved across the uneven ground.

With Buck at the wheel and Tatum next to him in the front passenger seat, Andrew was in the cramped backseat, still with his wrists handcuffed and his hands resting in his lap. He was looking straight ahead, intentionally avoiding eye contact with any of the three mercenaries but allowing his eyes to move furtively in an attempt to identify anything that might give him a chance to escape. Next to him was Curtis, sitting at a slight angle with his pistol out, pointing at Andrew's torso.

'Man, we should have brought ourselves some beers,' said Tatum flippantly. 'We could have had ourselves a little party out here. Just like last time we did this trip.'

Curtis and Buck chuckled dutifully. Wherever the two men were in the Ironclad pecking order, they were clearly below Tatum, who himself was almost certainly nowhere near the top. But that was the thing about ex-military employees. They were used to operating within a large hierarchy, and taking orders had become second nature to them. This in turn made it easy for someone like McKinnon to exert complete control over them, even when what he wanted them to do was illegal or worse. And having successfully spun his men a tale about lost pride and future glory, there was now nothing they would not do for him.

Eventually, the pickup truck arrived at the rusty old wreck of the minivan next to the firepit where Andrew and Donna had made their gruesome discovery a couple of days earlier. Buck parked the truck, and Tatum then leapt out, pulled his gun and opened the door to the backseat.

'Get out,' he said to Andrew, jerking his gun to make the point. 'I've got something to show you.'

Carrying a torch and flanked by Curtis and Buck who both had their pistols out, Tatum then led Andrew through the dusk past the minivan and in amongst the bushes. When they arrived at the spot where Barton had been buried, Tatum stopped dead in his tracks, pointing the torchlight at the disturbed shallow grave. Then he turned to Andrew with a look of mild incredulity.

'Did you do that?' he asked with a grin tinged with surprise. 'Did you come out here and dig up your own friend?'

'I found him where you bastards left him,' said Andrew coldly. 'He deserved better than this.'

'Actually, he didn't,' said Tatum. 'See, from what I understand, he was trying to screw the general over. How exactly he was fixing to do that, I'm not sure. But that's what they told me. And ain't nobody getting away with that.'

'Maybe he spent enough time with you lunatics to finally realise just how totally fucking crazy McKinnon is,' said Andrew evenly, staring straight ahead at the grave.

'You just keep running your mouth,' said Tatum with disdain. 'It won't make any damn difference to how this ends. Now, pick up that shovel and start digging. Over there'll be fine.'

Tatum indicated to a spot next to Barton's grave, took a step back and pointed the gun at Andrew's head.

'Get on it,' he said with a snarl. 'Or I'll put a bullet in your head right now.'

Andrew looked past the gun and into Tatum's eyes for a moment, and he saw a readiness to follow words with deeds. But he also saw a sliver of apprehension, as if the mercenary, for all his bluster, was less than perfectly convinced that he had the situation under control. Andrew averted his eyes, shrugged and walked to pick up the shovel.

As he began digging his own grave, scooping shovelful after shovelful of pale sand and dirt into an elongated heap next to the emerging man-sized trench, Tatum and his two companies lit up cigarettes and watched in silence. At one point, Andrew glanced towards them with sweat running off his brow, and behind the bright glow of cigarette embers, their faces spoke of hard cold vengeance for their dead friend Thornton. In a strange sense, Andrew knew exactly how they felt. This was now a case of retribution pitted against revenge.

When the grave was about a metre deep, Tatum took a step forward.

'That's enough,' he said. 'Step on out of there. Lose the shovel.'

Andrew stopped and panted for a couple of moments. He briefly considered throwing the shovel at Tatum, but he would be dead before it could hit him. The only way out of this was to appear defeated and then try to use the complacency of the three mercenaries against them. Making sure to look exhausted and out of breath, he tossed the shovel into the bushes and stepped out of the freshly dug grave with a grimace.

'On your knees,' said Tatum coldly.

He was now pointing the pistol at Andrew while the two companies flanking him moved out to the sides a few metres behind him. They were still holding their weapons in their hands, but they appeared to sense no threat as they stood there. Andrew lowered himself onto his knees and sat back with his hands in his lap.

'This is where it ends for you,' said Tatum. 'You looking forward to joining your old buddy?'

Andrew looked up and gave him a look as cold as ice, but said nothing.

'Jesus Christ,' said Tatum, briefly glancing back at his two comrades. 'I swear to god, this guy's a smartass even when he's not talking.'

'Why don't you go fuck yourself, you amateur,' said Andrew derisively, now intentionally attempting to rile the mercenary.

'Now, that's not very cordial of you,' said Tatum with mock disappointment. 'You just seem to not understand how things work around here. See, if you fuck around, then eventually you're gonna find out. And you've been fucking around.'

'That's more or less what Sheriff Hogan told me,' said Andrew.

'Doesn't make it any less true,' said Tatum.

'I guess you're still really sore about your boyfriend Thornton,' said Andrew scornfully. 'If it makes you feel any better, he suffered. A lot. He looked like someone had spent a week putting a cheese grater to his whole body. It was nasty.'

Tatum gave a shake of the head and produced a bitter smile before glancing at Andrew again.

'Well, I am here to put that right,' he said. 'See, I'm an Old Testament kind of guy. An eye for an eye. That type of thing.'

He then racked the slide on his pistol and moved to stand a couple of metres from Andrew with the weapon pointing at his forehead.

'Any last words?' he said.

'Just don't fuck this up,' said Andrew as he looked up at Tatum, his words laced with derision. 'Put the damn muzzle on my forehead so you don't miss. I don't trust you fucking rednecks to hit a target from more than a few inches away.'

Tatum scoffed, gave a small shake of the head and glanced over his shoulder towards his two companions who chuckled.

'Can you believe the fucking lip on this guy?' he said. 'Alright. Have it your way.'

He then stepped close to Andrew and pressed the muzzle against the forehead of the kneeling and handcuffed prisoner in front of him before narrowing his eyes and speaking again.

'Say goodnight.'

In the blink of an eye, Andrew's cuffed hands left his lap and came up to grip Tatum's pistol around the top of the slide and the bottom of the receiver. At the same time, he jerked his head to one side and yanked Tatum's arm violently towards himself, using the mercenary's heft to pull himself up onto his feet.

Still holding the gun with one hand and shifting the other to grip around Tatum's trigger finger, he rotated his upper body so that his back was pressed into Tatum's chest, and the gun was now in front of him. As Curtis and Buck fumbled with their weapons, Andrew twisted himself and Tatum around to point his weapon at Curtis, pulling the trigger twice in quick succession. The dry pistol reports raced out across the desert as the two bullets smacked audibly into the mercenary's chest and he started going down.

Without delay, Andrew then wrenched Thornton's gun arm around to point towards Buck who had now managed to raise his own weapon. However, the mercenary hesitated to fire out of fear of hitting his superior, and this allowed Andrew to force two more shots from Tatum's pistol. One of them missed, but the other ripped through Buck's throat, sending a spray of blood shooting from his neck, and then he went down, dropping his gun while desperately clutching his throat. The whole thing had taken just a few seconds, and Tatum was only now beginning to regain his composure to fight back.

Still standing inside Tatum's embrace with his back to the mercenary while gripping the pistol, Andrew brought his head forward slightly, only to ram it backwards as hard as he could. The back of his head connected with Tatum's nose amid a wet crunch of cartilage and a cry of pain. The shock of the impact on his face caused Tatum to release his grip on the gun, and this allowed Andrew to rip it from his hand and push himself away from him. As he did so, he spun around, raised the weapon and fired again.

The bullet punched through Tatum's chest and heart, exiting his torso and cutting through the bushes behind him. With his heart punctured and suffering an instant loss of blood pressure, Tatum's legs gave way under him, and he collapsed onto his knees and keeled over sideways onto the ground in a puff of dust. With his mouth opening and closing like a caught fish and blood pouring from his mangled nose, his eyes bulged in shock at what had happened and at the realisation of what was coming next.

Slowly, Andrew raised himself to his full height, took a deep breath and exhaled slowly. Then he took a couple of steps towards his would-be executioner and went down on his haunches next to him. Tatum's mouth was still working, but no sound came out, and his wide eyes blinked a couple of times as they found Andrew's face staring up at him in disbelief. A croaking sound emanated from his throat, followed soon after by a final dry hiss as the air from his lungs was expelled for the final time. With his eyes staring vacantly up into the night sky, he moved no more.

'An eye for an eye,' said Andrew coldly as he looked down at the dead corpse of Travis Tatum. 'I'll remember that.'

He began retrieving his phone, passport and credit cards from Tatum's pockets, and he also extracted the dead man's phone, which he quickly searched for messages. Seeing that Tatum had recently sent a message to Roy Cobb saying that Andrew was in his possession and about to be taken into the desert, he quickly typed up a new message informing McKinnon's righthand man that Andrew was now dead and that they would be returning to the ranch soon. After a few moments, a reply from Cobb pinged in, congratulating him and his companions on solving a serious problem and then telling him that a bonus was on the way for all three of them.

Andrew grabbed his own phone and checked the time. The delivery truck from the catering company would have left the warehouse in Sweetwater already, thereby denying Andrew the opportunity to sneak aboard. But perhaps all was not lost. He quickly called Donna and told her about what had happened. She was driving, and he could hear the noise from the car in the background.

'Holy cow!' she said. 'Are you alright?'

'I'm fine,' said Andrew as he stood up and looked down at the three dead mercenaries lying on the ground around him. 'Lucky to be alive, but fine. But we have a problem now. I won't be able to make it to Sweetwater in time to sneak onto the delivery truck.'

'I know,' said Donna, sounding anxious. 'We need a new plan.'

'Is there anywhere we could interrupt the van's journey?' asked Andrew.

'Well,' said Donna. 'There's a final intersection on the outskirts of Revelation on the way out of town. The truck will have to pass through there before heading out along the country road towards the ranch. We could try to somehow hold it up there, but I just can't get there in time. I'm too far away.'

'Shit,' Andrew said. 'And Scarlett won't be able to get out and then back in again without someone realising that something is up.'

'I think I know what we can do,' said Donna. 'I'll call Paige. She'll help me out.'

'Are you sure?' said Andrew. 'We can't put her in any danger.'

'We won't,' said Donna. 'All she's got to do is drive her car to exactly where I tell her and block the truck. And then you have to lie in wait and get ready to get inside.'

'Right,' said Andrew, pondering the idea. 'I guess that could work. If you think she's up for it, then let's give it a shot. It's our only option right now.'

'Alright,' said Donna. 'Let me just tell you where you need to be waiting at about 7:45. And then I'll call Paige. Don't worry. She'll definitely help us out.'

*   *   *

There were about thirty mercenaries in the tightly packed ops centre, in addition to the usual crew of mission planners, technicians and members of the Intel team. Towards the front of the room near the display-covered wall was the Nightcrawler team, and there was a palpable sense of respect being given to the Tier 1 operators by the rest of the soldiers and guards.

At the very front, facing all of them, was General John McKinnon, wearing his midnight blue general's dress uniform consisting of a pair of trousers with two stripes of gold braid running down their sides, a jacket with his medals and commendations, as well as two stars on its shoulders. He was standing on a raised podium behind a small lectern which he gripped with both hands as he surveyed his men with a steely expression. No one said a word as they all waited for their commander to speak.

'Good evening, gentlemen,' he said gravely. 'And thank you all for being here. Tonight, we're going to change history. Some of you already know what is about to unfold, but most of you don't yet know the full details. Once I'm done talking to you, Roy Cobb will lay out everything you need to know.'

A murmur ran through the crowd, but it was one of excitement rather than concern or reticence. Several of the men gave each other meaningful looks, but the Nightcrawlers didn't seem to stir at all. With Cormac and the others keeping their gazes held firmly in the direction of the other men, Ironclad's Tier-1 operators had already been briefed several weeks earlier.

'Now, as you all know,' continued McKinnon solemnly, 'this country is in the midst of a crisis. And if we don't do something about it, then pretty soon there won't be a country left to defend. The president and the politicians in Washington have been taken over by greed and special interest organisations that are bleeding us dry and allowing the fabric of this nation to come apart at the seams. Yet, at the same time, the federal government is choking the life out of this country's citizens, with more laws being added every minute to restrict the free American spirit.'

McKinnon paused for dramatic effect while his men nodded and murmured their agreement.

'And if someone should rise up against it,' he continued, 'then we all know what would happen next. They'd call it an insurrection so that they could send in the army to quell it. And then they would put on the thumb screws and begin to take away your rights one by one. This has happened many times before. In the Civil War, during which my ancestor Thomas Stonewall Jackson was heroically killed, the politicians in Washington enacted the Confiscation Act of 1862. This act allowed the federal government to confiscate land and property from so-called *"disloyal citizens"*, meaning anyone who was fighting for the Confederacy. And there ain't no reason why they wouldn't do this again. Next, it'll be the 2nd Amendment. They'll come for your guns, boys. Trust me on that. And then finally, they'll take your freedom and lock you up unless you comply. And we can't let that happen. This is our last chance to correct the course of this nation's proud history.'

The crowd murmured again, this time more vocally, as McKinnon tugged at their patriotic heartstrings.

'This is the tyranny that our founding fathers warned against,' McKinnon went on. 'This very nation was forged in the crucible of insurrection. Had it not been for the battles at Lexington and Concorde in 1775 and the uprising against the tyrannical British, there simply would have been no United States of America. That's a fact. So, that insurrection was a beautiful thing, and sometimes this type of creative destruction is necessary in order for a nation to survive. Now, we have again arrived at one of those moments in history when action on the part of true patriots is required. The head of the snake in Washington has to be cut off for this nation to continue to live free. And it is the duty of every man here to make that happen. Your oath when you joined the military was to the United States Constitution. Not to the president. To the constitution. The Constitution that promised us freedom to live our lives free from the interference of the federal government. Tonight, we shall make a stand. With this one deed, we shall rise up to defend our constitution. To defend this nation. It wasn't for nothing that the battle cry of the insurrectionists of 1775 was Live Free or Die!'

At that, the room erupted in cheers and roars, and several of the men were pumping their fists in the air.

'Now, of course,' said McKinnon reasonably, once the clamour had died down, 'revolutions are expensive in both blood and treasure. That's why we have been doing what we have been doing. And our patriotism will continue to take a toll on us. But you all know what you signed up for, and you all knew this wasn't going to be a cakewalk. Yes, we've taken losses, which is what happens in war. And if it comes to it, I want you all to fight like hell. Don't let them take you alive. This is a fight for survival, not only for us but for this very nation, and there ain't no sense in living if all you do is end up living in chains. We are true patriots. Every last one of us here. And our cause is just. Our cause is righteous. And we *will* prevail!'

As McKinnon raised a fist in the air, saluted his men and stepped back from the podium, everyone in the room rose to their feet and saluted the former head of JSOC. He seemed to have them in the palm of his hands, and they continued to cheer as Roy Cobb emerged to present the plan for what was about to unfold. As he did so, McKinnon led the Nightcrawler team into the prep room where their cages were located. Once inside, he turned to them as they huddled around him.

'Everybody ready?' he asked.

'Ready as we'll ever be,' said Cormac gravely, with Knox and Tyler both nodding beside him.

'Good,' said McKinnon. 'Everything is all set to go. Now, I ain't gonna lie, we've had a couple of hiccups lately. As you know, there was a man running around this town causing all kinds of problems. Barton's old buddy. But he's dead now, so I want you to forget about him and focus on the job at hand. We're on course for something truly heroic tonight. And we cannot let ourselves be distracted from our greater purpose.'

'We're with you all the way, sir,' said Cormac.

'I know you are, boys,' said McKinnon. 'And don't forget, Willis died believing in our cause. We're not going to forget about his sacrifice, and we're going to remember his name and the names of all of our fallen brothers when we finally put things right. But it's all up to you now. Godspeed.'

With that, he stood up straight and saluted the Nightcrawler team. They snapped to attention and returned the salute. Carrying their weapons and kit, they then filed out of the prep room towards the stairs leading up the helicopter pad where the V-280 was waiting with its engines running.

TWENTY-SIX

At half past seven in the evening, it was now almost dark, and Andrew was waiting at a bus stop about thirty metres from the last intersection before the country road led south and out of town. Having parked Tatum's pickup truck well out of sight, he was now simply waiting for the delivery truck to pass by.

As he sat there, he suddenly heard the unmistakable sound of the twin-rotor aircraft he had spotted several days earlier. Turning to face the direction it appeared to be coming from, he soon spotted it coming almost directly towards him out over the high desert. Flying low and fast through the relative darkness, it cut across the terrain at impressive speeds and passed the western outskirts of Revelation at a distance of a few hundred meters. It then continued racing away from the town, and soon it had disappeared in the distance. Andrew's heart sank. Was he too late?

About ten minutes later, exactly as Donna had planned, Paige's small silver hatchback appeared around the corner a couple of hundred metres away, coming from the centre of town. She was driving at a sedate pace, seemingly not accelerating much after making the turn. A few seconds later, a delivery truck with its sides covered in images of fruit and vegetables followed, and it made the same turn and headed for the intersection about fifty metres behind her car.

Paige kept her speed down so that the delivery truck would catch up with her, and she had timed it perfectly because when she was almost level with the bus stop, the lights turned red and she coasted forward. The delivery truck closed the distance to her car and also slowed down as the two vehicles approached the intersection. When the gap was just a couple of metres, Paige suddenly slammed on the brakes, and the delivery driver was forced to do the same. However, his delay in reacting and the fact that the truck was much heavier than the small car meant that he was unable to slow down in time, and he ended up bumping into the back of Paige's vehicle. The truck's tyres squealed briefly as its front bumper connected with the rear of the hatchback, but the impact was not hard enough to cause much damage. However, as soon as both vehicles had come to a stop, Paige flung her door open and exited the vehicle, seemingly in a highly distressed state. She was shouting at the truck driver and rushing back to inspect the rear of her car.

As the truck driver opened the door and began climbing down from behind the wheel, Andrew was already moving. Out of sight of the driver, he swiftly pushed up to the back of the truck and got up onto a raised step that allowed him to grip the handle of the rear door's bolt and lever locking mechanism. While Paige remonstrated loudly with the beleaguered driver, Andrew began rotating the metal handle, wincing in anticipation of the corroded metal lock squeaking and giving away his presence.

In the end, the lock disengaged quietly, and he was able to slip inside and close the doors behind him. It was possible for him to jam the locking pins partly in place to prevent the doors from flying open in transit, but he would be unable to slot the exterior handle back in its original position. Quietly moving out of sight of the doors behind a set of tall metal trolleys containing fresh fruit, he pulled out his phone and sent a message to Scarlett. Somehow, she had to find a way to make sure that she was the first person to greet the truck after it arrived at the ranch in order for no one to realise that its rear doors had been tampered with. And then she would hopefully be able to distract the ranch's catering staff while Andrew would sneak out of the vehicle.

Outside, Andrew could hear the driver attempting to placate the irate female driver, and Paige was now speaking slightly more calmly. After another few minutes, he felt the truck shift marginally as the driver climbed back up into the cab, and then he heard the sound of Paige's car speeding off. The truck driver then mumbled something unintelligible to himself and re-started the engine. The time was now 7:52 p.m., and the driver was bound to be late for his delivery, although only by a few minutes, and Andrew could only hope that this wouldn't arouse any suspicion.

At 8:07, the truck slowed down and came to a stop, and a few seconds later, Andrew recognised the sound of the metal gates to the ranch estate open. As the vehicle began trundling along the treelined avenue towards the compound, a text message dinged in on Andrew's phone. It was Donna saying that she had just finished sabotaging the police cruisers and that she was about to leave the rear courtyard of the sheriff's office.

Within minutes, the truck drove around to the back of the compound, and then the automated beeping noise sounded as the truck began to back up. Andrew gripped his Beretta, ready for anything that might be on the other side of the rear doors. As soon as the truck came to a stop, the doors were pulled open. To his relief, it was Scarlett standing there wearing her black waitress uniform. He was about to join her when two members of the ranch's catering staff wearing dark blue uniforms emerged from a doorway on the other side of the open area adjoining the truck loading bays. As Andrew swiftly moved back behind cover, Scarlett immediately turned around and headed for a different door. On the way, she waved and greeted the two others cheerfully.

Andrew remained where he was as the two catering staff began pulling the first couple of trolleys off the van while talking loudly about the latest baseball results. One of them greeted the driver briefly, but he appeared to be happy to remain inside his cab while the consignment of fresh fruit and vegetables was being unloaded. The two staff members returned for another set of trolleys, and unless Andrew came up with a way to get out, he would be discovered within seconds.

Then he suddenly heard a cascading crash of glass, followed by Scarlett's voice shrieking and then swearing loudly. One of the staff members called out to her to ask if she was OK.

'Oh darn it! I dropped a whole case of beer,' she replied, sounding furious with herself. 'Could you guys come help me? I don't want glass lying everywhere for you to step on.'

'Sure,' came the reply.

Scarlett had come through, and it was now up to Andrew to get out of there. He moved out from his cover, and as soon as he spotted the two staff members walking away from him towards Scarlett who was on her haunches picking up shards of glass amid a foaming mess of beer and broken bottles, he slipped out of the truck. Quietly, he then moved across to a corner of the large room where several blue plastic barrels were stacked on top of a wooden pallet.

Waiting until Scarlett and the two staff members had cleaned up the mess, all of the fresh produce had been rolled off the truck and the vehicle had left, Andrew finally re-emerged. Scarlett and the two others were nowhere to be seen, but within seconds, his phone vibrated as it received a text message from her sent from the basement bar. It contained nothing but a question mark. He replied with the words, 'All good'.

Recalling her hand-drawn sketch of the ranch's interior layout, which he had now memorised, he moved purposefully towards the door behind which the two staff members had just disappeared. Pushing through it cautiously, he found himself in a wide empty corridor with dark grey walls. About five metres ahead on one side was an open door, which by the sounds emanating from behind it led to the kitchen. Opposite it was another door, and next to it was one of the tall metal trolleys that had now been emptied of its contents.

As Andrew moved past the two doors, he could hear someone rummaging around inside what appeared to be a food storage room. Moving quickly and quietly, he came to the end of the corridor where a stairwell curved up to the first floor and down to the basement level. This was the stairwell that would allow him to access both the upstairs mansion where McKinnon's office was located and the ops centre down in the basement. As he pushed up towards his first planned target, the décor changed from muted and utilitarian to light and elegant.

When he found himself in a hallway connecting two corridors and a large living room, he followed the corridor to his right towards McKinnon's office. He had only just set foot inside the corridor when the door to the office opened some ten metres further along and Roy Cobb stepped out. He was wearing a light grey suit with a white shirt and a blue tie, and under one of his arms was a folder with documents. Andrew pulled back into the hallway and out of sight while Cobb closed the door to the office and strode along the corridor in the opposite direction. Soon, he turned a corner and was gone.

Andrew moved up to the office door and used his thumb to flick the Beretta's safety off. If McKinnon was in there, Andrew would most likely need to subdue him, although opening fire with the unsuppressed weapon would attract a lot of attention. He looked at his watch. It was another twenty minutes until Emmett was due to arrive, but when he did, that should give Andrew the opportunity to head back down to the ops centre in the basement. For now, however, he had to push inside the general's office and take his chances there.

Opening the door and stepping inside with his gun out in front of him ready to fire, Andrew was relieved to find the spacious room empty. Closing the door quietly behind him, he looked around the office to take in the many old weapons with which the walls had been decorated. There was a Model 1816 Musket seemingly in mint condition, a Springfield Model 1861, and two repeating carbine Henry rifles hung across each other on the wall above the mantlepiece of a large open fireplace.

On the wall directly behind McKinnon's office chair was an oil painting of a man with a lean face and dark medium-length wavy hair parted on his left side. He had short sideburns and a small goatee under his chin, and both were greying slightly. His nose was somewhat hawkish, and his steel blue eyes were directed off to one side. Wearing a black tailcoat and a waistcoat over a white dress shirt with a standing collar and a cravat, he looked the image of a 19th-century statesman. Approaching the painting, Andrew read the text on the small brass plaque attached to the lower section of the gilded frame and then realised who he was looking at. This was Jefferson F. Davis, President of the Confederate States of America from 1862 to 1865, and the commander in chief of the Confederacy until its defeat and dissolution. Andrew looked up at the former president for a moment and wondered why McKinnon would have a painting of Davis hanging there when he might have chosen a depiction of his own supposed illustrious ancestor, Stonewall Jackson.

A bit further along the wall on a large wood panel was another reproduction of an old oil painting. According to the brass plaque below, it was called 'American Progress'. It had apparently been painted in 1872 by a man named John Gast, and it seemed to capture perfectly the spirit of what McKinnon had talked about when he had held forth about the idea of manifest destiny. It showed a blond woman in white flowing robes moving across the plains from right to left while holding a book. Behind her on the right were sunlit fields, cities and railroads, and in front of her on the left was darkness, empty plains with nothing except fleeing native Americans and buffalo herds. It was a perfect representation of the white man seen as liberating the continent from its darkness, and in the process, displacing natives to make room for the progress alluded to in the painting's title.

Sitting down at McKinnon's desk, Andrew pulled the keyboard towards himself and moved the mouse to make the computer monitor come alive. As expected, the computer was locked, and an input box sat in the middle of the screen with a cursor blinking mockingly at him, as if daring him to guess the correct password and then lock him out of the system when he got it wrong. The default setting for the number of allowed password attempts before a PC locks the user out is ten, and Andrew figured that McKinnon would have been unlikely to change that setting. This meant that he had ten attempts to guess the correct password, which would then almost certainly give him access to a good deal of compromising information.

He began by typing in 'Jackson', but that didn't work. Then he tried 'Stonewall', but that failed too. After that, he attempted 'Davis' and 'Texas', followed by 'Freedom'. None of them worked, and he was now down to five remaining attempts. Next, he typed 'Manifest Destiny', but that too failed. Beginning to feel the pressure build, he furrowed his brow as he rubbed his temples with his fingertips. He was convinced that the password would somehow relate to McKinnon's obsession with ideas about freedom, tyranny and the soul of the nation being under threat. It had to be related either to the Declaration of Independence or to the United States Constitution. He typed in '1776' for the year when the Declaration of Independence was written, but that proved incorrect. Three attempts left. Then he typed in the year when the Constitution had been created. '1787'. The screen went from blurred out to a desktop with a crisp image of the Stars and Stripes fluttering in the wind with an out-of-focus Capitol Building in Washington D.C. in the background.

Andrew breathed a sigh of relief, gripped the mouse and began trawling through the general's files and emails. It didn't take him long to discover a set of files containing a ledger that showed hundreds of payments of various amounts of money to local people, the most prominent of which were Sheriff Hogan and Mayor Meeks. There were dozens of others, and there were even a few for Assistant DA Bremmer in Nolan County. It looked as if McKinnon had bought the entire county in order to keep himself insulated from any kind of investigation or interference in what he and Ironclad were doing at Stonewall Ranch.

Andrew then found an extensive trail of detailed communications with a man called Jean-Pascal Mokri with whom McKinnon appeared to be preparing for some sort of upcoming event on Wall Street. After some more digging, it became evident that the two men were anticipating a major stock market crash, which they would then exploit through the use of a host of financial instruments set up by Mokri.

Soon after, he came across references to 'the weapon' and 'the Capitol'. Only then did the penny drop, and when it did, he could practically hear the metallic sound of the copper coin bouncing off the hard bottom inside his skull. McKinnon and Mokri were engineering a stock market crash that would make them insanely rich, and they were going to make it happen with an attack on the Capitol building using a weapon they had somehow stolen from a chemical weapons depot. Andrew felt the hairs at the back of his neck stand on end as the full horror of the plan unfurled inside his mind. Any weapon stolen from a military chemical weapons depot would be powerful enough to inflict massive numbers of casualties if released in a crowded area. Such an event would almost certainly cause a huge reaction on Wall Street, if only temporarily, but it was probably enough to allow him and Mokri to successfully carry out their diabolical plan.

He thought back to earlier that evening when he had watched the black aircraft heading northeast directly towards Washington D.C. With the sorts of speeds that such a tilt-rotor plane could achieve, he estimated that it would take it somewhere between three and four hours to get there, and he had spotted the aircraft about an hour earlier.

He had to warn someone, but who? The only person he knew and trusted implicitly in Washington was Captain Jack Lynch from the U.S. Navy. Lynch worked for the ONI, the Office of Naval Intelligence, and he had been instrumental in helping Andrew prevent a global disaster almost two years earlier when the rogue captain of an Ohio-class nuclear submarine and his deranged industrialist co-conspirator had attempted to engineer a nuclear Armageddon.

The naval intelligence agency was headquartered in Suitland, Maryland, less than ten kilometres from the Capitol Building. If he could get a message to Lynch with credible evidence of the plot, he might be able to help avert it. But it would take more than a couple of emails between a retired general and some Middle Eastern financier. He would need tangible proof. Precise and actionable information that would allow the FBI or the NSA to take immediate action. But time was against him. If he remembered correctly, today was the day of the president's State of the Union address, and this meant that the commander-in-chief and the entire Congress would be gathered inside the Capitol Building. It would be a perfect time for such an attack.

Quickly gathering all of the files and emails he needed, he packaged them into a small zip file and emailed it to himself. A couple of seconds later, the email came in on his phone, so at least now he had some evidence. But he would need a lot more, and he was certain that he would be able to find it inside the ops centre in the basement. He looked at his watch. It would still be another five minutes before Emmett would make his appearance. Andrew got up from the desk, not because he was about to leave the office, but because tension was now building up inside him, and walking around usually helped him think.

As he stood up, he walked over to the large oil painting by John Gast. It was clearly a reproduction, but the detail was impressive. Glancing down towards the floor for a moment, he realised that the skirting board on that section of wall panel seemed to be floating a couple of millimetres above the floorboards, and when he pushed his foot against it, it moved ever so slightly. In fact, the entire wall section moved. Pushing harder, it suddenly swivelled on hinges mounted on one side to reveal a small passage lit up by soft lighting from above. It extended about two metres, and then it turned right.

Andrew stepped inside, closed the wall panel behind him and pushed further along through the passage. After the right-hand turn, the passage opened up into a small room no larger than two by two metres, but it was like nothing Andrew had ever seen before. Reminiscent of a miniature museum, its walls were decorated with what appeared to be authentic Civil War paraphernalia such as torn authentic Confederate flags, old revolvers, framed documents and handwritten texts. Against the back wall was a varnished wooden desk with more documents, a worn and very old-looking pocket knife, a quill pen with a silver ink well, a disc-shaped pocket watch on a gold chain, and a small .22 four-barrelled pocket gun of a kind that used to be popular with officers during the civil war.

Andrew wondered who all of these items used to belong to, but as he looked up at the wall above the desk, he soon found his answer. Hanging inside a tall glass box was a white flowing rope with a rope arranged loosely around the waist. It came with a pointy hood that also worked as a full-face covering with cutouts for eyes. Next to it was a thick hemp rope tied into a noose. On the left side of the white robe's chest was a circular symbol in red and white. Inside the circle was a symmetrical cross similar to that of the Order of Christ, and at its centre was a small square with a stylised drop of blood. Andrew had seen this symbol before, and the noose next to the robe left no doubt about what he was looking at. It was the so-called Blood Drop Cross used by the Ku Klux Klan, and the white robe was almost certainly that of McKinnon's grandfather. Andrew stared up at the robe and the hood with its menacing hollow eyes, reflecting on the bloody history that this outfit represented. He could only guess at why McKinnon kept all these items hidden in here, but they appeared to be heirlooms collected to make some sort of shrine to his dead grandfather and his Ku Klux Klan affiliations.

Andrew decided to take a couple of pictures, slipped his phone back into his pocket, and was about to leave when he heard the door from the corridor to the office open and someone enter. There was then the sound of swift but heavy footsteps approaching, and then the faint squeak as someone sat down in

McKinnon's office chair. This had to be the general himself, and that was bad news. Andrew was now trapped inside the shrine, and he suddenly grew concerned that McKinnon might be able to see that someone had been accessing his computer. He looked at his watch again, wondering if the whole plan was about to come apart, but at that very moment, Emmett finally arrived.

TWENTY-SEVEN

Andrew both heard and felt the aircraft as it swooped low over the mansion, making the windows rattle and the whole structure of the building's roof vibrate. The ageing Grumman biplane cropduster was a small aircraft, but its single yet powerful Pratt & Whitney turboprop engine was huge for its size, and with its three-bladed propeller, it produced noise equivalent to that of World War Two fighter planes such as the Spitfire or the Hurricane. As Emmett completed his first pass over the ranch, Andrew could hear McKinnon leap up from his chair and hurry over to the window amid a growling stream of profanities. Then he heard the cropduster return, and this time McKinnon's reaction was even more forceful.

'Jesus Christ!' he yelled. 'What in the hell is going on?'

Andrew knew exactly what was happening, and he could easily picture the look of shock and rage on McKinnon's face as Emmett began dropping Molotov cocktails made from petroleum and old beer bottles onto the ranch below.

'Son of a bitch!' swore McKinnon, and then he stormed out of the office.

Andrew wasted no time and opened the panel to step back out into the office. Outside, across a large courtyard, he could see flames billowing up from the roof of one of the other buildings as the burning liquid ran down the roof tiles into the gutter and down the side of the exterior wall. As he watched, Emmett returned in the small but fast and manoeuvrable yellow cropduster, banking hard as he threw another Molotov cocktail that disintegrated across two pickup trucks, lighting them both on fire. Then the plane was gone again.

Emmett's fiery harassment was evidently extremely effective because the whole ranch was now in a state of uproar, but it also proved dangerous. Andrew could now hear the sound of the first rifle reports, followed by a burst from an assault rifle. McKinnon's men were trying to shoot him down. As Andrew exited the office and headed back towards the stairwell, he could only cross his fingers and hope that the small plane would prove too difficult to hit as it raced low and fast over the compound.

When he arrived at the stairwell, an alarm began blaring throughout the ranch complex, and he could now hear men shouting from different directions both inside and outside the mansion. One of the voices belonged to McKinnon who sounded irate. Holding his Beretta out in front of him as he descended, Andrew followed the curving stairs down to the kitchen level and then further down to the basement.

Everything down there was painted black, and the lighting was muted and cold. When he emerged into a long wide corridor, he had only taken a couple of steps along it when two men emerged from one of the doors which he knew from Scarlett's sketch led to the ops centre.

Both men were wearing camouflage cargo trousers and t-shirts, and they were carrying assault rifles on their backs along with what looked like Glocks in shoulder holsters. As soon as they spotted him, they both realised that he was not one of their own, and they immediately went for their holstered weapons. However, Andrew was ready for them, and he fired four shots in rapid succession as he kept pushing forward. All four bullets hit their mark, and both men went down hard onto the grey concrete floor. Without slowing down, Andrew kept advancing until he was next to the two men. They were both dead.

He reached down and grabbed one of the assault rifles. It was an MK16 SCAR that was chambered with 5.56mm ammo, and it was fitted with a suppressor. He extracted the extra magazine that the mercenary had been carrying and shoved it into a side pocket in his trousers. He reached through the loop of the carry strap and pulled it over his head, tucked the stock of the rifle into his shoulder and flicked the fire selector to single shot. Then he pushed through the door to the ops centre.

The centre was empty except for a single operator who was looking at various streams of live security camera footage while appearing to be busy directing members of McKinnon's guards to different locations around the ranch. It would appear that they were expecting some sort of larger assault on the compound.

When Andrew entered, the man turned his head and stared for a brief moment as it dawned on him what he was facing. Then he reached for his sidearm, but Andrew pulled the trigger and a single bullet smacked into his head and sprayed the wall behind him in red. Then he slumped down on the desk in front of him.

Andrew closed and locked the door behind him, slung the MK16 onto his back and moved to one of the computer terminals. On the split screen monitor in front of the dead man, he caught glimpses of Emmett's small yellow cropduster as it raced briefly into view of some of the cameras, only to disappear into the night once more. As far as Andrew could see, Donna's uncle had now run out of Molotov cocktails and was simply using the aircraft to keep the pressure on the mercenaries and distract them for as long as he could. When the aircraft was passing over the ranch, Andrew could also see the muzzle flashes of the weapons trained on Emmett as he flew over. Before long, he would have to retreat to avoid being shot down or worse.

Andrew's fingers flew across the keyboard to type in various search requests, and he managed to find references to a plan for a mission in Galveston and another one in Pueblo, Colorado, but nothing tangible enough to prove what had happened. Then he remembered that Scarlett had marked another room at the end of the corridor, which she didn't know what was for, but she had once seen McKinnon and one of his intelligence specialists exit from there.

Andrew got up, unclipped a keycard from the dead man's jacket, and then he unlocked the door to the ops centre and exited out into the corridor. He could still hear the faint noises of the chaos unfolding upstairs, but he ignored them and swiftly moved to the far end of the corridor where he swiped the keycard across the card reader mounted next to the door.

As he pushed it open with his foot and moved inside with his assault rifle up and ready to fire, a single person was sitting by a computer terminal holding a phone to his ear. It was a man in his mid-thirties of medium height with short dark hair, and he was wearing dark slacks and a light blue shirt. As soon as he saw Andrew, he froze and locked eyes with the intruder. There was palpable fear there, and Andrew reckoned that this man was not a trained shooter. In fact, he appeared not to be armed at all.

As the door clicked shut behind him, Andrew brought his index finger up to his mouth, and the man immediately understood. Saying nothing more, he very slowly placed the phone on the desk and slid it towards Andrew. Then he carefully raised both hands above his head, never breaking eye contact with the man in front of him holding the assault rifle.

Andrew advanced towards him and picked up the phone. While still pointing the rifle at the man, he held the phone to his ear, and over the background noise of shots fired, he could then hear someone shouting orders, but it did not appear to be McKinnon. Removing the phone from his ear, he then hit the 'End call' button and tossed it on the floor.

'What's your name?' he asked.

'Ryder,' said the man, staring at the MK16's muzzle.

'Listen, Ryder,' said Andrew. 'You're going to help me find what I am looking for. Do you understand?'

'Yes, sir,' said the man nervously, giving a quick nod.

'Good,' said Andrew. 'If you do exactly as I say, I'll let you live. Is that also clear?'

'Absolutely, sir,' nodded Ryder.

'Good,' said Andrew. 'We don't have much time, so you need to work fast. Can you do that?'

'Yes, sir,' said Ryder. 'Just tell me what to do.'

After about five minutes, Ryder had produced a memory stick containing all the plans, timetables, maps, crew rosters and objectives for the hit on Galveston, the theft of the JSX agent from the Pueblo depot, and the upcoming attack on the United States Congress that was now mere hours away.

Easily persuaded by Andrew's words as well as the feeling of the cold steel of the MK16's muzzle at the back of his head, Ryder then also emailed the package to Andrew's own email address. Andrew would then forward it to Captain Lynch at NOI headquarters in Maryland. It was all Andrew could do at this point, and he could only hope that Lynch would receive the message in time and be able to mobilise some sort of response to find and bring down the Nightcrawler team, who would soon be touching down in a public park across the Anacostia River just a couple of miles from the Capitol Building. From there, they would board a van and head straight for their target, carrying the deadly nerve agent in a container that was kept inside an innocuous-looking briefcase.

'There,' said Ryder, glancing nervously up at Andrew. 'It's done. Are you going to kill me?'

'No,' said Andrew coldly. 'You probably deserve it, but I gave you my word. Go sit by that radiator.'

Ryder did as he was told and went to sit with his hands behind his back while Andrew ripped some electrical wires from the computer system's power supplies. He then used them to tie Ryder's wrists together, and then he tied those to the radiator.

'What's the best way to get out of here?' said Andrew. 'I don't suppose there's some secret hidden underground escape tunnel?'

Ryder peered up at him, looking reticent and confused, as if he were trying to work out whether Andrew had been serious.

'No,' he said haltingly. 'McKinnon has a private helicopter out on the pad. And he has a bunch of his personal vehicles parked inside the big grey hangar at the back. But that's all I can think of.'

'OK,' said Andrew. 'Now, listen carefully. Don't move. Don't make a sound, alright? Your best bet right now is to stay quiet and hope that the FBI gets here before McKinnon does. I don't know what the odds of that happening are, but I am sure that gamble is better than being dead.'

Ryder nodded with a defeated look on his face, and then he lowered his head to his chest as Andrew turned and left the room.

★   ★   ★

As Andrew moved swiftly along the corridor in the basement, he fished his phone out of his pocket. There was still no message from Donna. She was meant to have reported back a while ago to say that she had returned safely from the sheriff's office to the abandoned silver mine where she would wait for Andrew and Emmett to come and find her. He sent her a brief text asking if she was OK, and then he slipped the phone back into his pocket.

Arriving at the stairwell, he stopped for a moment to listen for noises from upstairs. He could still hear people shouting, but with less urgency than before, and there seemed to be no sound of the cropduster. Either Emmett had been forced to retreat, or worse still, the plane might finally have been brought down by the gunfire from McKinnon's men.

Andrew headed up the stairs and emerged on the ground floor where a narrow passage led towards the front of the house. Shortly thereafter, he found himself in the mansion's lobby where Roy Cobb had greeted him a few short days ago. When he strode across the lobby, he could hardly believe what he was seeing through the windows and the open front door. It seemed as if almost the entire ranch complex was on fire, with several buildings now completely enveloped by tall flames that were busy devouring the mostly wooden structures. Armed men were running across the open courtyard amid shouting and yelling, but there appeared to be no coordinated effort to put out the fires.

As he approached the front door, he slung the assault rifle onto his back and picked up speed in order to match that of the people outside, hoping to be able to blend in and move to the rear of the compound unnoticed. Walking swiftly along the front of the mansion, he turned the corner and headed for the grey hangar that Ryder had pointed him to. Its large sliding doors were pulled shut, and a couple of mercenaries were walking around near it, looking agitated. As he came nearer, he spotted a small corporate helicopter parked on its own pad next to the one used by the much larger twin-rotor aircraft. If he could get to it quickly without being noticed, he might be able to fire up the engines and take off.

He immediately began heading for the pad, but a couple of seconds later, three people came out of the back of the mansion and jogged along a gravelled footpath towards the chopper. Two of them were familiar to Andrew. It was General McKinnon and Roy Cobb, and they were both carrying assault rifles. For some reason, McKinnon appeared to be in full army dress, and Cobb was wearing a grey suit. Judging by his clothes, the third man looked to be a pilot.

Halfway between the warehouse and the helicopter pad, Andrew veered off for fear of being spotted, and within seconds, the three men had reached the chopper. The pilot climbed up into the cockpit, and soon after, the generators began spinning up the engines. McKinnon gripped the handle on the door to the rear passenger compartment and slid it aside, and as the turbofan engine began its high-pitched whine and the rotors slowly started spinning, the general climbed up inside the compartment and sat down in the seat directly behind the pilot.

Realising that they were seconds from getting away, Andrew decided that he had to roll the dice and attempt to prevent the chopper from taking off. He went down on one knee, brought up the assault rifle and began firing at the engine compartment. The distance was about seventy metres, so he had to fire single shots one at a time since bursts would be impossible to control. He couldn't afford to kill McKinnon. At least not yet. Not until he had got a confession out of him.

Without hesitation, Cobb suddenly gripped his assault rifle and swung around to aim at Andrew who was sitting exposed out in the open. The speed and control on display by McKinnon's mild-mannered number two caught Andrew off guard. He did not have the demeanour of a military man, but he was fearless, and he knew how to handle the weapon.

With bullets ricocheting off the ground and zipping through the air close by, Andrew ceased firing and sprinted for cover behind a tree. Sliding in behind it, the bullets kept coming and smacked into the trunk one by one. Cobb had zeroed in on him, and he was walking forward as he fired, closing the distance as if he had no fear of being hit himself. Still prone, Andrew peeked around the tree trunk to see that behind Cobb, the helicopter's main rotor was now at full takeoff revs. To Cobb's apparent surprise, the chopper began to lift off from the ground inside a whirling torrent of dusty air. Clearly expecting McKinnon to have waited for him, Cobb half turned around and stopped firing for long enough for Andrew to line up the MK16 on Cobb's torso and fire. Squeezing the trigger twice, he delivered a quick well-placed double-tap to Cobb's chest, and

McKinnon's second in command flailed and went down hard.

Other mercenaries had now realised what was going on, and some were taking shots at Andrew lying prone behind the tree. As soon as Cobb had hit the ground, Andrew leapt up and made a break for the hangar. Bullets pinged off the corrugated metal sheets with which the hangar was clad, and as Andrew pulled the sliding door aside, he was greeted with a view of a range of vehicles spanning from sportscars in bright colours to large understated luxury SUVs. He threw himself into cover on the concrete floor and pushed the door closed with his foot. Several of the incoming shots landed uncomfortably close to him, and one or two of them punched clean through the metal sheets and smacked into a couple of the vehicles.

Still sprawled on the floor, Andrew spun around to see what was inside the hangar, and it only took a few seconds for him to spot his ticket out of there sitting at the very back. Painted in green and yellow flaming livery and towering over everything else was a huge monster truck. It was three times taller than the largest SUV in the hangar, and its four massive tyres were as tall and as wide as a fully grown man. Its chassis was raised onto a heavy-duty suspension system, its front grille was shining chrome, and on top of the cab were a row of six large floodlights. Why someone like McKinnon would want to own such a beast was a mystery, but right now it was Andrew's way out.

With bullets still smacking into the hangar door, he sprinted along the wide centre aisle, along which all the different cars had been parked. The only vehicle facing the door was the monster truck, and Andrew leapt up onto the elevated footrest by the driver's side and tore open the door. As he had hoped, the keys were in the ignition, and as he slumped down into the seat behind the wheel and the huge dials and gauges, he felt like he was strapping himself into a 1950s rocket ship.

He turned the key and pressed the ignition button, and with a deafening roar that reverberated around the hangar, the oversized methanol-fueled engine growled into action. He shunted the gear lever into 1st and slowly released the clutch. As soon as it connected, the imposing vehicle jolted and began creeping forward as the engine idled, and Andrew looked out of the reinforced windscreen to the hangar door and wondered how much speed he would need to barge through it.

Suddenly, the door began sliding aside, and outside stood a haggard and furious-looking Roy Cobb. His ballistics vest had stopped both of Andrew's shots but had knocked Cobb over into the dirt, which had made Andrew think that he had gone down for good. As soon as he spotted Andrew behind the wheel of the monster truck, he slammed in a fresh magazine and pulled back on the charging handle. Andrew realised that it was now or never. Soon, there would be many more mercenaries joining Cobb at the hangar entrance, and then not even a rocket ship would be able to save his life, let alone a truck, albeit a very large one. He shifted into 2nd gear and throttled up as he released the clutch. The monster truck leapt forward and began accelerating rapidly towards Cobb amid a furious roar and two columns of smoke shooting up from its vertically mounted exhaust pipes directly behind the cab.

Instead of attempting to get out of the way, Cobb raised his assault rifle and fired. As the giant vehicle tore across the hangar floor towards him, he kept spraying bullets towards it until his magazine was empty. Some of the projectiles slammed into the windscreen and punched right through, but Andrew leaned down low to one side to get behind the huge engine block while keeping the accelerator depressed and the steering wheel fixed in the same position.

With an enraged bellow, Cobb released the empty mag and slammed a fresh one in, raising the rifle again as the truck was bearing down on his and closing the distance rapidly. He only managed to get another few shots off before the monster truck rammed into him, and its two right-hand tyres ground him violently into the dirt outside the hangar. When the truck had shot past him, he was nothing more than a mangled heap of flesh and bone.

With a handful of shocked mercenaries taking badly-aimed shots at him, Andrew sat back up in the driver's seat and drove the monster truck away from the light of the flames and out towards the darkness of the surrounding high desert. He crashed through several hedges and flowerbeds, leaving a trail behind him mostly akin to a freshly ploughed field. Within seconds, he was out in open terrain and he switched on the lights. The truck's large collection of headlights lit up the desert as if it were daytime, and he quickly turned the truck north, crashed through the perimeter fence as if it wasn't even there and continued on until the burning ranch appeared like a small orange flame in his rearview mirror.

After several kilometres of tearing across the uneven high desert terrain, Andrew veered back and joined the road leading north to Revelation. Once the truck was on the level blacktop, he was able to extract his mobile phone. He was about to attempt to call Emmett when he saw that there was a text message from him and a voice message from Donna. He tapped the text message and was relieved to see that Emmett had successfully returned to land the cropduster at Jim Scarborough's farm, although the plane now had a few bullet holes in its fuselage.

He then tapped the button for voice messages, and when it began playing the message from Donna's phone, he felt the blood in his veins turn to ice.

'Hello, Mr Sterling,' came Hogan's lazy drawl. 'I gotta say, I don't know how in the hell you managed to get away from Tatum and his pals, I surely don't. I suppose they underestimated you, but I won't do such a thing, believe me. Anyway, I thought I'd just call to let you know that we've got your little girlfriend, Donna Cooper, here with us. Seems like she got herself all confused about what constitutes decent behaviour. See, sneaking into a police parking lot and sabotaging vehicles is a pretty serious crime. She told me how you two are in cahoots with Emmett to stir up even more problems. Took some persuading, but she finally spilled the beans. Now, I understand there's been some trouble at Stonewall Ranch, and I'd bet just about anything you've got something to do with that. So, would you kindly call me back at your earliest convenience? That'd be mighty nice of you.'

The recording ended, and Andrew pulled over by the side of the road and sat inside the monster truck's cab, staring out of the windscreen for a while. Then he hit the 'Return call' button.

'Mr Sterling,' came Hogan's voice after a couple of rings. 'How nice of you to call back.'

'Talk,' said Andrew coldly. 'What do you want?'

'Well,' said Hogan casually. 'I just want to resolve all this unpleasantness. And I'd prefer it if you just went back to where you came from and left us folks alone.'

'I'm afraid I can't do that,' said Andrew. 'I am taking you and McKinnon down. Cobb's already dead.'

'Yes, I heard about that,' said Hogan. 'I spoke to McKinnon just now, and he ain't too happy about what's been happening.'

'Where is that coward anyway?' said Andrew. 'I watched him bail on his own men and run away as soon as things started heating up.'

'I am sure I have no idea,' said Hogan. 'And you don't need to worry about that. What you need to be concerned with is the welfare of one Donna Cooper. Her life is in your hands, and she will join her brother shortly if you don't do exactly as I tell you.'

'What is it you want?' repeated Andrew.

'Well,' said Hogan. 'McKinnon said to me that his men told him that you have stolen a whole bunch of information from the ranch. Stuff that the general wants back. So, it seems to me that we both got something the other person wants. And that's why I am proposing we make a trade. You get Donna, and we get whatever you stole. And then you go on your way back to England and never come back here. How does that sound?

Andrew was silent for a moment as he pondered Hogan's offer. McKinnon and Hogan clearly did not realise that all of the information he had obtained from the ranch had also been sent to an email address. Perhaps Ryder had omitted that detail. Part of him wanted to hunt down both McKinnon and the sheriff and deliver vengeance for Barton and Billy Ray without delay. But another part told him that the threat to Donna's life was very real and that if he did not comply with their demands, she might not be alive for much longer. Barton and Billy Ray were gone, but Donna was still alive. He simply couldn't allow himself to gamble with her life, regardless of how much he wanted payback. He was under no illusion that Hogan and McKinnon would just allow Donna to go on with her life after everything that had happened, or that they would allow Andrew to leave Revelation, but that was a problem for another day. First, he had to get her back safely.

'Alright. Fine,' he eventually said. 'You win. I have everything here with me on a memory stick. Let's make the trade. The stick for Donna's safe return. When and where?'

'Alright,' said Hogan, sounding pleased. 'I'm glad you finally managed to see some sense. Now, listen very carefully…'

TWENTY-EIGHT

It was late in the evening when the white van ostensibly belonging to a Capitol Hill-accredited cleaning company, was making its way leisurely along the wide boulevards of central Washington D.C. Inside the vehicle were Cormac, Knox and Tyler. Knox was at the wheel wearing dark blue overalls with the name of the phoney cleaning company emblazoned across his back. In the back of the van were Cormac and Tyler, both dressed in identical almost black Capitol Police uniforms. Both had standard-issue Glock 19s sitting in black leather holsters attached to their belts. Tyler was fingering the handle on the leather briefcase containing the lethal JSX agent, but his face was calm and emotionless.

'You alright?' said Cormac, stroking his moustache.

'Yup,' said Tyler, nodding sluggishly. 'Never better.'

'We're making history today,' said Cormac. 'Just like the boss said.'

'I know,' said Tyler. 'Everything is cool.'

'Good,' said Cormac. 'Just making sure you've got yourself squared away. Remember, one day they'll be making statues of us. I guarantee it.'

'They'd better,' said Tyler.

'Yo,' came Knox's voice from the front seat as he rapped twice on the metal partition to the van's rear compartment. 'We've got a problem here.'

Cormac slid the shutter in the partition aside so he could see out of the windscreen. Up ahead was a police roadblock consisting of several police cruisers and sets of waist-high plastic barricades with the words 'Capitol Police' written along the top. It was manned by a dozen officers armed with AR-15 semi-automatic rifles.

'Shit,' he grunted. 'What the hell is this now? There weren't supposed to be barricades here.'

'Well,' said Knox tensely. 'They're here, alright. What do we do?'

'Go straight through,' said Cormac.

'Are you serious?' said Knox.

'Ain't nothing else we *can* do,' said Cormac brusquely. 'The president's address starts in fifteen minutes. If we don't make it, it'll all have been for nothing.'

'Fuck me sideways,' winced Knox. 'Alright. Hang on to something, guys. This'll get bumpy.'

Knox floored the accelerator and the van shot forward towards the barricades. It took the Capitol police several seconds to realise what was happening, and that the white van was actually going to attempt to charge through the barrier. By the time most of them had scattered and a couple of them had brought up their weapons, the van tore through the barricades, sending them flying into the air. It then clipped the front of a police cruiser side-on and sent it spinning, but the van continued on at almost undiminished speed. The team now had a clear run the last half mile to the Capitol Building where they would continue into a pre-determined parking garage and be let through and up into the complex by a Texas congressman whom McKinnon had brought into the conspiracy many months earlier.

Several bullets fired by the police officers behind them smacked into the van's thin metal bodywork, but none of the three operators were hit. Knox jammed his foot down onto the accelerator and willed the van to go faster when, up ahead, he suddenly saw a single Capitol police officer run out towards the road holding something bulky. Shunting his arms forward, the officer released the bundle of metal road spikes, and the multi-sectioned concertina strip shot out across the road in front of the van leaving Knox no chance to swerve away from it.

The van raced across the spikes, and they instantly tore open all four wheels amid loud popping noises. Immediately thereafter, the van continued to shoot forward, grinding its wheel hubs and axles against the road surface and sending a shower of orange and yellow sparks shooting out from beneath it. Knox still had his foot jammed against the floor, but the van no longer had any purchase on the road, and it soon slid partly sideways and came to a stop inside a cloud of smoke.

'Fuck!' shouted Knox, reaching for the assault rifle concealed under a blanket on the passenger seat.

Outside, a black heavily armoured SWAT team van emerged from a concealed location near the broken barricades and raced up to come to a halt some fifty metres from the white van. As soon as it stopped, its rear doors opened and a team of SWAT officers wearing full body armour and carrying heavy weapons spilled out and took up positions around the van.

'Stay inside!' shouted Cormac.

'What the hell for?' yelled Knox. 'They'll get us if we don't get the hell out of here.'

'Wait!' repeated Cormac sternly, extracting a phone from a pocket. 'I'm calling the general.'

Tyler looked up at him, his eyes narrowing and his mouth a thin strip across his face. Cormac put the phone to his ear, and a few seconds later, the call was picked up.

'General, sir,' said Cormac. 'We're in the van, and we're surrounded by a SWAT team. We're about two hundred metres from the Capitol Building. What are your orders?'

There was a long pause during which time Cormac could hear the unmistakable sound in the background of a helicopter's turbofan whine and the rapid thudding of its rotor blades. For some reason, McKinnon was in a chopper.

'Sir,' Cormac said, insistently. 'We need your orders.'

When the general finally spoke, his voice sounded heavy with bitterness and regret.

'I'm sorry, boys,' he said. 'You did your best. You're true American heroes.'

Inside the chopper, some 2,300 kilometres to the southwest of Washington D.C. and heading for the city of Nuevo Laredo just across the border into Mexico, General McKinnon flicked open the transparent protective cover on the transmitter. Hesitating for a brief moment, he then pressed the button.

Back in Washington D.C., the explosive device that Cobb had built into the briefcase detonated. The explosion was roughly as powerful as that of a hand grenade, and it instantly shattered the nerve gas container and shredded the briefcase. The overpressure caused the van's rear doors to fly open as a cloud of smoke and aerosolised nerve agent shot out of the back of the vehicle.

Looking on in disbelief, the SWAT team and the Capitol Police officers watched as two wounded men wearing police uniforms tumbled out of the back of the van while a third man opened the driver's side door and fell out onto the road. They were all bloodied but just about able to get to their feet and attempt to get away. However, as soon as they did so, they began clawing frantically at their throats, their eyes and their faces, and they cried out in pain with desperate animalistic roars as the nerve agent seeped into their bodies and rapidly set them on their short path towards an agonising death.

Within seconds, they were on the ground, convulsing violently with mouths foaming and eyes bulging, looking like they were about to pop out of their skulls. The largest of the three, who was a barrel-chested giant with a large black moustache, somehow managed to pull a pistol from its holster, bring it up under his own chin, and pull the trigger. A lone shot rang out across the boulevard, and at that, the SWAT team opened up with a hail of bullets that ripped through the three men. They all lay there convulsing while being jerked around by the impacts of the many high-velocity projectiles slamming into them. After a few seconds, it was all over, and the SWAT team was then ordered to put on their gas masks and back off.

Just over a hundred metres away, a handsome dark-haired man in his thirties wearing a charcoal suit and a white shirt with an open collar stepped out of an unmarked vehicle and moved up to where the police barricade had been. He peered towards the scene of death and destruction up ahead, and then he took out a phone from his suit jacket pocket and hit a number on his speed dial. It rang three times, and then it went to voice mail. He proceeded to leave a brief message for his friend.

'Andrew,' he said calmly. 'This is Jack Lynch. I got your message. Everything you said turned out to be true. We managed to stop the strike team before they reached the Capitol Building. They're all dead. And thanks to you, no one else got hurt. The FBI is mounting a raid on that ranch you mentioned, or whatever is left of it by the time they get there. They probably won't be ready to move until around noon tomorrow, but they intend to round up whatever is left of that mercenary outfit out there. Anyway, let me know if you need help with anything else stateside. I'm sure I can convince my superiors to step up if I remind them of what you did for us a couple of years back. I'll talk to you soon. Take care, buddy.'

★   ★   ★

Half an hour before sunrise the next day, Andrew was making his way south across the high desert. He had retrieved the Jeep from the motel parking lot and was coming towards the end of a long drive. Ahead of him, the foothills of the mountain ranges that stretch across southwestern Texas began to rise up. They started out as gentle undulating low hills but soon became rocky ridges and steep escarpments through which the road now wound itself as it stretched further towards the southwest.

Following Hogan's directions, Andrew had stayed on the main country road and kept going until he could spot a distant peak against the pale pre-dawn sky to his left. After another twenty minutes, he had taken the only turn for many miles and headed towards his final destination where Hogan had promised to meet him and hand over Donna in exchange for the memory stick. He was approaching the location by himself since this had been part of the agreement, but he was expecting both Hogan and Fuller to be there along with their hostage. He was struggling to make sense of precisely what might be Fuller's motivation for being Hogan's lapdog, but it almost certainly had something to do with money. Money that had probably passed from McKinnon through Hogan to Fuller, and the sergeant was now beyond anyone's ability to reach with reason or appeals to his moral side. He had clearly made his choice.

Eventually, the potholed road became a dirt track that meandered through the arid hills and wide ravines until it stopped in a shallow valley at a site that looked most of all like an old movie set. There were only a couple of dilapidated wooden structures and several foundations where buildings had once stood, and there was a small stone well in the middle of a wide open square. Behind the well was the only structure that still looked to be vaguely intact. It was a tiny church built from rendered stone blocks in a Mexican colonial style similar to the Alamo mission building in San Antonio, about 350 kilometres to the southeast. Large patches of render had fallen off, it had no windows, and much of the slate roof structure looked to have caved in. Next to the church were several low cactus plants.

Towards the east was a tall escarpment, and the sun was now just beginning to inch above it to bathe what was left of the small ghost town in its warm glow. Near the well in front of the church was parked a white Ford Ranger pickup truck that Andrew assumed was a personal vehicle belonging to either Hogan or Fuller. He slowed down as he approached, and then he parked up on the other side of the well, where he stepped out of the car and stood next to the vehicle.

At first, there was no movement except for a large hawk circling languidly high overhead, and the only sound was of his own boots on the dry compacted soil. However, after a few seconds, Fuller emerged from the church entrance holding a shotgun, and then Hogan came out behind him, holding Donna and pressing his pistol into her side. Her slender wrists were tied in front of her, her face was bruised and there was a trace of blood on her lower lip. She looked tense and scared as she was marched out of the church with a weapon pointing at her, ready to fire. However, there was also a defiant look in her eyes. The look of someone who was down but not out.

'Mr Sterling,' called Hogan, as the three figures emerged in front of the church, where Fuller moved over to one side while still covering Andrew with his shotgun. 'You just stay right where you are.'

'Donna, are you hurt?' Andrew said, as Hogan pushed her forward until they were roughly three metres apart.

'I'm fine,' said Donna, wincing as Hogan jammed the pistol into her ribs. 'Except for the sheriff's bad breath.'

'That's enough from you,' said Hogan tersely as he tugged sharply at her arm and then looked towards Andrew. 'Have you got the memory stick?'

'Right here,' said Andrew, fishing the stick out of his shirt pocket and holding it up for Hogan to see.

'And you ain't been making copies or nothing?' said Hogan. 'Because if you have, things will turn out real ugly for this little lady here. You can't keep her safe for the rest of her life. I'm sure you understand that.'

'No copies,' Andrew lied. 'I just want Donna to be let go. Here it is.'

He held the memory stick forward towards Hogan who was still holding Donna in front of himself.

'Go on,' he said to Donna. 'Go get it for me. And don't you get any ideas.'

He shoved Donna forward and then kept the pistol trained at her back as she walked towards Andrew.

'That goes for you too,' said Hogan, looking straight at Andrew. 'Raise your hands. Fuller here will gladly turn you both into mincemeat if you try anything stupid.'

Andrew raised his hands above his head, and Donna continued walking until she could reach out and take the memory stick from his hand. As she did so, their eyes met, and Andrew gave her a small nod of encouragement. This would soon be over. Just a few more minutes, and they would be out of there.

'Alright,' called Hogan. 'Now turn around slowly and bring it back to me.'

Looking visibly nervous, Donna turned and began walking back towards Hogan who took a step forward and reached out his hand. As soon as Donna had placed the memory stick inside it, he suddenly lunged forward and pushed Donna forcefully away from himself towards Andrew while yelling at Fuller.

'Now!' he shouted.

Fuller pulled the trigger on the right-hand barrel, but it didn't move. The safety was still engaged, and that was what saved both Andrew and Donna's lives. While Fuller flicked the safety off and raised his weapon again, Andrew flung himself forward, wrapped an arm around Donna's waist and hauled her off her feet and into cover behind the stone well just as Fuller fired. The shot went wide by a few inches and a shower of shotgun pellets sprayed the front corner of Andrew's Jeep. Hogan was scrambling in an ungainly fashion towards the church entrance while he reached back, pointing his pistol at the well and firing wildly as he went.

'Shoot'em, damn it!' he shouted.

Fuller's second shot clipped the top edge of the well just where Andrew was pushing Donna into cover. Most of the steel pellets ripped into the well amid an explosion of dust and stone fragments, but a handful of them smacked into Andrew's shoulder with a hard slap. He instantly knew what had happened, and the sharp sting was quickly replaced by a hot burning sensation.

At that moment, there was the distinctive sound of a high-velocity bullet zipping through the air followed immediately by a loud rifle report from up on the escarpment above. The 7.62 copper-jacketed lead projectile from Emmett's hunting rifle slammed into the centre of Fuller's back, tore through his spine and punched out through his chest in a spray of red. Fuller fell to his knees with a shocked but strangely vacant expression, and while still holding the shotgun, he toppled forward and smacked face-first into the dusty ground.

Now in cover behind the well, Andrew reached behind his back for the Beretta, rolled out to one side with the pistol out in front of himself and aimed at Hogan who was scrambling through the church entrance and trying to escape inside. Andrew squeezed the trigger twice. One bullet hit the sheriff in the upper back slightly on the right-hand side, and the other punched through his lower right hand, making him drop the pistol. Somehow, the large overweight man managed to stay on his feet as he lumbered further into the church and out of sight. Andrew kept his pistol trained at the entrance for several seconds in case Hogan re-emerged, but then he spotted the sheriff's pistol lying on the floor inside the small vestibule that led into the nave of the church.

He glanced briefly to his side where Donna was curled up, pressing herself against the well.

'Are you alright?' he said.

'I'm OK,' she said, sounding shaken. 'I'm not hit. You?'

'I took a couple of pellets from the shotgun,' he said. 'I'll be fine.'

'Who shot that rifle?' said Donna.

'Your uncle,' said Andrew. 'I guess his days as an Army Ranger finally paid off.'

They both glanced up towards the top of the escarpment to see Emmett give them a wave.

'You guys alright?' he shouted.

'We're OK,' shouted Donna.

'You can come down,' Andrew shouted. 'Hogan is holed up inside. I'll cover the exit.'

A couple of minutes later, Emmett appeared from behind one of the ramshackle wooden houses, cradling the hunting rifle. When he walked past Fuller's corpse, he glanced at him but didn't slow down as he approached the well, and as he came closer to Andrew and Donna, he pointed his rifle at the church entrance.

'He still in there?' he said, not taking his eyes off the church.

'Yes,' said Andrew, getting to his feet. 'He dropped his gun, and I don't think he was carrying another.'

'Well,' said Emmett, sliding the bolt back and slamming it forward again to load another round. 'I best go talk to him. There are some things I need to say. You two stay here. Donna, try to patch Andrew up until we can get him to a doctor. I'll be right back.'

When Emmett stepped inside the church, it was dead quiet. With the roof gone and lying in broken pieces across the floor and what was left of the pews, the blue morning sky overhead made for a surreal sight inside the small space. When he was halfway through the nave, he heard movement behind the stone altar at the other end.

'Elijah, is that you behind there?' said Emmett.

'Yeah,' grunted Hogan. 'It's me alright.'

'Why don't you come out?' said Emmett. 'Ain't no sense in hiding no more. And you ain't got much of a chance of runnin' neither.'

After a moment, Hogan got to his feet unsteadily and stepped out where Emmett could see him. He was still wearing his hat, his white sheriff's shirt was soaked in blood around the right shoulder, and he was gripping his lower right arm with his left hand as blood trickled from it onto the dusty flagstones.

'Are you here to make a citizen's arrest?' scoffed Hogan with a sneer. 'Or have you just come to gloat, you good-for-nothin' bastard?'

Emmett ignored the jibe and stepped closer to Hogan while keeping the rifle pointed at him.

'You know, this whole mess got me to thinkin',' said Emmett pensively. 'As I am sure you'll recall from Sunday school when we were kids, 'Elijah' was the name of a prophet in the Old Testament. Sent to show the people of Israel the evil of their ways when they had begun worshipping the false god Baal. That's in Kings, if I am not mistaken.'

Hogan looked up at him from under his hat with a puzzled expression, as if he thought Emmett had now finally lost his marbles.

'I wonder if the irony of that is lost on you,' continued Emmett, 'or if you can now see what you have become, and how you are no longer worthy of such a name.'

'What in the hell are you talking about, Emmett?' spat Hogan derisively. 'Have you been drinking?'

'Not any more than usual,' said Emmett.

'So, what are you trying to say to me?' said Hogan, raising his voice and grimacing from the pain.

'I am talking about Billy Ray!' shouted Emmett, a sudden flash of fury in his eyes. 'You let McKinnon's men kill that boy, you goddamn heartless bastard. And you did that knowing that his and Donna's parents died when they were both young. Those two kids only had each other. And you took him away from her. Left her alone in this world.'

'Bullshit,' said Hogan dismissively. 'It was his own damn fault. If he'd just kept himself to himself, there wouldn't have been no problem. But he wouldn't do that. So, he had it coming.'

'I'm sorry to hear you say that,' said Emmett. 'I surely am. I was hoping you might repent.'

'Repent?' scoffed Hogan loudly. 'You've always been a dreamer, Emmett. You're nothin' but a damn fool.'

'Well, maybe it's all the same,' said Emmett. 'You see, Elijah, there ain't no forgiveness for what you've done. And that's the truth.'

Hogan eyed Emmett warily as he spoke, and his jaw worked nervously.

'What's that supposed to mean?' said Hogan.

'What it means,' said Emmett, 'is that all that's left for you is the righteous punishment that you deserve.'

'And what's that?' said Hogan mockingly. 'You think you're a lawman now, Emmett?'

'Damn straight,' said Emmett coldly.

The report from the hunting rifle exploded with a deafening blast inside the small space when Emmett pulled the trigger. The weapon recoiled in his hands as the bullet slammed into the centre of Hogan's chest, tore through his torso and smacked into the wall behind him, taking a gory red spray of blood and tissue with it.

'A lawman of a kind, anyways,' said Emmett quietly, as tendrils of smoke rose from Hogan's dead body on the floor in front of him. 'Hell, I might even run for sheriff.'

TWENTY-NINE

Two days later, Andrew, Donna and Emmett were sitting in a booth at Donna's Diner, and Andrew's shoulder had already begun to heal nicely. They had all spent the better part of the past couple of days in various interviews with teams of FBI agents that had descended on Stonewall Ranch and the town of Revelation. By the end of it, the agents had detained around a dozen mercenaries, along with Mayor Meeks and a handful of others, including two deputies from the sheriff's office. There were also rumours that Assistant DA Bremmer, flanked by state troopers, had been forced to take the short walk of shame from his office in the Nolan County Courthouse to the jail just across the street.

The bodies of Roy Cobb, Sheriff Hogan and Sergeant Fuller had all been recovered, and the federal agents seemed to have accepted that their deaths had been the results of self-defence and the attempt to rescue Donna Cooper from her kidnappers. Of General McKinnon, there was still no trace.

It was now early morning, about an hour before the diner opened, but the chef was already setting up the kitchen and cooking the trio breakfast consisting of stacks of pancakes layered with yoghurt and berry compote and drizzled with maple syrup.

'Hot diggety dog,' said Emmett as he tucked into his meal. 'This is just about the tastiest breakfast I've ever had. Maybe I'll ask your chef to teach me how to make this. Mind you, it'll be a few weeks until my house is fixed back up again.'

'I'm glad you like it,' said Donna with a gentle smile as she watched the big man devour the pancakes. 'I'm just happy to be back here where I belong. The whole thing seems like a bad dream now. But I know that it wasn't, and I also know that Billy Ray will never come back. Still, I realise I am lucky to be alive, thanks to you two.'

'Don't think nothin' of it,' said Emmett. 'We did what needed doing. Ain't that right, Andrew?'

'I couldn't have said it better myself,' said Andrew with a slight nod. 'We all lost someone close to us, but we did what we could to put things right. And I think we did our best, given the hand we were dealt.'

'Wise words,' said Emmett. 'Mostly, you don't need to go look for trouble. Oftentimes, trouble will find you. And what matters then, is what you do with it. Do you roll over, or do you try to do something about it? And I gotta say, Donna, I'm very proud of you. And I know your parents would have been too.'

'Thank you,' said Donna with a hint of sadness in her voice. 'Hopefully, this town can move on now. Get back to normal.'

'I am sure it will,' said Andrew. 'It seems like the rot is being ripped out. I think they are even planning to raze Stonewall Ranch to the ground so that there's nothing left. Not that there was much out there after the fire.'

'So, what are you fixing to do now?' Emmett said as he looked at Andrew.

'I'll be heading back to London,' said Andrew. 'I have someone waiting there for me.'

'Oh,' said Emmett. 'You mean… like a lady friend?'

'Yes,' said Andrew. 'Her name's Fiona.'

Emmett seemed to ponder that for a moment as he finished chewing his last pancake.

'Right,' he finally said, wiping his mouth with a napkin. 'That's a damn shame, if I'm honest. See, I had been kinda hopin' maybe you and Donna here might…'

'Emmett! Stop talking like that,' said Donna incredulously, as embarrassment flashed across her face.

'What?' Emmett said, spreading out his hands. 'You two were a great team. And you seemed to get along real well. Now, call me old-fashioned, but I think a nice girl like you needs a good man. And there's one sittin' right here. That's all I'm saying.'

'We've become friends,' said Donna reasonably, shooting Andrew an apologetic look. 'Good friends. But it ain't like that.'

'She's right,' said Andrew with a quiet smile. 'The woman I love is thousands of miles from here, and I can't wait to see her again.'

'Alright, alright,' said Emmett. 'Well, it was worth a shot.'

Donna shook her head and couldn't help smiling at Emmett's attempt at playing matchmaker.

'Uncle Emmett, you crazy old man,' she chuckled. 'Don't ever change.'

'I suspect I won't,' said Emmett, giving Andrew a wink. 'It's way too late for that now, anyways. Everything that's happened in my life has done brought me to this place, and I ain't gonna complain about it. No, sir.'

'A lot of people could learn something from that,' said Andrew, giving him a nod and a smile.

'Here she is,' said Donna, her face lighting up as a small silver hatchback pulled up and parked in one of the staff parking spaces.

Donna scooted out of the booth and went outside just as Scarlett emerged from the vehicle. The two women hugged as Andrew and Emmett watched.

'It was mighty nice of Donna to offer her a job here at the diner,' said Emmett as he looked out of the window. 'It surely was.'

'Scarlett came through for us all,' said Andrew. 'She would be a great asset to any business. And with McKinnon gone, she needed a new job.'

'I'm sure she'll fit right in,' said Emmett. 'Speaking of McKinnon. Any idea where that bastard might have run off to?

'No, I don't,' said Andrew. 'Not yet.'

'But you're fixin' to find him, are you?' said Emmett.

Andrew gazed out of the window impassively for a moment before looking straight at Emmett with quiet determination in his eyes.

'One way or another,' he said, 'McKinnon will get what he deserves. He's not going to get away with what he did to my friend. Not a chance.'

'Well, I hope you'll take care of yourself, you hear?' Emmett said, looking straight at Andrew.

'I will,' said Andrew. 'You too.'

'So long, friend,' Emmett said, offering his large calloused hand across the table. 'And remember, you've always got family right here in this town.'

'Thank you,' said Andrew as the two men shook hands. 'I hope I'll be back some day.'

THIRTY

Six weeks later, Andrew Sterling walked off the Airbus Boeing 777 at Bahrain International Airport a few miles northeast of the capital of Manama, and headed for immigration. The British Airways flight from Heathrow had taken just over six and a half hours, and he had managed to catch one hour of sleep along the way. It was now mid-afternoon, and the sun was slowly moving towards the horizon as it bathed the island kingdom in its warm orange light.

Consisting of fifty natural islands and almost as many artificial ones, the largest island belonging to the small Persian Gulf nation was Bahrain Island, at roughly sixty kilometres in length from north to south. Most of the smaller islands were man-made and housed sprawling high-end residential communities.

Andrew was wearing a dark grey suit, a light blue shirt and a dark navy tie, and he was carrying a briefcase with official UK diplomatic tags. This meant that he would not have to submit the case to scrutiny by Bahraini border officials. Twenty minutes later, he walked out into the dry desert heat and headed for a taxi stand. With their characteristic white bodywork topped by a red roof, they stood out amongst the black limousines waiting to pick up VIP visitors.

He ordered the driver to go north around the two-runway airport complex and head straight for the Amwaj Marina, which was adjacent to the blandly named artificial island, Block 257. Once there, he paid the driver in US dollars and stepped out. Then he walked across to the large circular marina and proceeded along the main jetty until he arrived at mooring berth No. 27. Tethered to the jetty and moving gently on the wavelets lapping around it was a gleaming Oyster 565 sailing yacht. Its white twenty-metre hull reflected in the virtually still marina, its dark brown varnished wood deck gleamed in the afternoon sun, and its tall single mast rose almost thirty metres up into the air.

Andrew stepped aboard and used a keycard to enter the interior. The cabin was spacious and luxuriously decorated, but he had no time to enjoy his new surroundings. Placing the briefcase on the table in the dining area, he headed for the bedroom where a locked hard plastic suitcase lay on the bed. He entered the correct combination, opened the lid and went through the various clothing items placed inside. Satisfied that everything he needed was there, he changed into casual wear more befitting of someone enjoying an afternoon on a yacht.

Now wearing light beige slacks, navy deck shoes and a white short-sleeved shirt, he went back to the dining table and opened the briefcase. Inside was a black Glock 17, a suppressor and three magazines, all neatly arranged in custom cutouts inside its foam interior. He screwed the suppressor onto the pistol's barrel, checked all three mags and slapped one up into the magazine well inside the grip. Then he racked the slide to chamber a round.

Leaving the weapon on the table, he headed upstairs and cast off. Using the onboard engine to navigate out of the marina, he eventually raised the 150-square-metre main sail, taking up position behind the shiny steel starboard wheel and steering the vessel south along the east coast of Bahrain Island. Out on the water, there was a moderate breeze, and as the luxury yacht cut across the water at an impressive speed, Andrew donned his sunglasses and settled in for the trip.

After about an hour, he could see his destination in the distance near the island's southern tip. It was the enormous residential complex of Durrat Al Bahrain. The complex consisted of a number of artificial islands packed with large luxury villas sitting on eight vaguely horseshoe-shaped atolls and five smaller fish-shaped islands. Access to the sprawling artificial archipelago could be obtained via a road system from the main island, which included several checkpoints along the way. The only other way inside was from the sea via the Durrat Marina, and this was where Andrew was now headed. Having studied detailed maps and satellite images of the area, Andrew knew exactly where he needed to go to find what he was looking for.

During the FBI raid on the smouldering remains of Stonewall Ranch, the federal agents had discovered additional evidence of General McKinnon's financial activities, including the investment company he owned jointly with a now-deceased Lebanese businessman by the name of Jean-Pascal Mokri. Along with several other properties in Bahrain, the investment company owned the largest villa on Durrat Al Bahrain's Atoll No. 2.

Given Bahrain's status as one of the relatively few countries in the world with which the United States does not have an extradition treaty, Captain Lynch had decided to covertly provide Andrew with everything the FBI had uncovered at the ranch. Based on this information, Andrew had then been able to determine precisely where General McKinnon was now located. Finally, Colonel Strickland, working from the HQ of his special investigative unit in London had pulled some strings to get Andrew a set of UK diplomatic papers that would allow him unfettered entry into Bahrain. The sailing yacht had then been rented and provided fully fitted and ready to go by two MI6 staffers at the British Embassy in Manama, who officially worked there as trade envoys to the island kingdom.

Andrew sailed towards the Durrat Marina entrance, and when he was roughly half a kilometre away from it, he lowered the sail and once again engaged the diesel engine. Humming quietly below deck, the engine then propelled the boat around the northern breakwater and into the marina's interior, where he pulled alongside one of the concrete piers and moored the ship at one of the many available berths. There were only a handful of other yachts and pleasure crafts in the marina, but they were all large and luxurious, which gave a hint at the type of clientele that had bought properties on the atoll.

Still wearing his sailing clothes, Andrew stepped onto the pier carrying only a large black holdall, and he then walked casually towards the shore where a border official wearing a white uniform greeted him politely. After a quick exchange of some words and an envelope containing a fistful of crisp £100 notes, the official retreated to his air-conditioned shed, and Andrew proceeded into a large leisure complex. He walked to the restaurant and asked for a table on the first-floor terrasse overlooking the artificial atoll's bay, and then he set down his holdall and ordered a meal.

Extracting a powerful pair of binoculars from the bag, he sat back and scanned the horseshoe-shaped beach that wrapped around the bay. The sand was almost white, although it had taken on a golden colour as the sun began to set, and the water was a clear emerald green. As he sat there looking through his binoculars at the grand villas whose properties backed out onto the beach, he wondered what it might be like to live here permanently. For all its apparent luxury and idyllic nature, he knew that he would end up bored rigid within just a couple of days. But McKinnon had been there for over a month now, and his aim was not entertainment. His plan was apparently to lay low under a false name for as long as it took for the world to forget about him.

But Andrew had not forgotten. He would never forget, and he was here now to settle a score that could not be ignored. Barton's ignominious death at the hands of McKinnon's goons, no doubt at the direct orders of the general himself, would continue to haunt him for the rest of his life unless he finally put things right once and for all.

Pretending to be watching the marina and the boats out to sea when the waiter brought his food and drink, Andrew then focused in on the largest of all the villas in the bay. It was a two-storey structure built in the same vaguely modernist style as all of the other villas, with white rendered walls, large tinted windows overlooking the bay and a flat roof. It sat back from the beach by about fifty metres, and in front of it at the top of the garden set into a wide veranda under a frosted glass roof, was a large private swimming pool.

At first, there was no movement, but then Andrew spotted a man in a dark suit strolling from one side of the veranda to the other, looping down through the garden, and then disappearing behind the building along a footpath towards the front of the property. He was wearing dark sunglasses and an earpiece, and judging by the way he moved and the way he was scanning the beach and the bay, he had 'mercenary' written all over him. After about ten minutes, he returned and retraced the same route again. This continued several more times as the sun sank beneath the horizon and the light began to fade. Eventually, he returned and took up position by the ground floor sliding doors to the interior where he stood immobile with one hand clasping the other wrist in front of him.

A few minutes later, one of the large glass doors slid aside and a man wearing a white robe and holding a champagne glass stepped out and walked casually towards the swimming pool. He was tall and powerfully built with a short crewcut, a strong jaw and hard eyes, and Andrew would have recognised him anywhere. General John McKinnon. Former marine and JSOC deputy commander. Mass killer. Insurrectionist. Fugitive. But most importantly, the man responsible for Eddie Barton being callously killed and dumped in a shallow grave in the Texas high desert.

Andrew's jaw clenched as he watched McKinnon toss his robe on a sun lounger, proceed to down the champagne and then dive into the pool. Andrew watched the general do lengths for about ten minutes until he climbed out and put his robe back on. Then he walked down the path to the edge of the private garden where the beach began, and he stood there for several minutes with his arms folded across his chest and gazed out across the bay. At one point, he seemed to be peering at the restaurant, and Andrew could have sworn that he was looking straight at him. But at a distance of a couple of hundred metres, he knew this wasn't possible.

Eventually, McKinnon turned and walked back up to the house where he disappeared behind the closing sliding door. The suited guard immediately resumed his duties, and soon after, the villa's tasteful exterior lights came on, including several around the garden paths. Then another identically suited guard showed up and walked down to the beach where he took up position just inside a low white-painted metal gate.

Andrew lowered the binoculars and leaned back in his chair. He reached for his drink and sipped it as he contemplated his options. After another half hour or so, he put down the drink, asked for the bill and picked up his holdall. He walked through to the leisure centre and headed for the restrooms where he locked himself inside a cubicle and changed clothes. Now wearing black trousers, a tight-fitting dark navy long-sleeved t-shirt and a dark baseball cap, he slung the holdall over his shoulder, exited the building and began walking along the beach near the water's edge.

With the small waves gently lapping at the sandy shore inside the bay, he continued past McKinnon's villa, where the guard by the gate eyed him briefly before returning his gaze to his lit-up phone screen. Andrew couldn't help a small shake of the head. Watching a bright screen during the evening would play havoc with the man's ability to see in the dark, as well as severely impair his peripheral vision. Having probably stood there every night for more than a month, his boredom was understandable, but it was exactly this sort of lazy mistake that had cost many an armed guard his life when faced with a highly trained special forces operator.

As he walked past, Andrew noted that none of the other villas in the vicinity appeared to be occupied. Their dark windows looked out to the bay like large hollow eyes, and none of their exterior lights were on. Most likely, these were investment properties that no one had ever lived in.

Andrew continued on for another twenty metres along the beach where he stopped and dropped his holdall onto the soft sand. He bent down, unzipped the bag and extracted a telescopic fishing rod along with a rod holder with a metal spike which he pushed into the sand. He extended the rod, whipped the float out into the water and mounted a small night fishing torch to the rod holder, adjusting its beam so that it pointed just below where the float was bobbing in the water. The light-coloured sand beneath it was now lit up. Soon, various bait critters would converge on the torchlight, which would in turn attract the fish.

Andrew sat down next to the rod holder and reached into the holdall for a drink. Popping open the soft drink, he glanced over his shoulder towards the guard who was still watching his phone but appeared to be glancing up every once in a while. He evidently did not appear to regard the night fisherman as a threat.

Sipping his drink as he sat there quietly and watched the float, Andrew periodically pretended to check his phone until he suddenly made a show of placing a call to someone. Speaking loudly enough to make sure the guard could hear him, he exchanged words with the non-existent person on the other end of the line before terminating the call and slotting the phone into his pocket.

As he got to his feet, he surreptitiously extracted the black suppressed Glock 17 from the holdall and stuffed it under his belt at the small of his back. He then grabbed another two drinks from the bag and headed for the guard. As he walked, he cracked one of them open and took a swig, making an effort to appear unsteady on his feet. Fifty metres behind the guard, Andrew could see that there was now light in the windows of the villa's top floor.

'Hey there,' he said casually as he approached the guard who had now put his phone away. 'Care for a drink? I saw you standing there, and I figured you might be thirsty.'

The guard remained silent but unbuttoned his suit jacket as he regarded the man coming towards him.

When they were a few metres apart, he held out his left hand, showing his palm in an attempt to ward off the oncoming stranger.

'I'm fine,' he said in broken English that sounded Eastern European. 'No, thank you.'

'Are you sure?' said Andrew insistently, slurring his words slightly as he continued to move towards him. 'I've got plenty here.'

'I am sure,' said the guard, his right hand hovering in front of his chest. 'Please don't come any closer, sir.'

'Come on,' said Andrew with a grin. 'No one's going to know. You must be bored out of your mind standing here all night.'

He was now about a metre from the gate, and the guard was taking half a step back. Andrew took a large swig of his open can with his right hand and placed the other can clumsily on top of the metal gate with his left. As he did so, the can seemed to slip from his grasp, and it clonked onto the stone path by the guard's feet where it spun and shot out a spray of fizzy drink. The guard involuntarily looked down, and that was all the opportunity Andrew needed.

Reaching around to his lower back and gripping the Glock 17, he whipped it around in a flash to point it at the guard. The man's eyes returned to look up at Andrew as his hand instinctively reached inside his jacket for his own weapon, but by then it was too late. The Glock popped twice as Andrew fired two shots in quick succession, both of which thudded into the guard's chest. With wide eyes and a brief noise that was halfway between a choking sound and a cough, the guard staggered backwards a couple of steps before falling back into a low hedge surrounding a large flowerbed.

Andrew swiftly climbed over the gate and knelt next to the dead guard as he rifled through his pockets. He soon found what he had been looking for. An electronic keycard that would grant him access to the villa. He also took the guard's weapon, a MAG-08 pistol made by the Lucznik Arms Factory in Poland. The relatively compact but powerful semi-automatic gun was based on a design that had used the Soviet 9mm Makarov cartridge but which had now switched to the western 9mm Parabellum cartridge. This meant that Andrew would be able to use its ammunition if required.

Moving up towards the house along a footpath that wound its way lazily along the left side of the property, Andrew managed to remain in relative cover behind bushes most of the way there. When he emerged near the lit-up swimming pool, he moved to the path that ran along the house where he had seen the other guard patrolling earlier. Pressing himself into a tall and thick hedge that sat on the boundary to the next property, he waited several minutes for the other guard to appear.

It took much longer than he had expected, and he was beginning to fear that the alarm had been raised when the guard finally showed up. He was ambling along as casually as before, and halfway along the side of the villa, he lit a cigarette. This would ruin his night vision for several seconds, so Andrew took his time to step out onto the path, raise his weapon, aim and fire. The single 9mm bullet slammed into the suited guard's forehead, and he instantly crumpled to the ground in a heap, having never even seen the dark figure in front of him.

Andrew returned to the back of the house with his weapon out and ready, walking along the swimming pool towards the sliding glass doors. Once there, he stopped and swiped the keycard across the reader unit mounted on the exterior wall. The lock in the door clicked open, and he pushed it aside as slowly and quietly as he could.

Stepping inside, he paused for a moment to listen, but the house was completely quiet except for the faint sound of a voice droning on upstairs. After a few seconds, Andrew realised that it was the sound of a TV, possibly some sort of news show. Moving quietly across the wooden floor of the open-plan downstairs living area, he pushed upstairs through a stairwell.

He emerged on the top floor on a wide landing with access to a large bedroom as well as a corridor leading towards what appeared to be an office from where the TV sounds were emanating. Proceeding towards the office, he could hear the news presenter's words clearly now. It was some sort of financial news show, and the presenter was talking about the overnight performance of the Asian stock markets.

Andrew moved silently across the carpeted floor on the landing until he could peer through the open door to McKinnon's office. It seemed to take up almost a third of the expansive top floor of the villa, and with its huge floor-to-ceiling windows, it afforded an uninterrupted panoramic view of the entire bay of Atoll 2. Or rather, it would have done if McKinnon had not closed the wide wooden French blinds. And had the blinds been up, he might also have noticed that the guard at the metal gate by the beach was missing.

However, as it was, he was fully focused on the screens in front of him showing financial market information and charts and on the voice from a small picture-in-picture tile on one of the monitors that was streaming the news show.

Sitting behind his desk in a leather office chair, he was wearing white slacks and a dark burgundy shirt with the collar wide open. Near his left hand was a large glass of red wine next to an open bottle, and lying on the corner of his desk was a pistol. It was a chrome-plated Colt 1911 with a pearl grip. Loaded with .45 ACP rounds, it packed a heavier punch than a 9mm weapon, and as such, it had greater stopping power. However, because the Colt 1911 was made from steel and thus more than fifty percent heavier than the Glock, which is made from high-strength polymer, it was also much more unwieldy to use in a tight situation.

'Counting your millions?' said Andrew calmly as he stepped inside the office. 'How many people had to die so you could sit here watching those numbers on that screen?'

McKinnon seemed to freeze for a moment, only turning his head towards Andrew enough for him to be able to see the intruder out of the corner of his eye. Then his gaze shifted to the 1911 about a metre from his left hand.

'Nope,' said Andrew firmly, taking another swift step forward and keeping the Glock aimed straight at McKinnon's head. 'Don't do it. You'll never make it.'

McKinnon appeared to realise that he had been outmanoeuvred and was at his intruder's mercy, and after a couple of seconds of indecision, the tension in his shoulders seemed to dissipate.

'Well, wouldn't you know it,' he finally said, wearily. 'Andrew Sterling. You're like a bad smell that I can't seem to get rid of. Sticking to me like shit to a shovel.'

'Stand up,' said Andrew coldly. 'Pick up the gun by the barrel with your left hand, put it on the floor and slide it over to me.'

McKinnon hesitated as he glared at Andrew through narrow eyes, but he eventually rose slowly from his chair, picked up the gun and placed it on the floor. Then he gave it a kick so that it slid across the varnished wood floor to where Andrew was standing.

'What do I have to do to get you off my back?' said McKinnon, standing up straight with his arms by his side. 'How much do you need?'

Ignoring McKinnon's attempt at bribery, Andrew lowered himself slowly to pick up the 1911 while keeping his Glock aimed at the general. He then stood up and released the magazine from the chrome-plated pistol. He shoved the pistol under his belt and began flicking the bullets inside its magazine out onto the floor one by one, where they bounced off and rolled away.

'What in the hell are you doing?' asked McKinnon, watching Andrew empty the bullets out onto the floor until there was only one of them left inside the magazine.

'I'll tell you in a minute,' said Andrew, still keeping the Glock trained on McKinnon. 'First, you need to answer some questions.'

'Really?' said McKinnon doubtfully. 'Are you here to interrogate me? You know they ain't gonna send me back to the States, right? No extradition treaty.'

'I know,' said Andrew. 'That's why I am here. To do what the FBI and the CIA either couldn't do or wouldn't do.'

McKinnon looked puzzled for a moment.

'What the hell is in this for you?' he asked, looking mildly perplexed and amused at the same time. 'Why are you doing this?'

'Because someone has to,' said Andrew. 'Tell me about Jean-Pascal Mokri. Did you kill him too?'

McKinnon looked straight at Andrew for a moment before speaking, his eyes seemingly attempting to drill through the intruder's eyes to work out what he was thinking.

'Mokri met an unfortunate and untimely death, as far as I understand it,' said McKinnon blithely. 'Damn shame.'

'And you two were planning to make a killing on the stock markets after releasing the JSX agent inside the Capitol Building, right?' said Andrew.

McKinnon said nothing but just proceeded to glare contemptuously at Andrew.

'Alright,' nodded Andrew slowly. 'I'll take that as a yes. And you didn't mind killing your own men in the process. Men who were loyal to you. What an All-American hero you are.'

'Those men were loyal to the cause,' said McKinnon, finally. 'They died fighting for something they believed in. There's honour in that.'

'That's true,' said Andrew. 'But all that stuff about patriotism and the fight against tyranny. You never believed a word of that yourself, did you? It was all just a ruse. A tool to make those men do what you wanted them to do. To help you carry out this master plan of yours, which was never intended to do anything except make you rich.'

'You limey bastard,' sneered McKinnon. 'Sheriff Hogan told me you think you're judge and jury all rolled into one, and he was right. Who in the hell do you think you are?'

'I am the guy setting things right,' said Andrew. 'And as I am sure you know, you won't be hearing from Hogan again. They practically had to scrape what was left of him off the walls.'

'You really think I give a shit about him?' scoffed McKinnon. 'He was just another useful idiot. Sure, our families go way back, but I would be a fool not to exploit the fact that he was a couple of Buds short of a sixpack.'

'I found your little shrine to the KKK, by the way,' said Andrew. 'Very touching. Seems like their hateful nonsense is the only thing you really believe in, aside from money.'

'Those people have defended the whites of America ever since the end of the civil war,' said McKinnon, seemingly becoming agitated. 'And I hope they will continue to do that for many years to come.'

'I don't have time to debate history with you again,' said Andrew, shaking his head. 'Let's talk about the reason I'm here.'

'Alright,' sighed McKinnon. 'Let me guess. Your buddy, Eddie Barton.'

'Bingo,' said Andrew icily. 'You had him killed. Why?'

'Bastard was trying to blackmail my ass for money,' said McKinnon, sounding as if he thought that was more than enough reason to have someone murdered. 'Told me, if I didn't pay him a million dollars, he'd go to the feds. Now, I obviously couldn't let that stand. Think of what that would have done to the morale of my men.'

'So you had your goons shoot him in the back of the head and bury him out in the desert,' said Andrew.

'I could have done a lot worse to him,' McKinnon said with a menacing intonation in his voice. 'As far as I'm concerned, he got off lightly.'

'I'm afraid I don't see it that way,' said Andrew, raising the Glock slightly to point at McKinnon's head. 'But thanks for admitting that you were behind it. That makes this next part easy.'

'I ain't ashamed of anything I've ever done,' said McKinnon defiantly. 'And that includes getting rid of your boy, Barton. He was dead weight.'

'Spoken like a true psychopath,' said Andrew, lifting the unloaded 1911 from his belt and slipping the mag containing a single bullet up into its magazine well. 'Catch.'

He tossed the chrome-plated pistol through the air towards McKinnon, who caught it with both hands, and then froze for a moment as he regarded Andrew with a look of confusion and distrust on his face.

'What's this bullshit now?' said McKinnon.

'I am going to give you the best offer anyone has ever given you,' said Andrew. 'I am going to let you end this yourself. There's a single bullet in that magazine. Just put the gun to your head and pull the trigger. Or am I going to be proven right in thinking you are nothing but a damn coward?'

McKinnon's hard suspicious eyes stared straight at Andrew for a long moment before a sly smile slowly spread across his face.

'You're one hell of a piece of work,' he said with a small shake of the head.

Then his gaze shifted to the 1911 and he moved slowly towards himself, his right hand closing tightly around the pistol grip.

'Enough talk now,' said Andrew, his suppressed weapon still pointing at McKinnon's forehead. 'What's it going to be?'

McKinnon said nothing, but his left hand closed around the 1911's slide. Squeezing it tightly, he pulled back and racked it, and then allowed it to slip forward again with a metallic click as it shaved the last remaining .45 ACP round from the magazine and pushed it up into the firing chamber. Then he shifted his gaze back to Andrew. The moment seemed to stretch for minutes as the two men regarded each other across the room. Then there was the tiniest narrowing of McKinnon's eyes as he clenched his jaw.

With lightning speed and agility, McKinnon flung out the gun hand towards Andrew in the blink of an eye, but by then, Andrew had already pulled the trigger. The Glock 17 produced its characteristic suppressed pop, and the pistol's 9mm Parabellum bullet screamed through the air, tore through McKinnon's head and burst out of the back of his skull with a spray of blood and brain matter that slapped onto a computer screen behind him. As the general's dead body slumped heavily onto the varnished floor by the desk, rivulets of red ran slowly down the screen, obscuring the numbers and digits displayed there.

Andrew stood silently for a while without moving. Then he lowered the smoking pistol and let his arm hang by his side. As he regarded the corpse of General McKinnon lying in an expanding pool of blood, his thoughts turned to Eddie Barton.

'I'm sorry I couldn't save you, mate,' he said quietly. 'Rest in peace.'

THE END

EPILOGUE

The distinctive puttering sound of the motorcycle's single-cylinder engine echoed through the narrowing Shenandoah Valley as the road curved northeast towards the rider's destination. The Harley Davidson Model B had been launched three years earlier in 1926, and its rider had bought it with cash upon his arrival in Washington D.C. on a flight from Berlin a few days earlier.

Born on the 15th of November in 1891 in Heidenheim, Germany, the man was tall, blond and lean. His face was somewhat gaunt, and he had a thin mouth and cool blue eyes. He was 37 years old and had travelled to the United States as part of a research project, leaving behind his wife Lucia, whom he had married in November 1916 in the city of Danzig, later known as Gdansk, Poland. During the First World War, he had fought in the trenches near Verdun in northeastern France, receiving an Iron Cross, Second

Class for his bravery and also being promoted to the rank of *Oberleutnant.*

He had recently resigned his position as a company commander with the 13th Infantry Regiment based in Stuttgart, and upon returning to Germany a couple of weeks later, he would soon take up a new position to become an instructor at the Dresden Infantry School. In anticipation of this assignment, he had decided to travel to Virginia to study the most famous battles of the American Civil War. As part of that plan, he intended to ride his motorcycle west from the city of Fredericksburg to the Shenandoah River and then proceed north all the way along the Blue Ridge Mountains to the small town of Harper's Ferry. His aim was to trace the famous 1862 Valley Campaign of Thomas 'Stonewall' Jackson, whose tactical genius the man had come to revere.

As he rounded a bend in the road that meandered through the forested hills alongside the river, he spotted the confluence of the Shenandoah River in West Virginia and the Potomac River in Maryland up ahead. After their merger, the mighty Potomac would then continue on as the effective border between the two states for almost 300 kilometres, all the way to Washington D.C. and out into Chesapeake Bay and finally the Atlantic Ocean.

He drove up through the small town to its highest point on a steep rise next to the Potomac, stopping the motorcycle and dismounting in front of the Hill Top House Hotel, which overlooked the valley and the two rail bridges stretching east across the river and into Maryland. Originally built in 1888, the hotel was famous for its vistas across the valley and the river, and among its most celebrated former guests were Mark Twain and Alexander Graham Bell.

The tall man took off his helmet and ran his fingers through his sandy hair, placed the helmet on the Harley-Davidson's seat and detached his small suitcase from the motorcycle's rear luggage rack. Carrying the suitcase, he then proceeded up the wide wooden stairs through the doors and inside the hotel lobby where he approached the reception and met the clerk's gaze.

'Hello, Mister,' said the clerk amicably, putting down the newspaper where he was reading about how the New York Stock Exchange was setting new record highs almost every week now. 'How can I help you today? Looking for a room?'

'Yes, I am,' said the man with a noticeable German accent. 'I would like a room for one night. And could I have one where I can see the valley, please?'

'Certainly, sir,' said the clerk, checking the ledger and noticing the man's accent. 'Say, you're not from around here, are you?'

'No,' said the man. 'I am from Germany.'

'Oh,' said the clerk, intrigued. 'Are you here on holiday?'

'I am riding my motorcycle through Virginia,' said the man. 'I came to see the places where your Stonewall Jackson fought his battles.'

'Stonewall Jackson,' said the clerk, raising his eyebrows. 'Well, he was a serious son of a gun, that's for sure. A lot of people around these parts still look up to him, despite… you know. Despite things not going the way he wanted them to.'

'He was a great general,' said the tall man. 'I've come to study him and to see the battlefields for myself.'

'Well,' said the clerk. 'I sure hope you'll have an interesting time doing that. May I have your name, please?'

'Rommel,' said the man. 'Erwin Rommel.'

NOTE FROM THE AUTHOR.

Thank you very much for reading this book. I really hope you enjoyed it. If you did, I would be very grateful if you would give it a star rating on Amazon and perhaps even write a review.

I am always trying to improve my writing, and the best way to do that is to receive feedback from my readers. Reviews really do help me a lot. They are an excellent way for me to understand the reader's experience, and they will also help me to write better books in the future.

Thank you.

Lex Faulkner

Printed in Great Britain
by Amazon

41515066R00294